THE CONSEQUENCES

SARA CARROLL

For Jon, with love always

Part One

A dying man needs to die, as a sleepy man needs to sleep, and there comes a time when it is wrong, as well as useless, to resist.
Stewart Alsop

JANUARY

Chapter One

"Today's the day," Tom said, looking up.

"Is it?" Mark was only half-listening as he sat down at the kitchen table.

"I decided for sure this morning. There's no point hanging about now that I'm ready."

Mark glanced over at him and noticed that the old man looked unusually smart.

"You mean, the...what we have to do? Already?"

Tom started flattening the surface of his porridge with the back of a spoon and the cosy feeling in the kitchen faded as Mark's irritation grew.

"Tom?"

"Today, yes," Tom said at last.

"Why? What's happened?"

"Nothing's happened but when I heard the weather forecast it made up my mind. I'm ready now so today it is. That's what I want, look." Tom pointed to the kitchen window and smiled. There was frost on the glass but a weak sun was warming the room after days of January greyness. Mark's chair grated against the stone tiles as he stood up.

"Let me just get some toast, I'm starving."

He put the bread in the toaster and frowned as he stared out of the kitchen window, grateful for the delay. When Tom started whistling Mark closed his eyes against a shaft of sunlight until red and orange was all he could see. He'd never really thought Tom would go through with it. It had been easy to agree to something like this in theory but that was months ago now. Since then the rest of Tom's planning had masked what he and the others had to do to get things started. As the acrid smell of burning toast reached him he gave up on the idea of breakfast. He turned around and saw that Tom was watching him with an obstinate look on his face.

"There will be other sunny days you know Tom."

"Of course there will, but I'll take this one. I made up my mind on New Year's Day that the first sunny day would be it for me."

"You're sure about this?"

"I am - and no more questions, you know the drill. Just make the calls to get everyone here for dinner tonight and then we can take it from there."

"Can we not just give it one more day - to make sure we've got everything ready for a start?"

Tom stood up with the help of the table and leant on his walking stick as he walked over to Mark.

"No, it needs to be today and if anyone can't make it tonight, tough. Anyway it's better this way, without any build up, better for you as well."

After running through everything Mark left the room feeling unsettled by the lack of warning. He didn't feel ready. Deciding to make the quickest call first he flopped into an armchair and called Ray.

"It's me. About Tom, it's tonight."

Ray's reaction was similar to his own but Mark finished up the call quickly. He didn't have time to talk theories with Ray who was a nice enough guy but not his concern. He decided to make another call before ringing Kirsty who was the one person he needed to be on side. He rang Alice and was about to hang up when he heard her cut-glass tones as she answered.

"Alice speaking."

"Hi, it's Mark. This will seem out of the blue but Tom's moved things forward a bit. Well, a lot."

"When does he want us?"

"Tonight."

"Good grief. Is he sure?"

After another mercifully brief conversation, Alice confirmed that she'd tell Brian and they'd both see him for drinks at seven as planned. Two calls down he took a deep breath and called Kirsty. Ten minutes later he was still talking to her. He knew this would be the most difficult call, but he was starting to lose patience.

"It's been more than a game for a while now Kirsty."

"He's seemed really well since he's been on those new meds and he's loved all the planning sessions. I just thought it was all an excuse to have us over regularly, as if he didn't think we'd come if it was just for dinner."

Mark wondered if Kirsty was being deliberately naïve. They were all deeply involved in Tom's plan but it was the only thing that kept them together. Would they have come round on a weekly basis just to socialise? Would he himself have chosen to spend so much time with

Tom if not for a ready-made apartment?

"Would we though?" Mark asked.

"Would we what?"

"Come over every Monday night, week after week, no matter what."

There was silence on the other end of the line.

"After all Tom's done? I would have expected Brian or Frank to say something like that, but not you."

"I don't mean it like that. I might have got into the habit of dinner with Tom," or you, he thought, "but with everyone together like that? Just for fun – would you?"

"Alright, I know," Kirsty said. "I just don't like how it makes us sound."

"All of Tom's planning and getting everyone together, it's always been leading to this. I'm not ready for it either but he's serious. Everything else has been a distraction for him."

"I know and I'll be there but it doesn't mean I have to look forward to it."

Mark sighed and he was relieved to hear a smile in Kirsty's voice when she spoke again.

"Sorry. I'm not being very helpful am I? It was never meant to be so sudden, that's all," Kirsty said. "Look, don't worry Mark we'll make it a good farewell for him, exactly how he's planned. He still wants all that does he?"

"Yes, the works. All dressed up and ready to celebrate."

"Right, okay. We can do it – let me know if you need anything and send him my love will you?"

Mark exhaled slowly when he hung up the phone. She was the only one he'd been unsure of. Deciding to make a coffee before he called the others, he walked back into the kitchen to find Tom still at the table, humming to himself as he read the newspaper.

"Coffee?" Mark asked.

"Why not." Tom put down his paper.

"Kirsty said to remind you it's fine to change your mind later if you need more time to think about it."

"That's the last thing I need to do - I'm tired of thinking."

"You've been so well lately though, that's what I don't understand."

Tom shook his head.

"I take a lot of pills lad. Anyway, I'd rather go early than leave it too late and I've only got myself to think about."

"You've got all of us Tom. Wasn't that the whole point of getting us

9

together?"

"I know I have but it's not the same as being someone's priority is it? Not to downplay how much I've loved being a part of a group and getting to know everyone especially you and Ray. And Kirsty of course."

Mark didn't know what to say.

"Here, pass me that photo on the dresser will you, I want to show you something."

Mark passed the framed photo to him and sat down.

"Did you ever wonder at how quickly I took to you? When we met I mean."

"It was a good interview."

"Yes, well it was but I was only looking for someone to research my family tree, not a housemate. Look at this and see if you notice anything."

Mark saw two men in suits with carnation buttonholes and wide grins. "That's me and Teddy, my younger brother. He was my best man, must have been about your age there. He died a few months after that was taken."

"I remember you talking about him. 1970 was it, when you got married?"

"That's right – take a closer look at Teddy though. Here, use this."

Tom handed him a magnifying glass and Mark looked more closely at the photo. Both men were wearing blue double-breasted suits and Mark could easily recognise Tom. Next to him was Teddy, taller and leaner than his older brother with strong features and a mop of dark hair.

"You can tell that you're brothers."

"Can you see the resemblance though?" Tom asked eagerly. "You look just like him."

Mark looked again but couldn't see it. "Maybe," he said. "We share the same sort of build and… we're both got brown hair although mine's shorter."

Tom shook his head. "I suppose it's hard to see from this but take it from me - it's the expression and the easy way you both have about you. As soon as you walked in I saw it. Teddy had brown eyes but otherwise you're the spitting image of him."

"I'll take that as a compliment then."

"You should." Tom looked fondly at the photo. "Anyway, I just wanted to tell you. It's thanks to Teddy that I trusted my instincts that day."

"I'm glad you did - and I wouldn't normally have told a new client I was between addresses either."

"Well there we are. Imagine if you hadn't – we probably would have had a few meetings and then you would have sent me a report once you'd established my lack of family and that would have been that."

"I'm still sorry I wasn't able to find anyone for you." Mark said.

"Well I'm not, not anymore. I've spent the last few months putting together a family of my own, of sorts. I was thinking the other day that I could have chosen better with some of them but then I decided that makes it seem more like a real family. Naming no names."

Mark laughed. "You don't have to."

"At the other end of the scale if I'd been lucky enough to have a son, well I'd have been proud if he'd turned out anything like you."

"Thanks Tom. Same here, I mean…"

"Good, I know what you mean lad." Tom said. "Well, we'd best get on. Lots to do today to check everything through. You know It might take the full six months after I'm gone to find the answer, don't you? You need to be ready to stick with this for the long haul however difficult it gets."

"I know that – I'll be ready. I've just got two more calls to make then I'll give you a hand. Are you sure you don't want to ring Joan and Tony? They're more like family than employees."

"I can't Mark, I don't want to keep explaining myself. I'll see them at some point today anyway but I'll say my goodbyes to everyone tonight, like we've planned."

Mark left Tom to it and walked into the drawing room nursing his coffee. The room itself was magnificent, long and narrow with six high windows, but even after four months of living at Downsview Manor it was only the mess of clutter that stopped him feeling he'd strayed behind the velvet ropes. From where he was sitting he could just see smoke from one of the Lodge House's chimneys and wondered whether Tony was already out working in the grounds. He rang the house number for Joan and Tony. There was no mobile reception up here so he'd have to track one of them down if there was no answer. The phone went straight to answerphone so after leaving a message asking one of them to call him he called the home number for Sandra and Frank. After several rings he heard the loud boom of Frank's voice, "Hello?"

"Hi Frank, it's Mark. Listen, Tom's moved things forward to tonight so

I'm just ringing around to let everyone know."

"Ah, so the game's afoot then!" Frank said, "Wait a minute. No hang on, I can't make tonight."

"Why not?"

"I've got something on until about nine. I could come after that though. Sandra too - we'd still be in time."

"What is it, this thing?"

"It's more the people who are going. I know Tom said the call could come at short notice but people do have lives you know. "

"I'll tell Tom you had other priorities then shall I?"

"Oh come on Mark, don't be difficult – there's someone I need to meet tonight. It's all lined up."

Mark said nothing and after a while Frank sighed loudly.

"Fine. We'll be there."

Chapter Two

By eight o'clock, all ten of them were at the house. Frank and Sandra were the last to arrive, breezing in unapologetically late but adding a welcome burst of life to the proceedings. Looking at them now Mark thought again how alike they were, plump and sandy-haired with matching ruddy complexions. He always thought they seemed more like siblings than a married couple.

As though sensing Mark's gaze Frank drained his glass and waved it at him.

"While you're passing."

Frank wasn't the only one knocking back the pre-dinner drinks and Mark refilled Frank's glass before adding the nearly empty bottle to the collection on the side table. He was starting to feel like a waiter rather than a host and he'd been so busy helping Joan and Tony he hadn't seen Kirsty since she arrived. He wanted to check how she was holding up before heading back to the kitchen.

Kirsty was in conversation with Brian and Ray in a huddle of armchairs and seemed to be doing more listening than talking. She stood up as he looked across at her and Mark had to stop himself staring as she smoothed down her long evening dress. The pale green fabric skimmed the elegant lines of her body and her auburn hair was pinned up with a diamond clip. In the grand setting of the room she was like some bright young thing from the nineteen twenties.

"Hello. You look incredible Kirsty," Mark said, kissing her cheek. "I didn't see that dress when you arrived, just your big granny coat."

"It's not a granny coat, it's tartan! Anyway it's freezing out there."

"Not in here it isn't," Brian said, standing up to shake Mark's hand. "We had to move away from the fireplace, didn't we? I was just running through the renovations we made to this old house before Tom moved in actually. The fireplace was a wreck before Ray got his hands on it."

"Brian said he's found some more before and after photos."

Mark smiled as he caught the look in Kirsty's eyes. Brian's construction company usually featured in his conversations with the group and recently, it seemed, it also served to remind everyone that Brian was one of 'the originals' who'd known Tom the longest.

"Most of the masonry inside was Ray's work of course. The stonework was in a dreadful state wasn't it?"

Ray nodded and then gestured vaguely towards Frank before excusing himself.

"A lot of firms would have replaced it with something mass-produced, but for a house like this we'd always source the right materials and use proper craftsmen. English too, where we can. It's expensive but then that's not an issue for most of my clients."

Brian leaned back on his heels and took a sip of his whisky looking very pleased with himself and unusually smart in a well-cut dinner jacket that flattered his tall, bulky frame.

They spoke for another minute or so before Kirsty said, "I need another drink. Mark, shall I give you a hand?"

Mark walked with Kirsty towards the drinks table and poured them both a gin and tonic.

"Thanks, I need that," she said. "Dutch courage – cheers. Seems fitting as it's legal over there."

"Hey, none of that talk, not tonight anyway." Mark looked at her and could see up close how strained she was looking.

"What?" Kirsty asked.

"Nothing, sorry."

Kirsty frowned and tucked her hair behind her ears.

"The way Brian reminds Ray that he works for him," she said. "As if he doesn't already know."

"Alice does the same," Mark said. "She doesn't like him to forget she's the bosses wife. I'm not sure that Ray takes any notice these days though."

"He's getting there I think – we might need to keep an eye on him though when Tom's not around. Come on let's go and see the man himself."

Both assuming bright smiles, they walked over to where Tom sat serenely, surrounded as though by a court of admirers. Kirsty perched on the arm of Tom's armchair and kissed the top of his head.

"Hello gorgeous girl, you look like a film star," Tom said. "I wondered where you'd got to, and you Mark."

"I've been helping Joan out in the kitchen. We're just about ready to eat."

"Good, I'm starving!" Sandra said.

"Shall we go through?" Alice asked in a bored voice, one of her long legs swinging as she sipped from her glass. Mark paused as he thought about what would happen after dinner, but when Alice's leg became still he saw her glance at him and realised he'd been staring. He looked away and turned to Tom.

"What do you say Tom? It's your night."

"Well, if we're ready, let's get started." Tom maneuvered himself out of his chair. Leaving the others to seat themselves at the dining table, Mark noticed that Alice wore a self-satisfied look that softened her normally sharp features. Not surprising considering she'd thought a man nearly twenty years her junior was checking her out. He smiled as he walked back to the kitchen and his footsteps echoed along the wooden floor of the corridor as he left the noisy chatter behind him. After the soft lighting in the rest of the house, he was dazzled by the brightness of the kitchen and stood blinking for a moment in the entranceway.

"There you are!" Joan said, a frown deepening the lines on her usually placid face. She was carrying an enormous pan of roast potatoes to the table and kicked the oven door shut behind her. Tony stood to one side, carefully pouring bright red soup into a large tureen. Attacking the potatoes with a spatula, Joan turned them rapidly in the sizzling oil. "Blasted thing!" Joan sounded furious as a potato fell to the floor. Mark stepped forward to see if he could help, but Joan stopped him.

"Leave it, we've got plenty. Just help Tony and we'll be ready. I'm right behind you."

With his wiry strength Tony lifted the heavy tureen easily. "I'm all right with this - it's probably easier on my own."

As he walked past, he gestured for Mark to follow him.

"Joan gets a bit overheated cooking for this many. She'll be fine once she sits down."

A direct contrast of his wife in looks and character, Tony seemed as unruffled as ever after the fraught atmosphere of the kitchen. In the months he'd known him, Mark had only once seen Tony get angry and that was when Brian, after too many brandies, had said how amazing it was that Joan and Alice were the same age. Brian had apologised when his rudeness was pointed out, but the truth of his words had left Joan looking downcast and Tony furious on her behalf.

"Was she overheated?" Mark asked diplomatically.

Tom had settled on comfort food from his childhood for his last meal, choosing cream of tomato soup followed by beef stew and then bakewell tart to finish. Mark anticipated the look of horror on Alice's face, and wondered whether it would be the heaviness of the food or the tinned soup that would upset her most.

15

Chapter Three

Everyone was lively and noisy by the time they'd finished dinner without any sense of forced bonhomie now. Tom was laughing as much as anyone at one of Frank's stories as though even he could forget the reason they were all together. Mark felt reluctant to interrupt but they were running behind schedule and it was his job to keep them on track. He stood up as the laughter subsided and tapped a wine glass with his fork.

"Come on Mark, I want no speeches now."

"Yes, I know but can we at least raise our glasses to you?"

Tom smiled as they all stood up and toasted him. He gestured for them to sit down and said nothing for a while, seeming to collect himself.

"Yes, thank you. Especially to Joan for all your hard work and for being cook and guest at the same time. I know it was short notice but that was wonderful." He smiled over at Joan who blushed and looked pleased.

"While we're recovering, now seems the right time to let you know what's happening after today. First off though, I've had a great time this evening. Going out on a high note was just what I wanted so thank you – it can't have been easy for you but you've done me proud." He finished the wine in his glass as he toasted them back and his voice was steady as he continued.

"Looking at the empty bottles on the table, it's probably as well for me to tell you that I've already given instructions to Mark. We've had a busy afternoon, haven't we lad what with that and getting ready for tonight?"

"I've taken a lot of notes," Mark said.

"Yes, he may be one of the youngest, but don't think I chose him as leader just because he's lived here these last four months." Tom pointed to Mark. "He knows my thinking best and he's got guts, this one, but he's got heart too and that's what this adventure needs." He looked down the table at them. "You'll need to trust Mark like I have and you'll need to trust each other. No room for egos here."

Mark appreciated Tom's words because he knew that Brian felt he should have been put in charge. Kirsty smiled encouragingly across the table at him and Mark thought what an unlikely looking librarian she was. He'd never seen her so dressed-up, although he'd thought much the same about her when he'd first met, back when he'd run a series of genealogy seminars at Brighton Library.

"Hear, hear." Frank said. "We've got no choice but to trust each other and you'll keep us on the straight and narrow, won't you Mark?"
Mark smiled his thanks but wondered what Frank really thought. If nothing else, he must have resented that Tom hired him in a last-ditch attempt to trace any remaining relatives. Frank, with his background in historical research, could definitely have helped but instead Tom asked Kirsty if she knew anyone.
"Now, you've probably wondered about my circumstances – financially I mean. I know I've always been vague about it."
There was an expectant hush because none of them knew where Tom's money came from. Mark had often thought it was strange that Tom, who was so decent and likeable, didn't seem to have any friends. In the time that Mark had lived at Downsview Manor most visitors for Tom had been people like his lawyer and nurse. His only friends seemed to be people he'd met through their work for him - Brian and Ray because of the house renovations, Tony and Joan his gardener and housekeeper who came with the house and Sandra who he commissioned for a painting of Downsview Manor. Alice and Frank, spouses of Brian and Sandra, he'd met more recently once he started hosting his weekly dinners. Kirsty was the exception but even then they became friends through his regular chats with her at the library. He didn't seem to have normal friends.
         Tom seemed again to be collecting himself and he coughed again. It was clear that he hated talking so much about himself.
"You all know that I used to work on the railways. Different jobs and I did well but I was never what you'd call a boss type. It was a good living compared to where I came from though and I was always a saver, not that I could have saved enough to buy the roof tiles on this place. So there we are, I'm not a captain of industry and I obviously don't come from some rich family." Tom drummed his fingers on the table and took a deep breath. "As part of my fortune will be yours, I think it's only fair I let you know where it comes from."
Everyone sat up straighter and there was complete silence. Joan jumped as the chimes of the old grandfather clock in the hall sounded and a few people laughed nervously. Tom looked at his watch.
"Nine thirty already? Let's quickly get everything cleared from the table first and get some coffee. Then I'll carry on. Perhaps it's best if we just finish what's in our glasses and then put the drink away."
Frank quickly grabbed the nearest bottle of red wine and filled his glass while Joan headed straight out to the kitchen followed by an entourage

of helpers. As they headed down the corridor together Kirsty whispered to Mark.

"He means to go thorough with it doesn't he?"

"He was strolling around the grounds like he was saying goodbye earlier."

"I still can't get my head round it."

"I know. He was all business earlier though going through everything and double checking all the clues."

Joan, who was loading the dishwasher, must have heard Mark's words as they walked into the kitchen. Turning round she said to them,

"He amazes me with that computer at his age. He bought that new one at Christmas didn't he Mark?'

"He was obsessed with it."

"He was. He said he only wished he could see what would come next bless him, do you remember?"

"He's been in to them since the start. My guess is that's where the money comes from – some dot come thing. He knows more about coding than I'll ever do that's for sure." Mark said.

"I don't even know what coding is." Joan said. "I've got no time for any of that." With that she slammed the dishwasher shut

By the time they returned to the dining room there was a trail of seven people, all waiting for Tom to carry on, and laden with coffee and jugs of water. They placed everything on the dining room table and found Tom and Frank installed at one corner of the table.

"I thought we weren't having any more drink." Joan said as she noticed the large brandies they were cradling.

"I just meant we ought to slow down a bit that's all." Tom said. "We'll be alright."

Everyone grabbed their drinks, poured coffee or water and settled back around the table. Alice, leaning forward, was the first to break the silence and asked quietly,

"So where were we Tom?"

Clearing his throat, Tom walked over to the heavy oak sideboard where he collected a stack of cream envelopes from behind a silver tray. Moving slowly around the table he distributed them. "These aren't to be opened tonight. I'll explain later but it's important to keep these to yourselves, a sort of insurance if you like against anyone deciding to act on their own. I want you to put them somewhere safe right away."

Each of them looked at the envelope that had their name written in Tom's shaky writing and then put their envelope into pockets or handbags. When Tony automatically handed his to Joan, Tom reached across and said, "No that's for you to keep private. What's in here is the only time you won't be sharing information with each other." Tony nodded and put the envelope in his pocket.

"To stop anyone going rogue is it Tom?" Frank asked.

"That's right but just ignore those for now. I'll try to be brief as the evening's getting on. Now, going back a bit, some of you know my Annie didn't like going out. Agoraphobia it's called but we just said she didn't like leaving the house and that was that. We were never what you'd call sociable types anyway but in our last years what little family there was had long gone and our friends had either died off or forgotten us. When I stopped working that was an end of it."

Tom paused, seeing Sandra's sympathetic face. "No need to feel sorry for us - we were happy as we were. Anyway we both loved chess and logic puzzles, anything like that. Annie even used to set crosswords for the local paper. She was always the clever one. We loved our computer too and you can imagine how good it was for Annie to have the world at her fingertips. Now, we used to do the pools, partly because of the fun of choosing the draws and checking them afterwards. It was just something else we did together. We never won a thing…well, until one week we did. Not the jackpot mind, but a fair sum."

"So when was this?" asked Brian.

"How much was it?" Frank asked at the same time.

"Frank, really!" Joan said.

Tom nodded then exhaled loudly, as if relieved to get the worst over with. "No Joan, it's fine, that's what everybody's thinking. It was nothing like the amount the lottery winners have today but it was a long time ago and it seemed like a fortune to us at the time."

"A pools win does make sense of a lot of things." Brian said. "What so you just invested well then, did you?"

"Sort of. Annie and I were the kind of people that others would say the money was wasted on. It wasn't like we could travel or help our family and we didn't have extravagant tastes. We never expected to win."

"But someone has to with these things." Ray said. He looked thrilled. "Why didn't you tell us earlier?"

"Apart from my financial people you're the first people I've told. It's just…"

Tom seemed to run out of steam.

"Private?" Kirsty suggested.

"Yes, exactly. Old habits die hard I suppose and it wasn't done to talk

19

about money in my day. Anyway, the money wasn't enough for me to retire on but it gave us a cushion and it gave Annie a new hobby. She did online courses in finance and trading. I didn't understand half what she talked about but she did some clever stuff - learnt to back both sides if that makes sense. Like I say, she was always the clever one and before long I was able to retire. Then Annie had a remarkable run of luck and well it went up from there really."

"When did you start spending it then?" Frank asked.

"Not in a big way until this house really. Investing was just something else we did together - like the crossword puzzle. Change of any kind was hard for Annie and we loved where we lived so once we'd spent a bit getting it just as we wanted it, the novelty of buying things soon wore off. Mind you there was a time when we were getting deliveries every day."

"I'd go up and down Bond Street." Sandra said. "I'd walk into those shops with a security guard on them and they'd think I was just a tourist or something but I'd do the full Pretty Woman."

"Pretty Woman but without being a hooker - or is that another fantasy?"

"Stop it Frank." Sandra said hitting his arm. "Trust you to spoil things."

"I'd just go to Churchill Square and buy whatever took my fancy." Joan said. "I've always wanted to do that.

"All being well, you can." Tom said. "Annie had fun with the money but she always had in mind to leave it to charity so she took the investing side seriously. She never trusted banks though – I think that was the key to her success."

"Who does trust banks?" Brian asked.

"Yes, well. Annie's father lost everything in the great depression and that stayed with her. Alongside her investments, we bought a lot of gold and Annie went through a phase of buying jewellery. Posh stuff I mean, not just from the high street."

"That's what I'd do." Alice said. "Real investment pieces."

"She learnt all about that and went in for a lot of vintage stuff, diamonds mainly but also some really colourful modern necklaces. They cost a fortune but we had the money and she had had a lot of fun choosing things. She'd get so excited when a courier came up the drive and I often wondered what he thought, delivering parcels from Christies and places like Bulgari and Tiffany to our little house."

"How gorgeous." Alice said.

"She did love it although sometimes it made her sad too. All dressed up and nowhere to go, you know? There was one necklace she had, all diamonds and emeralds…I remember her looking at it and saying that jewellery like that wasn't made just to sit in its box. Anyway, Annie was in service at Downsview Manor before we met so when she saw the house for sale in Sussex Life she couldn't stop looking at the photos on the website. She kept ringing the estate agent about it but she wouldn't go and see it. He must have thought she was wasting his time but either he was very kind or he really was an optimist."

Tom smiled, remembering.

"In the end Annie made up her mind and we decided to buy it. She couldn't stand to think of it to become a hotel or a nursing home. I think back then this was more of a home to her than the one she left. She liked the idea of going from housemaid to lady of the manor too. We used to joke about her wearing all her grand jewellery while doing her knitting in the morning room. It made her happy all the planning, this is before even your time Brian, and I liked the grounds of course. I suppose I hoped that over time Annie would come for a walk around the lake with me or even just sit on the bench outside and look at the view. In truth though I don't know if she would ever have made it to the house at all, what with the way she was. It might always have been too big a step for her."

Tom swallowed and gestured for Sandra to pass him the coffee,

"As it was Annie's stroke put paid to all of that." Tom took a sip of his coffee.

"I lost my taste for the house after she went but the sale was in motion by then so I kept at it. You'll remember how much work needed doing Brian. It was something I could do for her so it seemed to make sense even when I didn't want to bother."

"I remember Tom." Brian said. "You were determined to see it through, very determined."

"It helped to have something to focus on."

"That was when you started coming into the library." Kirsty said. "You used to talk about your house being done up as if it was a little two up, two down. I remember asking you once what was taking so long."

Tom laughed. "You did. Problems with the builders I think I told you - sorry Brian."

"And there we were ahead of schedule." Brian said.

"I know. Anyway, going back to the question of money, Annie always made sure we took some out in cash." At that point Tom had another coughing fit.

"Do you need a break, Tom?" asked Joan.

Before Tom could answer, Frank asked, "how much are we talking, just to get an idea of the scale of this?"

Tom held up his hands to still the questions and sounded weary as he said,

"I should have talked to you about this before but I wanted to get to know you without the money. Then there never seemed the right time to bring it up. Last time I saw my financial advisor he told me I was worth about eight million but that's just the money he knows about and all that's going to charity once the house and everything is sold. Just like Annie wanted. I haven't named any of you in my Will, apart from a small bequest to Tony and Joan of course."

"Thank you Tom." Joan said.

"It would have been a lot more without this I promise you. I know you both came with the house but I wouldn't have got through my first months here without you."

"It's been a pleasure looking after you." Joan said, her eyes welling up.

"Now, stop all that. Tom said. "We're not there yet."

Tony patted Joan's arm while she searched for a tissue in her bag.

"I'm alright." She said. "You carry on Tom."

Tom nodded and looked around at them.

"So how much is our bit Tom?" Brian asked. "You still haven't said."

"I'm getting to it but first I want to say something about, about…later. As a Christian, I couldn't take the overdose myself. It might seem like I'm splitting hairs but I grew up in a time when suicides were buried in the corner of the churchyard."

There was absolute silence in the room, broken only by the crackle of wood from the dying fire. Mark thought this theological blurring of the lines was shaky at best but it was what Tom believed that mattered.

"I know you've all agreed to help my death but remember what came first. I told you when we first all got together that I was setting up a treasure hunt. Now, tell me - what did you think about that at the time?"

Nobody said anything for a moment then Sandra said,

"A bit eccentric, but fun, that's what I thought."

"When you said we'd be looking for something of great value, like proper treasure, that was enough for me." Ray said.

"Right, why not? So you agreed to give up an evening a week, partly to keep an old man company and partly to get to know each other ready for the treasure hunt. That's all you agreed to, remember. This next bit now, what you have to do, you agreed to that much later so don't think of the money as payment for services rendered, that's all I'm saying. Now, let me finish and then…" Tom halted, looking suddenly unnerved.

"What is it Tom?" Kirsty asked. It was a while before he spoke again but when he did his voice was steady.

"Nothing, I'm fine – really – but it just hit me that what I've planned for is happening now, that's all. That's how life is isn't it? Always thinking ahead, planning for the future and then whoosh it's here and then…gone."

Tom gestured to Mark. "You can take it from here. I'm done now."

"And you're ready?" Mark asked. His words hung heavily in the stillness of the room until Tom spoke.

"Yes, I'm ready."

At that, Mark stood up.

"Right. This is what Tom's got planned for us…"

Chapter Four

Tom's funeral took place at the local church two weeks later. It was a small turnout with just those who'd known Tom as a client and the nine people who had seen him last. The secret they shared drew them together and they huddled in a group under their umbrellas listening to the vicar's words. He was ancient, far older than Tom had been, and as his vestments billowed in the wind Mark had an image of him flying away like an oversized crow. Mark tried to concentrate on what he was saying but soon zoned out again until, abruptly, the droning monotone stopped. The vicar seemed as relieved as the rest of them when it was over, keen to escape the bleak January weather. He left after a few words with the mourners and headed for the relative warmth of his church while the group straggled back to their cars in twos and threes. Mark had Kirsty and Ray in his decrepit VW Golf and he allowed other cars to pass before reversing down the small country lane.

They were on their way back to Tom's house and there was a feeling of awkwardness in the car as they spoke about the dreary service. They hadn't seen much of each other since the night Tom died. Once they were on the main road Ray leaned forward from the back seat.

"You know the six months we've got to work out the clues?" Mark nodded. "Is that from today or from the day when Tom died do you know?"

"Jesus, Ray. We've literally just buried Tom." Kirsty said.

Mark glanced up as Ray sat back in his seat and felt a twinge of sympathy for him. It was like when Ray had announced, just before the funeral started, how amazing it was to have six months off work. Joan had given him a firm look but he'd known what Ray meant.

Mark's thoughts were far from work as he drove through the rain and like all of them he'd arranged everything so that he was free for the full six-month period. It was easy enough for him as he just had himself to answer to, but it was the money Tom had given each of them for expenses and living costs that meant he could afford to do it. As far as he knew Brian was the only one who still hadn't sorted everything out but they could start without him. Joan and Tony were the only ones carrying on as normal as they continued their roles as housekeeper and gardener.

"If my Mum could see me now." Ray said as they drove up the driveway to the house. "Talk about going up in the world."

"I still can't believe Tom used to live here on his own though." Kirsty said. "My Mum would have been very interested to meet him if she'd been between husbands. Tom wouldn't have known what hit him."

Mark laughed. "What did she think of you giving up your job?"

"Oh, she was really pleased - Mum despairs of my quiet life." Kirsty yawned loudly and stretched. " She told me to let her know if I needed money but otherwise she just assumes I'll be fine. In my family I'm the sensible one while my sister has the adventures."

"Where does she live?" Ray asked. "Your mum I mean."

"She's in Portugal with Luc…"

"Your step father?"

"Yes. Mum and Dad divorced way back – Luc is husband number four. Dad died a couple of years ago though."

"Sorry. I've heard you mention him…"

"No, it's fine Ray. I do still talk about him a lot I suppose. It was always him and me that were close and then Mum and Jenny, my older sister."

"Oh. Even worse." Ray said.

"I know, but I'm lucky I've still got Mum and Jenny and actually the three of us get on a lot better these days."

"What about Jenny, does she know about all this?" Mark asked.

"Not a chance. She'd be muscling in insisting she could help and Frank would let her just so she could liven things up. Anyway, I thought all this was supposed to be top secret. You haven't told anyone have you?"

"Not what's really going on, no, just that Tom commissioned me to write his life story along with the history of the house."

"The most unlike Tom behaviour ever."

"I know. It was his idea though and it's a great cover story for all of us. Explains a lot. Have you told Jenny you've given up your job?"

"She's still traveling so I've got the flat to myself. She's madly in love though so she's very distracted, probably won't even notice anything's different. I'll tell her when she gets back though. Have you told anyone Ray?"

Ray shrugged as Kirsty turned to face him,

"I've just said I'm working away for a few months."

"That's good. Joan's the only worry as far as I'm concerned."

"She knows not to talk about this though." Mark said. "Joan's been coming up to the house to cook for me like she used to for Tom."

Mark looked sheepish. "I keep telling her she doesn't need to but she insists. Not that I'm complaining - she's a fantastic cook."

"Definitely." Ray said as they arrived in front of the house, "Best food I've ever had by a mile."

Mark got out and pulled his seat forward to let Ray out. Looking around at the cars parked haphazardly on the circular drive in front of the house Mark saw that everyone else had arrived before them and he took a deep breath as he walked up the steps.

In the gloom of the rainy afternoon, the drawing room seemed almost as dark as when they had last been there together. A fire was burning in the grate and Joan was in the process of turning on the lamps around the room as they walked in. Everyone else was sitting down and conversation was muted as they nursed their drinks.

Once Joan uncovered the sandwiches she had left on a side table the atmosphere relaxed and after some discussion of the funeral, people began recounting their memories of Tom. Joan told them about when Tom first moved in.

"Oh it was awkward to start with, do you remember Tony? It was always 'would you mind?' and 'if it's not too much trouble?' until one day I said to him, 'Mr Stevens, you don't need to ask, just tell us what you want doing.'"

She looked over to Tony for confirmation.

"That's right."

"It took a while but we got there in the end."

"We did." Tony said. "Mind you he was like no employer I ever had. He even used to help me in the grounds sometimes, back when he still could, and then we took to playing the odd game of chess over a pint in the evening. Not that I gave him much a match."

"Well, he needed a friend most, love him, especially back then." Joan sighed. "Such a lovely man once you got to know him."

"I couldn't make him out when I first met him." Mark said. "We'd spoken over the phone but then when I came here for an interview it wasn't what I was expecting. That was when he had his little IKEA-style den. Do you remember?"

"God, I'd forgotten about that." Alice said. "When Brian brought me round to meet Tom and see the renovations I thought they'd missed a bit."

"What was this?" Kirsty asked.

"Tom used to have his old armchair in the corner with all his bits and pieces of teak furniture from his old living room." Joan pointed to the corner between the fireplace and the nearest window.

26

"That's it." Alice said. "He had his gallery of Annie photos in there too, all along the bookcase. She was lovely-looking when she was younger."
"She was." Joan said. "I used to dust all those photo frames. Even when she was an old lady you could tell she'd been beautiful."
"He spent a lot of time in that corner." Joan said. "Apart from when he made himself go out. Well you'll remember that Kirsty. He was usually off to the library for one reason or another."
"He was one of our regulars. I always kept an eye out for him especially in the early days of his grief. He practically radiated sadness back then poor thing."
"When was this?" asked Alice.
"Oh, ages. I've probably known Tom as long as Joan and Tony have. We used to chat for ages some days."
"And me." Brian said. "Don't forget I was meeting him about the renovations before he even moved in."
The reminiscences continued for a while but as darkness fell the atmosphere changed as though people were becoming impatient for the main event. Mark was about to say something when Brian cleared his throat and said,
"Well, I say again I'll miss the old boy but I must admit I'm wondering what's on those laptops upstairs."
There were murmurs of assent as people at up in their seats. Frank rubbed his hands together.
"It's been hard to wait until now."
"If all's gone to plan it went live five minutes ago." Mark said.
"As if we didn't know that." Brian said and Ray laughed
Half an hour later, after the laptops had been retrieved, all of them were seated around the long dining table. Mark sat at the head of the table, facing the empty seat where Tom had always sat. Each laptop case had an old-fashioned luggage label attached identifying it's owner and when the cases were opened there was some discussion about the fifteen thousand pounds that Tom had included. They had agreed to use it as needed and only put small amounts at a time in their bank. A verdict of suicide had been recorded but it made sense to remain cautious.
After connecting to the Wi-Fi they typed in the web address Tom had given them. The site slowly opened and they breathed a sigh of relief as they saw a photo of Tom and Annie on the opening page. The site was set up to look like a dull family newsletter. As instructed, they clicked through to access details of the web host and a technical page

appeared. They clicked onto the Contact us link at the bottom of the page and rather than filling in their name and address as asked, typed the word 'Treasure21', into the box where it asked for a phone number. After a lengthy delay, this took them through to a far more professional-looking home page, which said across the top, "The Treasure Trail".

The group broke into excited chatter and Frank boomed, "We're up and running folks!"

Mark said quickly, "Nobody touch anything now until we've read what's on here"

At this, Joan panicked and leaned away from her computer as though simply breathing on it would cause untold disaster.

Everyone else peered at the screen, reading Tom's instructions.

"Well that seems straightforward enough." Alice said. She read out Tom's words slowly,

"Whoever has the longest first name, please type it here, but don't do yourself short and in your typing be clear."

They sat and pondered it for a while before Sandra said slowly, "It's Kirsty or me, don't you think?"

Frank tutted. "No he says not to do yourself short, he must mean our first names, like Francis and…" he looked around the room, "and Anthony say."

"Oh yes, I see." Sandra muttered.

"Right let's make a list." Mark said, pulling a notebook towards him, "What about middle names let's include those too."

"I don't see why." Brian snapped. "He clearly says first names."

"Yes and Mark is my middle name which Tom knew."

"So what's your first name then?" Kirsty asked.

"Edward." Mark said, "but I've always been Mark."

"Edward Granger." Kirsty said thoughtfully. "You sound very distinguished.

"Teddy!" Frank said.

"Moving on, so it's Edward Mark for me," Mark scribbled into his notebook as he spoke. "Kirsty what's your middle name then?"

After everyone had answered Mark read out the list,

"Okay, we've got Edward Mark, Kirsty Louise, Sandra, Brian Andrew Robert, Alice May, Joan Evelyn, Anthony Thomas, Frank Peterson and Ray John. So…"

"That makes Anthony the answer then." Joan said. "Fancy that Tony."

"Wait! Hold on a minute." Ray said.

Everyone turned to look at him and he looked shifty for a moment before saying, "I was waiting to see if anyone else had a longer name but sure enough they haven't. My first name is Monterey."

Ray's cheeks burned and he stared at the table.

"I hate my name. I never normally tell people but Tom asked me straight out one day whether Ray was short for Raymond, and I told him. So he did know."

"Oh, it's not so bad. It's very unusual anyway." Sandra said.

"Yeah, well try going through school with a name like Monterey John. I got called cheese-straw when I was a kid."

There were puzzled looks around the table as everyone tried to work it out. In the end, Alice laughed and said,

"Oh, I know. Monterey Jack – it's an American cheese isn't it, very bland?"

"Come on Ray, you're not in the playground now." Brian said. "What if someone had typed in the wrong name?"

"Alright, let's not make a big deal about it. So we agree the longest name is Monterey?

"Yes Teddy." Frank said.

Mark ignored him.

Kirsty's hands shook slightly as she carefully typed in Monterey and asked Ray to check the spelling.

"Okay, we've got it. Just do it, Kirsty."

With everyone standing around her chair there was silence as they waited for something to happen. After a few seconds a new page came up with the words "Click here to see your first clue".

As Kirsty clicked the underlined word a series of bleeps announced that new mail had arrived in everyone's inboxes and everyone rushed back to their laptop.

"Here goes." Sandra said to nervous laughter and Mark felt excitement coil in his stomach as he opened the email from Tom Stevens and silently read the words that appeared.

Chapter Five

It was early evening and people were relaxing on chairs and sofas around the fire after their emotionally charged day. The funeral and its aftermath had drained their energy and the excitement of the first clue and subsequent debate seemed to have exhausted everyone. As if continuing a conversation, Mark interrupted their collective reverie. "Just wondering, has anyone thought about when they're going to move in to the house?"

People shifted in chairs and looked around at each other, as if waiting to see what other people would do first. Ray was the first to speak. "I'm ready to move in now Mark. I'm in a bed-sit at the moment so it won't take me long to pack. If that's all right with you?"

"Great. It's been a bit strange living here on my own.'

Ray grinned broadly and said,

"Well, I'll move in tomorrow then, won't take me long."

"Okay, anybody else?"

Mark avoided looking at Kirsty, but was glad when she spoke up next. "I've thought about it and now that my sister's got her boyfriend half moved in it would suit me to get out of there before they come home from their travels." Kirsty paused. "I don't want to sound anti-social but the only thing is that I'd need to feel I had privacy if you know what I mean. I wouldn't want to feel like a house guest for six months."

"I get that." Mark said. "You know how big this place is though and a couple of the larger bedrooms are more like apartments with dressing rooms and all sorts. If you don't want to see anyone just lock your door." He thought for a moment before adding, "You could put a kettle and fridge in your room if you wanted."

Kirsty laughed, "I'm not that much of a diva although that does sound good. Do we know how many there are like that?"

Remembering the hours spent wandering around the large empty house since Tom's death, Mark answered, "I worked it out. Leaving aside Tom's old rooms there are two main suites that have got dressing rooms. There are loads of bedrooms though and six of them have their own bathroom. A lot of them have interconnecting doors so it would be easy to set those up as suites."

"Well count me in then," Kirsty said. "What's everyone else doing?"

"Joan and I have decided not to." Tony said, "There's no point us upping sticks."

"No point at all." Joan agreed. "We're on the doorstep anyway and we'll be more comfortable in the Lodge House."

"We can practically wave at you from here anyway." Mark said.

"It would suit us to move in." Alice said. "We're finally having some work done to the house. This way, we can live here and let the workmen get on with it." Alice paused, smoothing her skirt before looking at Mark. "Of course as there are two of us I really think we ought to have one of the main suites."

"Right. Well, no problem I'm sure Ray won't mind, will you Ray?"

"It doesn't bother me, give Kirsty one of them and then you and Brian can have the other one." Ray earned a serene smile from Alice.

"Hang on!" Sandra said. "What about me and Frank?"

"First come, first served I say and Kirsty asked about a suite before anyone else."

"Oh I don't mind, Ray, I just want a bit of space that's all. I don't need the best room in the house."

"You should still have first pick though, it's only fair." Ray said.

"So, what are you planning to do?" Mark asked Sandra.

"It won't take us long to get ready. We'll have to see how we get on though. I'll miss the light in my studio and anyway Frank's hopeless unless he's locked in his study."

"That's true enough." Frank said, taking a large slug of whisky. We could always try it out I suppose and I'm sure we can find somewhere to work in this big old place."

"I thought we were taking a break from work until we've solved the clues," Brian said glaring at Frank. "If I'm expected to hand over the reins of my company for six months I can't see it's fair for you to carry on writing your bodice-rippers and for Sandra to be daubing away."

"Bodice-rippers!" Sandra said. "Frank was nominated for an award for one of his books. He writes history too you know, not that I'd expect you to understand it."

A flicker of anger crossed Brian's face but he said calmly,

"At least I take pride in my work. I tell you what I do know though…things tend to go wrong when you have unreliable people in the team."

Sandra looked to Frank for support but he ignored her, examining the contents of his glass instead. As the silence stretched Frank knocked back his drink.

"We've already agreed we won't be working while we're in the house so let's all just crack on shall we?"

"Good idea, Frank," Joan said. "Anyway I think your books are wonderful, really exciting plots and so many little historical details."

"Thanks Joan. That's the easy part for me. Just the characters I struggle with but I usually get there in the end."

"You wouldn't know that to read them," Joan said. "I think they're brilliant."

"Well, it the best way I've found to make a living without an alarm clock."

"And Brian, if this house is anything to go by you've every right to be proud."

Joan's unsubtle efforts to diffuse the argument seemed to work and Sandra smiled at her before saying in a softer voice than before, "Sorry Brian, I get a bit defensive about Frank's books."

The atmosphere lightened when Brian apologised in turn. After the stresses of the day it seemed they wanted to set the tone for the months ahead. Having agreed that everyone, except Tony and Joan, would move into the house, they decided on a tour of the upper floor to allocate rooms, and Mark had a coin at the ready to settle any disputes. The bedrooms had been done in modern country house chic with plenty of velvet cushions and heavy cotton drapes. The interior designer that Brian used had chosen neutral tones accented by splashes of colour so that each room looked different.

"The rooms are all so gorgeous." Kirsty said. "I can't believe Tom had all this done when it was just him living in it."

"It was his memorial to Annie." Alice said. "He told the designer he wanted nothing too showy but he wanted the best, didn't he Brian? He wasn't really involved other than that, apart from his own bedroom."

Brian nodded. "He kept his old bedroom furniture just like he did with his corner of the drawing room. Not sure the designer was pleased but otherwise he was a dream client really, pretty much left us to get on with it."

"I liked the room with the dusky rose curtains." Kirsty said. "Was that the one with the window seat looking over the lake?"

"Most of them look out on the lake." Joan said. "That one's got a nice feel about it though. It's got a bathroom and dressing room too, not the biggest, but still a lovely set of rooms."

"Do you want to stake a claim?" Mark asked.

"If nobody minds?" Kirsty said. "Yes please."

Alice chose the largest suite for her and Brian so Frank and Sandra automatically chose the other main suite. This was smaller but had windows on three sides and overlooked the woods at the back of the house as well as the lake. Mark relaxed once they were sorted, as he knew that Ray would go in a tiny attic room if needed. Instead Ray chose a large, airy room accented with green that was opposite Kirsty and in the same part of the house as Mark. It was a good end to their first day and Mark felt like they were making progress even if they had absolutely no idea where to start with their first clue.

Chapter Six

A week later, Mark woke to the sound of birdsong and stretched with a huge yawn. Opening one eye he could see from the alarm clock beside his bed that it was 7.30 and he exhaled noisily, burying himself back under the covers and relishing the prospect of more sleep. It had been another late night and he'd had too much to drink thanks to Frank's heavy-handedness with the wine. He reached for the pint of water on his bedside table and drank half of it in one swallow. Despite the hangover, he was enjoying having people around again and, even if they weren't his first choice of housemates, the house seemed a lot friendlier. He wasn't easily spooked but the house was too big and too old for one person. Since the group had moved in he'd been able to ignore the creaks and groans of the house settling at night and he was sleeping more soundly as a result.

Opposite his door he heard Ray's bedroom door slam and the boom of Frank's voice further down the corridor. He turned over and realised he wasn't going to get his extra hour after all. With the late nights and early morning noise, he might be sleeping better but that still didn't amount to much. He rubbed his eyes and decided, yet again, that tonight he would have an early night. With a huge yawn, Mark kicked the covers aside as the thought of coffee and toast stirred him to get up. After padding barefoot into his small kitchen he saw that he'd run out of milk and he put the carton in the bin where he also saw the bread wrapper. He swore as he remembered he'd used the last of his bread to make toast last night.

Walking in to the main kitchen for supplies a few minutes later, Mark found everyone except Joan and Tony sitting at the large kitchen table. Their discussion sounded familiar and he nearly walked straight back out again.

"I mean what the hell does it mean? Tom should have given us some sort of pointer," Frank boomed. "We don't know if we're supposed to take it literally, or whether it's some sort of code…?"

"Tom said this one would be easy." Kirsty interrupted.

"Easy, oh yes. Obviously." Brian said. "We've got less of an idea now that we did a week ago."

Mark walked over to the bread bin, not wanting to interrupt.

"There's no point going on about how difficult it is." Alice said. "We just have to keep at it. Morning Mark."

Mark let the conversation wash over him as put his toast on. He'd heard it before. He stared out at the frost-covered woods while he waited - still only half awake, and started when Brian called him. "Mark! This includes you. We need to all sit down together, properly I mean, and come up with some kind of strategy. What we're doing isn't working."

Brian's glare was unnerving and with everyone at the table turned towards him Mark was relieved when the toaster popped.

After some discussion and a quick call to Joan it was agreed to meet at nine-thirty, ready for what Brian called a brain-stormer. Mark headed upstairs, wondering if they'd been lulled into a false sense of security by Tom's assurances about an easy first clue. Admittedly last week had also been spent settling in and adjusting to their changed circumstances but even so it felt like they were getting nowhere. Moving in had been done with varying degrees of fuss, from Ray's arrival first thing with nothing more than a suitcase and yucca plant to Alice and Brian's stately entrance with a moving van and two helpers. Frank and Sandra had haphazardly unpacked their carload of suitcases, bags and a large easel, and in the midst of chaos the sight of a green and white taxi dispatching a beaming Kirsty had lifted Mark's spirits. She'd waved at him as he jogged down the steps to give her a hand and for the first few days the house seemed to come to life, its new inhabitants like weekend guests, eager to be entertaining and to get on with everyone. It seemed like nostalgia now to remember how relieved he'd been, even more so now that everyone's frustration was starting to show. It was the first clue that was doing it, the jaunty way it was written making it even more irritating. As Mark walked into his apartment he picked up a print out of the clue from his coffee table and read it absent-mindedly as he ate his toast.

This buzzing magician begins with Helen, and she ends in clay,
So when the chat peters away root through what you've found.
Need help? For a vision of the answer just look in the ground.

Reading it through, he found it more confusing now than when he first read it on the screen. He kept returning to it as though looking at it with fresh eyes would uncover something new but instead it felt like the words were becoming more meaningless. He dropped the tattered piece of paper back on the coffee table as soon as he'd finished his toast and stood up reluctantly. His coffee would have to wait. Mark showered in a rush and as he shaved he thought about how completely

Brian took charge earlier. Hard though it was to admit, even to himself, the older man had a presence that he lacked. Frowning at his reflection as he dried his face he wondered what he'd been thinking. His share of Tom's fortune was half a million pounds and he'd been treating this whole thing like a popularity contest. He'd always known it would take more than Tom's say so for him to be treated as leader by the group but he could tell his settling in time was at an end.

By nine-thirty everyone was seated around the large dining table while Mark set up a metal easel and attached a flipchart. The conversation was muted while they waited and Tony was leaning back in his chair with his arms folded.

"It's lucky there wasn't much to do in the grounds, that's all I'm saying." Tony said.

"Everybody's said from the start that you and Joan aren't actually working." Kirsty said. "You know Tom only set it up like he did to give you a reason to keep coming to the house."

"I know, but we're still paid to do our jobs."

"Give yourself a holiday then. Otherwise it's not fair if you're doing twice as much as everyone else."

Mark turned around to say he'd only be a minute and caught Sandra's look of panic at Kirsty's words.

He smiled as he and left them to it, unwrapping the pack of magic markers he'd found in Tom's study.

"Remember there are nine of us Kirsty," Sandra said, "so if we're squabbling over whose turn it is to cook or wash up, that doesn't work either."

Joan patted Kirsty's arm. "It's nice of you to think of me but I don't mind carrying on as we are for now. I'll leave the detective work to the rest of you."

"You're a wonder Joan." Sandra said. "Thank you."

"Mind you I don't want to feel left out, that's the only thing, and you know you're all responsible for your own rooms."

"I'll make sure you're not left out Joanie." Tony said, squeezing her hand.

"Right, I'm ready." Mark said. "I thought we could do with something a bit more formal."

"Seems like a plan." Frank said. "We just need a bottle of lime cordial and we could call this a conference room."

Frank was right. The walnut dining table looked very boardroom with the eight of them sitting around it, notebooks in front of them. The grand vista down to the lake and the country house setting completed the picture. The only wrong note, had they been delegates, was the wide interpretation of any dress code. Alice was her usual immaculate self with the deep burgundy of her heavy silk blouse exactly matching her lipstick and nail polish. By contrast, Sandra seemed to embrace the stereotype of an eccentric artist with colourful layers and random accessorising that included pearls, wooden beads and a rhinestone brooch. Everyone else was somewhere in between although Mark, in honour of the occasion, was wearing a smart pair of navy moleskin trousers and his best shirt.

"At least we've got a back-up plan now." Tony said. "If it looks like we can't solve this then we can sell some conferences while we're here."

"Don't. If we think like that we're done for." Mark said, only half joking. "The main thing to hang on to is that Tom wanted us to solve this. That was his plan - a nice easy one to get us started"

"Well, it's only easy if you know the answer." Brian said

"Isn't it always?" Mark asked in reply.

Mark ripped the cover off the pad of paper. "Let's start by getting everything on paper and then we can see how we've all been getting on." He wrote out the clue and stuck it to the back of the door.

This buzzing magician begins with Helen, and she ends in clay,
So when the chat peters away root through what you've found.
Need help? For a vision of the answer just look in the ground.

"Frank and Sandra, you've been on the case with Helen of Troy. How's that going?

"Painfully." Frank said holding up a book about Greek black figure pottery. "The Trojan wars were a popular theme so there's loads of stuff out there. There's an ancient Greek called Exekias who's been described as an artistic visionary, which is almost like 'vision of the answer', but that's it." He shrugged. "I've got an appointment with a pottery expert in London so that could lead to something."

"Sounds like you've covered a lot of ground." Mark said, writing down Exekias on the flipchart. "Have you got any other angles to look at or are you done for now?"

"No, but I'm not done yet, not even close. I'm starting to feel like a pottery expert myself."

"I've been looking at Helen of Troy in literature." Sandra said. "I started with the myths and then anything connected to a magician but it's a massive task. The best thing so far is when I found out Helen of Troy had a daughter called Hermione. Not sure if Ray, Kirsty and Tony are getting anywhere with that."

"I was going to ask how the Harry Potter lot are getting on next," Mark said, writing 'Hermione' underneath Exekias.

"Oh and I was looking at Dr Faustus yesterday so that's new," Sandra continued. "It's slow going though so if anyone's free to help out..."

"Sounds good." Mark said. "Let's just work out how everyone else is doing and see where we are."

"Nothing doing from us yet." Kirsty said. "I'm books one to three, Tony's four to five and Ray's on six and seven. We're going to swap when we've gone through them."

"At least someone's having fun." Frank said.

"Have you seen the size of those books?" Ray asked.

"The difficult bit is analysing rather than reading." Kirsty said. "I haven't read them in years so it's hard not to get carried off by the story."

"Anything at all?" Mark asked.

"Not yet." Tony said. "I know the books - read them to Andy when he was growing up and then we saw all the films..."

"I remember the night before a new book was coming out," Joan interrupted. "They'd both be so excited."

Tony laughed. "We even did the trip up to London for the last one. There we were standing in line like idiots waiting for the countdown at midnight. Anyway, I know what Kirsty means about analysing rather than reading, takes a bit of doing."

"We've all got a big focus on Hermione while also looking for anything that jumps out. It's sort of the know it when you see it approach." Ray said. "We haven't seen it yet though whatever it is."

"Plus, the problem with the Hermione angle is it sort of contradicts our first idea that the buzzing magician is Harry Potter." Kirsty agreed. "We really like 'ends in clay' for Potter but although Hermione could 'begin with Helen', sort of, she never becomes Hermione Potter so...I don't know, it just feels like we're forcing it."

"Clay means pottery rather than Potter as far as I'm concerned." Frank said.

"That was the whole point of us splitting into teams though wasn't it?" Kirsty said. "We're all zoomed in and focused on our particular theory rather than all of us trying to cover everything."

"Yes, but what if we're on the wrong track altogether?" Brian said, folding his arms. "There's nothing in the house about Greek mythology or Harry Potter is there? Mark, Alice and I are the only generalists in the group which seems a bit risky to me."

"It's a shame we haven't got more of an idea about Tom's style really." Alice said. "Mark, you keep saying that one of us will have an insight into each clue, but could Tom have told you that just to add a bit of fun. A red herring, you know?"

"I don't think so. He kept saying that we'd have to think back on our conversations with him."

"It's bloody annoying, is what that is." Frank said.

Mark shrugged. "If nobody can remember Tom talking about Helen of Troy or Harry Potter then later on we might need to forget both of those ideas."

"So all of this would be for nothing?"

"Make your mind up Brian." Frank said shaking his head.

"What? No, none of it is for nothing." Mark answered. "It's just we can't know which bit is going to count, can we? Anyway, it sounds like we're nowhere near ready to abandon the Helen of Troy or Harry Potter angle yet."

"Not even close." Sandra said.

"Right, so why don't we share what we've learnt – all of us - so we get some fresh eyes on what we've done so far. I've finished cataloguing all Tom's books now. I've emailed the list but I've got a print-out for you as well." He handed them out as he walked around the table. "I've included everything – from his Len Deightons and Frederick Forsyths to the old books that probably came with the house. The books are numbered in the order they appear on the shelf so…"

"Put them back where you found them?" Alice asked.

"Yes and have a glance through the list to see if anything jumps out - probably later. First how have you and Brian getting on with the word analysis?"

*

By late afternoon, the flipchart had half its pages covered in writing and they had a lot of new ideas to explore. When it came to solving the clue though Mark felt like they were no further forward and, if anything, they'd confused themselves even more. They'd battled through the mid-afternoon slump but as darkness fell he could tell they were all struggling.

"Mark. We're done for today, aren't we?" Alice asked." My head hurts and I've stopped taking anything in."

There was a chorus of relieved agreement.

"Yes, definitely but I thought I'd quickly run through the main points before we finish up."

"Oh, bugger off Mark." Frank said, and strolled to the sideboard to pour a drink.

Tony said, "I think everyone's done in Mark. Best leave it to the morning when we're feeling a bit more lively."

"I should think about what I'm making for dinner." Joan said, as though this settled the matter.

Mark closed his notebook with a snap. "Why don't we get out of here instead?"

There was a pause as everyone weighed up the effort of getting ready to go out against the novelty of escaping the confines of the house for a night.

"It would save me cooking I suppose." Joan said.

"Oh come on, it will do us good!" Alice said. "Where's your enthusiasm?"

"Where shall we go?" Sandra asked.

The others were soon persuaded and in better spirits they agreed to meet up in the drawing room for a drink in an hour or so. After a few calls Mark booked a restaurant and a couple of taxis and then ran up the stairs to get ready.

Chapter Seven

They ended up in a large brasserie restaurant in Brighton that had tables on the ground floor and a lounge bar downstairs. Lunch had been too long ago to remember so they went straight to their table, weaving their way through the busy restaurant to reach a long table at the back. Frank had called ahead to order three bottles of Champagne and by the time they got themselves settled into their seats it was already on its way. Once the drinks were poured Frank stood up from his seat at the head of the table and proposed a toast to inspiration. They all raised their glasses and chorused after him with enthusiasm but once they'd agreed to his request not to talk shop there was a lull as they cast around for something to say. Just as the silence was becoming awkward, their waitress, Amy, arrived with a full beam smile and started dealing menus to them. She was very pretty and coped well with Frank's flirting, answering his questions politely before leaving them to study the menu. When she returned, the chaos of nine people placing an order kept her busy but there was steel in her eyes when she had to remove Frank's hand from her hip. She moved away from him and then collected menus, her bright smile back in place again.

When the waitress left there was a pause until eventually Alice spoke, her years of charity lunches hard-wiring her to fill any awkward silences.

"Are you missing the library at all Kirsty?"

"Not really. I miss a couple of my colleagues but it feels amazing to have left. I should have done it years ago."

"Didn't you like it then?" Ray asked.

"I didn't not like it, it's just that it was a good job and I hadn't really thought about doing something else."

"It's so quiet though, surely." Sandra said.

"Sometimes, but it wasn't just shelving books. I set up reader programmes like the family research one Mark did and worked on the ordering side so as well. It didn't feel like I was there six years."

"Six years?" Mark said.

"I know. I'm the only person I know who's been in their first proper job that long."

"It's all about whether you like the job if you ask me," Tony said. "In my day more people stuck with the same job and there's something to be said for it. Look at Joan and me. We've been working at the house for nearly twenty years. Different owners mind but there's real

41

satisfaction in it especially for me where I get to see saplings I've planted grow into trees."

"I think it depends on what you're used to." Brian said. "These days all the kids have been to university and expect to be Managing Directors within five years."

"If only." Kirsty said. "A lot of my university friends have been working as interns or they're in some basic job. They're hardly living the dream."

"Where did you go Kirsty?" Frank asked.

"Just down the road. I was at Sussex Uni for a couple of years doing French but I didn't finish the course."

"Why not? Didn't you like it?" Sandra asked.

"There were a few reasons." Kirsty said and the expression on her face closed the subject.

"What about you Mark?" asked Joan.

"I was at Durham doing history. While I was there I did some research for one of my tutors who did genealogy on the side. That's how I got into it all."

"And were you a Managing Director within five years?" Joan asked.

Mark laughed "Sort of but I'm a company of one so I wouldn't call myself that."

"I thought you had an assistant?"

"Only sometimes. A friend of mine helps out when I'm busy but mostly I'm on my own."

"So did you set up straight after you finished your course then?"

Mark sensed Joan wasn't just asking casually and realised she was probably thinking about Andy who was due to graduate soon. Before he could answer, Brian jumped in to tell her how he had started his construction company all those years ago. Mark had already heard the story and tuned out. Instead he found himself thinking about the row he'd had with his mother in the run up to Christmas. He couldn't imagine Joan behaving like his mother did in her eagerness to make him fit her world. She had a habit of trying to fix him after a few drinks so he should have let it wash over him but he'd been irritated already by her matchmaking at lunch. They'd been sitting companionably on the sofa when she'd started.

"I know you like doing your own thing darling but if only you'd try the City. Paul could make some introductions and you just have to stick it for a few years and you've got it made."

"Like Dad you mean?"

"Honestly Mark, why do you insist on talking about that? Your father's bankruptcy was, well it was part of something that wasn't entirely his fault."

"Come on Mum, I remember the arguments. Dad was more concerned with covering his mistakes than getting people their money back."

The sigh she gave was familiar.

"I only ever wanted the best for you. Surely you've always known that, even back then?"

"It's not like you were there to ask."

"Oh Mark, honestly – you sound like a petulant child."

He wondered why she brought out the worst in him.

"You're right, I'm sorry."

"I wrote to you every week during term time and sent those lovely parcels. Every single week Mark even when I was abroad, but when you had to leave school after your father's problems, well it was a difficult time. Once I'd made the decision to leave him I had to look to our future. Beauty doesn't last forever my love, much though I pretend otherwise." She was still beautiful, but her taut features bore no resemblance to the face he remembered from his childhood.

"The husband-hunting years."

His mother laughed. "Let's face it darling, if I'd left it up to you to provide for my old age I wouldn't be living somewhere like this." She patted his arm and sighed again. "Besides, you didn't speak to me when I stayed home anyway."

"The teenage years."

"Yes! God, I hardly recognised you once you started at Southwood. You wore those awful trainers, do you remember?"

"Everyone did Mum."

"Oh, and it was then that I became Mum." She pouted at him. "Your lovely speaking voice disappeared overnight."

"I was the posh kid with the Dad in the papers, I had to lose the drawl to fit in and I'd have been beaten up if I'd talked about 'Mummy'."

"I know but why you won't let me help you now, I just…"

"Not again Mum, please." Mark knocked back the rest of his wine.

"Yes, fine. Pax?"

They stared at the fire for a while but Mark knew she wasn't done yet. He stood up to fetch the wine bottle but she grabbed his arm.

"Wait, Mark, there's something I want to ask you."

He sat back down and folded his arms but she tapped them.

"Body language darling, it's rude."

43

"It's protective." He unfolded his arms and put his hands deliberately on his knees. "Better?"

"Yes, thank you. So, are you and Jemma definitely over?"

"How many times Mum?"

"And there's still nobody else?"

He shook his head.

"That's what I thought. Look, Mark, I want you to know you can tell me."

"Tell you what?"

"I've often wondered what we were thinking sending you to boarding school so young. It was what everyone did though."

Mark closed his eyes and listened to the fire spitting and rumbling in the grate as the wind picked up outside.

"Let me just say this - it's been on my mind for a while." She turned to face him on the sofa. "Look at me darling. Jenny was telling me about her son being gay. Alistair if you remember him, not Rory – he's engaged. Anyway she said they get on beautifully now that he's come out." She looked meaningfully at him. "I won't lie to you, Mark, I'd be terribly sad to miss out on grandchildren, but otherwise..."

"I'm straight Mum."

"Are you? Anyway, what with the Houghton boy as well, their eldest, and Johnny Thurston, it started me wondering. Being gay is no big deal these days."

Mark took a deep breath as his mother patted his hand again.

"This is because I refuse to pair off with any of the girls you wheel in front of me isn't it?"

"Well you just don't seem at all interested. At lunch today, that delicious girl Ginny was all over you and you were barely civil."

"She's horrendous."

"Well, if she's not your thing then there are so many other lovely girls you would meet if you'd only get out and about."

"I'm not doing the season Mum, I've told you."

"You're so handsome but you still scruff about in jeans carrying around that ridiculous chip on your shoulder. Coming from a good background isn't something to be ashamed of..."

"A good background - what does that even mean?"

"Now you're being silly. You're twenty-six Mark, not sixteen – it's time to grow up."

Their row had started from there.

Mark took a deep breath. Even thinking about his mother made him

44

feel tense and he'd said some things that he still hadn't apologised for. He noticed that Joan was looking over at him and she was holding an empty glass. He topped up her drink and gave her an encouraging look while Brian carried on talking. His mother's ability to push his buttons was unsurpassed but he should try more. Topping up his own glass, he smiled as he wondered if she'd get off his back once he had half a million to his name. Probably not – and anyway, they had to find the money first.

Amy returned, bearing more drinks, and by the time dinner arrived everyone was in a relaxed frame of mind. Sandra was too busy talking to take any notice of Frank's continued flirting throughout dinner, and the talkative side of Joan had also come to the fore. Joan could be very entertaining and Tony looked on fondly as she told them about the antics of one of the past owners of the big house. Apparently the son of the family had been a successful author and this led Alice to ask Frank about his books. He answered her questions reluctantly before explaining, "The thing is, what I don't like about the kind of throw-away books I write is how the heroine always ends up with her man. It amazes me really that people bother to read them." Frank paused, seeing the look on Joan's face, before continuing, "Of course, people like a bit of escapism which I understand."

"I won't bother buying your next one then if there's no point reading it."

"You tell him Joan!" Kirsty said, squeezing her shoulder. "Honestly Frank, how can you have written all those books thinking like that?" Sandra jumped to Frank's defence,

"Oh, he's not being disrespectful. It's just Frank has different tastes, haven't you darling? I mean he's a history buff writing romantic fiction."

"The thing is Joan I'd rather be writing about the history than the people."

"Well you should do that then." Joan said.

"Sadly there's not much of a market for that or I would. To be honest, once Tom's money's in the bank, Frances Fletcher will be retiring so we'll see."

"Anyway, I think it's clever of him." Sandra said loyally. "They say writers should write the sort of books they'd want to read themselves, so to be able to write his Fletcher novels is quite something."

Frank sat up straighter as Amy reappeared at the table and started clearing their glasses. Another waitress joined her, explaining that they needed the table but she could offer them a table in the lounge bar instead.

"Not a problem, sweetheart. Lead the way." Frank said.

After the bill was paid, they all headed downstairs to the large dimly lit room. A long copper-topped bar and row of barstools was across one side of the room and there was even a small dance floor in the centre with a mirrored disco ball hanging above it. Around the room were leather sofas and scuffed tables softened by jewel bright tea light holders. It was a shabby mixture of kitsch and style in the old room that just about worked, much like Brighton itself. The waitress guided them to a horseshoe shaped banquette and explained that they'd need to order at the bar.

"This is lovely." Sandra said.

"As long as we have a seat I'm happy." Joan said, looking around. The bar was relatively quiet, with diners waiting for tables or having a drink after dinner.

Frank went to the bar to start a new tab and Mark and Kirsty went along to help carry the drinks.

"This was a good idea Mark. To come out I mean." Kirsty said as Frank spoke to the woman behind the bar.

"I know. We should do it more often."

"Maybe at a steadier pace though." Kirsty gestured towards the row of drinks that was lining up.

"With Frank around?" As Mark carried back their drinks to the table he could see everyone chatting animatedly around the table and felt relieved at how well they were getting on. There was clearly no intention of anyone leaving yet.

An hour later the bar was full and it was harder to hear what anyone was saying. Joan was the first to suggest going home after pointedly looking at her watch a few times. Brian and Alice suggested a nightcap somewhere quieter but when there were no takers they decided to head back instead. Sandra looked undecided but as Frank had no intention of going anywhere she settled back in her seat.

"Do you want to stay here?" Mark shouted to them, "Or go on somewhere?"

"We might as well stay as we've got this table." Kirsty said and waved goodbye to the others who headed outside to find a taxi.

Ray and Frank went to the bar to order them another round of drinks and Mark leaned back on the sofa feeling a rush of happiness to be among noise and other people. Kirsty was seated next to him now that the others had left and he turned towards her.

"How are you?"

She smiled at him. "Good, thanks - better anyway. How about you?"

"Same. I needed to get out of the house."

"You were really good today though Mark, up there with your marker pen."

He laughed. "Thanks, I think."

"No, you were. It can't be easy especially with Brian on your back half the time."

"It is a bit weird. I've been trying to rub along with everyone and acting like it's no big deal that Tom put me in charge,

"It was to Tom."

"I know. I think I realised that this morning."

"Well you could definitely tell the difference. Sandra noticed as well. She said it was good to see you stepping up. Mind you, Frank didn't look pleased."

"He wouldn't." Mark looked across the wide table at Sandra who was watching Frank chat to a couple of women at the bar.

"The hardest thing is being so out of touch with everyone."

"Tell me about it." Kirsty said. "It's made me realise how addicted to my phone I was. No social media allowed and no phone reception at the house? I was dreading that but yesterday I left my phone in my room all day and didn't even notice."

"I'm still struggling with it but I'm getting there. Have you got a good story?" Mark asked.

"What story?" Sandra asked, moving along to sit closer to them.

"The whole isolation thing." Mark replied.

"Oh right. Kirsty's story is probably the best of all of us, lucky thing."

Mark could see that Kirsty looked embarrassed.

"I was literally just going to tell you Mark."

"Tell me what?"

"It's nothing really. Just that Mum's been on at my sister to find out what's happening with me. In the end I had to tell Jenny I'd got a job helping you out with Tom's memoirs and that…you know?"

Mark smiled. "One thing led to another?"

"Exactly." Kirsty looked relieved. "I had to say it was all a bit whirlwind."

"So, did I sweep you off your feet?" Mark asked.

"Who knows, it might have been that I swept you off your feet." Kirsty answered with a laugh.

"Anytime, whenever you're ready." Mark said. His tone was light but when he looked at Kirsty she didn't meet his eyes. "Seriously though, it's a good story. Makes sense of you moving in."

"Thanks Mark. How about you Sandra?"

"I'm all set. Tom commissioned me to create a series of paintings of Downsview Manor."

"Did he really?" Kirsty asked.

"Not really no, but please don't tell Brian. I'd go stir crazy if I couldn't do a bit of painting and at least now I'm just adding to my cover story."

"Brilliant."

"I know, good isn't it? Shall I take a couple of photos of you lovebirds? For the cover story."

"Do you mind, Mark?" Kirsty asked.

"Of course not. Come here." He slung an arm casually around her shoulders but Kirsty shuffled along and then snuggled against him, putting her hand on his chest. Her girlfriend impression was very realistic and he swallowed as he felt the warmth of her body pressed against his. She smelled amazing up close and he wondered if Kirsty could feel his heart beating.

"One more," Sandra said. "That's it, perfect." He went to sit up but Kirsty stopped him.

"Hang on, I'll just take a selfie." Kirsty said. He smiled again for the camera then removed his arm once Kirsty sat back up.

"There, I'll send you both the photos." Sandra said. "What a gorgeous couple you make. Actually Mark, I wouldn't mind drawing you sometime. That aquiline nose of yours is divine and those eyes..." Sandra fanned herself and Mark laughed.

"Okay, uh…thanks. As long as it's not a nude."

"Spoilsport." Sandra said with a wink but then she smiled. "I'm only teasing you - I always find dangly bits distract the eye. I'd love to do your portrait though."

Mark wondered where the drinks were and looked over to the bar in time to see the dark expression on Ray's face.

"I'll just give them a hand." He said.

Ray gave him a thin smile as he approached. "You didn't waste any time."

"What, you mean Kirsty? No…"

"Why wouldn't you?" Frank said, slapping Mark on the shoulder.

"Hold up." Mark looked back at Kirsty and was glad to see she was too busy talking to Sandra to have noticed. "Nothing's going on."

"You could have fooled me." Ray said.

"It's not real though. She's told her sister we're together but only to explain why she's moved in." Mark said.

"You can take that as an insult then." Frank said.

"What?"

"If she's pretending that you're an item. Sandra told me - something about Kirsty only goes out with ugly fellas."

"What do you mean?" Ray asked.

"I don't know, ask Sandra." Frank knocked back the contents of his glass.

"She only goes out with ugly men?" Ray repeated.

"Apparently. I think Sandra said Kirsty won't get involved with anyone too good looking. Something like that - I can't remember now."

"That makes no sense." Ray said.

Frank shrugged. "Either way, you two are out of the picture. Never mind eh."

Chapter Eight

By the end of the second week morale was at an all time low. The night out together had been good but their increased camaraderie hadn't survived the frustration at being stuck on the first clue. They were bickering more than ever so it seemed fitting that an argument inspired their breakthrough. Sandra was at a meeting, but everyone else was having lunch in the drawing room after an uneventful morning. The large formal room seemed cold and cheerless as rain drizzled outside and the lamps created pools of light but did nothing to dispel the gloom. Talk was desultory and people were eating Joan's sandwiches with varying degrees of enthusiasm. Ray had a log pile of crusts on his plate, much to Joan's satisfaction, while Alice had abandoned her two triangles of ham and mustard after one bite. As she sat perched on the edge of her armchair she looked as though she'd rather be anywhere else.

There was silence as they ate. They had explored so many avenues between them all now but they were no further forwards. An update meeting was planned for the afternoon but as though prompted by the thought of this, Ray said, "I wonder if we should take a break from all this. We could let things sink in a bit and then come back to it in a couple of days."

"I can see why you've gone so far in life." Alice said, putting her plate on the table with a clatter. "Let's all give up now it's difficult shall we?"

"I didn't mean it like that." Ray protested.

"What a thing to say!" Joan said.

"Well it's true. Like having a little holiday will help matters."

"There's no need to talk to Ray like that though." Joan continued.

"Have I hurt your feelings Ray?" Alice asked.

"Come on Alice, that's enough." Mark said. "Maybe Ray's got a point. We spend all our time trying to come up with something but it seems like we've run out of steam."

After a pause, Tony said, "I agree. We can rabbit on all day long but if we're going around in circles we're just going to wear ourselves out."

"Rabbit on?" Frank said. "I haven't heard that in years. I'm with you though. It feels like we have less of an idea by the…"

"Rabbit on," interrupted Kirsty. "Rabbit on means chat doesn't it? Brian, Alice do you remember?"

"What do you mean?" Brian asked.

"When you were analysing all the clues - did you come across rabbit when you analysed chat?"

"I can't remember. It doesn't ring a bell." Alice said. "Brian?"

"Not sure. Let me look it up." The gloom seemed to have evaporated while everyone waited to see what Kirsty was on to.

"Interesting." Brian said. "Rabbit's not listed under chat but when I Google 'rabbit on' it is here. It's cockney rhyming slang. Rabbit and pork for talk."

Kirsty's lips were moving as she went through the clue in her mind. Then, without warning, she threw herself out of the chair and ran from the drawing room to the library next door.

"What?" Mark called after her.

"In a minute!" she yelled back.

"Please let her have come up with something new." Joan muttered. Nobody said anything, but they were all watching the entrance to the dining room waiting for Kirsty to return.

"What's she doing?" Joan asked impatiently.

"I'll go and see." Mark said and started to rise from his chair, but at that moment, Kirsty came rushing into the room.

"I've got it!" She said.

"Come on Kirsty, don't keep us waiting." Frank said.

"What have you got?" Mark asked.

"Right, it was when Tony said 'rabbit' and I remembered..." Kirsty's words were tumbling out. She took a deep breath before continuing more slowly, "Not remembered. You know when your brain makes word-associations?

"Yes, yes – and?" Alice asked in a clipped voice.

"When Tony said rabbit I immediately thought Peter Rabbit. I don't know why but it reminded me of a conversation with Tom. He said Peter Rabbit was his favourite book when he was a boy." Kirsty's voice was shaking and she took another deep breath. "He couldn't believe I hadn't read it and - here's the thing - he said I'd have to read his old copy of Peter Rabbit sometime."

"Yes, and?" Alice said, her voice rising.

"Think about it! Where it says, 'when the chat peters away'. Change chat to rabbit and you've got rabbit and peters next to each other. Do you see?" Kirsty finished triumphantly.

"Yes, could be." Brian said slowly.

"What about the rest of it?" Tony asked.

"Look, just listen will you!" Kirsty said. "After I'd thought Peter Rabbit, I googled Beatrix Potter and it turns out her full name was

51

Helen Beatrix Potter."

"At last!" Mark said. "That has to be it."

"Oh yes well done you clever thing" Joan said warmly.

"Not wanting to dampen the excitement here – well done and all that." Frank leant over and patted Kirsty's knee. "It still doesn't give us the password does it?"

Kirsty removed a small book from behind her back.

"Look what I found in the library? Do you want to read the inscription out Mark?"

Mark took the copy of Peter Rabbit and quickly scanned the flyleaf. He turned the pages and then heaved a deep sigh of relief.

"Yes that makes sense. I can't believe it…"

"Mark! What does it say?" Alice asked.

He read out the two sentences that Tom had written,

"Kirsty, I hope you enjoy Peter Rabbit. When you do, turn to page 12 – it will help you see things more clearly."

Mark turned the book to face everyone and pointed out the one word that had been scribbled in the margin,

"Tom's written 'carrot', that's the password.".

"Oh thank Christ for that!" Frank said.

"We said it was carrot!" Tony said. "For a vision of the answer look in the ground."

"And the bit about root for answers." Ray added.

"We couldn't have answered carrot without confirmation though." Alice said. "Not unless we were desperate."

"At least we've got some idea about Tom's style now." Mark said. "The first bit led us to the book but the last line was just about the password itself."

"Still very cryptic though." Alice said. "I can just about see why Tom would have thought it was easy but it makes me wonder about the rest of them."

"Let's find out then." Brian said. "What are we waiting for?"

"When's Sandra due back?" Mark asked.

"She said she'd be back for lunch." Kirsty said.

"Frank, do you want to ring her – we ought to wait."

"As long as she's not long." Brian said while pacing the room.

"I thought Tom would do something more obvious to get us started." Ray said, not for the first time.

"We all did." Tony agreed. "But there we are, we got there in the end."

"I'm only sorry I didn't remember about the Peter Rabbit conversation before." Kirsty said. "I did study the list of Tom's books but it didn't stand out."

"Ah well, that doesn't matter now." Joan said.

"Very generous of you Joan but let's not pretend it doesn't matter." Brian stopped his pacing as he spoke to Kirsty. "I mean he actually included 'peters' in the clue and we all thought of Potter. I can't believe you didn't connect the dots."

"Can you remember every conversation you ever had with Tom? I spent a lot of time talking to him about books."

"Hardly the point. He gave you an obvious clue but maybe you were distracted by other things?" Brian looked meaningfully at her. "To be honest I would have expected better from you."

"You sound like a disappointed teacher, Brian." Mark laughed in an attempt to diffuse the tension. "The main thing now is that we've got the answer."

Sandra walked in just as Mark spoke. "What, we've got the answer? To the Helen of Troy clue?"

"Hello old girl," Frank said. "Yep, we cracked it."

"Brilliant! Who got it? What's the answer?"

"It's carrot. Kirsty worked it out." Tony said.

"Nothing to do with Helen of Troy or Harry Potter as it turned out," Frank said with a shrug.

"You're kidding. After all that." Sandra shook her head. "So what was it?"

"It's Beatrix Potter – you know, Peter Rabbit? We think buzzing magician meant bee tricks." Mark said.

Sandra frowned at him, looking blank.

"Bee tricks, Beatrix? Although it turns out her first name was Helen."

"Wait…and the first clue was supposed to be the easy one was it?"

"When you know the answer it sort of is," Mark said. "'Begins with Helen and ends in clay'. He told us her name."

"But it's just so random."

"Well, sort of." Kirsty said. "If I'd remembered a conversation I had with Tom it would have led us to his old copy of Peter Rabbit next door…"

"Which had the answer in all along." Brian said. "We've just been talking about that."

"Yes and I'm sorry! Believe me, I wish I'd remembered earlier…"

"Nobody's blaming you Kirsty." Mark said, giving Brian a firm look. "Come on, let's find out the next clue. I've got my laptop next door."

Once everyone was in the dining room, Mark began the process of logging into Tom's website for the first time in almost a month. He typed 'Monterey' into the contact box and breathed more easily as the real website came up.

"Have you got the book, Kirsty?"

She handed it over to him wordlessly.

"So, I'll type it in just as it's written, all in lower case then?"

Mark wanted reassurance even though there could be little doubt. Holding his breath he typed it in and pressed enter. After a pause a blank screen was revealed and the second clue appeared,

Mark this place where Hope was born, a place that wealds to lake and lawn,
Where people wander far from home and herds of deer are free to roam.
Look at the red bridge until you see the password in front of you – times three.

There was silence as everyone read it and then Ray said.

"A place that wealds. This one's about the Wealdway, got to be."

"What's the Wealdway?" Alice asked.

"Tom talked about it a few times – he walked it once. It's a footpath that runs from Eastbourne up to Gravesend."

"It connects the North Downs to the South Downs." Tony said. "Tom was a keen walker in his day. He told me he did the South Downs Way once as well which is about a hundred miles."

"Not all in one go?" Sandra asked.

"I doubt it. People usually do it over a week or so. A mate of mine did it when he and his wife were expecting twins." Tony said. "He said he knew he wouldn't have a chance for years if he didn't do it then."

Mark was rereading the clue to see how it fitted.

"That works Ray. 'Mark this place' - you mark a map don't you?"

"So, we're looking for a red bridge where we'll see the password in front us times three. If we're right." Kirsty said.

"Why times three?" Sandra asked. "Why not three times?"

"Probably just a rhyming thing." Mark said. "I think there was a book about the Wealdway in the library. Hang on a minute."

"I'll come with you." Kirsty said.

They walked out of the drawing room together leaving a hubbub of chatter behind them. Mark was glad to see Kirsty looking so happy and she was practically skipping as she entered the double doors leading to the library.

"What a relief." Mark said.

"And it feels so good to be doing something new!"

"I know. Listen, you won't take what Brian said to heart will you?"

"No, it's fine. He's just being obnoxious. God knows what he meant about me being distracted though – I mean could he be any more patronising?"

"Just don't let me down again." Mark said in a pompous voice. "More importantly don't let yourself down..."

"You sound just like him!" Kirsty laughed.

They sat down at the table each with a copy of Mark's printout.

"What he said about being distracted...do you think maybe Brian meant..."

"Hmm?" Kirsty was scanning the list of books.

"Well, do you think he meant you were distracted because of me?" Mark asked.

"How do you mean?" Kirsty glanced up from her page, puzzled.

"How do you think I mean?"

After a moment she looked at him and her expression cleared.

"Oh...oh yes that's exactly how he'd think."

"Or distracted by Ray I suppose? I don't know."

Kirsty shook her head.

"Bloody man. Anyway, that kind of distraction is the last thing we need in this atmosphere."

"Or the only way to get through it." Mark said without thinking.

Kirsty gave him a look that suggested otherwise and he was surprised at the stab of disappointment he felt.

"I know." He smiled at her then returned to the task at hand." Either way I'm starting to think we've got a long few months ahead of us."

FEBRUARY

Chapter Nine

Mark still couldn't feel his feet. He was in a gloomy pub in the middle of a forest and he felt like he'd never be fully warm or dry again.

"I'm not going back out there today." Ray said, his tone belligerent. "I mean it. We should call a cab."

"It's less than four miles to the car." Kirsty said. "Five at the most - let's just warm up a bit. You'll feel better after lunch and...table!"

Kirsty was already moving and headed over to a table and sofas that was next to a roaring fire, seemingly the pub's main source of heat. She hovered while the elderly couple finished putting on their coats, gloves and hats. Mark and Ray joined her with their drinks and the woman smiled as she passed them.

"Surely you're not out walking in that?" She asked.

"We're doing the Wealdway." Kirsty replied.

"At this time of year! My goodness you're brave."

"They're mad, not brave." The old man said. "Which direction you going?"

"North." Kirsty said.

"At least you're not going against the wind," he said, "I suppose that's something."

"It doesn't feel like it." Ray said once they'd gone. He added a couple of logs to the blaze and rubbed his hands together as he sat down with a sigh. "That's so nice."

The three of them didn't say much while they warmed themselves next to the fire.

"This is the first time all day I haven't been jealous of the others back at the house." Ray said.

"Me too." Kirsty agreed.

"Yeah, well you've only got yourself to blame. Whose idea was it to volunteer us again?"

"Bugger off Ray." Kirsty said with a yawn. "You're only grumpy because you've got the wrong shoes on."

Ray laughed. "Believe me, it's not the shoes."

Mark closed his eyes and leaned back against the sofa while he waited for the food to arrive. This was their third day of bitterly cold weather and he was tired of walking for hours in bleak, desolate countryside. He'd done the same last week, just him and Ray on one thirty-mile stretch and Alice, Tony and Kirsty on another. The remainder had been split between the rest of the group with Frank and Brian driving where possible. There had been no sign of a red bridge.

"This is where we stopped last week." Kirsty said. "We managed to get the sofas then as well."

"Do we really need to cover the same ground so soon though, what with weather this bad?" Ray asked.

"If we cover the whole route we'll know we haven't missed anything." Mark said. "Anyway, we're half way through already."

"Exactly, and you know we can get it done the quickest." Kirsty said. "It needs three of us to do it properly though so please cheer up because you're doing my head in."

"Alright, I know. All I'm saying is that if the weather gets much worse we should mark our place in that stupid Wealdway book and join the others on the research side. Just for a couple of days. Mark, what do you reckon?"

Mark shrugged. Not for the first time he wondered about Tom's reference to Mark in the clue.

"Ray, how sure are you that this clue is yours?"

"I keep saying. I'm as sure as I can be. Tom spoke to me about the Wealdway a few times. He told me how you could see the South Downs and the North Downs from the house. When I was working up there this was."

"It's so broad though, that's what's bothering me. If you could see the Wealdway from the house that would give us something at least." Mark said.

"It's like with the deer." Kirsty said. "There's so much of the route where there are deer around."

"We're not going to find any in Eastbourne or Gravesend though are we?" Ray said. "Once we're through the Ashdown Forest I reckon we've passed the most likely bit of the route."

"We can't assume anything Ray." Mark said. "For all we know, Gravesend Pier has a mural showing a herd of deer."

"It doesn't though, does it?"

"I know but…" Mark sighed. "You know what I mean." He stood up. "I'm going to check on lunch."

*

The next day Mark was just as relieved as Ray that weather conditions had worsened. He was glad to rest his aching feet and spend some time by himself. He'd looked through everything in Tom's study already but he wanted to look again on the basis that he was the link for the clue. Nobody else thought that Tom was using 'Mark' as a noun rather than a verb, dismissing the idea as far too obvious, but whatever Ray said about his Wealdway chats, Mark felt sure this one was meant for him - Mark this place where hope was born, Mark this place, Mark, this place where hope was born...The more he said it the more meaningless it became but there was something that resonated beyond simply his own name. He sat down at Tom's desk and moved the nearest box file towards him.

"Right then, Tom."

It made sense to start with all his old research on Tom's family tree but he was surprised at how little there was to show for his months of work. Mark had traced Tom's family back to the seventeenth century on the maternal side helped by some unusual surnames and a lucky break with census records. He knew Tom had hoped to uncover distant cousins but there hadn't been anyone to find, not directly connected to him. It might have been different on the paternal side but Tom had no interest in that side of the family. He wondered what the story there was - at the time it hadn't felt appropriate to ask and now he'd never know. Mark picked up a stone rubbing he'd made from Tom's grandmother's gravestone up in Glasgow - 'Generous of heart, constant of faith.' Tom wasn't happy when he showed him, finding it disrespectful, but he'd been placated by Mark telling him about the flowers he'd left for her. A small lie but harmless.

He was still only half way through the first pile of documents when there was a knock at the door.

"So this is where you're hiding." Frank said. "We've already gone through everything in here."

"Who did?"

"Me and Sandra went through it between us last week." Frank said. "When we weren't walking."

"It's really tidy."

"That's Joan. I don't think she likes anyone being in here - asked if we'd finished 'poking around'. Look...I'll leave you to it shall I?"

"Thanks. Unless you need me for anything?"

"No. Just wondered where you were – I'll see you at lunch."

Mark frowned when Frank left, wondering what he'd really wanted. The centrally heated room seemed stifling after so many days spent outside so he opened a window and stood looking out at the grey water of the lake. After a few breaths of the damp, cold air he realised that was as much outside as he needed for now and he shut the window again.

Sitting back at Tom's desk he pushed the box file to one side and looked in the desk drawers for inspiration. All of Tom's important documents were with the lawyers and there was very little to look at. Even so, he felt like an intruder as he went through everything. At the bottom of Tom's desk there was a box that had once belonged to Annie. It was a large shoebox covered with an old piece of flower-sprigged wallpaper. Mark undid the faded green ribbon that was tied around it with care. There were a few old birthday cards that Mark placed to one side and a yellowing pair of white lace gloves that looked fragile and delicate. Mark removed those carefully and underneath saw a collection of oddments from seashells and pebbles to pressed flowers and old coins. He scooped these up and put them on the desk on top of a cross-stitched bookmark. Mark picked up a black and white photograph and saw a just-recognisable younger Tom standing next to Annie on their wedding day. Annie looked beautiful with black hair that curled in a bob around a heart-shaped face. Tom was tall but otherwise unremarkable-looking and Mark smiled as he remembered Tom saying he'd always felt that Annie was out of his league. As he looked at the solemn faces of the relatives standing next to the happy couple a memory stirred, something to do with Annie's parents. He sifted through the box some more and his nail caught on the lining at the bottom of the box. He continued to peel it back and realised there was something underneath. Swearing he emptied the box on the desk and ripped back the lining to reveal a large manila envelope.

"How did I miss this?" Mark muttered as he opened it and tipped the contents on the desk. Sifting through them he found everything from a school prize for reading to tickets for long-ago events but then he found a marriage certificate. He let out a groan as he looked at it and saw Annie's first names were Hope Faith Anne Charity. Tom had told him about Annie's background in their interview but he'd completely forgotten until now. Her parents were strict...something, Presbyterians perhaps? Something to do with Scotland - he couldn't remember but looking at the certificate he could see her Father's profession listed as Minister. Mark this place where Hope was born. Mark slumped back in his chair and closed his eyes. Of course Tom would have expected him to remember such a distinctive name. He'd always thought that feeling numb was just an expression but his whole body felt icy as he thought of the wasted time and the reaction he could expect from everyone. Hadn't Tom told them all that Mark had known his thinking best? He groaned again as he imagined Brian's reaction then stopped as it struck him that nobody knew about his conversation with Tom. Ray could claim this clue and nobody would ever know about the wasted days and miles of unnecessary walking.

He'd only just collected his thoughts when there was a knock on the door.

"Only me." Joan said as she elbowed her way into the room. "Thought you might like some coffee?" The grandfather clock chimed eleven from the hall as she placed a tray on his desk.

"You're an angel Joan, thanks." Mark said taking a biscuit "Look, what do you think of this?"

Joan frowned as he handed her the marriage certificate.

"What am I looking for?" She sounded impatient as she held the paper away from her. "You'll have to tell me - I haven't got my specs."

Mark read out Annie's full name carefully, smiling as he saw understanding dawn on Joan's face.

"Oh Mark! Quick let's tell the others." Joan was practically hopping from one foot to the other. "That poor woman though – no wonder she called herself Annie."

"You tell them Joan. I'll be right behind you. Let me just track down her birth certificate so we know where we're going next."

When he reached the drawing room he could hear excited voices inside and he brushed biscuit crumbs from his shirt ready to tell them the good news. As he reached for the door handle the door jerked open, making his jump, and Sandra stood there looking unnerved.

"What is it?" Mark asked as she stood staring at him.

She held out a letter to him.

"I was just coming to find you. We don't know what to make of it."

"Mark, I haven't had a chance to tell them about Annie yet." Joan said.

"What about Annie?" Brian demanded.

"Who's Annie?" Frank asked.

"Tom's wife." Mark said, irritably. "Hold on, one thing at a time – let me read this first."

When Mark had scanned the letter a few times he handed it back to Sandra. The words were printed on a scrappy piece of lined A4 paper and typed in a large, bold font.

I know what you lot are up to. Tom Stevens was my friend we go way back. He rung me up to say Good Bye the day he died. I knew something was up and let myself in. I heard everything and I got a photo of you preparing that poison you give him. I won't tell the Police what you done if you give me a half of the money. I'll be in touch.

"It wasn't poison was it?" Ray asked. "It was Oramorph."
"It was a whopping great overdose." Frank said. "Not really the point."
"I can't believe it." Joan said, her voice tremulous.
"No, neither can I." Mark said and he meant it literally. He wondered if the blackmailer was there in the room with them.
"Why did Tom never mention this old friend of his?" Mark asked. "It was because Tom had no old friends that we're here."
Alice looked sharply at Mark. "So, you're saying…"
"You can't think it was one of us?" Brian gestured to the letter and said, "Nobody here would could have written that, not even Ray. I mean look at the grammar."
"Yes, well that's rather the point." Alice sighed, "I think it's probably too badly written isn't it?"
"Not even Ray? You can't say that Brian!" Kirsty said but Ray shrugged.
"English wasn't my best subject to be fair Kirsty but I do know my past tenses and all that for what it's worth."
"No offence meant Ray, I didn't mean anything. But look, what about that wretched photo?" Brian asked. "What if someone's got a shot of us around Tom's deathbed with all that paraphernalia around!"
Mark thought of the nine crystal glasses, each with a shot of Oramorph mixed with whisky. The overdose was spread out so they were equally involved. It was a clever idea of Tom's but uncharacteristically dramatic with everyone gathered around his bed while he drank himself to death. It had taken about an hour. Could someone have taken a photo? Thinking back it was possible but more likely one of the group rather than an intruder.
"Do you know what? Let's not waste time on this at the moment." Mark said. "I can't believe Tom would have called someone – he was paranoid about us being secret, why would he risk that at the eleventh hour?"
"Tom didn't tell us everything did he?" Ray said. "He was really

private, like when he told us about winning the pools on that last night. There could be an old friend he'd lost touch with."

"Perhaps, but there's nothing we can do until we hear from them again anyway. If somebody is trying to liven things up around here though they need to think again." Mark said.

"Absolutely." Brian agreed. "We haven't got time for any nonsense, especially while we're stuck."

"No, listen," Mark said. "That's what I was coming to tell you - I know where Hope was born."

*

Once they knew that Annie was born in a small village called Buxted the rest was easy. They went online and quickly discovered that there was a hotel called Buxted Park that had an old deer park on the estate.

"I remember that place. I think we walked past the grounds of the hotel." Frank said.

"Looking at the map it goes right past it." Alice said. It was only about half an hour's drive away so they got everything they needed together and put on their walking gear. Joan was fretting about it being lunchtime so she packed some sandwiches for them to take with them. "Nobody's eating in my car." Brian said when she started handing them out, and Frank snorted, "Like you can't afford to get your car valeted."

They drove in convoy and parked near the hotel, a low-slung white mansion that was like a larger and grander version of Downsview Manor. Using a now crumpled map of the Wealdway, they walked past a thirteenth century church and followed the route past the hotel towards a large stretch of open land surrounded by woodland. A stunning view stretched in front of them and a lake twinkled in the distance, pinpointed by the rays from a weak winter sun breaking through the clouds. Some of them recognised the view from their previous Wealdway walk but there had been so much rain then they hadn't properly seen it.

"This is gorgeous." Sandra said, inhaling deeply. "I'll have to come back another time and make some sketches. I bet the light's wonderful at dawn."

"It might look gorgeous, old girl, but it's ankle-deep mud further down." Frank said putting an arm around her. "Especially near the river."

They plodded along the route for half a mile or more. They were in thick woodland by now and Mark was leading the way but feeling claustrophobic with all nine of them crashing about through the trees. He turned around and put up his hand, feeling like a reluctant tour guide.

"Hold up." He said as the stragglers caught up. "This doesn't feel right."

"No it's a waste of bloody time. I remember all this from the other day." Frank said. "We're getting further away from Buxted."

"That's what I thought." Mark said. "Why don't we go back to the hotel and regroup. See if we can talk to the locals."

"We can't go into a hotel like that looking like this" Alice said sounding appalled.

"Oh come on Alice." Frank said. "You look dazzling as ever."

"They'll be used to walkers I should think." Kirsty said. "Although I don't know how they'll feel about boots this muddy. My jeans are covered too."

Eventually it was agreed that just Mark would go inside, leaving his boots at the door, and ask the receptionist or concierge if they had any ideas about a red bridge in the area.

Trudging their way back through the woods they asked a dog-walker for directions. He told them the way and then laughed,

"It's right muddy further along but from the looks of you lot that won't matter too much."

"Yes, exactly." Alice said with a pointed look at Mark. "I wonder if you can help me." She continued. "I feel sure I've been here before, years ago now, but I remember a red bridge really clearly. Does that sound familiar? A red bridge and some deer I think."

The man looked slightly startled by the full-beam effect of Alice's attention but answered readily enough. "Could be. If it's deer you want then you can go the back way to Buxted Park and you'll see plenty in the distance near the woods. There are a couple of bridges, maybe more, but I don't know if they're red or not." He pointed them in the right direction and carried on, his brown coat and black boots disappearing into the trees. Less than five minutes later they went through a metal kissing gate into the grounds of Buxted Park estate and could see a rudimentary bridge ahead of them near a small lake. They squelched through the mud as quickly as they could and Mark cheered when he saw the thin metal sides of the bridge were painted red. It seemed impossible it could be this easy but spirits were high as they walked on to the wide bridge. While everyone looked around Mark handed his print out of the clue to Alice.

"As you led us this way will you do the honours?"

Alice smiled at him and read out the words,

"'Mark this place where Hope was born, a place that wealds to lake and lawn,

Where people wander far from home and herds of deer are free to roam.

Look at the red bridge until you see the password in front of you times three.'"

She looked around at them all. "Well, there you have it. We're on the red bridge so let's look for something we can see three of."

Chapter Ten

They were excited as they travelled back to the house. Kirsty had found the answer when she'd spotted three plastic circles on the bridge that each said 'Public Footpath'. Once Tony said these were called markers they had cheered and hugged each other. Mark had been near Kirsty at the time and she'd thrown her arms around him, her face alight with happiness. He had squeezed her in return and he might even have lifted her off her feet, he couldn't remember - although he could remember exactly how she'd felt against him. He'd noticed the blush on her face when they broke apart too and knew he hadn't imagined the look that passed between them. It had been a good day all round, especially as they'd solved two of Tom's clues in less that a month. Everyone was keen to get back to the house to find out the next clue but Joan's eagerness was mixed with agitation that she and Tony might have missed a call from Andy. It was bad timing as it turned out but his visit home from University wasn't something to be put off and Joan had been talking about it for days.

"He knows there's no point ringing our mobiles not with reception up at the house."

Andy would be staying with his parents at the Lodge but Joan was looking forward to showing him off and had concocted a story about Mark's friends staying up at the big house. Andy sounded like a nice lad and Tony's quiet pride and Joan's excitement about his visit were contagious. As Mark unlocked the door, the phone in the drawing room started ringing and Joan ran past him to get it.

"That will be Andy – I gave him this number! Hello?" Joan was breathless as she answered the phone in the hall but her face lit up when she heard her son's voice.

"Oh I know darling, I'm sorry. What time are you coming?"

Everyone had gathered in the dining room by the time Joan finished her call and they were turning on their laptops and talking excitedly about how quickly everything had turned around when she burst into the room.

"Tony, Andy's at the station already! He managed to get an earlier train. I said you'd leave straight away."

Joan was beaming and Tony smiled at her.

"Ah that's brilliant love, we weren't expecting him until tonight. I'll just wait to hear what the next clue is and then I'll be off."

"Oh Tony, no it could take ages what with double checking and everything. The poor lamb's been waiting for half an hour already - he couldn't get hold of us. Take your phone with you and I'll give you a call as soon as we know. Go on!"

"Never come between a mother and her son." Tony said drily to Mark. "I know my place in the pecking order."

Joan laughed and swatted Tony. Don't pretend you haven't been counting the days. You'll be playing pool in the Crown as soon as you've had your dinner!"

"All right." Tony's tone was grudging but the spring in his step betrayed him. "I'll get going now but make sure you ring once you've got the clue. It will need to be before I've got Andy with me. Will you be at home when we get back?"

"No, why don't you pick me up from here then Andy can say a quick hello to everyone."

Mark looked around at the mess of papers, scattered books and laptops.

"He can wave from the car." Tony said. "Mark, the timing's bad I know but after Andy's had a fix of Mum and Dad today he'll probably spend most of his time with his mates. We'll be back on it tomorrow."

"I didn't even think of that." Joan said. "Sorry, we weren't expecting him until later but I'll see what we've got in the freezer and I can…"

"Don't even think about all that Joan," Mark said. "We'll manage. You spend time with your boy and we'll see you when we see you. He's only here for a few days isn't he?"

After Tony had gone, giving Joan a hurried peck on the cheek as he left, the rest of them gathered around the laptop. It took a few minutes but the clue was unusually brief when it appeared on the screen.

This bleeding heart may have gone to seed,
But holds the answer that you need.

Over Mark's shoulder, Sandra read the clue out aloud.

"Is that all of it? Well, it's short. Come on everyone, who remembers Tom talking to them about bleeding hearts?"

"Depends what he means by bleeding heart." Brian said slowly, "a bleeding heart liberal, isn't that the phrase? Could be a person."

"Or a pub." Ray said, "I think there was a pub called the bleeding heart."

"There's definitely a restaurant." Kirsty added.

"What about those bleeding heart religious pictures? They always give me the heebie-jeebies." Sandra shuddered dramatically.

"The sacred heart." Alice said.

"That's the fellow."

"Hang on, let me ring Tony. It might mean something to him." Joan said, reaching for the phone.

"Put him on loud speaker!" Sandra said.

Kirsty showed Joan how to put the call on to loudspeaker and she dialled, her expression doubtful as the distorted sound of Tony's mobile ringing filled the room.

"Hello?"

"Tony, it's me are you on hands-free?"

The reception was patchy and it was hard to understand what he was saying but they heard him say,

"Just read it. I can hear." Having found her glasses, Joan slowly read the clue out to him.

"Say again?"

After a second reading, there was silence. When Tony spoke again he sounded excited,

"Could be two things…planted some…big patch…by the…"

"We can't hear you!" Joan shouted into the phone. "Shall I call you back?"

"No, I'll have Andy in the car. I'll show you where it is when I get back. I bet it's the…Tom liked…" The reception cut out again and just as it seemed they'd lost him they heard his voice perfectly. "Look I'm not on hands-free, I couldn't get the stupid thing to work, so I'll see you when I get back okay. Well done though hey, ruddy brilliant!"

Joan put the phone down and she was beaming.

"It sounds like he knows what it's about. Stupid reception though, he must be around Lewes."

"I don't see why he couldn't have waited five minutes before haring off." Brian said.

"That was my fault." Joan said. "But then it wouldn't have mattered normally would it? It's just typical if Tony is the one who knows what this clue is about."

"I think you should have asked him to wait for the clue Mark. I would have done. We're all in limbo now until he comes back."

Mark took a deep breath. "Fine."

"I'm only saying…"

"You're always only saying Brian!" Mark said. "If I could turn back time I would have asked him to hang on but it's done now. He won't be long. Joan once you've got Andy settled in will you ask Tony to pop around?"

"Yes, yes of course. I'll ask him to come straight over." Joan said. "Oh, I am sorry, what are the chances? I just didn't want to think of Andy waiting around by himself."

Mark patted her shoulder. "Joan don't worry, you weren't to know and it's delayed us by what, an hour? Let's get back to what Tony said. Was he saying something about planting?" Mark asked.

"I think so. I'll have a look in the plant encyclopaedia, there's one in the library." Joan went to get it looking very pleased at Tony's cleverness.

She looked even more pleased when she came back and triumphantly put the large book on the table. It was open to show a full-page description of Dicentra, more commonly known as Bleeding Heart.

"Good old Tony!" boomed Frank, rubbing his hands with glee. "I think he's cracked it."

"Let's not get carried away." Alice said cautiously. "How can a plant hold an answer? I mean one plant is much like any other, unless Tom wrote a message with seedlings like those awful displays you see on roundabouts."

They spent the next half hour looking up possibilities online and making lists of anything connected to Bleeding Heart or Dicentra.

"It's the 'holds' bit." Sandra said, returning to Alice's point.

"Well I don't know." Joan said, her mind elsewhere. "When they're back I'll quickly introduce you to Andy and then we'll get out of the way so that Tony can tell you what he knows."

Joan stood up and went over to the window, peering hopefully at the rain-soaked drive as though expecting to see Tony's green transit van arrive at any moment. Breaking the silence, Sandra cried suddenly, "Roots! It's roots of course."

As everyone looked at her, she explained,

"If Tom's buried something beneath the plant, then the bleeding heart would grow around it and the roots would hold the answer."

Grasping her point immediately, Alice said, "Yes! Going to seed, it all fits – and burying something would have appealed to Tom, don't you think?"

"That has to be it." Mark said. "Once Tony gets back he can show us where the bleeding heart is planted and we can get digging. That's great stuff Sandra."

Sandra glowed as Frank gave her a bear hug and everyone

congratulated her.

"I wasn't sure if I was going to get any of the answers to be honest." She said. "Logic's never been my forte so it would feel good to get one right." She sighed happily.

"Never mind logic." Kirsty said. "You've got the heart of an artist and that's much more useful." She spoke dramatically and Sandra bowed deeply, her necklaces swaying. The atmosphere was more relaxed than it had been since before Tom's death and they were almost giddy at the thought of getting so far ahead of their schedule. Frank was entertaining them with an anecdote about the time he was invited to give a talk to a big writer's circle but his agent had neglected to remind them that Frances Fletcher was a pseudonym.

"I mean, have you seen my author photo?" He asked, holding forth with a large whisky in hand. "I'm an absolutely stunning red head with enormous…well, just think Jessica rabbit but classy, you know, literary and you'll get the picture."

Alice rolled her eyes. "I'm sure you're very elegant."

"No, I really am Alice. I only wish that version of me came on book tours with me – that would liven them up. Joke, darling, joke." He said to Sandra, patting an arm around her.

"Anyway, you should have seen their faces when they saw me instead of Frances." He guffawed, remembering. "One of the men accused me of being a fraud - I could smell his aftershave from half way across the room."

After nearly two hours had gone by, Joan was stationed at the window pacing up and down in between phoning Tony and Andy's numbers. Her anxiety was palpable and the party atmosphere had vanished as quickly as it arrived. It was still too early to panic but Tony and Andy were so late now that reassurances about delayed traffic had stopped some time ago. Joan told them she didn't want anyone fussing around her, but it wouldn't have felt right to leave her so instead everyone was keeping busy while listening out for the sound of Tony's van. Mark had switched on the TV in Tom's old part of the drawing room and he and Ray idly watched a football game on mute, glad of something to do. Brian sat nearby reading a newspaper in between glances at his watch, while Alice sat next to him flicking through a magazine, the glossy pages swishing as she turned them. Nearby, Sandra was sketching in a small notebook besides Frank and Kirsty who were idly playing on their phones but mostly staring into space.

Ten minutes later when Joan slammed the phone down again, Frank looked up and said, "I still think Tony took him for a quick one in the pub on the way back and they lost track of time."

"Don't be stupid, he wouldn't do that without telling me. He just wouldn't."

Frank raised his eyebrows, about to reply, but Alice shook her head warningly.

"Are you sure you don't want me to take a drive out or make some calls?" Brian asked. "We can find out if…"

"No!" Joan said, and it was as if she feared that taking action would make the situation real. "Not yet. Just give it a bit longer."

After a while Joan repelled everyone's attempts to reassure her and she simply stood frozen by the window hugging her arms around herself. When the silence was finally broken, the hair on the back of Mark's neck stood on end.

"No, oh please no. No, no…"

The distant crunch of tyres on gravel could be heard but it was Joan's wail that had Mark bolting out of his seat. As he rushed to the window a feeling of dread settled over him in the face of Joan's despair. He put an arm around her but she pushed him away and instead curled in on herself, leaving him feeling powerless to help.

Chapter Eleven

A week later, Mark felt powerless again as he stood opposite Joan and watched the coffins containing the bodies of her son and her husband being lowered into the ground. The cold smell of mud reminded him of Tom's funeral and the dark clouds overhead threatened the same weather with weird light making the scene feel more surreal than it already was. The oppressive atmosphere gave Mark a heavy feeling in his chest and he took a deep gulp of the dank air to try to breathe past it. He hated funerals.

The car crash had been as random as most; a sequence of events that could easily have ended with Tony cursing bad drivers and forgetting his near miss within minutes. Instead, a driver had joined the dual carriageway too slowly and a speeding car was forced to swerve. This flipped Tony's overtaking van into the central reservation where it was hit head-on by a lorry. By the time the fire crews arrived to cut them out they were both dead. Joan had gone to formally identify them that same day and she had barely spoken since. There had been no tears either and her only coherent plan, according to Kirsty, was to stay on Valium as long as she could.

Joan stood next to but slightly apart from Shona, Tony's sister, who was sobbing uncontrollably and being supported by her husband, Phil. By contrast, Joan stood motionlessly, looking shrunken in a black coat that came almost to her ankles, and a veiled black hat that perched on top of her head like a malevolent bird. Joan's stillness was unnerving to watch as though it was due to more than grief and shock. Her body seemed to radiate hostility as if to repel any attempts to comfort her and she looked heartbreakingly alone with the crowd of mourners behind her. There had been a huge turnout in the church although most hadn't come to the burial - which was restricted to family and close friends only. The biggest group in the church was made up of Andy's local and school friends, mostly people in their late teens, that had done their best to dress appropriately. Among the older mourners were a lot of relatives from the Knight side of the family. Mark knew already that Joan had no close family of her own and that she had refused invitations to stay with Tony's sister. Instead she had insisted on staying at the Lodge House and they had all been uncomfortably aware of her at the bottom of the drive. Kirsty had visited her, not that Joan had wanted her company, but Kirsty had tried, especially as there didn't seem to be many friends.

The better Mark got to know the people in the group the more he noticed the similarities between them. Although different in so many ways the one thing they all had in common was a lack of close friends and family. He didn't know how Tom could have chosen them all using those criteria, but perhaps by some instinct he had. Mark didn't consider himself a loner but most of his friends lived away so he didn't see them often and he'd always been happy in his own company. Morbidly he wondered what the turnout would be like for his funeral. A few people would make the journey but what local friends he had were mostly through his ex-girlfriend and that hadn't ended well. Tom's offer of a place to live had come at just the right time. As for his family, it was really only his mother. His father was long gone, swallowed up by alcoholism and self-pity and Mark hadn't seen him in years. There were a few ancient aunts and cousins who'd turn out no doubt but there would be very few people he'd class as mourners. Frowning into the open grave that contained both coffins Mark put up his collar and thought again how much he hated burials. As though agreeing with him, the dark clouds overhead began shedding thick sheets of rain and the verger opened an umbrella, shielding the vicar as he raised his clear voice,

"...Thou knowest, Lord, the secrets of our hearts; shut not thy merciful ears to our prayer..."

Mark hunched into his collar and put an arm protectively around Kirsty as she stood shivering beside him. Neither of them had remembered an umbrella.

"How much longer?" She asked, her voice sounding hollow as fat raindrops mingled with the tears flowing from her eyes.

"Nearly over I think,"

At that moment the Vicar paused and nodded to Joan who picked up a handful of earth and slowly crumbled it into the grave. She winced as a stone sounded against the brass nameplate of Andy's coffin and as others threw in handfuls of earth or flowers, she closed her eyes, hugging herself so tightly that she looked like a child wishing for something so badly that it hurt.

Kirsty was sniffing noisily now and Mark felt a lump in his throat at the sight of Joan's silent grief, so much more painful to watch than her sister-in-law's anguished sobs. As the rain continued to drive down, Mark heard the familiar words of the Vicar with relief,

"...We therefore commit their bodies to the ground: earth to earth, ashes to ashes, dust to dust..."

When it was over the crowd surrounding the graveside moved away like oil on water, so eager were they to escape the rain. Joan and Shona remained where they were until Phil led them away to the large black Bentley that was waiting to take them on to their house. Due to the large numbers, they had restricted the post-funeral gathering to family and close friends only. Mark was guiltily relieved that he and the rest of the group were exempt from this although they had all arranged to gather back at the house for a small wake instead. Mark drove Kirsty and Ray back and followed Brian's green Jaguar XJS as it sped down the winding lanes. They caught up in time to witness Sandra's undignified scramble from the back of the low-slung car and Alice's poised exit, with knees held firmly together, from the front.

"Well that was bloody awful!" Frank shouted by way of greeting as he heaved himself out of the car. "I don't know why people have the full rigmarole of a burial these days. It's like they've decided it's not quite tragic enough so let's really pile it on in case anyone needs a good cry."

"Oh don't Frank! Just don't." Sandra said, "It's so hideous what's happened. I don't think Joan really knew what was going on."

"Good job if you ask me." Brian said, locking the car and unconsciously patting the bonnet as he walked past.

"Is Joan coming back here after?" Ray asked as he followed everyone up the steps to the front door.

"I'm not sure," Kirsty said. "I spoke to her this morning but it was like she couldn't take in what I was saying. She sat there with that little hat in her hands, just playing with the veil and looking up every now and then as though surprised I was still there."

"I think those drugs she's taking are too strong. She's completely out of it." Mark said as he opened the door wide and stood aside to let everyone enter.

"I rather think that's the idea." Alice said, shaking the rain off her umbrella and leaning it in the porch. "Anything to help her get through the first weeks. I remember when my mother died. What's happened to Joan though, well, it's unimaginable."

Mark turned on the lights to counter the gloom as they walked into the drawing room. There was no fire in the grate or trays of sandwiches laid out, as there had been after Tom's funeral and the room smelt musty as though it hadn't been aired out for a while.

"God, I miss Joan being around." Frank said.

"Frank, that is cold." Ray said shaking his head. "Seriously."

"I'm only saying what everyone else is thinking." Frank said. "Look at this place. I didn't mean it like that though, I know Joan's got her own stuff to deal with - "

"Stuff?" Kirsty asked.

"Don't look at me like that sweetheart." Frank said. "I'm an arse okay? Why don't I make a fire instead of speaking?"

Kirsty nodded. "Good idea. I'll make some coffee, or does anyone want tea?"

Mark began gathering up glasses and Ray joined him so that between them they had soon removed the worst of the mess. Sandra was arranging cushions and closing curtains while Brian poured drinks for those that wanted them. Alice was the only one doing nothing and perched on the sofa flicking through a magazine. After putting the magazine down with a sigh she watched them for a moment before saying.

"I think it's a poor show that people have been scattering their crockery around. Especially in a room like this."

Sandra's movements were precise as she finished folding a cashmere throw and placed it on the back of the biggest sofa. She stood looking at it for a while before turning to Alice.

"By people, you mean us I take it?"

"Not everyone of course but I do think we can do better than we have been over the last week."

"Unbelievable." Sandra said. "Alice. Just listen to yourself. You're not writing a report, you live here. Do you realise you haven't lifted one manicured finger to help all week?"

"There's no need to be personal Sandra. I'm not the one that's been creating the mess."

"What's this then?" Sandra snatched a champagne flute from Ray's hands. " You were the only one drinking Champagne last night. Obviously."

"Okay now." Mark said. "Why don't we do this tomorrow?"

"I should have known you'd take her side." Sandra said. "I've seen the way you look at her - and Kirsty, obviously. Whereas I'm just invisible aren't I?"

"What?" Mark was astonished. "Sandra, what are you talking about?"

"Oh nothing. Never mind - it's not you. Here, let me take some of those Ray." Sandra grabbed some of the glasses and walked out. Mark and Ray, still carrying their load of glasses and mugs, followed her into the kitchen and stopped at the look on Kirsty's face. She pointed to a letter on the kitchen table.

"Not another blackmail letter?" Mark asked.

"No, it's from Joan, she's leaving. She's going to Spain for a while. She gave it to me this morning and asked me to open it now. " Kirsty handed him the first page of the letter and Mark scanned Joan's neat writing quickly.

I'm not myself and I don't see how I ever will be again. I don't want to give up as I know that's not what Tony would have wanted, but I can't bring myself to carry on with it all especially now that Andy's gone. There's no point. I've had a great time, but even if everything worked out there'd be no joy for me now. I just want to escape. I'm sorry if this causes any trouble, although I think everyone will be better off without me anyway.

"Where's the bit about Spain?" Mark was frowning but read on when Kirsty handed him the second page,

I'm coming home after the funeral but I've arranged a flight to Spain in the morning and I'm going to live with my friend for a while. I know it's sudden but I feel like I can't breathe here. I can't face saying goodbye to everyone so I hope you'll let this letter speak for me.
If Kirsty would like to live here instead of up at the house, the spare key (purple fob) hangs in the kitchen. As for the money, I'm giving that up too of course and wish you well of it.
Thanks for all your support and good luck with it all.
Your friend,
Joan

"I was wondering about her friends, or the lack of them I mean." Mark said. "It's good she's got somebody. She looked so alone today."

"It could be exactly what she needs, just to escape all the reminders at home until the rawness has passed." Kirsty said. "It's awful to think of her going off on her own. She has to let us help her with that."

"We can try, but she doesn't seem to want to have anything to do with us, does she?" Sandra asked.

Sandra looked meaningfully at them and sat at the battered kitchen table, smoothing the skirt of her long black dress underneath her. What?" asked Mark.

"Well, think about it. I know from something Joan said ages ago that Tony was a cautious driver. She was teasing him, saying he'd rather drive ten miles behind a tractor than overtake it. When he had the accident wasn't he overtaking that lorry? That article said he was going about eighty miles per hour."

"But that was on the dual carriageway and even a cautious driver wouldn't mind overtaking there."

Sandra shook her head.

"No, I mean he was a really cautious driver. Remember when we all drove back from Tom's funeral? We were in Brian's car and we left ages after Joan and Tony. Even so, we overtook them on the A27 and Tony was crawling behind a lorry. He wasn't going anywhere near the speed limit."

"So you think Joan blames herself?" Kirsty sat down opposite Sandra.

"Remember when she called him on the mobile?" Sandra asked.

Mark groaned. "She thinks he was rushing because he wanted to show us where the bleeding heart was planted."

"If she blames herself then she definitely blames us too." Kirsty said.

"Look, there isn't a good way to say this but we still need to ask Joan for help." Mark was pacing up and down the kitchen. "She probably knows more than she thinks she does about what's planted where but even if it's just where Tom used to sit in the garden she can help. I was going to ask her at some point in the future."

Ray was absentmindedly wrapping the end of his black tie around his fingers.

"She may not know anything anyway. She said last week, you know when they…" Ray's grimace suggested the day of Tony's death. "She said to me that Tony would know exactly where it was planted, and when, and all that stuff but she only had the vaguest idea."

Mark landed heavily on one of the kitchen chairs and started pulled his fingers through his hair. "Shit! What are we going to do?"

"I don't know." Kirsty said. "Even talking about this makes me feel sick, Joan buried her husband and only child today and we're having to talk about this."

Mark's opened his mouth to speak but Kirsty continued quickly,

"Having to talk about this, I know. We can't wait a decent six months before bothering Joan but still, it's horrendous. I think we have to try and do this on our own first though. Before we do anything else we could get a metal detector and sweep the grounds in case Tom buried the clue in a metal box."

"Yes!" Mark said. "That's brilliant."

"We need to research the plant more and find out what sort of soil it needs. We could even employ a gardening expert if that fails."

"The gardening expert would be a last resort." Ray said.

"I know but we're ahead at the moment so I think we should give it a month at least…"

"Okay, but…" Ray interrupted but Kirsty talked over him.

"If we're no further along after a month I'll fly out to Spain and ask Joan for help. We just can't talk to Joan tonight about it. We can't!"

Mark placed a hand on her arm,

"I know Kirsty, don't worry. Nobody's going to do that."

Frank arrived in the room looking resentful, the whisky decanter dangling from one hand. Oblivious to the atmosphere he said,

"Have you got those glasses yet Sandra? I've been waiting ages out there. Brian's boring me senseless and Alice is doing her impression of a glacier. If I don't get a drink soon I can't be held responsible for my actions."

Sandra rushed over to the sideboard where glasses were kept,

"Sorry darling, but something's come up."

"Now what?" He sighed.

Kirsty handed him the letter and walked out of the kitchen, leaving Sandra and Ray to explain. Mark followed her,

"Kirsty, wait!"

She was striding along the corridor and Mark had to run a few paces to catch up. He grabbed her arm and as she shrugged it off. Mark saw she looked furious.

"What is it?"

"It's him!" Kirsty whispered. "It's just all about him isn't it? And the way Sandra treats him like a spoilt little boy."

"I know Kirsty. I know…"

"This whole thing. Today was Tony's funeral and I thought he was just lovely. He was such a decent, kind man and he and Joan obviously adored their son. Yet here we are worrying about stupid clues."

That will help us find millions of pounds, whispered a small voice inside Mark's head.

"As for Joan I honestly don't know how she'll get past this. I was thinking about Tom this morning too. He was so excited for us, all that planning he did and…" Kirsty's voice cracked. "If only I'd read that book Tom told me about earlier."

Mark stared at Kirsty and put his hands on her shoulders. She looked pale and tired, not at all like her usual vibrant self.

"Listen to me. You know there's no point thinking like that. It wasn't your fault and it's madness starting down that road. Maybe it's time for a break. The last week's been hard on everyone and we're starting to see people at their worst."

Kirsty looked at him, "Do you really think that's their worst?"

"I'm not convinced but let's hope so. Look why don't I say you've got a headache and you've gone upstairs to lie down."

"Would you? Thanks Mark."

"No problem." He paused. "If you like you could have dinner at mine tonight so you don't have to go downstairs?"

Kirsty looked surprised,

"Are you sure?"

"I can rustle up something."

Kirsty smiled, "I'm not sure how much of an appetite I'll have but that would be really nice, thanks Mark."

"So dinner at seven then?"

Mark walked back to the drawing room, but was interrupted from his reverie by Ray's voice at his shoulder.

"Got yourself a date then?" Ray said.

"Hardly a date." Mark said.

"I left the kitchen to get away from Frank but then I was stuck because you were trying it on with Kirsty."

"I wasn't trying it on." Mark snapped. "She just needs a break from everyone. So do I."

"What a coincidence."

"Just leave it Ray."

Mark walked into the drawing room and said abruptly, "Kirsty's got a headache. She's gone upstairs to lie down."

"Oh." Alice said, "No coffee then."

"Charming." Brian said, looking up from his iPad. "I could have made it myself by now."

"Now there's an idea." Mark muttered, flinging himself into an armchair and putting his feet on the coffee table.

Brian ignored Ray when he walked in, hailing Frank instead who followed behind with a decanter in one hand and three glasses in the other.

"Now that's more like it." Brian said. "Forget the coffee."

Frank was at his most generous when he had a bottle in his hand and he poured three large measures.

"What do you think about the letter then?" Frank asked the question as though commenting on the weather.

Brian choked on his drink but managed to halt a coughing fit by sniffing loudly and clearing his throat. Alice looked at him, an expression of disgust on her face, and asked if he wanted her to pat his back.

"I'm fine," Brian wheezed. "Blackmail letter is it?"

"No, from Joan." Frank replied. "She says she's going to live in Spain for a while. She doesn't want the money though which is a bit of a bonus."

"She's leaving tomorrow." Ray added.

"Tomorrow? Alice looked astonished, "Why the hurry?"

"Maybe she's finding living in the Lodge difficult." Mark spoke through gritted teeth. "And do you really think we wouldn't hand over her share Frank? Assuming we find the money."

Frank's blue eyes grew rounder as he swung round to stare at Mark. "She says – and I quote - she doesn't want it and wishes us well of it!"

"It's not like she decided to walk away in normal circumstances." Mark said. "We should still give it to her."

"She wouldn't know what to do with it." Alice's magazine slapped against the table as she put it down. "Look Mark. It's awful and I can't imagine what Joan is going through. We could consider giving her something of course but let's not make any rash promises now while we're upset." Alice smiled tightly at Mark as though the matter was settled and took out her lipstick and compact.

"Why don't we save this for another day, perhaps when Joan hasn't just buried her husband and son?"

"Mark, don't be ridiculous." Alice rubbed her lips together and clicked the lipstick shut. "It isn't the right time, of course it isn't, but there isn't going to be a good time for Joan, probably not for years. Frankly, we need a little more grit if we're going to uncover Tom's millions."

"A little more grit for what?" Mark snapped. "Forcing her to walk the grounds before she leaves, stopping her from going to Spain? Is a million not enough for you and Brian, is that it?"

"Sorry Mark…" Ray spoke tentatively. "I don't know how to put this but it's hundreds of thousand of pounds extra we're talking about here. We should give Joan something but you're treating her share like Monopoly money as if this isn't real."

Mark stood up. "Tom kept saying we mustn't let the money get to us, didn't he? To even think about cutting Joan out of this after what she's been through…that's not grit, that's pure greed."

"Well, that's me told isn't it?" Alice said. "Like I said, let's not do anything now."

"But remember it's not your decision to make," Brian said, glaring at Mark. "We can cross that bridge when we come to it. Anyway, Tony will have life insurance and all that too - I'm sure she's been well provided for."

"I'm going up." Mark said. "Leave me out of any dinner arrangements later, Kirsty too."

"Yes, alright. You realise you're the only one with a kitchen?" Alice asked. "It seems like you have the best rooms of us all."

Mark scowled. "Mine's more of a staffer's apartment. It doesn't have the same luxury feel as everywhere else."

"Yes, that's true." Brian said. "Tom wanted it in case he needed a live-in carer some day."

"I see." Alice said. "Well that seems more fair although I was thinking we could get a kettle for the room, Brian. What do you think darling?"

Mark left them to it and ran upstairs, so glad was he to escape the confines of the room and their company. As soon as he shut his door behind him, he stripped off his black tie and white shirt along with the mask it felt like he'd been wearing for most of the afternoon. He walked over to the window and rested his forehead against the cold glass looking out at twinkling lights in the distance. It was too dark to go for a run and it was too soon to start preparing dinner. He stood for a while, restless and yet strangely lethargic, before closing his eyes against the blackness.

Chapter Twelve

"This is really good Mark."

Mark was glad he'd chosen to play it safe with pasta rather than try to impress Kirsty, not that there was any sense that she wanted to be impressed. Her baggy jumper and scraped back hair sent a clear signal in that department and he'd received the message loud and clear. After the last few days it was enough just to hang out with someone of his own age like a normal person. Conversation flowed easily throughout the meal and they made inroads into a bottle of red wine. It was from Tom's cellar and Mark suspected it might be valuable, possibly very valuable. Having noticed the cellar keys in Tom's desk that morning he'd stolen down there after Kirsty agreed to come over. He'd grabbed a couple of embossed bottles of Chateauneuf du Pape that were nearest the door but it wasn't until he opened one that he saw it was dated 1997.

"Have I got a blackcurrant smile?" Kirsty asked. Mark nodded and wiped his own mouth.

"This is a dangerous path." Mark said, sniffing his glass. "I never understood people being into wine before."

"I know. Can you taste cherries?"

"Sort of but peppery. In a good way." Mark swilled the wine in his mouth before swallowing it. "God. I can see how you could get into it. My Mum's husband spends a fortune on wine but every time he opens a bottle there's always a lecture about the grapes and the producer. I used to make a point of knocking it back to piss him off." Mark laughed. "In my younger days of course. Poor guy, he's alright really."

They were both wrung out emotionally so their conversation so far had avoided anything to do with the recent tragedy or even anyone in the house. Mark stood up to put their plates in the sink and Kirsty joined him, helping to clear the table before moving to the sofa with their glasses. It didn't take long as Mark's kitchen counters hugged one third of the room, just leaving room for a small dining table, while the rest of the room contained his sofa, coffee table and TV. There was a long window behind the sofa, covered by floor-length curtains and to the side were two doors, one leading to his bedroom and the other to a small bathroom. It was true that the apartment had been created for a live-in carer rather than guests but Mark had underplayed to Alice how nice it actually was. The green curtains were plain but made of expensive linen that hung just right and the furniture was equally good, accessorised by plump cushions and paintings on the wall. Although small, the standard was a long way from the starter home he'd shared with his ex and the squalid flat he'd shared before that.

Mark grabbed the bottle of Chateauneuf du Pape and put it carefully on the coffee table before sitting down, next to Kirsty but with a clear metre of sofa between them.

Kirsty tucked her feet underneath and turned towards him. "So, tell me, how are you coping with being the boss then?"

Mark shrugged as he answered. "I don't know. Coping is probably the right word. I think I might have a mutiny on my hands soon."

"Brian?"

"Frank as well and even Ray now. He accused me earlier of acting as though I was dealing with Monopoly money. Then I had a bit of a run-in with Alice and accused her of being greedy."

Kirsty raised an eyebrow. "Ray? If anything he hero-worships you a bit."

"Does he?"

"He always asks where you are and he's usually on your side. I don't think Ray's used to people taking him seriously and you always act like you're trying to be fair to everyone, including him."

"Thanks Kirsty. I didn't want to lead the group when Tom first asked me but now…well, I know I don't want anyone else to do it."

"Don't they say something like that about politicians?" Kirsty looked at him over her wineglass, which was nearly empty again. "Anyone who wants to be an MP should be automatically banned from being one?" Kirsty laughed. "Actually, that came out wrong. I definitely think you should be leading us. I don't think you should be banned." Kirsty giggled. "Maybe some other people should be banned." Kirsty giggled again and Mark laughed.

"How much of that wine have you had?"

"Not nearly eneuf." Kirsty answered with a straight face, holding out her glass.

Mark smiled as he refilled her glass.

"Get it? Eneuf, not eneuf du Pape, baby."

"Thank you. Yes, I get it."

Mark shook his head at her as she took another sip then grinned as she caught his eye. This set Kirsty off but she had to try not to laugh so she could swallow her wine. Trying not to laugh only made it worse and twice she nearly spat out her wine before managing to compose herself. By the time she'd finally managed to drink it her eyes were shining and

Mark was laughing too. When Kirsty snorted with laughter over nothing Mark laughed even more and then got the hiccups. After that they couldn't stop, as if all the tension from the last few weeks was being released. Every time they thought they'd got themselves under control Mark would hiccup and set them off again until Mark was shaking with silent laughter and Kirsty was gasping for breath in between a strange mixture of sounds that combined cackling with wheezing giggles and the occasional snort. In the end Kirsty put her hand up.

"Stop, it hurts." She took a deep, shuddering breath and wiped her eyes. "Oh God, I can't even look at you." She leaned back with her hands on her waist.

Mark exhaled slowly and wiped his own eyes. He couldn't remember the last time he'd laughed like that. He looked at Kirsty and noticed that her baggy jumper had twisted around and was now clinging in all the right places. As she looked up at the ceiling Kirsty exhaled again and closed her eyes. Mark saw the pulse throbbing on the side of her neck and idly imagined kissing her just underneath her jaw. He could picture himself leaning over but as if sensing the direction his thoughts had taken Kirsty opened her eyes and caught his gaze. Her expression was unreadable but then she smiled brightly and straightened her jumper. The spell was broken and she stood up wiping her eyes again as she headed for the bathroom.

She was gone a while and her face was almost back to its normal colour when she returned.

"I haven't laughed like that in ages." Kirsty said as she sat back down.

"Me too. I needed that." Mark showed her the wine bottle. "16% alcohol, no wonder we were feeling it after a couple of glasses. What were we saying anyway? Before we lost it."

"I can't remember now. You were saying about Ray not being happy with you."

"I don't know, he's said a few weird things lately but then I think he's coming out of his shell more which is good. Depending what's in his shell I suppose." Mark shrugged.

Kirsty took a sip of her wine, "I think maybe Ray's feeling left out and that's why he's acting weird."

"How do you mean?" Mark asked

"If you think about it everyone else is coupled up one way or another. We knew each other from before so even we're sort of a pair."

"Even?" Mark asked.

"Sorry, you know what I mean…anyway now that Tom's gone maybe we should take Ray under our wing more." Kirsty said. "He's probably lonely."

"I think Ray and Frank get on."

"Maybe but it would be better if he teamed up with us than with the other lot, wouldn't it. We should try and make him feel more included."

Mark nodded and put his arms behind his head. He was sitting sideways on to Kirsty and as he thought about what she'd said he realised that Kirsty was staring at him. Was she checking him out? Kirsty had made her lack of interest plain so it bugged him that he was so aware of her. He noticed his set of weights in the corner and turned his head away while he stretched deliberately. Let her look. He was in good shape at the moment, mostly through boredom, although unfortunately that coincided with a lack of activity in other areas. What a waste. He looked back at her but she was facing away from him. He sighed and stood up.

"We could take more of an interest in him – I think he misses Tom for a start and with Joan and Tony gone now as well…"

They both jumped when there was a sudden hammering on the door. Mark was irritated even before he opened the door and the sight of a belligerent-looking Brian standing outside did nothing to improve his mood.

"I know you're busy but I need to talk to you." Brian's feet were firmly planted and he looked like he meant business.

"Can this wait Brian?"

"It cannot."

Mark opened the door wider knowing that Brian wouldn't leave until he'd said his piece. Brian stamped past him wearing his usual uniform of trousers, checked shirt and pullover.

"Kirsty." Brian inclined his head, oddly formal.

"What's this about?" Mark asked. Brian was scowling at him.

"You." He said at last, leaning forward so that his bulbous nose was only inches from Mark's face. "Who the hell do you think you are?" Brian jabbed a finger at Mark's chest as he spoke.

"Brian, stop it! What's wrong with you?" Kirsty stood up and moved between them.

"This has nothing to do with you my girl." Brian said, his eyes narrowed.

Mark suppressed the urge to laugh. "Come on Brian, out with it."

"Don't tell me what to do." Brain hissed.

"Right." Mark held his hands out, palms facing towards Brian even though his instinct was to push him out of the door. "Would you like to sit down and we talk about why you're here?"

"I'm fine standing thanks. We do enough sitting around here."

"I'll go shall I?" Kirsty asked.

"No, you don't have to leave." Mark said firmly.

"Joan's back at the Lodge House." Brian said. "The lights have been on for at least half an hour…"

"Okay, now I understand." Mark interrupted.

"Too bloody right! You can't insist that nobody's to bother her, not when there's this much at stake. We've been arguing about going over there tonight but then we realised Kirsty would be better."

"You said this was nothing to do with her."

"Yes, well it's not." Brian dismissed the notion of Kirsty airily. "She's not the problem, you are, and that's why I'm telling you that I won't…we won't put up with your weakness on this. We want you to send Kirsty over to talk to Joan and find out what she does know."

"Right." Mark said and he was quiet for a few moments. "Well thanks for that Brian. I think we're done for tonight." He looked at his phone. "It's late now so if Kirsty does choose to go round it won't be tonight."

"I was planning to see her in the morning anyway." Kirsty said.

"Why not now?" Brian asked.

"It's ten-thirty at night." Mark said. "She'll be exhausted after today, basic human decency…I could go on"

"That's what I've been saying." Brian shook his head. "You're too soft to lead anyone, let alone someone like me."

Mark laughed and in the reverse of their earlier positions, jabbed a finger at Brian's chest.

"Someone like you?" he said. "Why do you think Tom asked me to be in charge and not you, the big businessman, or clever old Frank, or perhaps Alice with all her committee experience? Why me, one of the youngest?"

"Because you wheedled your way into his affections," Brian spat. "I knew him nearly three years while you knew him two minutes and then moved in. You got your feet right under the table, didn't you?"

Mark could smell the whisky fumes coming off him in waves now as Brian swayed in front of him.

"Get out, Brian."

"What's your answer? Will you get Kirsty to go over tonight?"

"Get out!" Mark shouted, shoving past him and opening the door. Brian swayed again and stamped across the room, pausing in the doorway to glare at Mark before continuing down the corridor. Mark slammed the door behind him and threw himself down onto the sofa.

"That was ugly."

Mark nodded tightly. "I feel like fumigating the room."

"Do you want a coffee?" Kirsty asked.

"Thanks but I need another drink." He opened the second bottle of wine without ceremony and poured a large glass. "Do you want one?" He asked. She shook her head and he took a large swig then breathed out slowly. "So much for escaping."

"I was thinking about calling Joan tonight, you know? I couldn't decide whether she really meant what she wrote in her letter, about being on her own."

"Are you going to?"

"I don't know. I don't want to but maybe I should. Not because of him…them - just to see if she needs any help getting away. I get why she wants to leave so suddenly even if it is drastic."

"With Brian around I can see the appeal myself." Mark said, taking another large swallow of wine. "Sorry, bad taste."

Kirsty smiled ruefully and they lapsed into a silence that was less comfortable than before.

"Look, I'd better go. Thanks for dinner Mark, it was lovely." Kirsty stood up and Mark walked her the four paces to the door. "Just what I needed actually."

"Me too. You're welcome anytime – you and your bad jokes."

She looked at him questioningly and he pointed to the wine bottle.

"Oh!" Kirsty laughed and the good feeling between them was restored in an instant as Mark grinned at her then opened the door.

She pecked him on the cheek before walking down the corridor to her room. So near and yet so far Mark thought as he shut the door and returned to his wine.

Chapter Thirteen

Mark was in the drawing room staring out at the Lodge house as the dying sun turned the upstairs windows orange. It was a week since Joan had left and she hadn't said goodbye to any of them. Kirsty had gone over there before seven but her closed curtains had suggested an early flight. He hated the thought of Joan stealing away from her house in the dead of night even more than Frank's recriminations. The sun's glare made his eyes hurt and he turned away still seeing bright red rectangles in the gloominess of the room. He felt suddenly stifled knowing it would be dark soon.

"I'll just go and see how Ray's getting on," he said.

"He's been out there a while," Alice said. "Put the lights on would you?"

She murmured her thanks as he left but he found himself feeling irritated anyway. These days Kirsty was the only one whose company he sought and when she wasn't around he found himself making excuses to go to his apartment. Just shutting the door behind him made him feel better and he made a point of taking a few deep breaths when he remembered. Other times, he'd take out his frustration on the weights in his living room, sometimes swinging a kettle bell until the sweat poured off him and his back ached.

Mark let himself out of the back door, wrapping a scarf around his neck as he walked around the side of the house. It was a clear, crisp February afternoon and he stopped to look at the sky as the sun started to set over the woods. He could smell the wood smoke from a bonfire, and for a moment it felt like autumn rather than the last weeks of a dreary winter. Seeing a figure in the distance, he walked across the wide lawns to the edge of the woods.

"Found anything?" he asked.

Ray was concentrating intently as he swept a metal detector in slow arcs, and he didn't see Mark until his shadow fell in front of him. He nearly dropped the clumsy-looking device but recovered himself when he saw who it was and pulled down the headphones.

"The woods are getting me all spooked." He removed a cigarette from the packet he'd stowed in the back pocket of his jeans and lit it carefully. "I thought I felt something watching me earlier and when I turned around, I saw something in the shadows. It really creeped me out."

"Something or someone?" Mark said.

"Nah, it was probably only a fox or something. I'm still not used to being surrounded by this much countryside."

"It's the quiet that gets me." Mark said. "Have you found anything?"

"Nothing, literally nothing, and I've been out here all afternoon. I don't think there's any metal left to find now."

"Maybe. I thought you were taking it in turns with Frank today?"

"Yeah, so did I."

"Here, let me take over, you're shivering. Where have you been so far?"

Ray outlined where he'd already scanned for metal and Mark was impressed by the amount of ground he'd covered.

They'd spent the week before the funeral reading up about anything and everything to do with bleeding heart and it felt like they had exhausted every possible lead. Mark even spoke to a nursery owner about wanting to find his late father's favourite plant before the family home was sold. She was sympathetic but her advice was still to talk to the new owners in the spring. She showed him samples of Dicentra Spectabilis in her greenhouse, a tiny clump of red celery stalks, and explained it would be six weeks, maybe later, before any shoots appeared outside. Already though it felt like they were marking time until the plant started showing.

Ray gladly handed everything over. "Cheers Mark, and you were on earlier. Bloody Frank. Tomorrow I'm on research duty in the morning I think then back on later in the afternoon – I might get him to do a bit of that shift instead." Mark didn't mind taking another turn. There was a bit of the childhood geek in him that had always hankered after a metal detector. They were using the two they had bought on opposite sides of the grounds, taking shifts of a couple of hours each. They'd scanned the grounds and woods three times now and had found thick iron nails, belt-buckles and buttons, coins, a tin soldier and even a silver teaspoon with a hallmark that turned out to be from the 1870s. Mark had uncovered the blackened teaspoon himself and had imagined long ago owners of the house taking tea on the lawn. Mark still got excited when he heard the rapid stuttering of the beep that meant there was something underneath but the novelty was already wearing off as his collection of bottle tops grew. Alice had now refused to have anything more to do with it, citing circulation problems and he knew Kirsty wasn't keen either. Frank's absence was a sign that he'd try and avoid his shifts from now on and in a way he couldn't blame them. If there was anything to find they would have found it by now.

Mark put the headphones on and took over where Ray had left off, waving away his thanks. After a while he settled in to what he was doing and felt peaceful as he listened to the chattering of the birds as the sun went down. It was almost dark and when he nearly went sprawling over a large tree root he decided to finish for the day. Carrying the metal detector over one shoulder he whistled as he strolled up to the back of the house and waved to Alice and Sandra through the drawing room window although they didn't see him. After leaving all his kit in the boot room and putting the batteries on to charge he poured a coffee from the pot on the kitchen counter. He sighed when he heard a woman's heels walking down the corridor, but smiled when he saw that it was Kirsty. She looked guilty when she saw him.

"Hey, where have you been hiding?" Mark asked.

"Don't, you've caught me red-handed. I had to go into Brighton anyway but then I noticed there were loads of sales on. I was only a couple of hours."

"You haven't missed anything, don't worry. Apart from Ray I think everyone else has bunked off one way or another and Brian's spending more time at his office than here at the moment."

"I noticed."

"Anyway, did you have a successful trip?"

"Amazing, thanks. Almost everything I liked in the sale was in my size - that never happens. I haven't tried anything on so I'll probably need to take some things back but I think I've got loads of good stuff. Look." She went into the corridor and he heard rustling before she returned holding two bulging carrier bags.

"Wow." He said. "Impressive."

"I know. I've never seen so many places go full on with the hearts and flowers though. Here, have a love heart."

Mark looked puzzled but took a sweet from the tube Kirsty offered him.

"One of the shops was handing them out. What does it say?" She asked him.

"Sweet pea." Mark grinned. "Nice, thanks."

"Valentine's Day, the annual reminder for anyone single that they're on their own." Kirsty said as she put her bags down and went over to the kettle. "They had heart shaped balloons today, the works."

"Want anything?" she asked.

"Great." Mark said but he wasn't really listening.

"Tea or coffee?"

"What? No I'm fine thanks, I've got one already." Before he could change his mind, he continued, "Kirsty, if I can get a table. I mean if there's anywhere that's not full tonight..."

Kirsty smiled brightly at him and said, "Oh Mark, you don't need to take pity on me. I'm only joking."

"Pity?" Mark said. "Definitely not pity. It would be good to go out and…"

"It's lovely of you," she interrupted, "but no, really." She turned away from him and busied herself with the kettle.

Mark felt her rejection in the pit of his stomach. He was sure there was chemistry between them and it was becoming more obvious by the day. Lately, he'd noticed her looking at his mouth every time they talked – he knew that meant something.

"No to going out generally, or just no to me?" He didn't know what had come over him but suddenly he needed to understand where he stood.

Kirsty put the kettle down and turned to face him.

"Are you asking…?" Kirsty paused.

Mark nodded. He'd come this far. Kirsty said nothing for a while but her expression reminded him of someone deciding whether to refuse the dessert menu. His heart sank as she crossed her arms.

"It's okay." He was an idiot - he'd known that already. He'd known. "Sorry to put you on the spot." He managed to sound breezy as he leaned back against the counter. "Just good friends, right?

"Oh Mark." Kirsty said. "I'm sorry too. If it makes any difference you can take it as a compliment that you're not my type. Definitely good friends though, please - you're the only thing keeping me sane around here."

"Same here." He shrugged and put his hands in his pockets. "So what is your type then?"

Kirsty looked embarrassed.

"Just, well…not too good looking, you know?"

"What?" Mark smirked. Frank had been right.

"No, I know it sounds crazy but…"

"Wait, so I'd need to be uglier? That's discrimination."

"Don't. You make me sound ridiculous."

Mark looked at her and raised an eyebrow.

"I know. It's a long story - my friends don't understand it either, but it's sort of my one dating rule now."

"Listen Kirsty, it makes no sense at all but now we've established that we're both single and good-looking but absolutely nothing is happening about that, we could get out of here for a night anyway. Or, if that's too weird, maybe on another night?"

"Do you know what, I'd love that." Kirsty said. "This afternoon made me realise how good it is to get away from here and tonight's fine if you're sure. Why not?"

"Great, and if we go out in Brighton people will think I'm your gay best friend. Totally normal."

Kirsty laughed. "Perfect, you're on."

"Let's do it then." Mark said. "I'm not playing wing man if you see any uglies you like though - just so we're clear."

"Alright, and I won't set you up with any cute guys – or is butch more your thing?"

"You're hilarious Kirsty." Mark said. "Really hilarious."

They agreed to meet downstairs at seven to go for a drink before dinner. This gave them an hour so Kirsty left him to it and went off to get ready. He managed to book a taxi and after calling a few places, Mark found an Italian restaurant that had a table. He left the kitchen and went in search of somebody to pass on the message about an update meeting for the morning. He'd already decided that it was time to work out what to do next – they couldn't carry on like this. He found Ray in the drawing room sprawled out in an armchair. Ray looked bored and was idly flicking channels but he sat up when Mark asked him to let everyone know.

"What's there to talk about though Mark? I mean we keep having these meetings but there hasn't been anything to say for a while has there?"

"I know but that's why I want to get everyone together. I've had an idea."

Ray looked interested and started rolling a cigarette,

"Any chance of giving me a sneak preview?"

"Probably better to save it Ray - I want to talk to everyone together."

"Why don't I go and get everyone now though? You've got me thinking."

"I can't Ray, I'm going out. It's not that exciting though, nothing new - it will keep until the morning."

"Out with Kirsty are you?"

Mark nodded, now wishing he'd waited until tomorrow to say something.

"Nice little Valentine's Day outing is it? I bet you tell her."

Ray dabbed fallen shreds of tobacco from his jeans, and looked at Mark.

"You can't blame me for wanting to get out of here for a night, Ray but I won't talk about it with Kirsty, okay?"

"Yeah, whatever. Have fun."

"Thanks, and look don't make a big deal about meeting up tomorrow. Let's just have a coffee in the morning, say, in here at ten?"

"Uh huh." Ray moved over to the window seat and lit his cigarette. He'd just opened the window a crack when Alice walked in.

"Not in here Ray, you know Brian won't stand for it."

Mark left them to it. He shoved his hands into the pockets of his jeans and walked down the corridor into the library. He wanted to make a few notes before tomorrow's meeting but when he turned on the light, he was surprised to see Sandra sitting at the table. She looked like she had been crying but she rubbed her eyes and smiled round at him, blinking at the sudden light.

"Are you all right?"

"Oh yes, ignore me, ignore me!" Sandra said in a cheery voice. "I was watching the sunset, daydreaming really, and I just sort of forgot to put the light on when it got dark. I was thinking about a painting I'm planning."

"I'd better not interrupt then." Mark said. "I was telling Ray that I'd like us to all meet up tomorrow morning - I've got an idea I want to put to everyone. Ten o'clock in the drawing room?"

"Of course, yes that's fine and I'll let people know. See you then." She waved him away, the sleeves of her long cardigan flapping, and Mark left the room and headed for his apartment to make some notes before jumping in the shower. He was halfway up the stairs before it struck him that there was no view of the sunset from the library. He paused, wondering if he should go back. Reluctantly turning around he was startled to see Ray watching him from the doorway. His face was hidden in the shadows so Mark couldn't see his expression. Unnerved, he gave him a tight-lipped smile then turned around and continued upstairs to get ready – both Ray and Sandra would have to wait.

Chapter Fourteen

By eight o'clock they were at the restaurant and sat opposite each other at a small table near the kitchen. It turned out to be a very expensive Italian place although the old-fashioned décor suggested that it was on the way down rather than up. The food looked good though and the restaurant was busy and lively with waiters shouting to each other in rapid Italian in between flirting with the regulars. For Valentine's Day there was a special menu that included a page about aphrodisiacs - a man breaking open a fig and eating it in front of his lover is a powerful erotic act. Mark thought he'd better avoid the figs on this occasion. He looked around while Kirsty studied the menu. The whole room was packed with couples that seemed to be having a good time and there was a steady murmur of conversation and laughter overlaying the Italian music in the background.

Kirsty looked up from her menu. "It feels a bit like we could be in Italy." She gestured towards one of the waiters who wore a white apron tied around his waist.

"Have you spent any time there?" Mark asked.

"Not much, I've only been to Rome and Florence for long weekends but I'll definitely go back sometime. How about you?"

"Yeah, I like the culture they have over there, all the pavement cafes and the nightlife, especially in the smaller places where you can watch the evening promenade. It's like the worlds best people-watching." Mark didn't mention the long summers spent in Portofino or San Remo when he was growing up, as he still hadn't mentioned the privileged first half of his childhood. He changed the subject and asked Kirsty if she knew what she wanted to drink.

As if lip-reading, an elderly waiter came over at that point and insisted on them ordering a cocktail. He was a small man with thick white hair who peered at them over wire-rimmed glasses. Before they could acknowledge his suggestion he told them he'd bring them a Bellini and a Negroni.

"Bellini for bella, si?" He looked expectantly at them then said, "If you don't like it I'll bring something else, okay?"

Kirsty smiled at him as she said, "Okay, why not."

"Prego. You'll like it." He nodded and strode off scribbling on his order pad.

"It looks like I'm getting a Negroni then." Mark said. "Was it me or did he look like Geppetto?"

Kirsty looked blank.

"Pinocchio's dad."

Kirsty laughed and nodded her agreement. "That story always used to give me the creeps."

"You'd better like your Bellini then, you don't want to upset him." He drummed his fingers on the table. "Do you know what you want to eat because he'll probably try and order for us if we're not sure?"

Kirsty studied the menu and Mark glanced at it but he'd already decided on the fish.

"Shall we share some antipasto to start?" Kirsty asked.

"You go ahead, I was thinking about the calamari."

"No don't worry then, I'll have the salad with prosciutto and figs instead." Kirsty looked again at the menu and Mark saw she was reading the page about aphrodisiacs. Mark still felt hollow from her rejection of him earlier, especially for such a stupid reason. He'd get over it but he felt an ache of longing as he looked at her and wondered if it was because of how he felt or just because he couldn't have her. She looked particularly stunning tonight wearing a high-necked dress in jade green that contrasted with her auburn hair. He suppressed a smile as he saw a blush appear on her cheeks and quickly looked back down at the menu.

"So, a Bellini for the bella donna." The waiter was back and deftly put down their drinks and a basket of bread. "And a Negroni, here. Are you ready to order?"

They listened while he reeled off the specials and he accepted their order with an approving nod. They asked for a bottle of red wine to go with it, taking his recommendation of Valpolicella, and relaxed as he moved off.

"Cheers." Mark raised his glass and Kirsty looked at him.

"Cheers Mark and thanks for suggesting this, really." They chinked glasses. "I feel like I can breathe again away from the house."

"My pleasure. I know we're out of place tonight but we could try and get out sometimes even if it's just to the cinema or the pub."

"I'd like that. Why was Tom so insistent we stayed away from friends and family anyway?"

Mark shrugged. "He said he thought it would be safer for everyone. I mean, if I told friends you'd been walking the Wealdway in early February they'd know it wasn't for fun."

"That's definitely true. God that weather we had. I was so happy when we couldn't go out that last morning."

"Me too. I think Tom wanted to bring us together, plus it added to his sense of drama as well. He had a load of Agatha Christie books and he had the country house, so…"

"That doesn't sound good. There's usually someone bumping people off in those books." Kirsty's face lost its animated expression. "Sorry I didn't mean it like that."

"I know you didn't but…listen Kirsty, let's have a night off and forget about the crash and everything that's happened, just for a few hours. Me, I feel like eating and drinking way too much then falling asleep in the cab home – what do you say?"

Kirsty nodded and then smiled, almost visibly relaxing in front of him, "Yes - you're on. But no drooling on my shoulder."

After that they laughed easily, determined to enjoy their freedom, and the conversation flowed as though Mark's directness earlier had cleared the air between them. It was the first time Mark had told Kirsty about his childhood and she was fascinated by the whole story.

"I've only just realised that you always ask loads of questions whenever family or childhood stuff comes up." Kirsty said. "I can't believe I didn't notice that before."

"That's my mother for you, 'Think more about being interested than interesting, darling.' But yeah, I tend to avoid talking about it as much as I can."

"Sorry, I'll stop quizzing you, it's just…"

"No, I don't mean now! I just mean it's not something I mention casually."

"So what was it like going from boarding school to the local comp?"

"Terrifying to start with." Mark said. "I barely said a word on my first day and tried to lay low until people forgot about me being the posh kid with the dad in the papers."

Kirsty shook her head.

"No it was fine although I had to get used to being around girls, just at the stage when I had it all going on." Mark laughed. "Luckily I was a bit of a novelty and a couple of them took me under their wing. Once I made a couple of friends I was okay." He picked up a bread roll and broke it in half. "The hardest thing at the time was getting used to being broke – especially for my mum. She literally had no idea how to cope."

"How do you mean?" Kirsty asked

"My Dad's view was that he could fix anything by throwing money at it. He got rich really fast in the City and then had that whole work hard, play hard thing going on." Mark shrugged. "He basically delegated everything else - I hardly saw him. Mum's job was to spend the money and she created this whole lifestyle for them, did the ladies that lunch thing, had riding lessons, elocution lessons..."

"Elocution lesson, seriously?"

"All of it. If you met her now you'd assume she was from a very good family, darling. I love her to bits – she's my mother - but she drives me mad. Her life's work has been to pretend to be someone she's not so losing her money was like losing herself. She had to cope with the scandal around Dad as well."

"How old were you?" Kirsty asked.

"Just coming up to fourteen so I was completely useless. My biggest concern was the lack of stuff. I mean I had always had everything I ever wanted up until that point. Even things I never wanted."

"Like what?" Kirsty asked.

"Loads of things." Mark said. He thought for a moment. "Okay, so I wrote to Mum in my first term at boarding school and I mentioned this boy we called Cookie because he did an impression of the cookie monster from Sesame Street. Crumbs flying everywhere – we all thought it was hilarious."

Mark paused as their waiter brought their main courses. The fish came with a side of vegetables and a thick stack of chips he'd ordered separately.

"Is that enough for you?" He asked Kirsty, whose bowl of chilli-flecked ravioli looked meagre in comparison.

"Yes, it's fine – looks good." She smiled at the waiter as he topped up their wine glasses before moving away. "Anyway, I can always nick some of your chips."

Mark raised his eyebrows and gave her a firm look.

"I'd like to remind you about the just good friends thing." He popped one of the chips in his mouth. "Mind you, even if we were going out I still wouldn't let you have any of my chips." He looked at Kirsty and said solemnly, "It's my one dating rule."

"Ouch!" Kirsty shook her head and he grinned at her.

"Do you know, they taste as good as they look as well."

"Just one?" She asked, reaching towards his plate but Mark halted her hand.

"I'm not sure that's playing fair if you're going to break my one dating rule..."

Kirsty looked at him and something flashed between them that had nothing to do with food. "I'm actually quite tempted." She said quietly.

"Do you have everything you need?" The waiter was back. "Some more chips for the table, yes?"

"What? Oh. No, it's fine." Kirsty blushed. "I was just...no, thank you. " The waiter shrugged. "Water?"

He poured without waiting for an answer and when he'd gone, Kirsty asked.

"So what happened with Cookie?"

Mark was confused - had that really just happened?

"Cookie, the letter home?" Kirsty asked.

"Right, yes." He drank some wine and placed a couple of chips on the side of Kirsty's plate. "There, lucky for you I've never been big on rules anyway."

"Thanks - here, have a ravioli."

The moment had passed so Mark continued.

"So, Cookie, it was just a passing thing and I'd never even seen the show but when I came home for half term Mum had bought me a load of Sesame Street stuff, cuddly toys, DVDs, you name it."

"How old were you?"

"I was nine, with a Big Bird that was nearly as tall as me plus a load of toys aimed at pre-schoolers."

"Oh, Mark"

"No, don't feel sorry for me, Mum usually got it right, but you can see why it was a shock for us both when we went broke. God, I haven't thought of Cookie in years."

"Do you still see any of your friends from those days?"

"No, that feels like another life now. Anyway, Mum's fine, thankfully. It took her a while but she's married to Paul now. He's a lot older than her, but loaded, and she's found a whole new set of ladies that lunch."

"The marriage thing sounds a bit like my Mum." Kirsty said.

"Where is it she lives again?"

"Portugal. She moved out there with her fourth husband and they've since set up a gym together – he's a personal trainer. I'm not saying she was a lady who lunches but I'm sure she married her third husband for money. She denies it but he was so much older and definitely not her usual type." Kirsty paused as she chased a square of ravioli around her plate.

"So what happened to him?" Mark asked.

"Heart attack. The poor man died really suddenly. He was a real sweetie actually and he left pretty much everything to Mum. She was sad after he died but then she met Luc and...well, that was that."

"So how long has she lived in Portugal?" Mark asked.

"Coming up to two years now and the gym's going really well. I just hope Luc doesn't get distracted by any of his clients – that's how he and Mum met." Kirsty ate her second chip. "It's good to see her properly happy though. She and my Dad were terrible together - they married far too young. My sister was on her way and they were in love so…" Kirsty shrugged. "I'm not sure when the affairs started but they shouldn't have stayed together as long as they did."

"Did you know at the time?" Mark asked.

"Not really, I just knew they argued a lot and Mum went through phases of crying all the time. Jenny's told me about it since and apparently they had this really toxic thing where one of them would have an affair so the other would have a revenge fling. I know Mum had an affair with one of Dad's best friends and he was then her go to person whenever she was angry with Dad. Not that he and Dad stayed friends."

"Funnily enough."

"I know. Sorry, I don't know why I'm telling you all this." Kirsty looked embarrassed. "It's like an anti-Valentine's Day story – we'll get kicked out."

Mark laughed. "Definitely anti-marriage. So how long did they last?"

"Too long. I think they tried to stay together for Jenny and me but I was thirteen by the time Dad finally left. As a final insult Dad remarried someone who was the polar opposite of how Mum looked. Mum's slim and tall with strawberry blonde hair while Dad's new wife was the exact opposite, voluptuous and petite with black hair. Mum took it really personally."

"So is that where your one and only dating rule stems from then?" Mark asked as he topped up their glasses.

"Don't say it like that." Kirsty said, laughing.

"No, I'm serious. I'm guessing that your Dad wasn't backward in the looks department either?"

"No, even my friends used to fancy him which was obviously embarrassing." Kirsty toyed with her glass. "The looks thing is just something I've noticed though – among my friends too I mean. It's like the better looking a man is the more temptations they'll have, and so the more likely they are to cheat. They probably don't have to try as hard either so it can make them quite lazy with women and…maybe a bit arrogant, I don't know."

"Not generalising in any way then?" Mark asked.

"I'm massively generalising but that doesn't mean it's not true - in my experience anyway. And I'm not saying you're like that just because of the way you look."

There was silence and Kirsty looked away.

"This is why I don't try and explain."

"You don't have to explain yourself – that's our arrangement isn't it? That's the box I fit in, right?"

"Mark, don't be like that – I've had such a lovely evening."

Their waiter whisked their plates away and placed dessert menus in front of them without asking. There was an awkward silence between them and Kirsty said, "I suppose you want to go now…?"

Mark looked at her, surprised. "No, you idiot. It's a shame you think like that…a real shame, but I thought we've already agreed to disagree." Mark picked up the menu. "All I will say is that average-looking blokes have been known to cheat on their partners. Even downright ugly men can be lazy and arrogant – maybe ask around for some examples of that when compiling your research." Mark raised his hands in a surrender position. "Just in the interest of fairness."

"Good point." Kirsty smiled. "I know I sound ridiculous when you put it like that. It's just so much easier to stick to a decision if you make a blanket rule."

Kirsty picked up the menu and scanned through the options.

"I know. For your files though, I'm not lazy with women and I've never cheated on anyone either as it happens. So that's one tick for the non-uglies."

"Never cheated? Not even a little bit?" Kirsty asked looking up.

"What does that even mean?" Mark shook his head, smiling. "No, don't answer that. Seriously though Kirsty, you don't think your parents' affairs might have influenced you?"

At that moment their waiter returned to take their order and placed small glasses of liqueur in front of them.

"A digestif for you. Now, to finish I think you'll like the sharing plate, si?"

Mark looked at Kirsty. "This is your department – whatever you think."

"It does sound good, a little bit of everything."

"Prego. Very romantic."

They ordered coffee to go with it and made inroads into the plate of miniature Italian classics when it arrived – everything from Zabaglione to Tiramisu. Kirsty's face lit up when she saw it but they weren't even half way through it before they ran out of steam. Their conversation seemed to have ground to a halt too and Kirsty seemed distracted as they talked.

The restaurant was emptying out and Mark called for the bill, feeling ready for his bed. The people at the next table stood up to leave and Mark noticed the woman looking across at them. She was older than them, perhaps in her fifties, with a kind face. He smiled at her and she leaned over to them on her way past, "I just had to say something…you make such a beautiful couple." She beamed at them while her husband raised his eyes in mock-exasperation.

"Come on, leave these good people alone Julia." He nodded to them. "Good night."

"Good night. Thank you, I'm a lucky man, I know." Mark grinned at Kirsty and shrugged. "I didn't want to disappoint Julia. Hey, put that away." Kirsty had taken her purse out of her handbag. "Can you imagine Geppatto's reaction if we split the bill? Your turn next time."

"Okay, thanks. He would be appalled wouldn't he?" She lowered her voice and murmured, "Do you think he has connections?"

Mark laughed as their waiter returned with a card machine. After settling the bill he stretched and stifled a yawn.

"Shall we head home? I'll just…" He gestured to the bathrooms and stood up.

"Wait. Can we go for a walk before we go back?" Kirsty asked.

"What, seriously? I'm all ready for my snooze in the cab."

"Please Mark." Kirsty looked up at him. "I could really do with some fresh air, we don't have to be long."

"Okay, but if I drool on your shoulder in the cab it's not my fault."

"Deal." Kirsty said. "I'll get the coats."

As Mark washed his hands he wondered at Kirsty's sudden need for a walk. She was probably putting off their return to the house, reluctant to leave their little bubble of normality and face the others. Tonight had made him feel like his old self again so he could understand the feeling. His hand was on the door handle when the condom dispenser caught his eye. He paused. No, surely not…but some instinct made him get his wallet out. He saw he had some pound coins and, feeling slightly sleazy, inserted a couple of coins before he could change his mind. Not for tonight, of course not, but just in case.

Chapter Fifteen

It was nearly midnight when they left the restaurant and they huddled into their coats, buffeted by the wind that whipped along the narrow street.

"Christ, it's freezing. Come on where do you want to go?" Mark put his hands in his coat pockets and jumped up and down.

"If we head down towards Kemptown it's more sheltered - this road's always been a real wind tunnel." Kirsty put her arm through his and they strolled along the empty pavements, stepping around lamp-lit puddles from earlier on in the evening.

"You were right," Mark said after a while, "it's good to get some air before we go back."

"See it's not so cold now is it? For February, I mean?" She squeezed his arm and snuggled against him with an exaggerated brrr sound. Protected from the wind, the air felt refreshing rather than cold after the warmth of the restaurant. The clouds had cleared to reveal a bright moon that was nearly full and it was good to be in a city again after being so isolated for the last few months.

As they walked along Mark felt uncomfortable with Kirsty holding his arm tight against her. He could do platonic if she insisted but it would be easier without her breast pressed against his arm.

"Shall we head back towards the taxis?" Mark asked, stifling a yawn.

"In a minute, but I wanted to ask you something." Kirsty sounded nervous.

"What is it? "

"I don't know how you're going to take this."

"Go on." Still Kirsty said nothing. "Just say it Kirsty, whatever it is."

"What you said earlier, it got me thinking." She cleared her throat. "About…this whole looks thing I have, you know?"

Mark steered them around a large puddle and managed to suppress a delighted smile.

"This looks thing, your one and only dating rule?"

"Yes." Kirsty hit his arm. "That one. What you said tonight about me discriminating and about my parents really hit home."

"Uh huh. So what's your question?" Mark wanted her to spell it out.

"I'm…look stop, okay." They stopped and Kirsty pulled her long coat around her as she looked at him. They were standing underneath a streetlamp in a narrow road filled with shops that had all closed for the night. There was the sound of a car door slamming in the distance but there was nobody around apart from them. Finally she spoke.

"Mark, I was stupid to turn you down earlier just because of how you look." She paused. "Although I suppose we did end up going out anyway."

"As friends." Mark was leaning against the wall, his hands in the deep pockets of his coat to keep warm.

"As friends. But it's not your fault you're so…well, you know, so it's not right I wouldn't even give you a chance because of my stupid rule." Kirsty moved nearer to him and Mark noticed how the shadows accentuated her cheekbones and the fullness of her lips.

"Do you know the last date I went on? This new guy from work that I didn't fancy but I agreed to go out because he seemed quite nice and he was average-looking…normal. Safe, I suppose I'm saying." Kirsty smiled ruefully. "We had nothing in common and actually he was really arrogant as it turned out. I just, I never…all this time I've been rejecting anyone I actually fancied. I can't believe I've only just worked it out. No wonder I'm single."

"So what are you going to do now?" Mark asked in a casual voice, still with his hands in his pockets.

Kirsty took a deep breath and hugged herself tighter. "That was what I wanted to ask you but if you…if I'm not too late?" She looked at her shoes and then somewhere over his shoulder. "I've never done this before, sorry. I'm probably not making any sense…"

As she finally turned to look at him, Mark put a hand up to halt her words. It was too painful.

"Enough, please," he said, and he shook his head at the stricken look on her face. "Enough talking." He took one of her hands in his, lacing their fingers together, and leant across to kiss her softly on the lips. "Was that your question?"

"Yes." She spoke on a sigh and they smiled at each other as they squeezed hands.

Mark felt dazed at the sudden turn of events and as he lifted his other hand up towards her face he saw Kirsty's expression turn serious. He traced the shape of her lips with his thumb as she closed her eyes, before placing his mouth against hers, gently at first and then more firmly. Her lips were soft and warm and she tasted of chocolate and coffee as she kissed him back. When she moved her hands to the back of his neck he slid his hands down to her waist and pulled her against him.

After that, he lost all track of time – it could have been five minutes or it could have been an hour. They were standing in the narrow doorway of a second-hand bookshop and they had wedged themselves in the corner with Mark's back against the wall for support. Their coats were undone and he had one hand holding Kirsty against him while the other stroked her breasts through the thin fabric of her dress, savouring the silky hardness of her nipples against his fingers, and the softness of her tongue against his. Nothing existed for him apart from the two of them and the sound of their breathing and the heavy, warm feel of her body next to his as she pressed against him. She was standing with her legs weaved with his, one hand on the nape of his neck and the other moving under his shirt against his back and shoulders. He roamed his hands up and down her sides, enjoying the curve of her hips and the narrowness of her waist and then cupped her breasts, feeling their unexpected fullness, groaning as he squeezed them together. Kirsty arched her back and he moved one hand lower until he was beneath the skirt of her dress. He reached between her legs and she gasped softly and moved against his hand briefly before shifting herself away from him with a small shake of the head. They broke apart and Mark kissed her on the cheek and smoothed down the skirt of her dress before putting his hands loosely around her hips. They exhaled slowly in unison, then grinned at each other and stood for a while with their foreheads touching, catching their breath.

"Jesus, Kirsty."

"I know. I've been wondering what it would be like to kiss you for ages."

You haven't?" Mark groaned again. "Don't tell me that now." The temperature had dropped and without Kirsty's body against his he shivered involuntarily. He wanted to get them back to the house but he didn't want to break the spell.

"It's not the only thing I've wondered about." She looked at him with a small smile, and trailed her hand over his chest then moved lower and ran her hand slowly up and down the length of him.

He inhaled sharply and felt himself throb against her hand before she moved it away.

At that moment there was the sound of footsteps approaching on their side of the pavement. It sounded like a group of teenagers and they were shouting and singing as they moved nearer. Mark moved them back into the recess of the doorway and they straightened their clothes as Mark adjusted himself, trying to get comfortable. Moments later the group were past, having paused briefly in their singing, and Mark and

Kirsty smiled at each other.

From further down the street there was the sound of laughter.

"Get a room!"

Mark looked questioningly at Kirsty.

"I was about to say the same."

She nodded.

"Shall we get a cab back to the house?"

"No, I've got a much better idea." She grabbed his hand. "Follow me."

She started walking purposefully down the street. "

"What, a hotel?" He asked trying to think where was nearby.

"Better than that, you'll see."

A few minutes later they were outside the door of a converted Victorian town house. There was a row of buzzers next to the bell and Kirsty pointed to the top one while rummaging in her bag.

"Edwards, see? Home sweet home."

"This is your place?" Mark asked. "Amazing."

"My sister's away at the moment."

Mark put his arms around her from behind while she continued looking in her bag.

He kissed the side of her neck.

"I will probably die from disappointment if you haven't got your key." He murmured. "Literally fall down dead on the spot."

"No pressure then?" She giggled and started handing him things to hold. "Hang on. It's definitely here somewhere. No, don't worry, I've got it."

The light came on automatically once they were inside, revealing a scruffy hallway with black and white lino and a pile of junk mail on a small side-table.

"Come on." Kirsty whispered and she led the way across the threadbare stair carpet up three narrow flights of stairs. On the top floor were two doors and Kirsty quickly opened the one on the left to lead them up a final tiny flight of stairs that opened out into a small living room. A large, green sofa and a cluttered, magazine-piled coffee table took up most of the space. Kirsty turned on a standard lamp in the corner then took off her coat and turned to take his.

"Would you like a drink?"

"Just some water, thanks." He moved over to the bookcase and picked up a silver frame while she went in the kitchen. There was a photo of Kirsty in a black bikini and a sarong sitting with two women beside a small, vividly blue pool. He recognised the older woman with the

104

strawberry blonde hair from Kirsty's earlier description and guessed the other woman was her sister. She was grinning into the camera and had short platinum blonde hair and bright lipstick with huge black sunglasses.

"Jenny's the glamorous one," Kirsty said, returning from the kitchen. "That's with Mum at her place in Portugal."

"You don't look too shabby yourself," he said. "Nice bikini." He put the frame down. "So how long have you lived here?"

"About two years now - it's tiny but it's central. Here, let me show you the best bit." She moved towards the window and pointed towards the corner. "You have to angle your head a bit but you can see it really well from upstairs."

He could see the tops of the brightly lit, elaborate turrets of Brighton pavilion, only a few streets away.

"Nice. Good for work as well – well, I suppose it used to be."

She nodded and handed him his glass. He drank half of it in one go, only now realising how thirsty he was.

"Thanks." He put the glass down on the coffee table and wondered how to pick up from where they'd left off. He felt strangely nervous, but he sat on the sofa and patted the cushion next to him. Kirsty put her own glass down and he reached for her hand and pulled her towards him.

"You know you're the beautiful one, right?" She looked down at him as he ran his hands over her hips.

"I mean, seriously knockout beautiful?"

She smiled at him.

"Thanks, and you were on my forbidden list the moment I saw you."

Mark shook his head and pulled her down to sit on his lap, guiding her knees either side of him on the sofa so she faced him.

He leant forwards, still holding her hips, and kissed the pulse point underneath her jaw.

"I've been wanting to do that for a while."

She looked intently at him then leaned forwards so her mouth was next to his ear. She copied him and kissed just underneath his jaw, then whispered in his ear.

"Is there anything else you've been wanting to do?"

Mark swallowed. "Just a few things."

His hands fumbling, he undid the button at the top of her dress, kissing her hungrily while pulling her zip down at the back. He felt the softness of her skin under his hands and reached for her bra clasp, grazing the swell of her breasts with his palms once it was undone. He could feel her hands against his chest as she unfastened the buttons of his shirt and he quickly undid the last few himself so she could pull open his shirt.

He lifted her hair out of the way before sliding the dress down her shoulders. It pooled at her waist and he could hardly breathe as she shrugged off her bra. He reached for her but she put her hands up to block him.

"Let's go upstairs." Her voice trembled as she spoke and he saw she had goose bumps.

"Yes." He kept her in place against his lap. "Definitely." She froze as he leaned down and kissed one of her flushed pink nipples, then gasped as he took it fully in his mouth.

She gripped his shoulders then moaned as he brushed his hands up against her ribs and circled her other nipple with his fingers. Reluctantly he moved his mouth away and released her.

"Okay, now upstairs."

He took her hands, lifting them to help her stand, and was mesmerised as her breasts moved deliciously in front of his face while she unfolded her legs and wriggled herself off his lap. Looking up, he saw the mischievous look in her eye and realised that the wriggling had been for his benefit. She grinned at him and in that moment his feelings of longing and liking compounded and he fell a tiny bit in love with this woman who had previously seemed so out of reach. He stood up and took Kirsty's hand gratefully as she led him upstairs.

Chapter Sixteen

As the taxi drove up the lane to Downsview Manor it didn't seem possible that only the night before he'd still been smarting from Kirsty's rejection. Instead, just a few hours later they were holding hands and chatting softly as lovers. It was surreal. He had barely slept and his eyes felt gritty and tired but he'd spend the rest of his life feeling like this in exchange for nights like that. Part of him remained in Kirsty's bedroom and he smiled to himself as he pictured her as she'd been an hour ago, her cries masked by the sound of the seagulls circling outside. He lifted her hand to his mouth and kissed it. It was raining and the water ran down the window as Mark stared out of the car at the deserted-looking Lodge House. They were nearly at the house and somehow he had to get his thoughts together

"I wish I hadn't arranged the meeting for this morning."

"I wish you hadn't as well. I still think my conference call idea was good."

The taxi stopped and Mark handed the driver a twenty-pound note. He stepped outside out and stretched, enjoying the feel of the rain on his face as he held the door for Kirsty. She climbed out, wearing jeans and a cream, fitted sweater, looking somehow fresh-faced despite the lack of sleep.

"At least I don't need to worry about the rain." She lifted a hank of damp hair. He had just about had time for a shower too, but his clothes were crumpled from their night on the floor and he had to quickly change before he saw everyone. He needed to make a good impression, not least because there was more at stake now. He desperately wanted everyone to agree to his suggestion.

Mark opened the back door, hoping that everyone would have left the kitchen to head to the drawing room by now. His heart sank as he saw instead that Brian and Frank were still there.

He stood aside for Kirsty to enter then shut the door.

"You're cutting it fine." Brian said, leaning against the kitchen counter. "We've all been wondering what the big news is."

"Morning," Kirsty said. "We're here on time though, right Brian?"

"It is 'we' now, is it?" Frank asked with a leer. "We did wonder."

"It's none of your business Frank, is what it is." Mark already felt annoyed after being in the house for less than a minute.

"Don't be like that Mark. I'm only surprised it took you so long."

"I am here you know Frank." Kirsty said.

Brian sighed. "I haven't got time for this. I'll see you in there."

Frank laughed. "If he gets any more uptight I swear he'll burst. Right, see you in a mo. If you can keep your hands off each other." He winked at them and left the room with his coffee.

"Ah, it's great to be back," Mark said, shaking his head. "I just need to get changed, will you take a coffee in for me?"

"Of course. Deep breaths now."

"Thanks." He kissed her quickly on the mouth. "I'll be really quick."

He was heading back downstairs less than five minutes later and had thrown on a pair of smart black jeans and a blue shirt. He put his notebook under his arm and finished doing up his belt as he jogged down the stairs. Entering the drawing room he saw that he was the last to arrive.

Brian and Alice were by one of the windows but everyone else was sitting down. Kirsty had a trapped look on her face as Sandra leaned across the arm of her chair towards her, and she was blushing furiously. Mark saw her pat Kirsty on the arm as he walked in.

"Ah there he is." Sandra spoke approvingly. As everyone turned to look at him Mark was glad he wasn't prone to going red himself and he cleared his throat before saying.

"Morning. Thanks for being here." He sat down on an armchair, deliberately choosing not to sit near Kirsty. "I know it was short notice."

"It's not like we have any pressing engagements these days," Alice said, "unless you have news for us?" She tucked her legs underneath her and reached for her coffee.

"I know. That's why I thought we should get together." The smell of coffee was tantalising and Mark was relieved to see a cafetiere on the coffee table and a couple of empty mugs. He poured himself a cup and sat back down.

"So, now we're all here, what was it you wanted to say?" Brian asked, sounding belligerent.

"Let him catch his breath." Sandra said as Mark blew on his coffee to cool it down.

"He probably needs to," Frank said in an undertone. "I would."

Ray shook his head. "Give it a rest, Frank. Will you?"

"Right. I didn't mean this to be such a big deal." Mark opened his notebook. "We're so stuck though…anyway, I don't have any answers or new ideas but I want to run something past you."

Brian sighed heavily and Alice gave him a warning look.

"Until the bleeding heart plant starts properly showing," Mark continued, "there's nothing we can do - metal detecting aside, and we've already agreed that's a slim hope."

"Very slim considering we've covered the ground so many times already." Alice said.

"That contraption does my back in." Frank kneaded the small of his back, making his stomach stick out more than ever.

"It's not like it's comfortable for any of us," Brian said. "It's just some of us have more staying power than others."

Frank laughed. "Seriously Brian. Have you been on a charm course or is it just your time of the month?"

Sandra rolled her eyes. "You know you mustn't say things like that, Frank."

"Oh for God's sake."

Mark ignored them all and continued, "The woman at the nursery said it could be a month before we see any sign of the bleeding heart." He put down his notebook. "We're just getting on each other's nerves now. At this rate we're not going to manage another six weeks, let alone get to the end of the six months, right?" There were nods of agreement around the room. "I thought that instead of being stuck here going around in circles we could take a holiday, or go back home, or anything really just to get some space from the house and…I suppose, from each other."

"I am so in," Ray said, at once. "Absolutely brilliant idea."

"What if she's wrong though, the woman at the nursery?" Brian asked.

"I can stay here. This is home for me anyway for now," Mark said with a shrug. "I might go away for a few days but otherwise I'll stay on and keep looking. Everyone else can come back in maybe three weeks which is still way before we're expecting to see any shoots."

"What if you do find it though? What if she is wrong? What's to stop you getting a head start and closing everyone else out?" Brian asked.

"Darling, that's not very trusting of you." Alice said drily.

"I didn't build my business by trusting people, Alice. Besides, I'm sure he understands that, don't you Mark? It's nothing personal."

"I understand you Brian and, if you remember, so did Tom. That's why he set up the email accounts for us all. I've got nothing to gain by secretly entering the password unless I can work out all the other clues before anyone else checks their email." Brian nodded brusquely and Mark continued, "Look, I'm not forcing this on anyone, I just think we need a break that's all."

Mark sneaked a look at Kirsty who was sitting diagonally across from him. He was surprised to see a hurt expression on her face that she quickly masked. She smiled at him but the smile didn't reach her eyes and suddenly Mark realised what an idiot he'd been. In keeping his word to Ray, he hadn't told her what he was planning. It was hard to believe she'd think he wanted her to clear out too but then she must be as tired as he was so it was possible. He winked at her and was relieved to see a proper smile from her in return."

"I vote yes," Ray said. "I've got nearly fifteen grand in a case upstairs and I've never needed a holiday so much in my life."

"It's a good idea Mark," Alice said. "I'd love a bit of winter sunshine apart from anything else." She stretched her long arms languidly. "Oh it would be wonderful to get away from the rain and the cold."

"The office needs me," Brian said gruffly, pushing his glasses up his nose. "You'd have to go on your own but I could join you for a long weekend perhaps."

Alice waved away his suggestion. "Don't worry darling, you do your thing. Just remember that you're supposed to be recuperating so go easy. Oh, and you may need to tell a few fibs about where I am."

"What do you think, Sandra?" Frank asked.

"I've got a job waiting actually," Sandra said excitedly. "It's a bit of a jammy one and I've been trying to keep him on hold so this is perfect timing."

It was as though Sandra had come to life. Her careworn face was animated as she described the commission. "It's someone I've known for years and he's always been a real fan of my work." She giggled. "Sorry that sounds really immodest but, anyway, he's got this small hotel in France that he's nearly finished refurbishing…"

"Oh, is this that thing you told me about – for Freddy?" Frank asked.

"Yes. He's such a love and he wants me to come up with art for the hotel rooms. It will be a real blitz but he wants a load of sketches of the local area and some big pieces for the lobby. Isn't it wonderful?"

"Bloody hell, Sandra. Why didn't you tell us?" Ray asked.

"I didn't think I'd be able to do it. Not that I'll get it all done in three weeks but I can make a good start." She shrugged. "Anyway, I love your idea Mark. It's been really hard just twiddling our thumbs, hasn't it?"

"I know. It's been a tough time all round. Not really what Tom planned." Mark said.

Kirsty nodded and suppressed a yawn. "It would have broken Tom's

heart, all this but we're not going to find the plant by looking, not for a while and we've exhausted everything else. I think it's a great idea."
Mark felt relief wash over him that everyone had agreed, and as his stomach rumbled noisily he stood up.
"Great, I'll just go and get some biscuits. Let's have another coffee and sort out a return date and what we're going to do."
"Kirsty, will you give me a hand?"
They walked down the corridor towards the kitchen and Mark put an arm around her waist.
"Hello, only person in the house I don't need a break from."
She laughed. "Yeah, I got that, it's okay."
"Good. Once we're finished down here I'm going to get some sleep, but shall we get together later - maybe have dinner at mine?"
"I'd like that." Kirsty reached up to kiss him. "Thanks. I'm hopeless at sleeping in the day but considering what happened the last time you asked me out for dinner I'm going to try."

Part Two

The way to love anything is to realise that it may be lost.
GK Chesterton

MARCH

Chapter Seventeen

For over a week, Mark and Kirsty hardly left the haven of the house and its grounds. They went out for supplies but otherwise completely cut themselves off from the world outside, languidly ensconced in an orgy of box sets, board games and each other. Eventually though, the urge to get away from the house beckoned and on a whim they'd gone to Marrakech, somewhere neither of them had been before, and the explosion of noise and colour had blasted them back to wakefulness. They had skipped past the early dating stage of their relationship so it felt good to go out for long lunches and wander around Djemaa El-Fna, avoiding the snakes and the more gruesome cooking stalls, but relishing the variety in the souks and the feeling of being a world away from winter in England. The feeling of rewinding things between them was heightened by their discreet behaviour in public, so that in private there was a need to make up for the lost hours where they hadn't been physically close.

Back at Downsview Manor, a few days after their return, Mark woke up early and his first thought was that he was still in their large shuttered room in the riad. He could hear the regular rhythm of Kirsty's breathing and opened his eyes to find her face next to his in the gloomy half-light of his bedroom. He kissed her softly on the lips but she didn't move. Leaning up on to one elbow he watched Kirsty sleeping for a while and realised as he looked at her that he'd never felt so content. He'd been attracted to her ever since they met at the library two years ago but this was beyond desire. Absently, he wound a silky hank of Kirsty's hair around his fingers before lying back down. A ray of sunlight blazed through a crack in the curtains, the first sunshine since they were back, and Mark decided on impulse to take a quick look around the grounds before Kirsty woke up. He carefully moved out from underneath the duvet but as he walked around the bed Kirsty mumbled, "where are you going?"

"Just going out for a walk, won't be long." He kissed her briefly on the lips. "You stay there and I'll bring you a coffee when I come back." Kirsty mumbled something indecipherable and Mark went in to the bathroom to brush his teeth. He came back to find Kirsty looking much more awake and he wavered for a moment but then started to get dressed, all the while very aware of her gaze on him. Doing up his jeans he paused as he noticed Kirsty's nightdress crumpled on the floor. She'd been wearing it earlier.

He looked up at her as she let the duvet slip down to her waist.

"Don't mind me," she said.

"Seriously?" Mark asked with a laugh.

"It fell off." Kirsty stretched luxuriantly. "If you're busy though…"

Mark moved over to the bed and leaned over to kiss her, feeling her breasts brush against his bare chest.

"You're very demanding, " he said, looking down at her.

Kirsty lifted the duvet.

"Am I?"

Mark laughed again, unzipping his jeans and kicking them off. He dived back into bed and kissed her properly, feeling her gasp as he tweaked one of her nipples.

"Very," he murmured, as he moved his hand lower, "very demanding."

*

While Mark showered, Kirsty went next door to her room to get ready and by the time she came back he had brewed coffee and made some toast. The windows were open and they sat with their breakfast on the sofa, listening to the melancholy cawing of crows from the woods, and the noisy chirrup and twitter of birds from the ivy overhead.

"Lots of sunshine," Kirsty said, "that's exactly what we need." Their wait for the dicentra plant's shoots to appear was making them obsessed with the weather especially as it was their only hope now. They had no way of contacting Joan. Nobody knew the name of her friend, or even where exactly in Spain she lived, and Mark was starting to regret his restraint that evening, not that he'd admit that to Brian and the others.

"Fingers crossed for more days like this," Mark said, finishing his coffee. "Right, shall we get going?"

It always felt strange leaving Mark's apartment and venturing into the heavy silence of the house now that it had been empty so long. Dust motes drifted in the light from the hallway windows and Mark trailed his finger along the windowsill, showing Kirsty his dust-covered finger.

"We're going to have to clean the house before everyone gets back."

"I was thinking that," Kirsty said, then she giggled. "Why are we whispering?"

Mark laughed and spoke in his normal voice. "Sorry. I hated living here on my own after Tom died. All the creaks and groans you can hear at night had me completely freaked out."

"I don't know how Tom managed by himself."

"I know he started sleeping better after I moved in – he told me that once."

"I suppose he had Joan and Tony popping in as well," Kirsty said as they entered the cloakroom off the main kitchen to put on thick coats and boots. "Still, I'm not surprised he kept his furniture and made his own little corner downstairs."

The cold wind took their breath away when they stepped outside and for a moment they simply stood and enjoyed the sun on their face and the freshness of the air after so much time indoors.

"We could hire one of those cleaning companies to come in and blitz the house." Mark said.

"Yes, good idea. I can't believe Joan used to do it by herself." They both looked over at the lodge house. There had been no sign of the key on the purple fob so the curtains were still closed as if in mourning.

"Where to?" Kirsty asked after a moment.

"Let's do it methodically. Shall we start on this side?" Mark pointed to the woods that were to the right of them as they looked down the hill.

"There's just so much ground to cover," Kirsty said, sounding overwhelmed, as she looked at size of the area they had to search.

"I know but we're only doing a recce anyway - we're still too early, so it's just the most likely places we need to look."

"Okay," Kirsty said. "Anyway, even if it is still freezing out here I can think of worse places to be on a day like today."

"Or worse people to be with."

Mark put an arm around Kirsty's shoulder and they walked companionably along together through the woods. There was a lot of new growth since Mark had last been along here with the metal detector. The lush green shoots of Bluebells were coming up through the ground, ready to turn the ground blue, and there were various ferns starting to shoot among the rotted leaves. As they walked along the edge of the woods, they saw prickly green Holly bushes and a small oak tree, covered in dried brown leaves from the previous years growth.

"Does that mean it's dead?" Mark asked as he crumbled one of the leaves, but Kirsty shrugged. Neither of them knew much about woodland or plants and although they'd read up on plants when researching the dicentra plant and its growing conditions, the photos and encyclopaedic descriptions were difficult to match to the untidy reality. Just then Mark heard the sounds of rustling from beside them and turned to see a rabbit emerging from underneath a bush. It bounded away from them and as he watched it he looked over towards the Lodge House and froze in mid-stride, bumping Kirsty as she continued walking with her gaze down towards the ground.

"Look!" Mark spoke in a whisper. She followed his outstretched arm and they stared towards the house where a police car had pulled up outside.

A uniformed policeman unfolded his tall, gangling body from the car and his hair blazed orange in the sun before he put his cap on.

"Isn't that the same one that interviewed us after Tom?" Kirsty asked, "The Scottish guy."

"I know. What's he doing over at the Lodge though?"

"Maybe someone's reported suspicious behaviour. Or Joan could have called him I suppose." Kirsty said.

Mark's heart was hammering in his chest and he remained frozen in place. The nearest neighbour was half a mile away and surely Joan would have called the house if she wanted someone to check the Lodge.

"Should we go and see him?"

"No!" Mark said. "No, I think we should go back to the house, he probably hasn't seen us from down there."

They went back up the hill, hugging the edge of the woods and although they tried to walk, by the time they were in sight of the back of the house, they were almost running.

Closing the kitchen door behind them, Mark stood against it, his mind whirling with possibilities, none of them good.

Kirsty was tugging off her boots, her cheeks flushed and her hair wild from the wind.

"I've got a bad feeling about this Mark. I always felt like he suspected us of something."

"I know, me too. I remember how relieved I was when he left...Christ, what was his name? The way he looked at us..." Mark ran his fingers through his hair. "Right, pull yourself together. Come on."

"Look, it's probably nothing." Kirsty spoke soothingly as she stroked his back. "It could even be a community visit – he might be here to offer Joan counselling, or just to see how she is."

"Do they have time for that these days? No, you're right. It might not be anything and there's nothing that could come back on us from Tom's death."

Apart from the anonymous blackmailer, or someone in the group changing their mind he thought to himself. He pictured them all around Tom's bed, handing him the morphine, watching him die. "Okay, let's go into the living room and look busy, well, look normal," Mark said. "He'll probably be gone soon anyway once he finds that she's not in."

Relaxing slightly, they walked through the kitchen but both jumped when the loud peal of the doorbell echoed down the corridor.

*

PC Thomson sat opposite them on the same grouping of chairs where so often the group had sat and discussed things, or more lately sat and bickered. He had refused a cup of tea and Mark's poor joke about breaking the stereotype had been received with a thin smile.

"Just a couple of questions", he said. "We've received a call from a Mrs Paula Smith. I don't know if you know the name?"

They both shook their heads.

"She called us from Spain and said she'd been trying to contact Mrs Knight for the last couple of weeks."

"Ah." Mark said.

"You know the name do you?"

"No, not the name. It's just that Joan said she was going to stay with a friend in Spain." As what he said sank in, he said, "That's where she should be…"

"Are you saying she didn't arrive?" Kirsty asked.

"Apparently not. So you knew she was going to Spain. Do you know when she left?"

"She had a taxi booked for the day after the funeral," Mark said after a moment. "Hang on, let me look."

Mark looked at the calendar on his phone and was surprised to see that Joan had been gone nearly three weeks now.

"The funeral was February 7th."

"Has it really been that long?" Kirsty asked. "Her friend hasn't heard from her?"

"Mrs Knight was going to call to confirm arrangements but there was some confusion as to when she was arriving from the sound of it."

"Why didn't she call before?" Mark asked.

"So, did you actually see Mrs Knight get into the taxi, sir?"

Mark shook his head.

"And you, Miss Edwards?"

"What? No, I didn't, but I checked to see how she was the night before and she said it was booked for the next morning."

"So, she told you she had a taxi booked for early on the 8th – you're sure?" Kirsty nodded, her hands over her mouth.

"Did she mention which taxi firm she was using?"

"No, I ..."

"Can you tell me the nature of your relationship with Mrs Knight?" There was silence until at last Kirsty spoke. "She was the housekeeper here, that's all."

"Thank you. Right, I've spoken to her brother-in-law who says he had a key but lost it. Do you have a key?"

"No, I don't think so," Mark said, and it was only after he spoke that he remembered Joan had mentioned leaving a key for them in her letter. He felt Kirsty tense beside him and thought how simple a thing it would be to correct his mistake, yet he remained silent as the seconds ticked by.

"I'm sorry if you told me last time we met, but what exactly is your connection to this house? I need to know if you have any links to the house down there."

Mark thought carefully before answering. "I was working for the owner and after his death I was given six months to live here while I finished the work I was doing for him."

"And what work is that?"

"It's a history of the house. His wife was in service here but they ended up buying it so it's quite a story. His lawyers prepared an itinerary of the contents immediately after his death so I'm just babysitting really, but I have complete freedom. I mean there are no problems with Kirsty living here." Mark paused, aware that he was rambling as a result of the man's stare. "The Lodge House is completely separate from this house though - Tom gave it to Joan and Tony a couple of years ago."

"Very generous, Mr Stevens, wasn't he?"

"Yes. Yes he was."

"But he didn't leave you anything in his will, if I recall?"

"He left Mark six rent-free months in a mansion," Kirsty said. "With the cost of rent around here, I'd say that counts as something?"

"True enough, I wouldn't say no to that. Still, what about you, there was nothing for you or any other friends was there?"

Mark had reached his limit.

"Can I ask what all this has to do with Joan's disappearance?"

PC Thomson smiled at him and scribbled something in his notebook. "Now, I'm going to need to get someone down here so we can gain access to the Lodge House."

"Are you going to break the door down?" Kirsty asked.

"I have to check everything's okay in there. Excuse me a moment." He wandered over to the window and leaned his head towards his shoulder speaking quickly into the radio attached to his shoulder. Mark could just make out from the crackling reply that someone was being sent over.

"Right, I'll head down to the house and wait for my colleague there. I may need to talk to you again though. Did you have any plans to go out this morning?"

"No, not really."

"Fine, I'll come and find you later if I need to. No, don't bother getting up, I'll see myself out."

Listening intently for the sound of the door closing, they sat motionless until they finally heard it bang shut. Mark leapt from the chair and headed for the window. Standing to one side, he craned his neck forward to check that he had really gone.

"Careful, make sure he doesn't see us." Mark pulled Kirsty further back from the window and they silently watched him fold himself back into the car. After he had driven away, Mark broke the stillness,

"I don't believe this. We're going to have the police crawling all over the place if Joan's gone missing." Mark started pacing around the room. "What he said about us not receiving anything in Tom's Will, did you get that?"

Kirsty stood with her arms folded, biting her thumbnail.

"Joan will be all right, she just has to be. I felt awful saying she was just the housekeeper."

The worry in Kirsty's voice made Mark stop in his pacing.

"Ignore me," he said. "You're right, sorry."

Mark stood at the window and after a while he felt Kirsty's arms reach around him and the pressure of her face against his back.

"Mark, do you ever think about what we all did? About how Tom died?"

"No," he said honestly. "He didn't want to do it himself, but he was ready to go, wasn't he? You always said you were in favour of euthanasia."

"I know. I still am," she said. "It's just..."

Mark turned around and pulled her to him.

121

"Hey now," he said. "We did a good thing helping Tom. There's nothing to be gained by questioning things now."

"I'm not questioning things. I know we helped him but since then, all this with the money and feeling scared when a police car comes up the drive." She looked up at him. "It doesn't make me feel like we did a good thing that's all."

"Listen, what we did was for the right reasons. He was dying Kirsty and he was starting to suffer. Would you have helped him if there had been no money involved?"

"You know I would."

"There you go then. Tom told us to remember that, didn't he? What we did was illegal, yes, but it wasn't wrong and he needed us to be strong for him." He kissed the top of her head. "We have to stay strong Kirsty, now more than ever."

Mark continued to hold her and he felt the tension leave her body as she relaxed into him.

"You always make me feel better about things." She smiled at him.

"I'm sorry for my timing. Like we haven't got enough to worry about right now."

"Well that is one thing you don't need to worry about. For now we have to believe Joan is fine. Maybe she's gone to stay with another friend or perhaps she's taken herself off to somewhere she can be left alone. The bleeding heart will pop up any day now and when the others come back they'll all be in better moods."

Kirsty snuggled against him,

"Ever the optimist."

Mark laughed.

"Always. Right, in the meantime, let's go upstairs and see if we can see what's happening at the Lodge."

Chapter Eighteen

The attics made up a complete extra floor of the house and were the servant's quarters from long ago. The small white-painted door at the top of their staircase opened onto a gloomy corridor that had a series of rooms running off it at either side.

"I wonder which one was Annie's when she lived here?" Kirsty whispered.

"Don't start with questions like that. I came up here when I was in the house on my own, and lasted about five minutes. It's creepy the way the beds are still here - it must be decades since they were used."

"Imagine being one of the last remaining old-faithfuls and living up here on your own," Kirsty said with a grimace.

Mark opened the door to one of the rooms and a stream of sunlight poured through the dusty dormer window to help dispel the spookiness.

"Stop that talk now or I'm heading back down again."

"Where's the hidden room?" Kirsty asked.

"Right at the end." Mark said as he adjusted the binoculars. "The last room's got a panel in it that swings out if you press a floorboard on the floor, and there's a door behind it. I don't know how long it's been there..." Mark was distracted as the figure of PC Thomson came into view, as close as if he was fifty-metres away, rather than five hundred. He was leaning against the door of the car, his arms crossed and head tilted back into the sun. The young man jumped as a second police car slowly approached. Mark couldn't hear it from where he was but the car must have beeped him. A man got out of the driving seat and went to the boot of his car where he removed something that looked like a small battering ram. They spoke for a moment then walked up the path, their expressions serious as they knocked on the door, a modern white UPVC one that looked as out of place on the old building as the bright gleam of false teeth in a craggy face

"What are they doing? He said he's already tried the door."

Reluctantly, Mark handed over the binoculars.

"It looks like they've got...oh! Are they allowed to do that? Do you want to look?"

Mark took the binoculars back from Kirsty in time to see the two men recoil. He opened his mouth to say something but thought better of it. He didn't want to panic Kirsty over a pint of milk on the worktop.

PC Thomson jogged back to his car and returned with what looked to

Mark like a pot of Vicks. He was puzzled for a moment until they both wiped it under their nostrils and he understood. Kirsty was leaning against the window trying to see what was happening

"They've gone in."

Less than a minute later his worst fears were confirmed when both men came out of the house and inhaled great gulps of air.

"What's happening? What are they doing?"

Mark didn't know what to say as he watched PC Thomson begin issuing instructions into the radio of the car.

"Mark, what's happening? Tell me."

Mark lowered the binoculars.

"I don't know, but I think they've found something..."

"Something or someone?" Kirsty's voice was anxious as she reached for the binoculars.

"Something that smells, I don't know for sure, but..."

"They're not doing anything, just standing around chatting."

"Let's go downstairs. Come on."

Kirsty remained by the window, watching the house.

"Quick, Kirsty, I want to hide some stuff up here. This changes things"

Closing the door to the bedroom behind them, they raced back down the corridor, following the sharp imprints of their footsteps in the dust. They ran down the spiral staircase in a panic. Mark didn't know how much time they had but he wanted nothing left out about the clues they were working on.

They entered the dining room and looked at the chaos on the table. Luckily, everyone had taken their laptops with them when they left so it was mostly paper and scattered books.

"He might have noticed all this when he was here before, so we can't just clear it away. Just take away anything about the clues. This can be notes for my book."

"Mark, are you sure about this?"

"What? No I'm not sure." Mark stopped, putting his head in his hands as he thought. His hands were clenched into fists as he tugged on his hair but after a moment, he lowered his hands.

"Listen," he said. "I know this is cold but we have to assume the worst and we've got to be ready. Whatever the circumstances, questions are going to be asked – again – and we don't want to explain why everyone was living here. Whatever we say it will seem strange, and strange, to those two down there, means something worth looking at."

"What are you saying?"

124

"I'm guessing here, but it's likely Joan committed suicide, or maybe just overdid it on the drugs the Doctor gave her - you know how out of it she was."

Kirsty closed her eyes and shook her head

"I can't do this. If Joan is…if she's dead…and we have to lie to the police again on top of it all?"

"No, not lie, just…" Mark paused and looked intently at her. "We need to keep it as simple as possible. Ray's been staying here because he's a mate of mine. Brian and Alice stayed for a while because of their house renovations and Sandra was here because Tom commissioned a series of paintings. We all met through Tom but became friends ourselves. At the moment though it's just us. We don't talk about the others. We don't need to."

Mark stopped to collect his thoughts - this was the story they never expected to use. He was frazzled and rambling but he had to make Kirsty understand what was at stake.

"It's like we were saying earlier. We've done nothing wrong, but we have done something illegal. Really illegal – and the money complicates things. Would you want to be on trial with everyone else? Imagine Frank or Alice in the witness box."

She shook her head slowly, understanding dawning in her eyes.

"We have to be as normal as possible and me living here with my girlfriend is normal. The rest of them living here isn't. Anyway, it's just a white lie – they're not living here are they and…"

"Alright, alright I've got it." Kirsty snapped. "Come on, let's get this stuff upstairs."

They moved quickly now, creating a pile of books and papers and adding notebooks filled with strange scribbles about Helen of Troy and Harry Potter. Kirsty grabbed the instruction manuals for the metal detectors.

"No, leave that – it's just a hobby of mine, yes?"

"I nearly forgot this." He held out a rota that Kirsty had optimistically suggested as the best way of dividing the household tasks. "Let's get this lot upstairs first, we can fine tune things afterwards."

Kirsty was artistically rearranging the books and papers to look as scattered and messy as before but she left it to help Mark carry everything up. They trailed back to the top floor and up the narrow spiral staircase.

Kirsty nudged open one of the bedroom doors as she passed to give them more light and immediately the narrow corridor seemed less forbidding. They reached the end room with relief and depressed the lever, but Mark swore loudly when he found the hidden door locked. "Who was up here last?"

Kirsty opened the door opposite and dumped the papers she was carrying on the narrow bed inside. The mattress puffed out a cloud of dust and Kirsty waved it away, choking,

"Nobody since we got the laptops, I wouldn't have thought."

"Right, I'll go downstairs and look on the board in the kitchen. I just hope whoever it was put the key back. Can you go and look in all the bedrooms? Just get rid of anything to do with clues, anything incriminating. And try and make them look less lived-in if you can. Guests not residents."

Mark ran back downstairs, leaving Kirsty to decide what could be classed as incriminating. He paused at the small round window at the top of the staircase and was pleased to see that the police cars hadn't moved. He was out of breath by the time he reached the kitchen, more a result of panic than his exertions. He flicked the light on as he moved towards the old wooden board where keys were kept. The sun had moved away from this side of the house and the small windows made the kitchen gloomy.

There were probably fifty keys on the board, ranging from large iron keys that fitted some of the old gates in the boundary walls to shiny new Yale keys. Mark knew the one he wanted was a small old-fashioned key with a tag reading "Attic 8" in faded copperplate writing. He turned tags over to read them, entangling them in other keys as he did so and swearing repeatedly in a kind of mantra. Beads of sweat had appeared on his forehead and he was becoming frantic by the time he found it. He exhaled in relief and used the arm of his long-sleeved top to wipe his brow. Something had been nagging at him while he'd been hunting though the tangle of keys and it was the purple on his sleeve that brought it into focus - Joan's key, hadn't he just seen it? Muttering to himself, he started to scan the board and saw it again at once, a Yale key with a purple plastic cover and a luggage label attached to it with 'Lodge' written in thick black letters. Mark swore again, it definitely hadn't been there when they tried to find it after Joan left. He grabbed it, worried about what else he might have overlooked, but with no thought now other than to get back to the attics before the police came to break the news.

Half an hour later, although it felt like much longer, Kirsty was using a clothes brush to get rid of the dust from Mark's clothes. He did the same for her and they washed their hands and faces, talking all the while.

"Let's go down there." Mark said.

"He said he'd come and find us though."

"I know but we're concerned about Joan," Mark continued.

"Well we are."

"Exactly, so it makes sense that we'd wander down to find out what's happening." Mark rubbed his face with the towel Kirsty handed him. "Besides, we'll be nervous wrecks if we wait here."

Kirsty looked at him doubtfully. "Your call."

"Or I'll go on my own if you want." Mark said.

"No, I'll come with you, I just hope I can do this – I'm not a very good liar, I always end up going red."

"Look, you'll be fine. Shock does funny things to people and, one way or another we will be in shock."

Looking unconvinced, Kirsty agreed and they returned to the kitchen to put their outdoor things on.

"Wait," Kirsty said. "What if Joan didn't die in her sleep? He might think we're returning to the scene of the crime - isn't that a classic sign of guilt."

"But we haven't done anything."

"Mark, please I think it's better if we wait, I really do."

Mark threw his coat back onto the hook.

"Intuition?"

"If you like." Kirsty was standing in front of the door, chewing on her thumbnail. "I'll make us some tea. You go through to the dining room and make sure there's nothing I've overlooked."

The tea did nothing to calm their nerves but by the time PC Thomson came to talk to them, the reality of Joan's situation rather than their own had begun to sink into their overburdened minds and their reaction to the news was genuine.

"You think she's been there all that time?" Mark asked him.

"I can't confirm anything yet until the scene of crime officers have finished, but she died some time ago, yes."

Mark knew from previous visits to the Lodge House that Joan kept the house warm. She'd always complained about the cold in the Manor and he tried to shake away the gruesome images that his imagination supplied.

"Can you tell us how she died?" Kirsty asked in a whisper.

PC Thomson shook his head, with an expression of regret on his face.

"The only thing I can tell you is that she was found in her bed. I can't give you any other answers at this time, I'm afraid. Now, I do need to ask you some more questions."

Mark could almost see the change in the eyes as PC Thomson went from empathy to business and it reminded him of an actor assuming a role. To his surprise though, the questions that followed were not too demanding and Mark felt a lot calmer by the time he left. There were questions about Joan's state of mind and the accident, which they could answer genuinely enough, and a general filling in of the blanks. The only difficult moment was when PC Thomson asked whether anyone else had been at the Manor House on the night of the funeral. Without thinking, Mark told him that as far as he could remember it had just been the two of them. As someone who previously had no contact with the police other than a teenage misadventure and a speeding ticket, Mark was surprised by how easily the lie slipped out.

It was mid-afternoon by the time everyone left the Lodge House. They hadn't seen Joan's body leave the house, but Mark had seen the coroner's van leaving the driveway, its sedate pace a reminder that there was no hurry. After everyone had gone Mark needed to get out of the house and he and Kirsty decided to continue their walk around the grounds. They cut across the lawns to the opposite side of the grounds, their elongated shadows overlapping as they walked. "We're going to have to call the others aren't we?" Mark asked as he kicked a soggy branch out of the way.

"I was thinking about that but if they come back now, they'll have to go to their own homes – they can't come here at the moment."

"I doubt they'll return straight away though. I mean, let's face it, after Tony's death half of them were more concerned about the lack of Joan's housekeeping than anything else."

"Don't, I just can't get my head round it."

"I know, it hasn't sunk in yet for me either and…"

"All that time she was there," Kirsty interrupted, "that's what I can't stop thinking about. Remember she said in her letter that I could use the house - do you think she wanted me to find her?"

Mark squeezed Kirsty's hand. "I don't know. Whatever she did she won't have been thinking straight."

"But is that why she left the light on do you think? Oh Mark, what she went through…her whole family gone." Kirsty's expression crumpled.

"Hey, come here." Mark held out his arms. "Let it all out…that's it."

Mark held her while she cried, her sobs muffled against his shoulder. As her hair tickled his nose he was reminded of his feeling of contentment that morning – it felt like a long time ago.

"I'm alright," Kirsty said after a while. She sniffed and wiped her eyes. "Sorry, I just…" she shrugged.

"I know." Mark handed her his scarf. "Here, I haven't got a handkerchief."

Kirsty smiled. "Thanks. It's okay, I've got a tissue."

They resumed their walk, holding hands tightly.

"I'll phone everyone when we get in and tell them we'll call again when we know more," Mark said. "Alice knew Joan from school so it will be a shock for her."

"I think it will hit Ray the hardest although Sandra…"

Mark stopped dead, an expression of disbelief on his face.

"What, what is it?" Kirsty asked sounding worried.

"Down there…" Mark pointed at an oval-shaped patch of cultivated earth next to the lake. It was thick with daffodils still in bud but in the centre was a cluster of tiny, wine coloured shoots.

"See those?" Mark asked. "They're right next to one of the benches where Tom used to sit."

They picked their way over the wet soil and hunkered down to examine the tiny curling leaves at the top of the shoots. He brought up the photo on his phone and enlarged it before holding it next to the plant.

"These seem a bit smooth," Mark said. "When I went to the nursery the stalks had grooves running down them, like celery."

"There are so many different varieties of things though. What do you think?"

Mark stood up. "Stay there and I'll be back with a spade in a minute."

Half an hour later, Mark had dug a hole that was a metre across and over a metre deep. His hands were the colour of baked beans from sifting among the lumps of clay soil lower down.

"There's no way Tom could have dug this deep," Mark said in frustration.

"I think we should get it back to how it was," Kirsty said. "In case the police notice it." She kicked a clod of earth back into the hole.

Mark had placed a plastic bin liner on the grass outside the oval so he could replace the soil easily enough, but it would be harder to fix the plants trampled underfoot. Mark slammed the spade into the ground and climbed out of the hole.

"Have we got the clue wrong? After all this waiting around, did we have the answer wrong this whole time?"

"This bleeding heart may have gone to seed, but holds the answer that you need." Kirsty said automatically. "Mark, we didn't just latch on to Tony's response, you know we didn't. We looked at every possible option. Besides the clues always relate to Tom and to someone in the group who can make the connection and 'gone to seed' – it's got to be a plant."

"Maybe that was too obvious." Mark's voice was flat. "It was such an easy clue, well it would have been…"

"Why don't I take this to a nursery before we write it off. This poor plant might be something else altogether."

Mark looked at the huge pile of soil waiting to be replaced. "That would be great. I'll get this cleared up."

After Kirsty left Mark concentrated on his task, trying hard not to trash any more plants in the process. It took him longer than he thought to fill in the hole but even after his best efforts it was still fresh ground surrounded by trampled, soil-covered plants. When he got back to the house, he stepped out of his sweaty, soil-covered clothes in the kitchen and bundled them into the washing machine in the large cloakroom. Stopping only to down a pint of water at the sink, he headed straight upstairs. The shower in his room was a good one and the hot water ran out in a pounding spray. He was in a kind of heat-induced trance under the spray, slowly revolving in circles, by the time he heard banging on the door.

He lifted his head and smoothed his hair back to see, but the bathroom was thick with steam.

"Kirsty?"

"Peony," she said, standing in the doorway waving the plant at him. "It's a peony bush. Well, it was – the woman at the plant centre told me off for digging it up."

Mark turned the shower off and stepped out.

"Come here you gorgeous creature," he said, wrapping a towel around his waist.

"With or without the plant?" She threatened, and he grabbed it from her and dumped it in the sink.

They held each other tightly, the zip of Kirsty's coat cold against Mark's skin.

"You're soaking!"

"Don't care," Mark said. "I'm just glad it wasn't the right plant."

"Me too," Kirsty said. "Next time we'll have to go somewhere else though."

"Let's hope next time we get the right plant. The sooner we get this done the better."

"Now you're talking," Kirsty said pushing him away, "but you really are soaked."

Mark held her even tighter and shook his head, causing droplets of water to rain on her face

"Mark, stop it!" Kirsty squealed.

He let her go, glad to see her smiling again as she left him to dry off.

Chapter Nineteen

"I don't understand why you did that, Mark?"

"Honestly Alice! What should he have done then? Told the Police we were living in some kind of commune? I'm sure you did the best thing, just keeping it nice and simple." Sandra gave Mark an encouraging smile.

"Dodgy business Mark," Brian said, "it doesn't do to lie to the police. I've seen it at first hand with a former client of mine. He wanted me to do up his place then six months later he was bankrupt and on his way to the Fraud courts. How that started…"

"Yes, alright darling." Alice interrupted. "I don't see how that helps us with this." She turned to Mark. "So we now have to say that we were visitors. That's not going to gel with the neighbours, they know we haven't been at home."

"Look, all I said in my statement was that you weren't here the night of Tony's funeral. Anyway, the party line was always that you were staying here for a while and I didn't want to say you'd outstayed your welcome."

Alice glared at Mark and Frank muttered something under his breath.

"I'm not saying you have," Mark said. "It's just what I would say if anyone got curious. Anyway, with you and Brian having work done on your house it's plausible enough."

"What about us?" Frank asked.

"Sandra's staying while she's doing the series of paintings that Tom commissioned and you're keeping her company, while researching your next book. How's that?"

"And Kirsty?"

"We just say she's my girlfriend."

"I was wondering about that," Sandra said, her eyes bright with curiosity. "So do we have an extra bedroom free?"

"Don't be shy now, Sandra." Kirsty said.

"Let's just say the cover story should hold on that one." Mark added. This was the first time the group had all been in the house since their holiday and Mark was surprised by how easily they had slotted back together, even to the extent of automatically sitting in their usual chair or bit of sofa. Much though he hadn't missed them, a part of him was pleased to see them. They were meeting to decide what to do next and to properly search for the dicentra plant now that they were approaching time for it to appear.

Looking around the room, he could see how well everyone looked, more relaxed somehow even though they hadn't long finished discussing the latest about Joan. There wasn't much to tell as the police hadn't told Mark anything but he had spoken to Phil, her brother-in-law, to find out when the funeral would be. There was no date yet as the body wouldn't be released until after the Coroner's inquest, still a week away. The cursory police interest, combined with learning that she'd left a note confirmed Mark's guess that it was suicide. The local papers had reported the story of a family unit being wiped out in tragic circumstances with as many details as they could muster, but as they could only hint at the cause of Joan's death the story had soon faded away. It seemed to Mark, listening to everyone chatting about their holiday, that Joan and Tony had faded from the group's memory just as quickly.

"That's me in a helicopter flying over the Grand Canyon," Ray said, showing his photos to Sandra. "Hey, Mark will it be okay if I move back in today, it's just I've been staying at The Grand since I got back and it's getting a bit expensive."

"At the Grand? What do you only do five star now?"

Ray was unabashed. "Yeah, well that was the posh hotel when I was growing up - I wouldn't even have gone in there back then."

"You understand that we haven't actually found the money yet?" Brian asked.

"Just move back in when you're ready Ray." Mark said. "I don't think anyone's going to be questioning our living arrangements now, but it might be an idea for the rest of you to wait until after the inquest."

"I've got no argument with that." Alice said. "It's been wonderful to be at home actually, being surrounded by my own things and, well…I'm sure you won't take offence when I say I've enjoyed having the house to myself."

"I could do with more time at work too. It's a busy time and my deputy's doing a good job but it's not the same as me being there." Brian sighed heavily, the picture of a weary executive. "I want to be kept up to date though. Alice, will you be able to liaise with everyone from home?"

"Hang on!" Frank said. "Why should we do all the grunt work while you look around your building sites, or whatever it is you do?"

Mark realised that the novelty of being pleased to see them had already worn off. In the end, it was agreed that as it wouldn't take seven people to wander around the grounds everyday, Brian could continue at work.

After everyone left Mark found himself driving Ray back into Brighton to collect his things. The hotel doorman didn't like him parking outside the front while Ray checked out, but grudgingly allowed it on condition that Mark stayed with the car. The sea was sparkling in the sunlight, a rare deep blue rather than its usual murky green and after waiting a while Mark got out of the car. Stretching lazily, he leant against the bonnet and whiled away the time by people watching. He'd forgotten his phone so couldn't call Ray to find out what was keeping him. After another five minutes he snuck past the doorman while he was busy and walked into the echoing lobby, immediately spotting a miserable looking Ray at the reception desk. Ray's face lit up when he saw him,

"Mark, over here!" Ray was with a young receptionist, a sleek looking brunette with scraped back hair and immaculate make-up, who tactfully shuffled papers on the desk while Ray explained the situation.

"There must have been a mistake at my bank, so I was just coming to find you. Do you think you could…just until we get back?" Ray gestured to the bill.

"Eight hundred? Jesus, you were only here a couple of days."

"I know but I had the chance to upgrade my room when I arrived."

"Right." Mark handed over his Visa card to the receptionist.

"Thanks Mark, I owe you one."

The doorman gave him a tight smile when they walked past which Mark returned apologetically as they hurried back to the car. He opened the boot for Ray before throwing himself into the driver's seat.

As Mark maneuvered his way onto the main road Ray thanked him but Mark shook his head.

"Have you spent it all? The fifteen thousand, is it gone?"

"No, nothing like that. I've still got loads. I left half of it in my room at the house so I can sort you out when we get there."

"Well, that's something. It's nothing to do with me, but if you run out before the six months is up because you've spent it on helicopters and hotel rooms don't come to me for a loan, that's all."

"I know, I just got a bit carried away and the credit limit isn't very high on my cards so..." Ray shrugged. "Anyway, thanks again for bailing me out back there."

"No problem, although I wasn't sure I had enough credit to cover the bill either to be fair. They might have kicked us out."

"What, two soon to be wealthy men about town like us? Anyway, rich folk are notoriously tight, I heard Brian say once that poor people need

134

a bargain but rich people want one. Not me though, there's no point in having it if you don't spend it."

"Probably best to wait until you've got it though," Mark said. "Have you even looked at any of those books on money Tom left? He kept saying we needed to get ready."

"I know. I will get round to it but they're hardly holiday reading are they?" Ray sat silently for a while. "Hey, I bought presents for everyone - I'll show you when we get home. I hope Kirsty likes hers." Ray paused. "If that's all right now that you two are together."

Mark was surprised. "It's nothing to do with me if you want to give her a present. Well, as long as it's not underwear obviously – not sure how I'd feel about that." There was silence for a moment. "So what is it?"

"Just something from Victoria's Secret but it's no big deal." Ray shook his head as Mark looked at him. "No, it's a watch. You know how she said her other one kept playing up."

"A watch? Wow, very generous of you. Don't be offended if she sticks with her Longines number now she's had it repaired though - it turns out she's into watches like some women are into shoes."

"I know. I remember an old housemate of mine spent her first month's salary on a handbag so it could be worse."

They drove past the Lodge House, their eyes drawn to the blue and white police tape over the door.

"It's bloody terrible," Ray said. "I really liked Joan and Tony and they seemed so happy."

Mark nodded.

"They were. I think that's what did for Joan – they never needed the money in the first place."

"No they were fine as they were. I think I need money to be happy though. It definitely makes me more confident especially when talking to women. Plus, in America I had the accent thing, which was brilliant, and everyone seemed a lot friendlier. It seemed okay to ask someone if they wanted a drink, not so much of a thing you know."

Ray seemed more self-assured and Mark wondered if it would last once he had spent more time with Brian, Alice and the others.

They walked into the house and made their way to the drawing room where Mark saw Kirsty stretched out on one of the sofas with a book. She was lying in the sunlight and looked as contented as a sleeping cat.

"Comfortable?" Mark called.

"Hello!" She removed her glasses. "You've been ages."

"We had to sort out a few things with the bill. After that it was just traffic."

Ray smiled his thanks. "I'll just take these up."

Mark sat on the sofa beside Kirsty.

"When did they go?"

"About half an hour ago. It's been lovely to have the house back again. I'm going to miss this place when our time's up."

Mark looked around the bright, sunny room.

"Maybe we could buy it afterwards?"

Kirsty snorted, "We'd barely afford the attics. This place must be worth millions – way out of our league."

"Well, we could come and stay when it's been turned into a hotel."

"Do you think it will be?"

"I'm just guessing but I wouldn't be surprised. Anyway, budge up."

After rearranging themselves, they managed to both get in a comfortable position.

"Is this all right, with Ray here?"

"We're only lying next to each other Kirsty, I don't think he'll be too shocked."

Kirsty swatted him with her paperback.

"You know what I mean, he'll probably feel enough of a gooseberry as it is."

"Yeah, well he'll have to get used to it. Anyway, it's not like he hasn't been surrounded by couples when he lived here before."

"But there were three of us then, now he's the only one on his own."

"Stop fretting, he'll be fine. I think America's been good for him. He loved it out there."

By the time Ray came down they were both absorbed, Kirsty reading her book and Mark scrolling through something on his phone. The sense that he was being observed made Mark look up and he saw Ray staring at them from the doorway.

"I didn't know if I was intruding."

They both scrambled upright onto the sofa, ending up on opposite sides,

"Hi Ray, of course you're not intruding...what's that?"

Ray was clutching two brightly wrapped parcels and he looked nervous as he walked towards them.

"I was telling Mark I'd brought everyone presents from my holiday."

"Oh Ray, you shouldn't have," Kirsty said. "Still, as you have...how exciting!"

She beamed at him and he looked pleased, although a little wary.

"Just to explain, I bought a little something for everyone. But when I was in Vegas I had a bit of a win on the slot machines, well quite a big win really. Anyway, I knew I'd only end up losing it if I carried on so I went to the shop to spend it instead." Ray's words were coming out in a rush. "I didn't see anything I wanted and I'd had a lot of free drinks and well, you'll see Kirsty. This is yours Mark."

Mark opened his parcel and found a Guinness tee shirt inside with the legend, 'Drunk in New York, New York' inscribed above the distinctive black and white pint glass. He held it up against him.

"It's brilliant - thanks Ray, was that your hotel?"

"Yeah, I was playing at the Wynn when I hit the jackpot though."

"I like the little four-leaf clover stitched inside the 'o', it's really nice quality." Kirsty was rubbing the fabric between her fingers.

"Okay, so this is what I bought you before my win so you may as well have it as well. It's not much." He handed over a small parcel and Kirsty unwrapped a pale green scarf,

"Ray, it's gorgeous! This is silk isn't it? I can't believe you - 'it's not much'. That's one of my favourite colours too, you clever thing - thank you!" She leaned up to give him a peck on the cheek.

Ray looked embarrassed and held out the final present. He'd been holding it behind his back and when he handed over the glossy red bag, Mark saw the distinctive scrawled logo.

"Cartier? What, really?" She held the bag in her lap, and stared at Ray, looking puzzled.

"Go on. See what's inside, you might not like it anyway."

Kirsty removed a rectangular box from the bag and opened it. For some time, she simply gazed at the elegant white gold and diamond watch and Mark was astonished to see tears in her eyes when she looked up.

"Kirsty. Are you alright?"

"Sorry, I just…oh my God. Ray, I can't - this is too much."

"Don't you like it?"

"No, I love it. This is the ultimate watch and it's so pretty." Kirsty gazed at it again before closing the lid firmly. "I really can't accept it though. Thank you but…it's just too much." She handed the box back and Mark understood now why Ray had asked him about the present. Something from Victoria's Secret would have been better than this - at least they could have joked about it. He was surprised to feel a twinge of jealousy as well as irritation.

"If you like it, you should have it." Ray looked hurt when Kirsty shook her head. "I tell you what. If we don't find the money, you can give it back and I'll sell it, but if we get the money you keep it and then it's no big deal. That sort of thing will be a trinket to you then."

"You're sure about this?"

"Please, just take it."

She opened the box again. "It's so beautiful. I don't know what to say." She hugged him and Mark felt another stab of irritation. He didn't like the expression on Ray's face and wondered if Ray had bought it in the hope that he and Kirsty were just a fling.

"I'm just glad you like it."

"I won't be wearing this one round the house." Kirsty laughed, taking it out of the box and trying it on. "Special occasions only, the rest of the time I'll just look at it."

She twisted her wrist towards the sun and smiled as the diamonds sparkled. "I'm just borrowing it until we find out what happens with the money though. If it all goes wrong you might need it." Holding out her wrist she said, "Look Mark, isn't it gorgeous?"

"Hmm? Yes, very nice."

"You don't mind?" Ray asked him.

"It doesn't matter if I mind. I'll just remember not to leave you in charge of the kitty on a night out." He looked at the watch again. "I've made some drunken impulse buys in my time Ray, but nothing as spectacular as a diamond watch."

"A Cartier diamond watch." Kirsty murmured as she continued to admire it.

Ray moved over to the window, his hands in the back pockets of his jeans as he stared outside.

"Well, I think I might take a stroll around the grounds." He turned to face them. "I really missed this old place when I was away. It'll be hard to go back to the sort of digs I'm used to living in if things don't work out."

"We were saying the same thing earlier," Kirsty said. "I never thought that such a grand house would feel like home but I'm starting to get used to it."

"Yeah, I don't know about living here on my own though, like Tom did. You need a few other people rattling around the place and a few cleaning staff too from the looks of it."

Ray was right. The house was taking on a pronounced air of neglect. All the windows needed cleaning, the wooden corridors needed to be polished and a layer of dust was settling throughout the house.

"Let's get a cleaning crew in for a day while it's quiet." Kirsty said. "What do you think, Mark?"

"Definitely. We never got round to doing that. We should give the place a good clean before the others move back in. Will you sort it out or do you want me to?"

"No, it's fine, I'll do it."

Kirsty left the room in search of a phone signal and Ray moved quickly over to Mark, fishing an envelope from his back pocket.

"Thanks again. It's all there, you can count it if you like."

"Don't worry, I'll take your word on it. So, helicopters, five star hotels and diamond watches – which, for the record, I do mind by the way."

"What can I say Mark, they give you free drinks in those places. When I won on the slots everyone was crowded around me – I was buzzing." Ray's face was wistful. "Have you ever been to Vegas?"

Mark shook his head.

"They have these designer shops in the hotels. That watch was in the window at Cartier as I was leaving. It just seemed like such a brilliantly frivolous thing to do, to replace Kirsty's broken watch Vegas style. Anyway, even after that I had some money left."

"Will you have enough money to last?"

"I'll be fine now I'm back here. It's only three and a half months."

"Four clues to go." Mark said.

"I'll be fine. I've got another credit card on the way in case I do need more money. It's one of those high interest ones but what else can an unemployed man in rented accommodation do?"

"He can stop buying stupidly expensive presents for other peoples girlfriends," Mark suggested.

Ray shook his head. "You really do mind about the watch. Look, I've got it – hands off. Noted." He put his hands in his pockets. "Anyway, no offence because Kirsty's lovely, obviously, but she's really not my type."

"Okay, well…good." Mark said. "Talk about setting the bar for presents though. Seriously Ray, I bought her some nice earrings in Marrakech and wondered if that was too much."

"Don't worry about it, we're on a treasure hunt, remember? We all keep talking about the money but there's Annie's jewellery as well. Just make sure you get your share of that and you'll be all set. Anyway, talking of which, I'll get going and see what's new outside."

They went to the kitchen together and Mark switched on the kettle while Ray put his coat and boots on. He and Kirsty had already done their shift that morning after breakfast. Once Ray had left, Mark wondered whether to go the drawing room or to his apartment with his coffee. It was strange having someone else around and he felt restless. He considered going for a run instead as it was such a nice day but, before he could decide, Kirsty walked in with a triumphant look on her face.

"Aaah, the power of money. I explained about the size of the house and said I'd hire whichever company could come out first. The lady I just spoke to said she'd have a full crew here by tomorrow."

"Is this the Kirsty Edwards I know?" Mark asked. "Give someone a diamond watch and look out."

"I'm still a mild-mannered librarian at heart but it did feel good, I won't lie. I can see how money can turn your head – the way people treat you – and being able to buy whatever you like? I mean, that watch - I don't know what Ray was thinking but it's just so beautiful."

"The trick is to appreciate the perks and the stuff without needing them." Mark said. "Then it's no big deal and you're less likely to turn into a power-crazed shopaholic."

"No guarantees Mark, I've never had money so anything could happen. Prepare yourself." She laughed. "I keep forgetting you speak from experience. You don't act like you used to have money – in a good way I mean."

"I completely took it for granted when I did, not that it was really mine, but my parents were terrible examples. I had a watch once you would have liked though. What's that Swiss one beginning with P?"

"Not a Patek Phillipe?"

"That's it. It was a back to school present but I lost it that same term – or it was nicked, I'm not sure. I never even told anyone that I'd lost it but that was a nice watch."

Kirsty snorted. "That's like saying an Aston Martin's a nice car. You had that at school?"

They looked up as they heard Ray's voice from outside. He was shouting something as he ran around the side of the house.

"What's he doing?" she asked.

"He's going around the back." Mark was already moving towards the kitchen as he spoke, his heart sinking. Ray couldn't have found the plant as he'd only been out there a few minutes. It must be the police back again. The door crashed as it opened and as a grinning Ray barrelled towards them, Mark could see he had it wrong. Ray leaned on a chair to catch his breath then reverently placed a small soil-covered box on the kitchen table.

"Another gift from Lady Luck," he said with a flourish.

Chapter Twenty

"What's bloody keeping them?" Frank asked. He and Sandra had arrived half an hour ago and tempers were fraying as Mark insisted on waiting for Brian and Alice.

"They're on their way. They're stuck in traffic on their way back from Lancing." Brian was on a building site over there and it took Alice a while to track him down.

"There's no harm in just unwrapping it, we don't have to look inside even," Frank wheedled.

"Frank, we're not opening it until they get here. Ray found this half an hour before you arrived and we wanted to open it then".

"Too right," Ray said

"It's been six weeks already so we can hang on another few minutes – you'd have been livid if we'd just called you with the answer."

"No, I wouldn't," Frank said. "I wouldn't have minded at all." He stared at the small box on the table.

"Come and sit down, love. They'll be here soon," Sandra said. "Look, I've poured you a drink."

Frank snatched the glass from her hands, glaring at Mark. He swigged the drink back and handed his empty glass to Sandra, wiping his moustache before returning to his post at the window.

"Thank Christ for that…"

"There they are…"

Frank and Ray said together.

Mark hurried to open the front door, to save the time it would take for them to walk round the back of the house. He was gratified to see Alice break into a restrained jog and Brian pounding along behind her.

"Did you wait for us?" Alice asked sharply.

Mark nodded. "Oh you are a treasure. Brian said we'd be too late but I told him you'd wait. I'm sorry we were so long - the traffic was dreadful."

Alice was twittering as she hurried into the room, as flustered as Mark had seen her since the night of Tom's death.

"Sorry everyone," Brian panted as he walked in. "It's just typical that I had an important meeting in Lancing, I've spent most of my time about five miles from here until today."

"Perhaps if you weren't working you would have been more available," Frank muttered.

"Well, this is just like Christmas morning," Alice said, smoothly changing the subject. "Who's going to open it?"

"Ray found it, so…" Mark gestured to the box and Ray hurried over. He picked up the small rectangular box and examined it carefully, before picking up the scissors that were ready on the table.

"Where did you find it?" Brian asked. "Was it somewhere we've been looking?"

"It was a total fluke," Ray said. "I sat down for a smoke just on that bench by the lake and noticed there was some dug-over earth…"

"That was us," Kirsty said. "Mark and I dug up a peony bush a while back."

"Right, so I was looking at that and trying to work it out when I saw a little plant on the other side of the bench. It looked just like the picture so I just prodded around it and there it was."

"After all that," Frank said. "Come on then."

"Yeah, Tom hadn't buried it deeply at all," Ray said as he cut through the multi-layered green plastic that was probably a garden rubbish sack from Tony's tool shed. He placed the wrappings to one side and everyone crowded round to look at the old cigar box that Ray held up. It was taped shut and he sliced it open using a scissor blade. "Ready everyone?"

With the lid open, there was nothing inside except a folded piece of paper. He opened it with trembling fingers and read out,

"King Edward. That's all it says, King Edward?" Ray repeated, turning the paper over. "What's all that about?" Frank pointed to the box he was holding and Ray laughed. "Oh, yes." He closed the box, revealing the portly image of Edward VII.

Mark was already entering Tom's website on the laptop and soon everyone was crowded around, more interested in the information on the folded piece of paper than in its container. "Ready?"

He paused to check that it was entered correctly and then, with encouragement from the others, he hit the return key. At once the screen changed, revealing a clue that was longer than the previous ones. Mark scanned it quickly before reading it aloud.

Angle yourself towards the East for this famous tinker's town,
For long ago he dreamed of gold and earned local renown.
In this town there are signs of him still, especially in the church,
Just find the name of his companion to progress in your search.

There was silence as everyone continued staring at the screen, trying to make sense of the rhyme.

"That one's going to be harder to remember." Ray said.

"As long as it's not harder to work out, I don't care," Kirsty murmured, frowning at the screen.

"Oh, I don't know, we worked out the last one quickly enough. I'd rather this one was harder to work out but quicker to solve, myself," Brian said.

Mark thought he had a point.

"So does this mean anything to anyone?" Mark asked.

"Give us a bloody chance!" Frank said. "I'm still trying to get to grips with it."

Mark gave it a couple of minutes. "So, nobody's got any light bulbs flashing then? It looks like we're going to have to do this one the hard way, word associations and all."

"Before you break out the flip chart Mark, it may mean something to me, and to Brian if I'm right."

Alice leaned back from the screen and looked to Brian for confirmation. Brian looked blankly at her and she sighed.

"Well to me, anyway."

"Go on," Mark said as everyone turned towards her.

Alice sat up straighter and took her reading glasses off.

"Well, it's just an idea, but where it starts with 'Angle yourself to the East', that suggests East Anglia to me. If he was talking about the East as in the Orient or even East of here wouldn't he have said 'look to the East' or 'go East' rather than 'Angle yourself'. I mean it's quite an awkward start otherwise."

"Does that mean something to you?" Mark asked.

"Yes, Tom told us about that little town he visited, somewhere in Norfolk, I think? Do you remember Brian, no? It definitely was Norfolk because I told him I visited the Norfolk Broads when I was at school. Come on now darling, you were right there!" Alice spoke tersely as Brian shrugged. "Anyway, he was saying something about the legend of… somebody or other…and there was something about a church. I remember because he said he got chatting to the vicar." Alice shrugged. "That's as much as I remember but it seems to fit. "

"It could be." Mark said. "What you said about East Anglia makes sense."

"So did he mention what this town was called then?" Frank asked.

144

"He did because I remember thinking what a quaint-sounding name it was. I can't remember now though. Honestly, Brian isn't this ringing any bells with you at all?"

"How am I supposed to remember some anecdote from Tom about a trip to a town somewhere in Norfolk? I've never even been to Norfolk!" Brian said sounding exasperated.

"You could try listening to people," Alice said.

"I do listen to…" Brian puffed, but Mark interrupted in an attempt to keep them on track.

"Well, that's a good start anyway. So all we need to do…" he peered at the screen and re-read the clue. "I think all we need to do is go to this town, probably in Norfolk, look in the church, and then name the companion of this famous tinker." He looked up. "If you're right Alice, then that's huge. I have no idea what it all means but I think you're onto something. Right, shall we get started then? Let's see what we can find online."

"Before we do I would really like a cup of tea or a drink of something. We've got time, haven't we?"

Once everyone had drinks, they gathered in the dining room where the table was still loaded with their books from last time they'd been together around the table.

"This all feels very familiar," Frank said thickly, his mouth full of digestive biscuit.

It did feel familiar but it was strange to be back together in the dining room after so long. It made all the difference to have a fresh clue to work on though especially as it already seemed promising. Mark retrieved the flip chart from its position behind the door.

"Just for you Alice," he said. "You know you've missed this."

The first thing Mark did was write the clue on the flip chart in large green letters. Kirsty called it out to him and he managed to fit it all onto one page. Tearing off the sheet, he pinned it to the enormous corkboard standing against one wall. Next he wrote 'East Anglia - Norfolk town?' and underneath 'famous tinker'.

"Okay, who wants to give me some other words for tinker?"

Sandra had looked up 'tinker' and began shouting out the words.

"Mender, meddle, be unskillful, be cunning." Remembering the first clue, Mark wrote down everything no matter how irrelevant it seemed, "Not, complete, pedlar, tinker's cuss. That's it for tinker. What shall I look at next?"

"Wait!" Brian said. "It's pedlar, the something pedlar. I remember now

because one of my supplier's is called Swain & Pedlar and...."
"Are you sure?"
"That's it Brian, you were listening! I remember now..." Alice said excitedly.
Brian spread his hands in a modest gesture of acknowledgement, "It was something about a dog. That's what Tom was excited about - the vicar of the local church had tracked down the name of the pedlar's dog after hundreds of years or something."
"That could be the companion!" Kirsty exclaimed. "Let's look up pedlar and see if there's anything about it."
There was a flurry of activity, and Brian and Alice basked in the glory of their rapid recollection of Tom's story.
Ray congratulated them with all the rest but Mark noticed he seemed subdued. It was unlucky for Ray that his discovery of the bleeding heart plant had so quickly been forgotten.
Kirsty typed in 'Pedlar Norfolk' and let out a delighted yelp.
"Swaffham?" She asked Alice.
"Yes, I think it could be. Quaint little name isn't it?"
"That's the one." Brian said. "It wasn't just pedlar that rang a bell, Swaffham pedlar reminded me of Swain & Pedlar. Tom agreed they sounded alike. They were on my mind because I'd had a visit from James at Swain & Pedlar's only the day before to talk about…"
"It's got its own website." Kirsty interrupted. She clicked through and triumphantly turned the screen round to show everyone the page she'd found,
"The Pedlar of Swaffham. Look at the picture." She said. "It's even the town sign."
They could see a colour reproduction of the sign that showed a pedlar and his dog that could have walked straight out of The Canterbury Tales. Kirsty turned back the screen to read more about it.
"This is definitely the one. Listen, this is what it says on the town sign - ye tinker of Swaffham who did by a dream find a great treasure."
Mark sat down heavily, relieved that they seemed to be back on track with the clues. This one seemed half solved already and if all they had to do was find out the name of the dog, they might even be able to crack it online or with a quick call to the local Tourist Information Centre – if there was one. He logged in to the Swaffham website on his laptop. Bringing up the home page, he clicked through to the page about the pedlar and read through the text, tuning out the sound of Frank reading it aloud on the opposite side of the table.

The pedlar, a man called John Chapman travelled to London Bridge with his dog after a dream told him he'd meet someone offering great advantage. While he waited, a shopkeeper asked why he was standing there and then mocked him for following his dream, telling him of his dream that there was treasure buried under a tree in a garden in a town called Swaffham."

"I can see why Tom would have liked that story." Sandra said.

"Especially for this," Kirsty said. "He'd love the treasure thing."

"Hang on there's more," Frank said. "It says the pedlar kept the gold and sold the brass pot he'd found it in and a monk translated its Latin inscription as 'under me doth lie another much richer than I'. So he found an even bigger pot of gold and used it to restore the church."

Mark read on and saw there were church records showing that a man called John Chapman had funded the North aisle of Swaffham's church in 1454. He wondered whether the same church was still there.

"This is definitely it, isn't it darling?" Alice craned her neck up to look at Brian, who nodded. "Tom was telling us about a visit he'd made to Norfolk and asked if we'd ever heard of Swaffham. That's when he started telling us about the Pedlar."

"And his dog." Brian added.

"Yes, and his dog. He was really tickled by that I think, that the vicar had discovered the dog's name after so long."

"So, did he say what the dog's name was?" Mark asked.

Alice tapped her teeth with one dark red fingernail while she thought. "No idea. If he did I can't remember anyway."

They spent the rest of the afternoon trying to track down more information but didn't get any further online. After calls to the library, the Tourist Information Centre – which was closed until April – and the company behind the town website, it seemed they would need to go to Swaffham to talk to the vicar.

"It's only three or four hours from here." Mark said. "Brian, do you and Alice want to go – as you were the ones Tom spoke to about it?"

Alice looked keen but Brian jumped in before she could agree.

"There's no way I can go before next week. That meeting in Lancing today needs a lot of follow-up and I've got to be involved."

"That's more important than this is it?" Frank asked.

"I thought it was agreed that I'm off duty for a while. It's not like you and Sandra have been doing much as I understand it," Brian said.

"We agreed that was until anything came up. I don't see why you..."

"Mark and I can go," Kirsty interrupted. "If you're too busy Brian, I'm happy to go and I've never been to Norfolk, have you Mark?"

"Not for years. I went to the coast when I was a kid, but that's a long way from Swaffham by the looks of it. Does anyone mind if we go?"

"Can I still stay here?" Ray asked, looking worried.

"You live here, Ray. Of course you can stay, we need someone to look after things anyway. The inquest won't be before next week and I want to get back for that."

"When shall we go?" Kirsty sounded excited,

Mark looked at his watch and saw that it was just gone five.

"We might as well get up there tonight, ready to make a start tomorrow. How soon can you be ready?"

"Oh!" Kirsty stood up. "Right, I'll go and get packed. Where will we stay? No, don't worry we can sort that on the way. I'll see you all later - will you still be here? Oh, and we've got a cleaning crew coming in tomorrow. Damn! Do I need to be here for that?"

Mark smiled at Kirsty's uncharacteristic dithering.

"Ray can look after the cleaning crew. Just get ready in your own time – we'll get there when we get there. Unless you want to set off early tomorrow morning, I don't mind either way."

"No, no let's go tonight. It won't take me long."

After she'd left, Mark turned to Ray,

"Will you be okay looking after the cleaning crew? Just tell them to go through the whole house apart from everyone's rooms."

"No problem. What if the Police come here to talk to you though, what shall I say?"

"Just say Kirsty and I have gone to Norfolk for a short break and let us know if there are any updates about the inquest."

"There aren't likely to be, are there?"

"No, but if there are. Oh and will you clear away all this stuff." Mark gestured to the mess of papers and laptops on the dining table.

"Probably best to store it in the attic room while we're gone, you know where the key is don't you?"

Ray nodded. They all knew that the key was hidden in plain sight, tangled in with all the other keys on the board in the kitchen.

"And the rest of you are staying at home until after Joan's funeral?"

"Definitely." Brian said.

"I don't mind either way," Frank said. "Are you going to keep us up to date with your progress though? I don't want to find out you've got the password by getting an email from Tom's site. Wait until we're all back here, won't you."

"Frank, you shouldn't need to ask that." Alice said. "I think today demonstrated their restraint. You did really well to wait for us Mark, you must have been dying to know what was in the box."

"We all were. As soon as I dug it up I wanted to rip it open," Ray said.

"Right, I'm off to pack." Mark dug into his back pocket for the money that Ray had given him earlier. He divided it and gave half to Ray. "For the cleaning crew and just in case something else comes up."

"Thanks Mark." Ray pocketed it. "I'll sort it out."

Mark left the room and ran up the stairs feeling excitement bubble at the thought of a few days away with Kirsty again, even if a small, land-locked Norfolk town wouldn't usually be his first choice for a weekend break.

Chapter Twenty-one

Mark woke up to the sound of traffic and peered at the alarm clock on Kirsty's bedside table. Six-thirty, he saw, much too early to be up. He reached an arm underneath Kirsty and pulled her towards him, smiling as she murmured something drowsily. He lay there for a while with his eyes closed, trying to quiet his mind and drift off again but when the quarter hour chimes of the church bells sounded, he gave up on sleep. After a while he disentangled himself and got out of bed, wincing at the noisy creaking of the floorboards as he padded over to the window. The sun was just rising and he could see shadows on the tall grey church to his left and part of the town to his right. They'd driven through the place last night and his impression of it had been of a sleepy town with a triangle of shops and pubs centred round a large pillared dome that looked like it had been transported from a stately home. Mark watched an old man crossing the street with a newspaper under his arm and wondered why so many old people woke up so early – Tom had been the same. He shivered at the draught coming through the windows and looked back at the bed. It didn't matter if he couldn't sleep he wasn't going to get up yet, not while there was a beautiful woman wearing something silky in his bed. He inched his way back under the covers and pulled Kirsty towards him.

When Mark next woke, it was to the sound of the kettle boiling and he lifted his head over the tangle of sheets, blanket and bedspread to see Kirsty looking out of the window. As he yawned she turned around.

"There you are – I was about to wake you up."

Mark looked at the alarm clock and saw that it was gone nine. The heating was on now and he felt uncomfortably warm. He threw back the covers and sat up.

"I can't believe I nodded off again." Mark said, "I was wide awake earlier but you were fast asleep."

"Well, we were quite late last night, weren't we?" Kirsty said.

"I suppose so." Mark yawned and stretched again as he stood up.

Kirsty lifted the curtain to cover the lower half of the windows.

"You could close those curtains," he suggested, "now that we're both awake." He reached for her but she twisted away.

"No time. Look I'm dressed."

"I can soon change that for you."

Kirsty laughed and swatted him away. "Come on - let's get going. The shower's really nice."

"You can't be rejecting me in a hotel?" Mark asked. "We've only been together a month - it's practically in the guest rules."

"We'll have plenty of time later." Kirsty said. "Go on, I want to get out and have a look round the town."

"And you'll make it up to me later?"

Kirsty rolled her eyes at him. "Come on, hurry up – I'm really hungry! There's a place called the Pedlar's Hall Café near that dome thing we passed, the Butter cross it's called. I thought we could go there and see if they know anything."

"Okay, sounds good. Actually I'm starving."

"Thank you." She kissed him lightly on the lips. "And yes I'm sure I'll make it up to you later."

Twenty minutes later they walked downstairs and left their room key with the old man on reception. Once outside, they breathed in the crisp morning air and Mark's eyes were drawn again to the church.

"Shall we go and have a quick wander through the church yard?"

"Breakfast first," Kirsty pleaded.

"Breakfast it is then." He put an arm around her and kissed the top of her head as they crossed the road and headed towards the café, walking past the gated front entrance to the church. In the light of day Mark could see how old it was.

The café was busy but they were relieved when the waitress took their order within a couple of minutes of them sitting down. Almost immediately she brought their coffee and they felt ready to start planning their day.

"The church first?" Kirsty asked.

"Definitely. We need to check the companion bit of the clue. You never know, in the church he might have a griffin or something with him rather than a dog."

"A bit unlikely."

"I know but we might as well check while we're here."

Kirsty nodded as she blew on her coffee to cool it down.

"I like old churches anyway," Mark said.

"Do you?"

"Part of the job I suppose. I've spent a fair few hours looking through parish records and after a while you start to notice where you are."

"Well that's this morning taken care of then. After we've found out the dog's name from the vicar of course."

After breakfast, they walked back through the Butter cross and headed over to the church. There was a notice board with a list of forthcoming services and details of the vicar,

"It's even got his phone number – why wasn't that on the website?" Kirsty grabbed a notebook and pen from her large handbag, and scribbled down the number.

"Job done," she said. "I've got a feeling this is going to be easy." They walked up the path to the church, craning their necks up at the tall, square tower with its large circular clock. At the entrance to the church they stood in the lobby for a moment breathing in the cool chalky smell of the old building.

"I love the smell of old churches," Mark said.

"Weirdo," she whispered, squeezing his hand. Noticing a bank of leaflets and brochures to their left, Mark put a pound in the box and took a brochure, 'The Parish Church of St. Peter and St. Paul'. He was reading it as he walked out of the lobby but Kirsty stopped him.

"Oh, Mark look…"

He glanced up and saw the long clean sweep of the nave and the arch of the ceiling high above them.

"Isn't it gorgeous?"

Mark nodded. It was a beautiful medieval church with tall wide Perpendicular windows and high above them, rank after rank of angels carved into the wooden hammer-beam roof.

"So where's the pedlar?" Kirsty asked.

They wandered down the aisle of the silent church while Mark read the brochure. He found a photo of the carving of John Chapman, the Pedlar, and scanned the text.

"The finials on the front pews - down here."

Kirsty skipped ahead.

"Here he is," she whispered, "and look his dog is there."

Mark looked at the two pews each with a carving of the dog and pedlar either side.

"That's our man." He was pleased to have what they already knew confirmed. "So where's the vicar?"

They looked round the church and eventually spoke to a lady with vividly white hair who was polishing the brass. She told them that she had no idea where Revd James was but they could see him at one of the Sunday services the next day. They thanked her and looked around the church some more before going outside to call the number on the notice board again.

"Now what?" Kirsty asked when the number rang out.

"I don't know - maybe have a look around the town, get chatting to the locals, look in the library. I'm not sure how much of a thing the pedlar legend is even if it's on the town sign."

The sun was shining on them in the churchyard but it was still cold and they huddled into their coats as they picked their way through the moss-covered gravestones, trying to read the writing on the oldest ones.

"We know how to have a good time, don't we?" Mark asked, when Kirsty pointed out a seventeenth century gravestone.

She looked embarrassed. "It's just interesting, imagining them coming to this church hundreds of years ago. I wouldn't rummage around a modern…"

"I know - I'm with you," Mark said, hunkering down to look at the inscription more closely. "That's what I like about my job, when it feels like you're going back in time. I like it best when I manage to track down someone interesting rather than trying to prove someone's great-great grandfather was related to Queen Victoria or whatever."

"Do people ask you to do that?" Kirsty asked.

"Sometimes. People like to feel a connection to someone well known although it's usually someone like Brian who wants to find a grand connection somewhere." He stood up. "So much is online these days though, it's a lot easier to find out things than it was."

"Will you go back to it if things don't work out."

"Probably. I've even missed it a bit these last few months. Not so much the hours spent poring over records until it feels like your eyes are bleeding. The buzz when you have a breakthrough though, I like that, and peoples excitement when you talk them through what you've found. What about you? Would you go back to the library?"

"I don't think so." Kirsty sighed, digging her hands into the pockets of her coat. "No idea what I would do though. I could put an ad in the paper, 'ex-librarian and failed treasure hunter seeks interesting, well paid work."

"You could be my apprentice," Mark said. "There's the eye-bleeding thing but you like old gravestones so you'd probably find it interesting work."

"You make it sound so tempting." Kirsty said, then added in a dignified voice. "If I'm available I'll let you know."

"Very well, Miss Edwards," Mark said.

She smiled at him and they looked at each other for a long moment, motionless as the leaves rustled in the trees around them and the sun warmed their faces. Mark drank in the sight of her in the same long navy coat she'd been wearing the night they got together, her tumble of auburn hair and flushed cheeks contrasting with the daffodil-filled churchyard.

"I can't cope with how gorgeous you are," he said, not having the words to sum up how he was feeling.

"Thank you," Kirsty said softly. "Same here."

Mark kissed her gently on the lips and although he hadn't said anything he knew she'd felt it too. She squeezed his hand.

"Come on, let's head back into town," she said. "The sooner we go through our list of chores, the sooner we can get back."

"Okay, let me take a photo of you first. Stay exactly where you are." He took out his phone and frowned when he saw the screen.

"I've got four missed calls from Ray. He's probably wondering why we haven't checked in."

Just then, Mark's phone rang again and he remembered he'd put it on silent when he went in the church. He stiffened when he heard Ray's panicky voice.

"Is everything all right Ray?"

"What? No, it's not all right. Why haven't you been answering? Mark this is serious! I found it this morning on the doormat. I was just passing, checking everywhere was locked…I've only just noticed."

"Ray, calm down. Start from the beginning. What did you find?"

"A letter," Ray said. "Another letter from him. No postmark so he must have hand delivered it. I'm still on my own but he must have come to the front door since last night, because it wasn't there then, I'm sure it wasn't."

"What is it?" Kirsty asked.

"Another blackmail letter I think," Mark murmured. "Ray, take a breath - what does it say?"

"Can't you come back? You can see it then."

"Calm down, it's only a letter."

"That's easy for you to say! You're not rattling around here on your own. I don't like it Mark. I don't like the idea of someone creeping around."

"Alright, I know but hold it together. It's only a letter and whoever put it through the letterbox will be long gone by now. Come on Ray, what does it say?"

"Hang on, let me get it."

Mark gestured for Kirsty to move closer and put the phone on speaker so that she could hear.

"Right, ready? It says, 'I haven't forgotten about you and what you all done and this photo shows I mean business.' God his spelling's terrible."

"A photo. So it does exist then, what does it show?" Mark asked.

"It's pretty bad. In both senses of the word, terrible quality, really blurry and the angle's tilted so…"

"And?" Mark said impatiently.

"Well, you can see Tom sitting up in bed and you're there pouring the stuff into glasses - all the glasses are laid out on the bedside table. Then you can see a bit of Kirsty, she's turned towards you with Joan and Tony opposite. And Mark, it's from a proper camera, not a phone, and it's got the date and time on the photo."

"What, no way - how is that possible?"

Kirsty looked at him disbelievingly.

"I know. It looks like what it is, no doubt about it. You can see why I'm shaken up."

"Right," Mark said distractedly. "Does the letter say anything else?"

"He says, 'You've got less than three months so I hope you're getting on with it. I know you had seven clues so you should have at least three of them done now.' How are you and Kirsty getting on by the way, is the fourth one nearly done?"

"It's looking good," Mark said. "Hopefully we'll know more tomorrow. What else?"

"That's about it really. He just says that he wants us to put some big ornaments in an upstairs window. He says one object for each clue then when he sees seven objects he'll be in touch again. That's it."

"Great." Mark said tightly. "As if we haven't got enough to think about. If we don't find the money someone could send that photo to the police anyway. Or if we do find the money we have to hand over half."

"You can see why I don't want to be on my own can't you? How can it be someone in the group when they've got a photo? And they'll probably be lurking around spying on the house now as well."

"Listen Ray, don't get carried away – it could still be someone in the house. Let me have a think and come back to you."

"Okay," Ray said reluctantly.

"I'll call you back in half an hour. Just sit tight and lock the doors, okay? Stay calm. Even if there is someone around they've got no reason to come to the house, have they?"

155

"No, I suppose not."

"Half an hour, all right?"

Mark hung up and turned to Kirsty who looked pale.

"Come on, it's cold out here, lets go back to the hotel."

They crossed the road to the hotel in silence and, as the church bells chimed the quarter hour, Mark remembered that he hadn't taken the photo of Kirsty.

Chapter Twenty-two

Mark and Kirsty sat at the back of the church, trying to be as inconspicuous as possible. Mark felt like an impostor but he liked the hymns which all seemed to be ones he remembered from his childhood. He was amused to discover that Kirsty had a terrible singing voice but as the service went on he found it endearing that she happily sang along to her favourites anyway. Mark bowed his head for the final prayer and could see Kirsty's knee jiggling up and down. They planned to return to Sussex straight after church and their bags were packed and waiting in the car outside. Mark only hoped they had the right vicar and wouldn't need to unpack and check back into the hotel. They'd calmed Ray down by agreeing not to stay longer than they needed to and he was expecting them this afternoon. Yesterday, after researching the legend locally they distracted themselves from his unsettling news by being tourists for the afternoon. They'd driven to an old coastal town called Hunstanton where they found the sea at low tide revealing a beach that stretched far into the distance. The sky seemed to go on forever and after a long walk they sat and ate ice cream and watched the sky turned pink and orange as the sun set. Driving back to the hotel they hadn't said much but when they got to their room the intensity of their lovemaking was bittersweet, as though touched by their need to make the most of their last night away from the group.

Mark squeezed Kirsty's hand as the choir proceeded past them to the exit, led by the vicar in flowing robes, and they hung back waiting patiently for the church to empty. Mark watched the two jackdaws that had cawed loudly throughout the service and were now resting on the beams between the carved wooden angels. There were still people milling around and it seemed that everyone wanted to chat to the vicar, who despite his solemn robes, was laughing loudly with an elderly couple up ahead.

"I hope he doesn't have to rush off," Kirsty whispered.

"I know. I wanted to catch him on his own but I don't think that's going to happen."

They continued to lurk in the background until, finally, it was their turn and the vicar turned to them with a smile and his hand outstretched, "Hello, I don't think we've met."

The vicar was a tall man in his fifties with a mop of thick blond hair and a kind face.

"No we're just visiting for the weekend."

"It was a nice service." Kirsty said as the Vicar shook her hand.
"Thank you. Always good to have visitors – the more the merrier, especially these days." He looked at them quizzically. "Can I help you with something?"
"Thank you, yes, we're hoping you can." Mark said.
"It's about the Pedlar of Swaffham." Kirsty said.
"Oh, our own John Chapman." Revd James said. "Have you seen the finials at the front of the church?"
"Yes, they're lovely," Kirsty said. "I love that the dog has one too."
"Come with me, there's a bit of a story to them if you've got time." He steered them back into the church, waving over his shoulder at a smart looking man in a suit who was hurrying towards the church gates.
"Thanks Jim, see you next week!" He called. "My churchwarden - he's got a busy morning. Now, you've seen these?"
Revd James was pointing to the finials of the Pedlar and his dog on the front pew. They nodded. "Well these are Victorian. Eighteen-fifties, but a few years ago someone walked off with this one."
"What, they stole the dog?" Kirsty asked.
"I'm afraid so," he said. "We had a craftsman make this one though and we're delighted with it. He's done a wonderful job."
"You can't tell the difference." Mark said. "Do you know much about the dog?"
"Funny you should ask but…yes. I've got something that might interest you - let me just show you this first."
He led them to the clergy stalls and pointed out an effigy of a weary-looking Pedlar with a pack on his back and his dog next to him.
"Now these are fifteenth century, from John Chapman's family pew. They would have had their own closed-in pew as they were such important benefactors to the church, and over here," he led them to the opposite stall, "now this is his wife. Supposedly, she's leaning over a shop door, but see, those are her rosary beads so I prefer to think she's leaning over the door of her pew. That's just what I think though, we don't know that for sure." He shrugged.
Mark nodded. The man's enthusiasm was contagious but he wondered how to steer the conversation back to the dog as the vicar wheeled a flat mirror out so Kirsty could see the angels in the roof more clearly.
"One hundred and ninety two of them, including the ones on the wall, and all the ones in the roof are different. Amazing how they did it and cleverest of all, they carved them in chestnut. They knew a thing or two back then." He began ticking things off on his fingers. "Chestnut's a

hard wood so insects won't burrow in it. No insects means no spiders and with no spiders there are no cobwebs and so no dusting." He beamed at them and they admired the spotless roof.

"Thanks boys, lovely singing today," he said, as a handful of young choirboys walked past them.

"The Pedlar's dog?" Mark blurted out, unable to stop himself. "You said there was something we should see."

"I did indeed. So what's made you so interested in the dog?" He asked, leading them towards the vestry.

"Sorry," Mark mouthed to Kirsty who smiled at him, shaking her head. "Oh, it's more me really," she said. "I love dogs and we've got a friend who visited here a couple of years ago. I think he might have spoken to you actually. He told us the legend and said that John Chapman really existed."

"Oh yes, he's in the church records."

"Well, I thought it was a lovely story and I remember him saying that you even knew what the dog's name was. I can't remember now what he said it was but I thought, while we were here, it would be good to find out."

"Your friend," Revd James said, turning to them, "an elderly gent is he? From Sussex I think."

"Yes!" Kirsty said. "That's right. I'm amazed you remember."

"It helps to have a good memory with this." He tugged at his dog collar.

"Besides we had quite a long chat when he visited – it wasn't long after his wife died. Anyway the day he was here was only a few days after I'd received this." He tapped a large cloth-bound book. "An old parishioner asked if we'd like it. You won't find the dog's name anywhere else but here you know. How is he by the way? Stephen, is it?"

"Tom, Tom Stevens but…"

"That's it. Nearly right…oh, I see."

"Yes, three months ago now."

"I am sorry to hear that, lovely old chap. He seemed lost without his wife I think but really trying to get on. Yes, I'll remember him in my prayers tonight."

"Thanks, I think you made an impression on him."

The vicar opened the book. "Yes, Tom liked this. Look - 'John Chapman and his faithful dog, Shock.'"

Mark felt relief wash over him as he looked at the illustration.

159

"I see you like it too." Revd James said.

"Thank you, so much," Kirsty said, excitement making her voice shake.

"Well I'm glad I could help," he said, shutting the book with a snap.

A mobile phone rang and Revd James winced and pulled a phone from the pocket of his robes.

"I must have forgotten to switch it off," he said. "Now that could have been embarrassing."

They left him to it in a flurry of thanks and good byes, and once outside and away from the main entrance, Mark picked up Kirsty and kissed her. He swung her around feeling jubilant.

"Mark, stop it!" She wriggled free, laughing.

"We've done it!"

"I can't believe how easy it was," Kirsty said.

"I know. Four clues down, three to go - we're back on track."

"How amazing that he remembered Tom," Kirsty said.

"Come on, let's get going. The sooner we get back, the sooner we can find out what the next clue is."

"Yes - I'll call Ray once we're in the car." They started walking back to the car but on impulse Mark took Kirsty's hand and started jogging. Kirsty laughed and broke in to a run. Mark fumbled for the car keys as they ran back together and it then took all his efforts to keep up with her.

"God you're fast," he said. He was breathing heavily as he started the car while Kirsty seemed barely out of breath.

"I used to win the one hundred metre race every sports day," she said, "not that I ever did much with it."

"Impressive though." He exhaled and then grinned at Kirsty.

"What?"

"Nothing, just that this is the kind of thing I pictured when Tom spoke about a treasure hunt. Driving up and down the country, racing around after clues with a beautiful companion."

"Companion. Is that what I am?" Kirsty asked.

"You know what I mean. Escort – is that better?

Kirsty slapped his arm.

"Partner, I meant partner."

"Right, let's go," she said. "I'm ringing Ray."

Kirsty put him on speakerphone and told him what they'd discovered. Ray sounded overjoyed.

"Brilliant, just brilliant – well done guys. What a relief!"

"Thanks Ray, such an easy one this time. We're on our way back now if you want to get everyone together."

"Okay, that's great. Alice and Brian are on standby and Frank and Sandra are here already – Sandra said they'd keep me company after I told her about the blackmail letter. Sorry about yesterday, I don't know why I freaked out."

"It's the house, that's all," Mark said.

Ray said he'd call them once Brian and Alice arrived so they passed the time discussing their theories about the blackmailer.

"If it is one of us then Brian's the one who said that when the money's shared out it didn't amount to much 'in today's climate'," Mark said.

"I still can't believe he said that!"

"I know although that was when we were still dividing the money between nine. It will be more now."

"I still can't imagine him doing it though," Kirsty continued. "He and Alice must be loaded - he was showing me pictures of their house the other day."

"Just because they've got a big house doesn't mean much. They could still have money troubles or maybe a problem with the business." Mark shrugged. "I don't know. What about Frank and Sandra then, they could be working together and it was Sandra who found the first letter."

Kirsty dismissed this at once,

"No, not Sandra, no way - Frank maybe, but he's too unimaginative to try something like that. I don't know Mark the photo changes things - I think there must be someone else."

"Frank's not unimaginative though is he? I mean he can't be."

"His books you mean." Kirsty said. "It's weird but because he writes under a pen name I kind of forget that it's actually him. Surely he's too lazy though, well – laid back?"

"Maybe. What about Ray?" Mark asked. "He had the opportunity on the second letter."

Kirsty laughed. "What, seriously?"

"Why not?"

"Okay, I tell you why I don't think it could be Ray, apart from the obvious," Kirsty said. "I just can't see him asking for half the money."

"How do you mean?"

"He'd probably say he wanted 'a hundred grand' not half of the money, don't you think?"

"You know him better than me."

"What does that mean?"

"Well, you're the one he bought a five grand watch for."

Kirsty turned to face him, and Mark glanced at her, taking in her astonished expression. He hadn't meant to sound so critical.

"Where's that come from?"

"Nothing. I'm just saying."

"No, come on, out with it."

Mark glanced at her again and saw that she was frowning.

"It's just that giving a friend a present like that is a bit much that's all."

"Well, of course it is! That's why I tried to give it back. You were there, remember?"

"Yes, okay…I know."

"Have you been sitting on that ever since Friday? Thinking that Ray…thinking I might decide Ray's a good bet because he'd buy me pretty things?"

"No, nothing like that." Mark shook his head. "Look, I'm sorry. He just put me to shame that's all. He's given you a diamond watch and I've given you a pair of earrings from a market stall."

"Oh Mark, don't be silly. That watch is incredible but if I had to choose I know which present means the most to me." Kirsty paused and then asked. "If it bothers you that much I can give the watch back."

"No, just forget I said anything."

"Okay," she said. "Anyway, Ray's not my type - he's much too good-looking."

"Ouch!" Mark shook his head. "I suppose I asked for that. If you had to choose though, keep the watch and we'll fly back to Marrakech to replace the earrings."

She laughed. "Seriously though, I don't get any vibes like that from Ray. It's crazy what he did but I think he's just after connection."

"I'll bet he is." Mark said, his tone lighter now.

"Mark! No, I mean it – he doesn't have anyone, does he? I don't think he's used to having female friends."

"True."

They drove a while in silence and Mark regretted his earlier flash of jealousy. It wasn't Kirsty he doubted, but he'd noticed how Ray looked at her sometimes, and the expensive watch seemed to him like a declaration of intent, a marker, rather than a moment of madness - for all that he claimed Kirsty wasn't his type. Mark glanced across at her.

"Alright?" Kirsty asked and he nodded.

"Just thinking how gorgeous you are."

"And…?"

He laughed. "And I'm a bit gutted to be going back that's all."

"Me too. I've got that end of holiday feeling after these last few weeks. Just think if we solve the next three clues as easily as this one though - we'll be free again in no time."

Mark squeezed her leg in reply. They could only hope.

Now that harmony was restored the journey back seemed to fly past. It seemed like one moment they were surrounded by fields, with lines of tall, narrow trees so far away they looked like feathers against the horizon, the next they were approaching the Dartford bridge. It was as they were crossing the wide expanse of the Thames estuary that Ray finally called.

Mark had his phone connected to the hands free so Ray's voice boomed out as the car crawled along in the traffic.

"Sorry it took a while to come back to you. Long story but we're all here now."

"Great. We're only an hour and a half away but you go ahead – Kirsty can read the email out to me."

"We hoped you'd say that," Ray said. "I've got Tom's website up and we're ready to go if you want to hang on a minute. We may as well all hear it together."

"I'm typing in 'Shock' now, Mark," Brian said. "Capital S and the rest lower case, yes?"

"That's right. S – h – o – c – k as in electric."

"Okay, we have it," Brian said. "It's a long one this time."

His voice was harder to hear as the car sped up so they listened intently as he read the clue out.

She's a sight to behold - delicate as a feather with a heart that is cold.
Made as one of the three, fairest of all, she will last for eternity.
Seek her out more than diamond or steel and then turn her about.
You'll delight in her words more than the other two thirds.
What is her name? You know already but why not play the game.

After Brian hung up Kirsty opened her email and read out the clue line by line. It meant nothing to either of them but they knew it by heart by the time they passed the Regency markers to Brighton. When at last they arrived at the house they let themselves in the back door, eager to see how the others were getting on.

"How's Ray made this much mess in two days?" Kirsty asked as she looked around. The remains of a cooked breakfast were congealing in a frying pan on top of the Aga and there were unwashed plates piled in the sink. Kirsty wrinkled her nose at the stale, greasy smell and opened a window.

"Let's hope they've been busy," Mark said.

They dumped their bags at the foot of the stairs and walked towards the dining room where they could see Brian standing in front of the flip chart. The others were slumped around the dining table but perked up immediately when Mark and Kirsty walked in. Ray started clapping and the others joined in.

"You've shocked us awake!" Sandra said.

"So how are we doing? Any ideas?" Mark asked as he pulled out a chair for Kirsty and sat down next to her. Brian remained standing, poised to continue his work with the flip chart.

"Let me bring you up to speed," Brian said. He pointed to 'Sight to behold' and 'fairest of all' then to the word 'beautiful', which was circled in green marker pen.

"We thought he might be pointing us in the direction of someone in particular, maybe someone like Helen of Troy, you know renowned for their beauty." Brian flipped over the page.

"Not Helen of Troy again," Frank groaned.

"Tom's reference to more than diamonds or steel as well as eternal..."

"Wait, isn't it diamond singular rather than diamonds?" Mark asked.

Brian folded his arms. "Does that matter?"

"Not if Tom made a mistake, but so far he's been precise with his words," Mark said.

"You're right Mark," Sandra said. "Normally you'd say more than diamonds, not diamond."

"So what does it mean?" Brian asked.

Mark shrugged. "It might be a pointer to someone. Diamond means nothing to me but it might to one of us."

"Fine, we'll bear it in mind. Anyway..."

Brian lectured them for another twenty minutes on what they had discussed, summarising every last detail.

"Brian?" Sandra raised her hand as though she was in a classroom. "I should think Mark and Kirsty would like a drink after their journey. Anyone else?"

"I'll help old girl," Frank volunteered immediately.

"No, don't worry Frank, I can give Sandra a hand," Alice said.

"We haven't finished going through this. Can't it wait a minute?"

"It's all right darling, you've been through this already with us, I'll catch up with anything new."

Frank looked wistfully after them as they left for the kitchen and then stood up.

"I'll just help them carry things in," he said

"Now where was I?" Brian asked.

"Play the game," Ray said in between a large yawn, and Brian was off again. After ten long minutes Frank, Sandra and Alice came back with the tea things and by this time Mark had reached his limit.

"Brian. That's great, thanks but shall we all have a break now?"

Brian shrugged. "There are still a couple more points to cover and..."

"Shall we do that afterwards," Kirsty interrupted. "It will give us a chance to digest what you've told us already.

Mark followed the others through into the drawing room and sat down next to Kirsty.

"I thought he'd never stop," she whispered to him.

Mark smiled and reached for a copy of the local newspaper that was lying on the coffee table.

Alice passed it to him. "Has anyone told you about the inquest?"

"No?" Mark and Kirsty said in unison.

"Oh. Ray said he would tell you. You were the last to see Joan weren't you? I'm surprised you haven't been asked to give evidence."

"I saw her briefly the night before the funeral," Kirsty said.

"It seems odd they haven't got in touch then. There's a small piece in the paper and it says the inquest will be held tomorrow." Alice pointed to the paper.

Kirsty looked worried. "When they took my statement they said that it could be read out in my absence. I was planning to go, but..."

"We still could," Mark said, flicking through the paper, trying to find the story. "It's good they haven't been in touch, it must mean it's straightforward. What do you think - it won't seem odd if we go, will it?"

"Mark you really are turning paranoid." Brian said, sitting down opposite them. "You were here when they found the body and Kirsty was the last one to see her alive. It stands to reason you'd want to know what's happened - it's not like they've kept you in the loop."

Mark scanned the write-up in the paper.

Triple Tragedy Family Waiting to Grieve
A Coroner's inquest will be held in Brighton on Monday morning for Joan Knight,

46 whose body was discovered by local police at home on 5th March. Mrs Knight buried her husband, Tony, 45, and their only son Andrew, 19, on 10 February this year after they were killed in a lorry collision on the A27 near Lewes. Cause of death is yet to be confirmed but Police have said there were no suspicious circumstances...

Mark handed the paper to Kirsty, who read it quickly. She sighed. "I think I do want to be there and it's natural that we'd go together. I can't see a problem."

"Fine, we'll have to try and find out what time it is tomorrow. We could ring the police station - they should be able to tell us. I don't want to talk to that Scottish guy though, the less we have to do with him the better."

The rest of the afternoon was spent separately. It was Alice's suggestion to come up with their own ideas about Tom's clue and everyone agreed it was a good idea, not least as it kept Brian away from the flip chart. Mark went up to his apartment and Kirsty went to her room to avoid distracting each other but it was strange being apart in the house after so long together. By the time the sun went down he was ready to stop. He knocked on Kirsty's door but she must have gone downstairs already. He heard her voice as he neared the kitchen and was about to say hello when he heard Sandra giggle and say something about Ray. He paused, hovering at the foot of the stairs. "Did you see the look she gave him?" Sandra asked, "I don't know what he got up to on holiday but he's definitely more confident."

"She likes it though doesn't she," Kirsty said, "him standing up to her?"

"That's what I mean – the look on her face, the poor boy wouldn't stand a chance if she...oh, hi Mark."

"Hi, what have I missed?" Mark asked.

"Nothing," Kirsty said, "Sandra's just being naughty."

"I'm not!" Sandra protested. "I was just saying that Ray is more sure of himself since he got back from America..."

"Is he?" Mark asked.

"Definitely, how can you not have noticed? Anyway, Alice seems to prefer this new version, that's all I was saying."

"If it means they get on better I'm all for it," Mark said.

Sandra shrugged. "Careful what you wish for. Anyway, talking of team work we're just taking some glasses through so you can give us a hand."

166

"Who cleared up?" Mark asked as he looked around the tidy kitchen.

"Ray did," Kirsty said. "Apparently he volunteered."

"To be fair it was mostly his mess," Sandra said. "Still, it gets us off to a good start."

They walked into the drawing room where Brian was lighting a fire in the huge grate and Ray was drawing the curtains. As ever, Frank was in charge of the drinks and by the time everyone was settled there was a cosy feeling in the room.

"Why don't we stay over tonight Brian?" Alice asked.

"I thought we were waiting until after the inquest."

"You might as well - we've moved back already," Frank said. "Here, let me top you up."

Brian yawned. 'I don't mind – we've still got our stuff here."

"Live a little," Frank said. "Why don't we celebrate cracking the fourth clue so fast.

"Let's raise a glass to Joan too, thinking about tomorrow." Ray said.

"Of course, absolutely." Frank said. "I hope she's at peace now, poor lady, or soon will be at least."

As the evening wore on the drinks flowed and Mark found he was enjoying himself and feeling unexpectedly at home. As he watched Sandra and Kirsty laughing with Frank about something he felt happiness wash over him. The fact that even Ray and Alice were getting on now gave him confidence that it was all going to be fine.

Chapter Twenty-three

Mark and Kirsty were both in black and wearing what had become their usual funeral clothes. The inquest was at half past eleven but they were setting out early to get parked up in plenty of time.

"I'm really nervous," Kirsty said as they walked downstairs and into the kitchen.

"Don't be - there's nothing to feel nervous about," Mark said.

Alice walked in behind them, carrying an empty cafetiere.

"I'm sure it will be very brief, just a formality really. I wouldn't bother with a suit though Mark."

"Too much?"

"Perhaps, but it's up to you. Here Kirsty, borrow my scarf – you don't need to look like you're going to a funeral." Alice removed the colourful silk scarf she was wearing and tied it around Kirsty's neck in a loose knot.

"That's better," she said.

"Thanks Alice. I wasn't sure what to wear."

"I'm going to stay as I am," Mark said, removing his tie. "If I take my jacket off too I'll look like a waiter."

"Actually, I'm going to change," Kirsty said. "Otherwise I think we'll stand out too much. I'll just be a minute. Thanks Alice." Kirsty handed back the scarf and Alice smiled at her.

"Good idea. Besides, black's not right for your complexion darling so only wear it when you need to."

"I'll bear it in mind. Mark, I really will only be a minute – we've got time haven't we?"

"Yes but be quick. Will you grab me a sweater while you're up there." Mark paced around the kitchen while he waited and realised Kirsty's uneasiness was rubbing off on him.

"How are you holding up?" Alice asked.

"Me? Alright thanks, why do you ask?"

Alice laughed. "Goodness Mark, you sound paranoid. I just meant how's your head?"

"Oh, I see, no I'm fine thanks – Kirsty and I went up quite early. How's Frank – have you seen him this morning?"

"He's the same as ever. I haven't seen Sandra though – they were both still going when I called it a night."

"As long as she's okay for this afternoon."

"She will be I'm sure. Listen Mark, Brian's got some good ideas to

share, well it sounds like we all have, but you'll need to…uh, take charge early on if you want to avoid a repeat of yesterday."
Mark looked at her, surprised. "Okay," he said, "I was thinking about that."
Alice leaned towards him and spoke quietly, "I'm not being disloyal you understand. It's just that we can't afford for people to zone out."
"Thanks Alice, I know what you're saying."
"Yes, last night was fun but it won't last and the sooner we get these clues solved…oh that's much better Kirsty."
"Good. Okay I'm ready."
Kirsty had thrown a green top over her black fitted dress and added some chunky amber beads. She handed Mark a pale grey pullover and he shrugged out of his suit jacket and put it on instead.
"Thanks. Right, are you ready?" Mark asked.
"I think so," Kirsty said. "I'll be glad when this is over."
"Poor Joan. Do you think we'll find out whether she meant to do it?" Alice asked.
"Perhaps. I've no idea how it all works," Mark said. "We should be back in plenty of time for the meeting this afternoon."
"We'll let you know when we get back. See you later Alice." Kirsty waved as they left.

*

Two hours later, Mark was in a state of shocked disbelief. He held tightly on to Kirsty's hand as they sat next to each other in the bland municipal room. Everyone started filing out past them but Mark felt unable to move.
"Come on, let's go," Kirsty whispered, tugging his hand. "Mark!"
"Right. Yes." He stood and walked out of the room with Kirsty following behind him, still holding onto his hand. He didn't think he could let go. PC Thomson was up ahead, his red hair standing out among a group of men all talking quietly together. Mark's heart was hammering and he steered Kirsty the long way around the room to avoid seeing him. Once they were outside Mark took a deep lungful of the frigid air and shivered, having left his coat in the car.
He exhaled and started to speak but Kirsty stopped him.
"Not here, Mark," Kirsty said urgently. "Not here, come on."
He realised she was right. There was a café across the road, a grimy looking place, but it shone out like a beacon.

"Let's get a coffee," he said, and seeing a break in the flow of cars he ran across to the traffic island dragging Kirsty with him. She removed her hand from his angrily.

"Sorry," he said. "I needed to get away from there."

"It's fine. It's just not easy to run in these stupid heels. Come on." The traffic lights changed and they walked over to the café.

They found a table in the corner, away from the window, and ordered coffee from an indifferent waitress.

"Just wait until we've got our drinks." Kirsty said softly and Mark nodded. The waitress returned to her task of decanting tomato ketchup into red plastic bottles and Mark watched her while they waited, trying to make sense of what they'd just learnt. When their coffees arrived, Kirsty poured three sugars into her mug. She stirred it slowly then looked at him.

"I can't believe it. When they started reading out the suicide note..." Tears were brimming in Kirsty's eyes as she spoke and Mark handed her a napkin.

"At first I thought she'd just copied the letter she wrote to us about leaving," he said.

"Me too, until they showed it on the screen with the same sentence scribbled out."

"It had to be the one she left for us."

"We left that letter in the kitchen – anyone could have taken it, well, taken the first page of it. Who would even think to do that?" Mark shivered again. Despite the overheated café he still felt cold.

"What are we going to do? Kirsty asked.

"We can't tell the police, that's for sure."

"Someone planted that note with her body Mark. We have to say something."

"You're not serious? You know we can't tell anyone."

Kirsty shook her head. "It had to be one of us, there's no other explanation is there? I broke the law for Tom, but not this. This is cold-blooded murder." Kirsty lowered her voice still further. "With Tom, it's not like we'd be treated like criminals even if we were caught – he was terminally ill and he wanted to choose his end. We helped him." Kirsty looked at Mark as though desperate for him to believe her. "What we did was a crime but for us it was morally right. If we don't say anything about this though we're protecting a murderer. I can't do that."

Mark stared at her aghast and knew he had to choose his next words carefully.

"Kirsty, listen to me. Euthanasia is one thing when a loved one helps to end someone's suffering and they can't get to Switzerland or whatever."

"I know what you're going to say but even…"

"We're talking millions Kirsty. Tom's fortune is worth millions – the whole pro-euthanasia thing doesn't work for us. Joan's gone - nothing can change that and even if we did tell the police, how are they going to prove which of us planted the letter and gave her the overdose? We'd raise suspicion around Tom's death for nothing and we'd lose the money. Tom wouldn't have wanted that." Kirsty didn't say anything and Mark continued. "We'd do more for Joan by finding the money and doing something good with it. We could set up a scholarship in Andy's name. We could campaign for road safety, I don't know but we could do something."

Kirsty blew her nose and then nodded.

"Okay. Just let me think."

Mark downed the rest of his coffee.

"Another one?" He asked and she nodded. Mark called the waitress over and ordered two more coffees, all the while trying to think what their next move should be. The café was slowly emptying after the lunchtime rush and he realised he was hungry.

"If we can't tell the police we should try and find out who it is ourselves," Kirsty said.

"Okay, good. We could start by gauging reactions when we get back to the house. Whoever it is will be waiting to see what we know. If the coroner hadn't shown the note we'd coming back to the house thinking it was suicide."

Kirsty nodded.

"How good are you at acting?"

"I'm terrible. It's the same with lying – I just go red, sorry. Why, what are you thinking?"

"That's a shame," Mark said. "I was thinking we could act as if everything was fine and see who seemed relieved. They must be anxious right now."

"I wonder who it is." Kirsty said.

"It could be any of them. It's a really cunning murder too so it could be a woman just as easily."

"Thanks."

Mark shrugged. "You know what I mean - when women kill it tends to be more subtle so an overdose fits that. It was clever really - someone saw an opportunity and took it."

"Why though? That's what I don't get – who would want to hurt Joan? It makes no sense."

"I've been wondering how they did it. It could be that they went around to talk to Joan and then helped her with her meds."

Kirsty shuddered. "Everyone was up until quite late – that whole thing with Brian."

"So maybe they went in when she was already asleep and…I don't know, made her swallow some pills or ground them up and made her drink them down. It was strong stuff from the sounds of it so wouldn't have taken much."

"I can't believe that any of them could do it. I mean they've all got their faults but this?" Kirsty shook her head. "What are we going to do?"

"We'll work out who it is and kick them out of the house for a start."

"Who do you think it is?" Kirsty asked.

Mark straightened up as the waitress bought their coffees.

"My first thought was Brian, but I don't think he's clever enough to have done it. Plus he'd know we'd all suspect him, don't you think, the way he bangs on about the money not seeming much once it's split between us?"

Kirsty nodded. "I agree. I'd be more likely to suspect Alice than him. Joan would invite her in as well if she went round there at night whereas I can't imagine Joan letting Brian in."

"She never really liked Joan either, I always thought," Mark said.

"Maybe there was something from the past that we don't know about. Alice definitely didn't want Joan talking about their school days. Did you notice how she always changed the subject?"

"True but I think that was as much because Alice hated being reminded they were contemporaries. Let's face it, Joan looked much older than her age especially with the way she dressed, whereas Alice treats Vogue as her bible and still looks in her thirties."

"What about Frank?" Mark asked. "He'd do it for the money and he doesn't seem to have much in the way of feelings."

"He's too lazy," Kirsty said at once. "I know what you mean but I can't picture him being bothered with it all."

"I bet he could have talked Joan into letting him past the door though. He can be really persuasive when he turns on the charm," Mark said.

"I just can't see it. He always seemed to really like Joan."

"Yes, but he was usually at his friendliest when he was after something from the kitchen or he wanted her to get him a drink."

"True. She used to let him get away with it too." Kirsty sighed. "I can't believe the way we let her fetch and carry."

"Okay, I'm not ruling out Frank but Sandra…no way. What do you think?"

"Definitely not - Sandra's harmless and she's not ruthless enough for something like that. She's lovely - I still don't know why she puts up with Frank."

Mark shrugged. "Why would anyone? So, if we rule out you, me - and Sandra, that leaves us with four suspects."

"Ray wouldn't kill Joan, he hasn't got it in him," Kirsty said. "He's not…assertive enough and he's a nice guy."

Mark snorted. "Exactly, and isn't that always what people say on the news when some nutter goes on a killing spree? 'Kept to himself, seemed like a nice guy, harmless…'"

"Don't sit on the fence, Mark."

"I'm not saying he did it but he's got a side to him and he's a bit of a loner, that's all."

Kirsty wrapped her coat tightly around her.

"I can't seem to warm up."

"Let's order some food, that'll help."

Kirsty wrinkled her nose. "Not for me, my stomach's tied in knots. Anyway, we need to get back and tell everyone the verdict."

"So what are we going to say then? Just come straight out with it?"

"I think so. If we make sure everyone's together and then you tell them and I'll watch their reactions." Kirsty shivered. "Don't tell them straight out though. Let them work it out when you tell them the letter Joan wrote to us was found with her body."

"Good idea." They maneuvered out of their seats, the café being the kind that had tables with plastic seats attached. Mark settled up while Kirsty waited outside and he came out clutching a paper bag containing two warm pasties.

"In case you change your mind. I'm starving."

He ate as they walked back to the car park, and brushed big flakes of pastry off his shirt before he got in the car.

The journey back flew past but Mark was feeling queasy from the greasiness of the food on top of all the coffee. He drank some water as he drove up to the house, thinking again about how to frame what he had to say.

*

It was evening before he and Kirsty were alone again. The news of Joan's murder had ignited an enormous row although they'd reached a consensus in the end. After that they'd had to have the meeting they'd planned to discuss their ideas about the clue. Mark had taken charge immediately, following Alice's advice, but he knew he could have been more tactful about it

"Well, that went well," he said once they were back upstairs.

"Thank God you've got your own kitchen and we can lock the door on everyone else."

"Thank God you got past your stupid rule," Mark said, handing her a glass of wine. "Can you imagine going through all this on your own? Once that door closes behind us I'm living the dream. Before, I was going out of my mind with boredom up here or hanging around downstairs in the hope of you being there."

Kirsty kissed him. "I just spent my time reading. Coming off social media was really hard and being so cut off still feels weird sometimes. Apart from Mum and Jenny I haven't even told anyone about you."

"Same here."

"My friends would freak out if they saw you though. Considering my usual type."

"In a good way?"

"Yes, in a good way. Honestly, you have no idea – especially my sister, and Rachel."

"You're making me nervous," Mark laughed. "That's one good thing about being in exile, no judgment drinks yet."

"No, they'd be lovely."

"Let's hope so - they'll probably think I've had you in some kind of cult."

"Don't worry, they think I'm being paid as part of some research project about social media addiction. Anyway, Rachel will probably be more interested in whether you have any single friends."

Mark sat down on the sofa and put an arm around Kirsty. She leaned against him, cradling her wine glass, and he kissed the top of her head feeling comforted by the familiar smell of her hair.

"So...?" she asked.

"You first, you're the observant one."

"Not today – I have no idea, although whoever it is must be a brilliant actor."

"That's what I thought. They all seemed completely themselves."

"I know. It was like Brian thought that if he kept saying, 'it's not on' he'd undo what's happened. It was sweet though when he tried to send Alice home." Kirsty said.

"Until Frank shot him down."

"Not that she was having any of it. Just as well though - Alice might shirk the dirty work but she's clever. Anyway, so far there hasn't been a clue directed at her."

"We can't lose anyone else," Mark said.

"I don't think we will, not after Frank's reminder that anyone leaving would forfeit their share of the money. As for the rest of them, I think Ray literally didn't believe it at first," Kirsty said. "He didn't get it for ages."

"I saw that. Do you ever think he seems a bit too slow on the uptake though?"

"No. That's just what he's like," Kirsty said. "He's sharp when you chat to him, but he's told me before that when we're all together it reminds him of school. He says he sort of freezes."

"That's helpful."

"Don't be mean!"

"No, to be fair he was really fond of Joan. The way he got angry when he realised what had happened seemed real enough." Mark stood up and went over to the window. The hills in the distance looked inviting. "Shall we go out?"

"Out where?" Kirsty asked.

"Anywhere."

Kirsty stood up and moved towards him. She placed herself between him and the window.

"I was just thinking it was nice to be snug in here. How badly do you want to go out? In my head I've practically got my PJs on already."

"I suppose it depends on how optional the pyjamas are...?" Mark asked, putting his arms around her.

"Completely optional."

Mark smiled and pulled her towards him. "See, living the dream right here," he murmured. Kirsty reached up to kiss him but they were interrupted by a knock at the door. He sighed heavily. "Trying to anyway. Hold that thought, okay."

Kirsty shrugged and sat down on the window seat as he went to answer the door. It was Brian.

"I just wanted to catch you before you settle in for the evening." He lowered his voice. "I need to have a private word with you."

Mark gestured for Brian to come in and shut the door behind him.

"Do you want me to go?" Kirsty asked wearily.

"No, it's fine. I trust both of you - that's why I'm here. I'll come straight out with it."

"Okay," Mark said, waiting for Brian to continue.

"I think we should keep a very close watch on Frank, that's all. I've never liked him and he strikes me as greedy enough to do something like this." Brian folded his arms. "I know we said earlier not to throw accusations around unless we had any evidence, but I couldn't not say something."

"What makes you think he's greedy?" Mark asked.

"You only have to look at him, he does everything to excess. He eats too much, drinks too much. He treats his wife like an afterthought. It's all about him – and it strikes me that if someone was in his way then it would still be all about him. The man doesn't care and he is always going on about the money. Just thinking about him makes my blood pressure rise, I swear it."

"Brian, take it easy. We were just saying we can't afford to lose anyone else."

"This isn't a joke Mark."

"I know it isn't but I have to be neutral, and we all go on about the money."

"I knew you'd take his side - just because he makes everyone laugh. Don't be fooled by him Mark. He's selfish to the core. I don't trust him, I really don't."

"So, not a fan then Brian?" Kirsty asked.

"Are either of you going to take this seriously? Listen, I want you both to look out for him and I will as well, Alice too of course. The question is whether we can trust Ray enough to ask him to do the same."

"I think everyone will be watching everyone now." Mark said.

"Good. Well, keep me posted," Brian said, sounding more like his usual self.

"Now that we know about Joan there can't be anything else or we'll have to stop," Mark said. "It's what we all agreed and the killer won't want that anymore than we do."

"Who knows what he wants."

After Brian left Mark joined Kirsty beside the window.

"Now, where we?" He took one of her hands and lifted her towards him.

Kirsty reached her arms around his waist and leaned her head against his shoulder. "Can you just hold me instead?"

"The moment's passed hey?" Mark asked.

"I'm sorry. I just feel so sad about Joan - I'm all over the place."

"I know." Mark stroked Kirsty's back as she leaned against him. After a while he twisted the soft strands of her hair around his hand. An image flashed through his mind of pulling Kirsty's head back and kissing her sadness away. He wanted to forget everything for a while. He moved his hands lower but Kirsty pulled away, as if sensing the direction of his thoughts. Mark swallowed a sigh of frustration.

Kirsty smiled at him. "I'm up for going out if you still want to?"

"Okay, why not - anything to get away from everyone."

As Mark grabbed a coat and scooped up his car keys from the coffee table it occurred to him that they'd only been back from Norfolk for two days. He shook his head in disbelief.

"What?" Kirsty asked.

"Nothing. Come on, let's get out of here."

Part Three

What you don't do can be a destructive force.
Eleanor Roosevelt

MAY

Chapter Twenty-four

Mark was startled from sleep by the sound of someone hammering on the door.

"What is it?" Kirsty mumbled.

Mark clicked the bedside light on and they both squinted at the sudden brightness. The hammering was repeated then there was a sob and they heard Sandra's voice,

"Please, somebody help me. Kirsty, Mark, are you in there?"

"Jesus. Sandra, hang on..." Mark flung the duvet aside and scrambled out of bed. Glancing at the alarm clock, he saw it was just after four am.

"I'm just coming." He shouted, pulling on a pair of shorts and lunging for the door. Kirsty was beside him, pulling her dressing gown around her and they both stepped back as Sandra fell into the room, now sobbing uncontrollably. She was unable to answer any of their questions as they steered her over to the sofa and sat her down. Sandra sat there looking lost and much smaller than usual as she hunched into herself. Her sandy blonde hair was sticking up in every direction and her face was bright red as if she'd been running. Kirsty put an arm around her shoulders, hushing her gently while Mark went to get a glass of water for Sandra. When he came back she was taking huge gasps of air and seemed calmer.

"Here Sandra, drink this." He handed to it her and she took it gratefully.

"Thanks. I'm sorry to wake you up." She gulped the water then winced and rubbed her throat. After a while, she handed the empty glass back with an attempt at a smile.

"Did Frank do this?" Mark asked.

She shook her head,

"Not Frank, I don't know who."

"Sandra, what's happened? Kirsty asked.

Sandra shook her head.

"Do you want me to leave so you can to talk to Kirsty?" Mark asked feeling out of place.

"No, it's not...no, just give me a minute. Stay Mark, please."

After another glass of water and several deep breaths Sandra was calm enough to tell them what had happened.

"It's my fault I didn't hear anything," she said in a hoarse croak. "I took something to help me sleep. You're not supposed to have it with alcohol though and I'd drunk quite a lot I think." From what Mark had seen before he went to bed, this was an understatement. "I was a bit upset about Frank going out. He stays out so late and I don't know what he gets up to." She looked at her watch and her face crumpled. "See, he's not back now and I...I need him. Where is he?"

Kirsty stroked her back, "Just tell us what happened Sandra, I'm sure he'll be back soon."

Sandra nodded and took a shaky breath before continuing, "I woke up and I was gasping for air. I didn't know what was happening - I thought I was having a nightmare at first. I started panicking and that's when I realised I had...I had a pillow over my face." Sandra hugged herself. "It was pressed against my neck as well as my nose. Whoever it was they were sitting on top of me and I was trying to push them off me but I started to feel a bit faint." Sandra shuddered. "I knew if I passed out that was it and suddenly, well I just wanted them off me and I felt this surge of strength from I don't know where." The memory of this seemed to bolster her and Sandra's shoulders lost some of their slump.

"So what happened?" Kirsty asked in a whisper.

"Well, once I could breathe I started screaming as loudly as I could and kicking...and I got my hands free so I was hitting him. I was struggling for ages and they kept shoving the pillow against my face. My nose really hurts." Sandra

Kirsty peered at it.

"It looks okay. A bit red but I don't think it's broken. How did you get away?"

"My head was pounding and I thought I was going to black out. They were so much stronger and I could feel myself getting weaker. You know how you see things in films when the victim gets more and more feeble and then the head lolls?" She took a deep breath and wiped away the tears that had started again. "I felt like that was happening to me and I just remember thinking I was going to die. Then my life started to flash before me – that really happens you know?" She sounded shocked. "Well, it made me really angry. I'm not ready to die and I thought about Frank and my parents and I decided my only chance was to play dead."

"Good idea." Mark said. "So they went away?"

"Well it was a good theory but I couldn't do it. I suppose it's a bit like holding your breath for any length of time. Instinct takes over after a while. Anyway, it gets a bit hazy after that. I think I heard something and it must have frightened them off." She shuddered. "That's the last thing I remember. I must have blacked out because when I came to, the pillow was shoved back underneath me and the covers were straight. It was as if it never happened."

"I can't believe it," Kirsty said, her voice hollow.

"I didn't make it up, honestly I didn't."

"No of course not. I meant I can't believe someone did that to you. When we were all here as well. It's just crazy."

Mark had pulled on a sweater and was putting on his shoes. "Sandra, I'm going to leave you with Kirsty, okay? I need to see what everyone else in the house is up to and then have a look around. How long do you think you were out for?"

"I don't know."

"Well looking at those marks, it can't have been long." Mark pointed to the sweat marks on her pyjamas. Sandra glanced down and looked stricken when she realised.

"Oh, sorry. That's horrible!"

"No, that's adrenaline, and you might not be here without it," Mark said. "I know you couldn't see anything but what was your impression when you were fighting them? Can you remember anything about their build, or the length of their hair, clothes – anything?"

Sandra thought for a moment and Mark tried to be patient, but he was aware of the seconds ticking away. Just as he was about to give up, Sandra spoke.

"I remember! A puffa jacket, he was wearing a puffa jacket. I know because it was all slippery and squidgy and I couldn't get a grip on it. I think he was wearing a balaclava, because I could feel wool too. I do think I might have scratched him though and maybe it was a scarf because I definitely felt flesh. I don't remember it being scratchy skin but…"

"And he was heavy?" Mark asked.

"He felt very heavy, I think he was sitting on my stomach. Oh, I don't know Mark…I'm sorry, I'm being so useless…I just…"

Mark leaned over and gave her shoulders a reassuring squeeze.

"You're doing brilliantly. I'll be back soon. Kirsty, lock the door behind me yes and don't open it to anyone but me."

Kirsty nodded as he left and he waited until he heard the sound of the key turn before he walked over to Ray's door. There was a light showing beneath the door and without knocking, Mark slowly turned the handle and pushed the door open. Ray was stretched out under the covers reading a book with his back to the door.

"Ray?" Mark said. "Get up." There was no way he could have missed the commotion outside his door. Mark strode over to the bed and grabbed Ray roughly by the shoulder but was startled by Ray's terrified yelp as he sat up and tugged down his earphones. Linkin Park blared tinnily from the earpieces as Ray turned towards Mark.

"What the fuck - what are you doing?"

He looked furious, but Mark glared at him.

"What are you doing up at this time of the morning?"

"What's it to you? I couldn't sleep, okay - I often can't in this happy household of ours. Anyway, why are you in my room? That door was locked."

"No, it wasn't, I just turned the handle."

"Wasn't it? Whatever. Why are you here?"

"Sandra's been attacked," Mark said. "Someone tried to smother her with a pillow while she slept."

Ray's mouth gaped. "You're joking?"

"Do I look like I'm joking?"

"Is she okay?"

Mark nodded. "She's had a scare but she'll be alright. Will you come with me? I need to talk to Brian…and Alice."

Ray jumped out of bed and started looking around for his trousers. He was wearing an old T-shirt and boxers and Mark threw him a pair of tracksuit bottoms that were draped over a chair. Ray caught them and put one leg in then stopped suddenly and looked up at Mark.

"Hang on, so you think it was someone in the house?"

Mark shrugged.

"Probably."

"Well, it wasn't me!" Ray said indignantly. "I couldn't sleep that's all. I was just…"

"Never mind that now. Come on, hurry up!"

They walked out into the dimly lit corridor and walked past Kirsty's room then past another three closed doors that led to empty bedrooms. Mark paused when he reached the central staircase, wondering whether he ought to check behind the closed doors for an intruder. He knew he was kidding himself though. Sandra's attacker was either standing next to him, pretending to be asleep in Brian and Alice's room or lurking in the grounds after another heavy night without his wife. They walked past the staircase and Mark looked down the dark hallway before continuing down the corridor that led to the other half of the house. Sandra's bedroom door was wide open and Mark glanced inside. His heart banged in his chest when he saw a man in a black leather jacket sprawled across the bed and he grabbed Ray's arm,

"It's Frank. See if you can wake him up, I'll be with you in a minute."

Ray peered around Mark's shoulder and swallowed nervously.

"Can't we come back for him? It looks like he's out for the count." An enormous snore reverberated through the room and Frank grunted in his sleep.

"Fine. Just stay there though and shout if he moves," Mark said, before lowering his voice to a whisper. "Make sure he's really asleep. From the look of Sandra I don't think it's been long since she was attacked. Definitely not long enough for her attacker to get back to sleep."

Ray nodded and Mark carried on down the corridor to the room at the end. He was tempted to burst in on them as he had with Ray. The occasion demanded it but the thought of Alice held him back. He banged on the door instead and within moments heard the creaking of floorboards as someone moved across the room.

"Who is it?" Alice asked in alarm from behind the closed door.

"It's Mark. Open up, I need to speak to you."

"Do you know what time it is?"

"Alice just open the door. It's an emergency."

The door opened a crack and Alice peered at him, looking annoyed.

"What is it - Brian's asleep?"

Mark explained and saw her expression change from annoyance to alarm and finally to disbelief.

"Oh, surely not - you know how drunk she was last night. She must have had a nightmare."

Mark needed to check the state of Frank lying on the bed a few doors down and after failing to convince Alice to let him in, he pushed the door open and turned on the light. He strode over to Brian, ignoring Alice's indignant complaints, and shook him roughly by the shoulder. Brian mumbled something under his breath and Mark shook him harder.

"Brian, wake up!" Mark shouted.

"He's a very deep sleeper," Alice said icily from behind him. Mark turned around and saw she was tying the knot on an ivory satin dressing gown.

"He's been finding it very difficult to sleep lately and if you wake him now he'll probably be awake for the rest of the night. Is it really necessary to disturb him?"

Mark looked down at Brian, noticing his slack jawed expression and even the drool that had pooled on the pillow beside his mouth. As he watched, Brian's eyes twitched.

"No, it's okay now, he's answered my question. I'm sorry but come and talk to Sandra and you'll understand why I had to check that Brian was sleeping."

"Fine," Alice snapped. "Just give me a moment will you?"

Mark stepped outside and walked down to speak to Ray who stood anxiously in the doorway to Sandra and Frank's room. He looked relieved when he saw Mark.

"He's definitely asleep," Ray said with a grimace. "I don't know how Sandra puts up with it – I can smell him from here."

"Okay, we'll wake him in a minute. I'm just going to walk Alice down to my room, so keep watching him until I'm back."

Mark walked back down the corridor and stood outside Alice's door. He could hear her moving around against the rhythmic background of Brian's snoring. He yawned hugely and shivered in the draught that tickled the back of his neck. It was as he turned to look out the window opposite Alice's door that the draught registered with him. They didn't keep any of the windows open at night. Ignoring Ray's bemused look, he walked back down the corridor checking each window. When he came to the one diagonally opposite Frank and Sandra's room he could see that the sash window was slightly raised. He pushed it higher and, looking down, saw that just below the windowsill was a tall aluminium ladder. Just as he was about to withdraw his head to point it out to Ray, Alice tapped him on the shoulder causing him to bang his head.

"Sorry," she said perfunctorily. "What exactly is going on?"

Mark rubbed his head, noticing that Alice had taken the time to brush her hair. "I'll take you to my room. Kirsty and Sandra are both there and they can explain better than me."

He ignored her questions as they walked quickly down towards his room and called for Kirsty to let them in. She opened the door looking worried.

"Are you all right?" He could see Sandra sitting on the sofa with a blanket and she looked much better than before although the quick smile she gave him was more of a grimace.

"We'll be fine. Come in Alice."

Mark left them to it and re-joined Ray.

"He's definitely asleep?" Mark asked.

"He's completely out of it."

They walked into the room together and Mark put a hand over his mouth. The stench of Tequila was so strong it seemed to be oozing from Frank's pores. Mark rolled him over and saw that he looked pale and clammy, and very deeply asleep - if not actually unconscious. Mark shook him vigorously but Frank didn't stir.

I've never seen him this bad." Ray whispered.

"I've never seen anyone this bad," Mark said, "This is beyond drunk."

At that moment there were retching sounds, and they jumped back to avoid what smelt like a jet of pure alcohol mixed with curry. They looked at each other incredulously, frozen in disgust, until eventually Ray volunteered to get a towel.

Mark checked Frank's position, reluctant to touch him but not wanting to ask Sandra to do it. He was lying on his side already so Mark removed Frank's leather jacket and arranged his arms into the recovery position. Ray returned with a towel and Mark threw it over the mess on the floor and opened a window.

"Do you think he'll be okay?"

"Probably," Mark said, but looking at Frank's prone figure he added, "I think we need to wake him up though. He's got some of it out of his system, but unless you fancy babysitting him?"

Ray shook his head.

"Me neither. Come on, let's get him in the shower."

Frank's body was a dead weight but between them they managed to half drag, half carry him into the bathroom. They rolled him into the bath and it was with some satisfaction that Mark turned the cold shower head onto his face. Even then, it took a while for the pounding jet of cold water to register and just as Mark was on the verge of giving up and calling an ambulance, Frank started batting ineffectually at the water. Mark kept the pressure on and after another few seconds, Frank came around, mumbling incoherently. His round eyes were popping and he seemed furious.

"Get it off me!" He glared at them in confusion. Mark turned it off then watched as Frank breathed heavily and shook his head, covering them in drops of icy water. His hair was streaming water onto his face, which went from pasty grey to green as they watched. He held up his hand. "Excuse me," he muttered, before turning his head to one side and throwing up into the bath. It seemed to last forever.

"Jesus," Ray muttered. "How is that even possible?"

The smell of Tequila pervaded the bathroom and Mark turned the shower onto the offending mess, washing what he could of it down the plughole. Frank was draped over the bath, sighing heavily.

"'That's better," he said.

"You're a mess Frank. How much have you drunk?" Mark asked.

"Not much," he giggled. "Tequila night. No lemon and salt for Frank though, just Tequila."

Frank slumped into a doze and Ray hunkered down to look at him.

"Is that enough do you think?"

"Yeah, that'll do," Mark said disgustedly. "He can sleep the rest off."

They manhandled him out of the bath and put him back into the recovery position on the floor of the bathroom.

"He can stay here," Mark said, prodding him with his foot. They flung the duvet over him. "With the hangover he's got coming I'll enjoy waking him up in the morning," Mark said.

They turned the lights off and walked back down the corridor to Mark's room. Sandra and Kirsty were both curled up on the sofa and Alice was sitting on one of Mark's kitchen chairs facing them.

"Is Frank back yet?" Sandra asked.

"He's back but he's been drinking Tequila and he's not in a good state. He doesn't know what's happened to you."

"He can't drink Tequila," Sandra said. "Why would he do that? It always makes him sick."

"We noticed." Mark said.

Sandra looked embarrassed so Mark changed the subject.

"You're looking much better. How are you feeling?"

"I'll be fine," she smiled. "Kirsty and Alice have been looking after me and plying me with tea and chocolate which always helps."

"That's good," Mark said.

He sat in the remaining armchair and Ray sat next to Alice on a kitchen chair. They chatted for a while and then, when he was sure Sandra was relaxed, Mark asked her again to try and remember anything about her attacker. She had clearly thought about it while he was gone but couldn't add anything, other than that it was a balaclava not a scarf because she had felt wool rather than hair. Mark nodded.

"Also, the more I think about it the more I'm sure it was a man. He was really heavy and his breathing sounded like a man, I can't describe it really but I'm certain."

"Okay. I've been thinking about this. You know we can't call the police because they'd want to question us all?" Sandra shook her head and Mark continued. "One of us is going to have to turn detective again like we did with Joan. I have an alibi as Kirsty was with me all night," Mark said.

"I'm a light sleeper," Kirsty agreed, "so I would have heard him going out and coming back in, especially as the bedroom door makes a terrible noise."

Mark went over to the door and demonstrated the loud creak.

"As you can hear. I keep meaning to WD40 that." He sat back down.

"Alice, you and Kirsty are both too light from what Sandra said so that puts you in the clear." The others glanced sidelong at Ray. "Before we start giving anyone a hard time though I'll search the house and have a look outside. That includes your rooms, okay? I'm hoping there's a puffa jacket and a balaclava lying around somewhere - that would be a big help."

Everyone nodded, including Ray who turned to Sandra.

"I haven't got anyone who can vouch for me Sandra, but you know I couldn't have done that to you. I haven't got it in me..." He trailed off and Sandra smiled and patted his arm.

"I know Ray, you're more of a gentle giant I'd say. The thing is I can't see how any of us could have done it. Brian's got his blood pressure problem and Frank was drunk and he just wouldn't do that to me even if we have been rowing a lot. Mark, you and Kirsty were together which only leaves Alice - who probably weighs half the amount of my attacker. Sandra took a deep breath.

"It was so horrible."

Outside, dawn was beginning to break accompanied by the noisy chorus of birds, and Mark stretched as he stood up, feeling exhausted. After asking everyone else to stay put until he was back, he left with Ray to have a look around.

Chapter Twenty-five

Mark walked into the house after a meeting in Brighton to be met with the news that Kirsty was packing.

"She's upstairs," Ray said, "says the way things are now she can't stand being here any more."

"She said that?" Mark asked. She'd spoken about leaving before but he hadn't believed her.

"I think she meant things generally not just you guys."

Mark sighed. "It's exhausting - we keep having the same conversation. Ever since Sandra."

Relations between everyone had been strained already in the weeks after Joan's inquest but since Sandra's attack the atmosphere in the house had been worse than ever.

"It doesn't help that we're so stuck," Ray said. "I still feel bad for screwing up on the last clue – maybe if we'd solved that one faster…"

Mark shrugged but he was the one who felt guilty. He should have owned up to his mistake on the Wealdway clue instead of letting Ray think he was the link. If he had then Ray might have registered the language of stone masonry sooner – feather, diamond and steel. It took Alice suggesting that a cold heart could refer to a statue for Ray to finally make the connection.

She's a sight to behold - delicate as a feather with a heart that is cold.
Made as one of the three, fairest of all, she will last for eternity.
Seek her out more than diamond or steel and then turn her about.
You'll delight in her words more than the other two thirds.
What is her name? You know already but why not play the game

Once they worked out they were looking for beauty, or Thalia, from The Three Graces, it should have been easy.

"Don't blame yourself Ray. We took so many wrong turns on that one."

"Maybe. We don't want to lose Kirsty though - see if you can talk her out of leaving. I didn't get anywhere."

"I will but to be honest Ray, there's part of me that wants to let her go."

Passing Tom's study, he remembered the argument after Sandra found a small statue of The Three Graces tucked away behind Tom's collection of board games. The answer had been there all the time

190

'beauty' as Sandra had guessed, written on the base of the statue. Instead of celebrating their win though Brian raged that the cleaning company booked by Kirsty could have moved the statue. This meant no more cleaning crews and since then the house was looking shabbier and more unloved by the day.

Mark unlocked his door but Kirsty wasn't there so he continued next door and took a deep breath as he knocked on her door. She stood back as she let him in showing little sign of the radiance that had taken his breath away when he'd first met her. As she lit a cigarette Mark couldn't stop himself. "I still can't get used to you smoking."

She'd started a while ago, at first just drunkenly nabbing the odd one from Ray, but recently she'd started buying her own. It was like a form of rebellion while she was stuck in the house. She shrugged and walked over to open the window before stubbing it out in the ashtray. She turned to face him and he could see she looked gaunt and pale with shadows under her eyes. She seemed to have lost her appetite for food and for everything, including him lately, so Mark was relieved when she hugged him. The smoke from her smouldering cigarette was tickling his throat but he ignored it, not wanting her to move.

"Don't go," he said.

She sighed before releasing him and standing back.

"I've got to Mark, I can't live like this anymore."

"But we're so close, just one more month."

"It's not worth it. What happened to Sandra brought it home to me and I should have gone after that."

She sat down heavily on the bed and Mark sat next to her, not knowing the words to make her stay. The breeze from the open window stirred the smoke from her abandoned cigarette and he leaned forward and ground it out in the ashtray. The views were spectacular from Kirsty's room and the sun was sparkling on the lake but April's grey overcast skies had suited the mood within the house better.

"I don't know if I can keep doing this without you," he said at last.

"Then come with me. Don't think you're safe just because a man hasn't been targeted yet."

Mark rubbed his hands through his hair, pulling hard at the roots.

"I can't leave it Kirsty, not now - we're so nearly there." He thought of the five vases on the table in front of the window in the hall.

"We've got a month left." Kirsty said. "If we run out of time it will all be for nothing anyway."

"Look, we're making progress with the sixth clue, I've finally got a meeting with that specialist at the university tomorrow. Come on, it's just four weeks of your life, that's nothing."

"It's not nothing if I don't survive those four weeks. We're living with a killer Mark! I don't understand how everyone seems to be okay with that apart from me."

"Nobody thinks it's okay but…listen, he won't try anything while I'm here."

"Then that makes you a target too. I've got a bad feeling Mark. If we solve this clue and the next one seems straightforward he might up the body count. He knows we can't go to the police."

"We can stick together Kirsty - I'll make it my job to protect you."

"How?" Kirsty laughed. "It's not just about who's got the biggest muscles is it? Anyway, it's not only that, it's the time I've already spent with people I can't stand to look at anymore. My head is spinning trying to work out which one of them did it. One minute I think it's Frank, then it's Brian, then Ray and before I know it Sandra or Alice has said something strange and I think it's one of them." Kirsty took a deep breath. "I told you I'm a terrible actor and I just can't carry on pretending I'm fine."

"You don't have to pretend…"

"No Mark, I don't want to live with someone who could kill Joan and then get up in the morning as if nothing's happened."

"I know, I know. I'm not saying it will be easy but if you leave now you're doing exactly what they want you to do, whoever they are." Kirsty sighed.

"I probably am but what's the alternative? You know how the money's weighted – you, me and Ray stand to get more per person than the couples do individually. If they get me out of the way it's an easy win." Kirsty stood up as though unable to stay still.

"Look at me - I'm a wreck," she said. "I know what you're saying but all this is making me ill."

"You could start by cutting those out." Mark gestured to the ashtray.

"Christ you sound like my mother! I'll stop again when this is over. Look it's not a problem - I can stop anytime I want." There was silence for a moment, before the corners of Kirsty's mouth curled upwards. She caught his eye and they smiled together. "I'll have hypnotherapy or something if I can't, don't worry. I started mainly to annoy Brian but now it's this or overdosing on chocolate."

"I'll get you some chocolate then. I'll get you one of those giant Lindt rabbits, the gold ones they had in the shops for Easter."

"The one kilo bunnies we saw? That's a serious offer."

"What if I say you're ill? You wouldn't have to see anyone then. Maybe you could go and stay with your sister for a couple of weeks."

"It wouldn't be allowed," she said and Mark thought she was probably right.

Part of the agreement to continue after Sandra's attack was that they worked and lived together for the remaining time to ensure safety in numbers as well as knowing where everyone was. Time away from the house was restricted to when absolutely necessary but Mark knew he wasn't the only one finding reasons to meet people rather than do things over the phone or online. With every day that passed he felt more stifled by the dusty confines of the house.

"You could be ill and stay in your room for a few days." Mark suggested.

Kirsty sighed heavily and plucked absent-mindedly at a shirt that was in the suitcase beside her.

"It's like Peter crying wolf, isn't it? Every time I think about leaving you talk me out of it."

"So you'll stay?"

"I don't think I can."

"Just let me say you're ill and then you won't have to see anyone for a while. Give it a week and if we've cracked the sixth clue by then that will change things. Look if you walk away now you'll regret it for the rest of your life."

"That's the problem Mark. The money feels so tainted now I'm starting to think I'll regret it more if I keep going."

Mark stood up and went over to the window. The lawns were so overgrown that the grass was waving in the breeze. The green stood out vividly against the cornflower blue sky.

"Look at it out here. It's hard to remember now what it was like when it was freezing cold and raining all the time and it's the same with all this. You'll forget the worst of it and in a month this will be over. You can do amazing things with that money Kirsty. Learn how to build assets then use it to do something useful, make a difference - all of that."

Kirsty sighed but she was smiling. "Emotional blackmail now?"

"Maybe, but it's true. Besides, it's not like anyone is going to be throwing money in the air and cracking open the Champagne when we get to the end."

Kirsty moved over to him and Mark put an arm around her waist as they looked out of the window together. After a while she turned to him. "Okay."

"You'll stay?"

"Yes, and thank you. Again."

"You're welcome, although you know it's all for my benefit."

"This would have been so much fun if it was just the two of us." Kirsty looked at him and then pulled him away from the window towards the bed. She leaned up to kiss him and Mark felt himself respond at once - he'd missed her terribly. She was so light now he lifted her easily and she wrapped her legs around him. When they finally broke apart she said breathlessly,

"Sorry, the smoking…shall I brush my teeth?"

"No." Mark said, placing her firmly on the bed. "No, I don't want you going anywhere."

*

It was some time before Mark came downstairs and the first person he saw was Ray, who was sitting at the dining table on his laptop, surrounded by books and note paper.

"Found anything interesting?" Mark asked.

"Not really, nothing new. What about Kirsty? You've been up there forever."

"Just catching up." Mark said, keeping his expression neutral. "She's going to stay on though."

"That's brilliant." Ray said, looking pleased. "Is she in her room?"

"She is but no offence Ray she won't invite you in. You're better off having a chat when she comes down."

"Right, no offence." Ray said.

"You know she doesn't think it's you but that's why she's been having such a hard time I think – not being able to take anyone on trust. Look I'll leave you to it."

"Okay. I won't take it personally. Tell her I'm glad she's staying in case I don't see her later."

Mark wanted to pass on the news to everyone else and he found Brian and Alice in the drawing room. He told them Kirsty would be staying after all and they seemed disinterested. What Kirsty said about crying wolf seemed to be true.

"We'll see," Alice had said, pinching the bridge of her narrow nose. "If

194

she stays, she stays, if not – well…"

"If not, she ought to go now rather than dragging it out," Brian said, keeping his voice calm in response to a worried look from Alice. Apparently Brian's blood pressure had skyrocketed so there were fewer outbursts of temper while he waited to see if his medication was working.

"It's making her ill this situation we're in, that's one of the reasons she wants to go. It's not that she means to mess anyone around." Mark said.

"Look at Brian," Alice said. "He really has been made ill by the stress but he's not creating a drama about it, is he?"

"Well, thanks for your support Alice and just so you know, Kirsty and I are going out for dinner tonight."

"Really? So the conversation we all had about staying here…"

"We'll be out rather than having dinner in my apartment. It doesn't really affect anyone else does it?"

"That's not really the point Mark but yes, fine, thanks for telling us." Alice put on her glasses and reached for the paperback next to her. "For the record, I'm not unsupportive of Kirsty. You know I like her very much but it does annoy me that she acts like she's the only one with feelings."

"It's not an act Alice and who knows, maybe she is the only one of us with feelings."

Mark left, not wanting to say anything more and he could hear raised voices coming from the kitchen. He walked in on Sandra and Frank, not caring if he was interrupting. They stopped once they saw Mark.

"That's good news," Sandra said when he told them Kirsty would be staying. "She's not looking well though, quite gaunt I thought. Why don't we make a nice home cooked meal for dinner tonight – get some good food into her?"

"Thanks Sandra but we've arranged to go out for dinner."

"I thought that was against the new rules," Frank said

"Never mind the rules," Sandra said. "It sounds like she needs to escape for the night. One evening won't hurt."

Frank shrugged. "Fine by me then."

"Thanks, I just want to get her away from here for the evening."

"Good. Well, I might still cook something for the five of us," Sandra said. "It's all become very haphazard lately."

For all of them, the news that Kirsty was or wasn't going was little more than a distraction. They were more concerned with the lack of progress on the sixth clue and Kirsty was right that they were running out of time. They'd been stuck now for weeks and if Mark's meeting with the history expert tomorrow didn't help he didn't know what their next move would be. He knew the clue off by heart and as he walked back upstairs he muttered it under his breath,

As these epic visionaries took a chance to win,
Be inspired to do the same.
But first look at war in 1815
As all you need is their name.

The previous weeks had been spent immersed in Napoleonic history, particularly the heroes of the battle of Waterloo, but nobody could pinpoint anything that was absolute. It was risky consulting someone outside the group but after trying everything from online forums to museums, they had to try. He ran up the stairs to Kirsty feeling excited by the idea of escaping everything for the evening and hoped she felt the same.

Chapter Twenty-six

By ten that morning, Mark was driving to the university for his appointment with Dr Mitchell, a history tutor and specialist in the Napoleonic Wars. He yawned when he stopped at the traffic lights, hoping he was alert enough to take in what she said. Kirsty's hands-off phase very definitely seemed to be over and last night reminded him of when they first got together. He didn't know what had changed but he was all for it as long as he got some sleep at some point.

Realising he was nearing the university, he tried to clear his head so he could concentrate on the meeting ahead. Mark felt like a Napoleonic expert by now after weeks of solid research and although he had read one article that referred to Bonaparte as a 'visionary statesman' there was nothing conclusive enough to risk trying it as a password. None of them could remember Tom mentioning any interest in Waterloo either, but there was the possibility that Joan had been the link to the sixth clue. They had found a couple of books about the Napoleonic Wars in Tom's library so had taken this as a sign they were on the right track. Mark parked up and got out of the car, stretching again before leaning in to retrieve his file. He made his way into the building and a few minutes later he was knocking on Dr Mitchell's door.

"Come in."

He walked in to the florescent lit, windowless room where there were books everywhere, some of them looking as old as the wars they covered. There was a vase of yellow tulips on the desk, clearly there in a hopeful attempt to cheer up the room. Then there was Dr Mitchell. She was a tall striking looking woman in her sixties with a thick bob of dark hair and a wide mouth. She stood up from her desk and smiled as she shook his hand.

"Nice to meet you Mark. Please, sit down." She gestured to the small green sofa to her left and joined him on it.

Mark felt unaccountably nervous and coughed, unsure where to start.

"I've been looking forward to seeing you," she said. "I like puzzles."

Mark smiled at her. "I've brought my research, just a list of what I've considered so far…and the riddle itself of course."

"How much longer have you got, before your friend wins his bet?"

"I've got a week and I know he's making good progress with the riddle I gave him so…"

"So, the sooner the better," she said. "You're fairly sure it's related to the battle of Waterloo are you?"

"I don't know what else it could be." Mark said handing her the clue.

"Right, let me have a look." She leaned back on the sofa, one leg swinging back and forth in front of her as she concentrated. He heard the pen tapping against her teeth and glancing across he saw her frown of concentration. After a moment he stood up and began inspecting the books on her shelves. He even recognised some of them. Just as he was about to remove one, he heard her bark of laughter and turning around was amazed to see her grinning at him.

"What?"

"Just come here a moment Mark," she said, gesturing for him to sit down. "I think someone's been pulling your leg."

He sat down and she laid the clue in front of him.

"Now look at this…"

Mark looked, even though the words were embedded in his brain.

As these epic visionaries took a chance to win,
Be inspired to do the same.
But first look at war in 1815
As all you need is their name.

"Notice anything?" She asked.

Mark looked at her blankly and shook his head.

"First look it says – see? Look vertically rather than across."

Mark looked again, feeling annoyed, "I've looked at it so often I…"

"Okay, what if I do this?" She took her pen and drew around the first letter of each line.

"A – B – B – A." He read out loud and then groaned. "Waterloo, Abba - how did I miss that?"

She smiled. "They are a bit before your time but lucky for you I saw them play at Brighton Dome back in 1974 and when they won Eurovision that song was everywhere."

"Very lucky for…oh, 'Take a Chance on Me.'" Mark said.

"Yes and perhaps 'Winner takes it all' as well? I've still got those singles in the attic somewhere so I can even tell you they were signed to the Epic record label. I was quite a fan."

Mark put his head in his hands, "I've spent the last month reading about Napoleon and Wellington," he said.

Dr Mitchell shrugged. "I can see how it could happen – you'd either get it straight away or not at all. A case of can't see the wood for the trees."

"It was right there though, wow." Mark couldn't believe they'd all missed it. "I can't thank you enough Dr Mitchell although I'm sorry to have wasted your time."

"Jane, please, and I'm happy I could help," she said, smiling at him. "Anyway, if you decide to follow up on your Napoleonic studies, you know where to come."

"I feel like I've had enough of that for a while, but thanks, I'll bear it in mind."

After fielding Dr Mitchell's questions about the bet and thanking her again Mark left the office feeling euphoric. One clue left and a whole month left in which to crack it.

*

Mark was whistling as he let himself into the kitchen but he stopped when he saw the expression on Ray's face.

"What?"

"Bad news. Her bags are packed."

"Again? I thought we'd sorted this out."

"Don't let her see you're annoyed mate, that's not going to help anything. How'd you get on with the Professor lady?"

"Right. Good thanks – I'll tell you in a bit."

"She was out by the lake talking to Sandra for ages this morning – just so you know."

Mark walked into the drawing room and saw Frank and Sandra were watching the TV in the corner. Kirsty was sitting in the window seat with a book. She lowered it when she saw him and smiled nervously, "I've been waiting for you before..."

"Before you leave?"

She nodded.

"How did you get on?" Frank asked.

"Later Frank." Mark said and held out a hand to Kirsty. "Shall we go for a walk?"

"Come on, don't keep us in suspense," Frank said in a cheerful voice.

"I said later," Mark snapped.

They left the room and walked back through the kitchen where Ray was now eating an enormous sandwich. He raised a hand to them, his mouth full, and Kirsty said hello as they passed. Mark ignored him, too distracted to respond, and once outside he blinked rapidly against the wind.

"Is it too cold?"

"No it's nice, " she said. "I love this kind of weather, sunny but with a chill in the air, you know."

They made their way down to the lake automatically and Mark tried to swallow his irritation and think of what he could say to change her mind.

"Will you stay while I put the password in to get the seventh clue?" he asked at last.

"You got the answer then?"

Mark nodded and waited for her to ask what the answer was. As the silence grew between them, Mark knew beyond doubt that she was leaving.

They sat down on the bench in front of the lake and both turned to look at the Bleeding Heart that had survived Ray's uprooting. The drooping pink flowers swayed back and forth in the wind.

"That all seems so long ago," Kirsty said. "I loved that time Mark, when it was just the two of us. I don't think I've ever been so happy."

"Me too," Mark said. "Just one more month until it's the two of us again."

"No, I'm sorry."

"You can't hang on until then?"

"No Mark, I really can't."

Mark sighed and sat for a while watching a family of ducks swimming on the lake.

"I feel like there's something you're not telling me," he said at last.

"It's everything I said yesterday - it's not safe here. The money's not worth dying for."

"So you're going."

"I am and I don't want anything more to do with it. With it or…with anyone."

"What are you saying?" Mark asked, feeling tightness in his chest.

"I'm sorry Mark."

"I can understand you're leaving but we're fine aren't we? I can carry on for both of us and then we'll pick up when it's over."

Kirsty was shaking her head slowly.

"No," she said. "I can't Mark, I can't be around anyone connected to all this any more, not even you." She gestured towards the house, her voice breaking. "We went from euthanasia to withholding evidence and then, what – protecting a murderer who has since tried to kill again?

That's the kind of person I've become."

"But that's not you and it's not me either."

"It is now though. That's my point. I just want to put it behind me now and that means a clean break. I think when we killed Tom we unleashed something, and we did kill that lovely old man, no matter how I think about it."

"It's what he wanted - it wasn't about him clinging on. We agreed that, all of us. What's happened Kirsty? What's changed?"

"Nothing. I just can't stand everyone carrying on as normal after what happened to Sandra. I mean someone tried to kill her and it wasn't even an option that we could call the police."

"But you know why we couldn't call the police," Mark said.

"Have you noticed how cowardly the killer is, whoever it is?" Kirsty asked. "An overdose and trying to suffocate someone while they sleep. Can you really stand to spend any more time with someone like that?"

Mark held out his hands. "Not really, no, but I've come this far. We all have."

"Exactly, but that's how we're different Mark. That's what I'm trying to tell you. I just can't be with someone who could accept it."

"Are you asking me to choose?"

"No!" Kirsty gripped his arm but Mark saw how she took her hand away immediately as if she couldn't bear to touch him. He felt numb.

"What happened Kirsty? Did Sandra say something?"

Kirsty shook her head.

"Did you decide yesterday, is that what last night was about? Wait, was that you saying goodbye?" He exhaled and shook his head. "I thought you said you couldn't act."

"No, Mark I…"

"What then? I thought we had something Kirsty."

"We did."

Mark felt sick. "We did? What's changed since I left this morning? Sandra said something didn't she?"

"No, I can't explain it."

Mark didn't believe her. There was something that didn't ring true about her words and he could see the blush in her cheeks.

"Tell me Kirsty. Try."

He reached out to touch her but she shifted away. Mark couldn't believe this was happening. He felt a lump forming in his throat as the silence lengthened between them. He stood up and took a deep breath but it was a while before he could speak.

"That's all you're going to say?"

Kirsty hung her head. "I'm sorry Mark."

"Is there someone else?"

"What?" Kirsty looked up at him and he could see the confusion in her eyes. "No, of course not. No, I just…can't."

There was silence again.

"That's it then is it, that's all you've got to say about us?" Mark asked. "Well, thanks for saying goodbye last night - I hope you enjoyed the ride."

"Mark, no – it's not like that." Kirsty sounded on the verge of tears.

"What then? What is it like Kirsty?" Mark spoke urgently but she refused to look at him.

"Nothing. Look, my taxi will be here in a minute. I have to go, I'm sorry. Sandra can ring me about the clue."

Mark looked at her in disbelief but when she said nothing else, he shrugged.

"Don't let me keep you then."

He marched off towards the cover of the woods, feeling he could hardly breathe. Once he was hidden behind the trees he turned around to see what she was doing but Kirsty was already heading back towards the house. He kicked out at a tree branch on the floor and then walked further into the woods, choking back furious tears and shouldering his way through the overgrowth. A blackbird's warning cry rang out nearby and small branches scratched his arms and face as he walked blindly, almost welcoming the pain, away from Kirsty. After a while he sat down heavily on the fallen trunk of an old oak tree and put his head in his hands. His face was a picture of misery as he stared at the ground and tried to work out what had just happened.

Chapter Twenty-seven

"You're just being annoying now," Frank said. "I keep telling you that Tom never spoke to me about wars or churches so stop trying to put the pressure on."

"I'm not putting pressure on," Brian said. "I'm just saying that we've all had some link to the clues apart from you and Sandra. Just think about it that's all I'm asking rather than insisting that you don't know anything."

"This is pointless," Mark said, looking up from the book he was reading.

"Yes, although if you'd been more forthcoming about the Wealdway clue we might have finished this whole thing weeks ago."

"Can we please not go there again?" Alice asked.

"If you didn't bore on about things Brian I might have said something earlier," Mark said. "How many times do I have to apologise?"

"It might have been Joan, remember," Sandra said mildly. "She might be the link."

"I thought the Abba clue was for Joan," Ray said.

"We'll never know for sure though, will we?" Brian asked. "Of course if someone hadn't killed her…"

"How is this helping?" Mark asked, lowering his copy of Cathedrals of Britain. "Seriously Brian, does it help you think?

"All I'm asking is that Frank and Sandra agree that this is down to them," Brian said. "I couldn't care less if I'm annoying."

"And all I'm asking," Frank said, "for the hundredth time, is that you please…for the love of all that is holy, please stop going on about it you tedious, dim-witted…"

"Now Frank…" Sandra put a hand on his arm.

Frank brushed her away. "No I mean it. If he says one more word about us being the link."

Mark slammed his book down.

"Enough!"

"Yes, come on everyone this is giving me a headache." Alice said.

"I agree," Sandra said. "Brian, we've racked our brains trying to remember talking to Tom about anything to do with religion or war or seats, we really have so you don't have to remind us. We know that thing word for word, upside down and backwards, I promise, okay?"

Sandra pointed at the clue that was written out on a piece of flipchart paper and tacked to the wall.

In World War II, I saved a crew even though I'm only teeny,
And now I'm on the highest seat while prayers are said around me.
So, what am I? Look beneath the seat and the password you will see.

Mark knew the twee, cheerful tone of Tom's last clue grated on everyone's nerves but his frustration with it had reached new heights. Tom couldn't have known how things would turn out but everything seemed to irritate Mark now and whenever he read the clue he heard the words in a mocking singsong voice.

"Thank you Sandra," Brian said. "It's a shame your husband isn't capable of a civil answer but there we are. Perhaps…"

"Anyone for a cup of tea?" Ray interrupted.

"I'll give you a hand." Alice offered after everyone said yes.

They walked out together but when they returned with the tea things twenty minutes later Alice was holding a grubby looking envelope by its corner. She waved it in front of them looking flushed.

"Look what's arrived at last – I'd say it's definitely second class."

Brian thrust out a hand and grabbed it from her almost before she'd finished speaking. He painstakingly opened it and read the note it contained to himself, shaking his head before reading it again.

"Extraordinary." He muttered.

Rather than giving Brian the satisfaction of asking him what it said, Mark asked,

"Did it come with the post?"

"Must have done, it was just on the door mat. I spotted it as we were walking out of the kitchen."

"You guys were gone ages," Sandra said.

"Were we?" Alice asked. "I suppose we were chatting for a while weren't we Ray?"

Ray nodded.

"Doesn't anyone want to know what's in this bloody letter?" Brian demanded.

"Yes darling of course we do," Alice said.

"You could just hand it around." Mark said.

"Right…" Brian coughed and smoothed the letter out. "I will, but first here's what our blackmailer has to say for himself."

Brian coughed again and said, "I saw that vase you put up and I've been watching you so I know there's less of you there now. When you got the last one solved add one more vase to the window. Then I'll say what you got to do for a handover. I tell you now I got a gun so no tricks."

"Same old thing," Frank said dismissively.

"It's about time we heard from him." Ray added.

"Is that all you've got to say about it?" Brian asked.

"It's not as if it says anything new," Mark said. "Add a vase, I been watching you. Whatever."

"Nothing new - are you serious?" Brian demanded. "He says he's got a gun."

"He says a lot of things. It doesn't mean we should believe him," Mark said, picking up his book.

"What about the photo?" Sandra asked.

Mark shrugged. "Not sure yet but I've got a lot of reading to do."

"Haven't we all?" Alice sighed. "Well, at least we know where we stand – for what it's worth."

As Ray started handing around mugs of tea Mark pushed thoughts of the blackmailer aside. He was sure it was someone in the group and whatever happened he wasn't going to reward Joan's killer by handing over half their money.

Chapter Twenty-eight

A week after the letter arrived Mark walked upstairs to his apartment feeling relieved to be away from the others for the evening. He sipped from his whisky glass as he walked and swore as he felt something sharp cut his lip. Examining the crystal tumbler he saw the rim was badly chipped inside and he paused on the step, wondering whether to go back for a new glass. It was a small thing but he didn't want to have his one drink of the night, a good single malt, out of the cheap glasses he had in his kitchen. He couldn't face going back downstairs though after already saying goodnight to everyone - he'd rather risk cutting his lip. He rarely drank now partly through trying to stay sharp, but mostly because it would be too easy to sink into oblivion. Kirsty had been gone two weeks now and he missed her achingly. He'd even lost his appetite after layering heartbreak, anger and frustration on top of the stress he'd been living with for months already. Despite this he forced himself to refuel so he had the energy to put in the hours but it was hard going. He let himself into his apartment and clicked on the light switch. Nothing happened so he moved quickly towards the table lamp, managing to switch it on before the closing door extinguished the light from the hall. He put his glass down and sighed, overcome with grey exhaustion but not yet ready for sleep. He could feel the tension in his shoulders as he rubbed at his neck and he winced as he tried to loosen a knot at the top of his spine. What he needed was a good massage but he'd have to settle for a hot bath using some of the muscle-relaxing salts Kirsty had left behind.

The bathroom was steamed up and fragrant by the time Mark sank into the bath, chest deep in the warm water. The lemon verbena smell reminded him of Kirsty but he pushed the thought away, another of his strategies for getting through the day. He was so angry with her for breaking up with him the way she did but he was starting to understand why she'd had to leave. The tense atmosphere in the house was becoming unbearable and he'd noticed how people tended to cluster together after dark or stay in their rooms behind locked doors. He closed his eyes and took a deep breath trying to clear his mind, then relaxed as he felt tiredness seep over him. When he opened his eyes the water was the cold side of lukewarm and he had goose bumps on his exposed flesh. He grabbed for his phone and saw it was gone eleven and he'd been in there for nearly two hours. He stepped out of the bath and quickly dried himself before putting on a pair of pyjama bottoms and a tee shirt. He felt a little warmer but he was still shivering. Going through into the living room he picked up his drink and took it to bed. He was about to sip his whisky when he remembered his cut lip earlier. He turned the glass around and held it up to the light but he couldn't see the chipped area. Carefully feeling his way around the glass he realised the chip wasn't there. He was puzzled as he stared at the glass and after his long nap the implication of this took a while to register. When eventually it did, Mark threw the duvet aside and went into the living room to check he hadn't left another glass lying around. There was no other crystal tumbler to be seen so someone, unbelievably, must have replaced his drink.

He sat down and traced back his movements and then remembered the light not working when we walked in. He went to the door and sure enough he'd forgotten to lock it. He shivered again feeling thoroughly spooked by the thought of someone creeping into his room while he was asleep in the bath. Had they taken advantage of his unlocked door and the sounds of him running a bath or had they somehow planned it out. Either way it was hard not to take it personally. He looked at the glass and sniffed it cautiously but could smell only the pungent peaty fumes of his single malt. His mouth watered but there was no way he was going to taste it. Swirling the amber liquid around, he wondered what to do about it. He thought about going to confront the others but with a two-hour window it was difficult. He didn't want to give Sandra nightmares either as she'd been sleeping badly enough since her attack. On reflection he decided to wait until morning. Perhaps it was better to play dead and find out afterwards which of them was most anxious to know why he wasn't up. Mark went to the door to check it was locked and moved a kitchen chair against the doorknob for good measure. He longed to call Kirsty but if she did speak to him she'd tell him to leave and he'd come too far for that. Instead he covered the glass with cling film and put it in the fridge, then dragged himself to bed feeling overcome with exhaustion despite his long nap in the bath and recent adrenaline rush.

Mark woke with a start from a nightmare and fumbled for the alarm clock. It was six-thirty and he lay back down, his heart pounding. In the dream he'd been standing in his bathroom and calmly strangling Brian with the white and yellow striped shower curtain from the bathroom in his old house. Just as Brian stopped struggling, his face morphed into Frank's and Mark had strangled him with the same calmness. When Frank had slumped to the ground, Mark had let go of

207

the shower curtain and had been straightening it into place when he'd realised that Kirsty and Ray were watching him in the mirror. It was the contemptuous look on Kirsty's face and Ray's grin that had brought him gasping into wakefulness. It still seemed vividly real and he lay there for a while concentrating on the sound of the birds outside and trying to think about something else. It was a measure of how much the dream rattled him that it wasn't until he reached for the water by his bed that the memory of last night came back to him and he paused in mid-reach. Carefully maneuvering himself out of bed so as not to make a noise, he crept towards the door and looked out into his living room. The chair was still wedged in front of the door and although he felt relieved to see it, the sight of it brought back his feelings of isolation and fear from last night. He moved back into bed and drew the duvet tightly around him, burying his head under the covers.

The next time he woke up, he was stunned to see that it was nearly ten o'clock. He hadn't expected to get back to sleep at all but instead he'd managed to sleep more than he had in weeks. By now he would definitely have been missed. He hadn't turned up for the meeting they held at nine every morning where they matched up any interesting finds and gave each other leads to follow. The two couples were concentrating on memoirs and accounts by ordinary British soldiers rather than dusty accounts of battles and strategy or the International effort. They hoped to come across the account of a crew's lucky escape this way. Whenever they did, they passed on details of the regiment so that Mark and Ray could concentrate on the area that they were from. Similarly, any interesting Word War II war memorial Mark and Ray came across, they asked the others to try to track the history of the regiments from the area. Usually they found very little – or too much – online so the dining room now stank of musty old books and documents. Between them they had scoured second hand bookshops and bought hundreds of books. Ray also had thousands of brochures like the one Mark had bought in Swaffham church. All these things took time and the material they gathered was useless until it was read and digested whether in print or online. Unfortunately for them, the average church was oozing with history and held so many interesting things that something 'teeny' that dated back to the 1940s was unlikely to figure.

Mark felt anxious just thinking about it as he lay in bed and waited for someone to come and see what had happened to him. After another twenty minutes, he couldn't stand it anymore. He had too much to do to stay in his room playing dead. Being careful not to make any noise, he dressed quickly and crept downstairs and along the corridor towards the drawing room. There was no-one in there and he headed into the dining room where he could see Sandra stretched out on the window seat, an enormous pile of books on a chair beside her. Alice was at the table, absorbed in something she was looking at on the laptop and Brian was standing at the head of the table sorting his notes into piles. Mark interrupted their silent concentration as he walked in and said good morning in a loud voice. They all looked startled and Sandra, who was very twitchy these days, dropped her book in surprise. "Oh, hello. You made me jump," she said.

"Nice lie-in?" Brian asked, his voice heavy with sarcasm.

"Yes thanks. Where are Frank and Ray?"

Sandra looked uncertain at the coldness of his tone but said, "Frank's got a meeting with someone at the university and Ray's gone to the post office – he won't be long. Why…are you all right?"

Mark pulled out a chair and sat down heavily.

"Sort of," he said, wrong-footed by the concern in Sandra's voice.

"Mark, what's wrong?"

He told them what had happened and was sad to see the return of Sandra's troubled expression.

"Are you sure?" Alice asked.

"Short of sending the glass off to be analysed, I am," Mark said. "I've no idea what's in it but I know my glass was switched. I think someone might have drugged me at dinner too. I couldn't stay awake last night."

Brian looked unconvinced and asked, "Are you sure you weren't imagining the chip in the glass. If you were tired perhaps you were thinking of another night you took a drink up?"

"No. I haven't had a drink for a few days. I'm trying to stay focused."

"Well, aren't you the sensible one?" Alice asked.

"As I've said before, we need all the help we can get."

"Unwinding with a few drinks in the evening is probably the only thing stopping us from killing each other," Alice said. "Although, apparently not any more," she added with a laugh. "Anyway, the odd drink won't hurt."

"I thought whoever did it would be desperate to know if their plan worked. That's why I stayed up there for so long."

Yet again they were faced with the uncomfortable reality that there were only five of them for Mark to point the finger at.

"Well I didn't wake you because I thought you must need the sleep.

You haven't been looking very well." Sandra said. "As for Frank, he went into town and didn't even ask where you were. I think he was busy planning for his meeting. Ray said he'd wake you up when he got back."

"Obviously I don't need to account for Alice's movements." Brian said pompously.

"Well, Frank wouldn't have done something like that either, of course he wouldn't." Sandra paused. "Let's face it, if Frank were involved you would have found an empty glass not a different one."

There were times that Mark understood what Kirsty meant when she said they'd lost sight of who they were. He smiled at Sandra's joke, but part of him couldn't believe how casually they were discussing this while the rest of him itched to know who it was.

JUNE

Chapter Twenty-nine

There were five days left until access to Tom's website expired and for the last week they had all been working long hours into the night. Everyone was so sleep-deprived that at first Mark wondered if he was so tired that he'd started seeing things. He stood frozen in place at the entrance to the library where he'd gone in search of Ray. His question for Ray would have to wait though because instead of being busy with research he and Alice were enthusiastically kissing each other while Ray roamed his hands over her body. As her skirt rode up Mark saw Alice was wearing stockings and it was this intimacy that broke the spell. He crept backwards, desperate not to be seen but his arm knocked against the open door, which banged against the wall and thudded noisily. They sprang apart guiltily and Mark raised his hands and smiled apologetically.

"I've seen nothing," he said.

"Wait, Mark," Alice said. "Please. You can't tell Brian."

"I know." Mark just wanted to get away.

"He has no idea – you promise you won't tell him?"

"Alice, it's fine. Pretend you haven't seen me. Really," Mark said, already moving backwards.

"Hang on Mark, come and sit down," Ray said as he sank into an armchair. "Now you know about us there's something I need to tell you."

"Seriously, this is none of my business. I don't want to get involved."

"No, it's nothing like that. We're just having a bit of fun, aren't we darling?" Alice said to Ray as she perched on the arm of his chair. "We're just keeping each other company, no drama."

Ray gave her a fond smile before turning back to Mark. "Something like that. Listen Mark, it isn't about Alice and me, it's about the night Sandra was attacked. You'll want to hear this."

"Please Mark," Alice said.

"Okay, I'm listening," Mark said, coming into the room and leaning against the wall with his arms folded.

"Right, I didn't say anything at the time but I was with Alice the night Sandra was attacked. She was in my room."

"What, the whole time?" Mark asked.

"No, but we worked out Alice must have returned to her room just before Sandra came to find you. Once she'd regained consciousness."

"So you were lying there waiting for me to come in?" Mark asked.

"What? No, of course not. I put my headphones on as soon as Alice left so I didn't hear a thing."

"My room's at the other end of the house so I didn't hear anything either," Alice said. "Do you see what it means though Mark? Ray and I had an alibi, as did you with Kirsty and your creaking bedroom door. Brian was fast asleep, practically comatose, so it wasn't him either. Do you see?"

"Oh," Mark said after a moment. "Christ, that puts a different complexion on things."

Mark paced over to the window then turned to them. "Why didn't you say anything before?"

"Why do you think?" Alice said.

"But you could have told me, I wouldn't have said anything to Brian," Mark said angrily.

"Look, Ray wanted to talk to you about it but you know how Brian tries to press your buttons. I was worried you might hint at something next time he's having a dig. Anyway, there's nothing we can do, is there? Not until the blackmailer makes their demand."

"But we have to warn Sandra." Mark said.

"We're already all sleeping in separate bedrooms," Ray said. "We're preparing our own food and drink and we've got locks on our food cupboards."

"It's like living in a student house," Alice said. "Except I doubt even they have padlocked storage containers in the fridge. We're on our guard already. The other thing though, and this is the really tricky bit, we don't know for sure that Frank and Sandra aren't in it together."

"Not Sandra, no way." Mark sat down heavily, his chair at right angles to Ray's. "You didn't see her that night, not when she first came in. She was in a real state."

"We've gone around in circles with this and it's the only thing that makes sense," Ray said. "Although I agree it's hard to imagine Sandra being so devious."

"We think there are three options." Alice said. "Option one is you somehow rigged the creaking door, or Kirsty slept through the noise, so it was you."

"Thanks," Mark said.

"You know this isn't personal and anyway we don't think it is you. As for us, we know we were together at the time Sandra was being attacked."

"And I was asleep next to Kirsty."

"Okay, so if we agree that we're all out of the picture then it could be Sandra on her own. That's option two."

"Definitely not." Mark said shaking his head.

"Unlikely, but it's possible – she's an artist, remember. For all we know, she's a fantastic actress." Alice said. "Option three is that it's Frank and Sandra working together."

"Otherwise it's an outsider." Ray said. "But that doesn't add up."

Mark exhaled. "None of it adds up. Frank, yes – I already thought it was him because Brian doesn't have the imagination, no offence Alice." She shrugged and he continued. "To be honest, I already wondered if Frank's got sociopathic tendencies even without knowing this. His drunkenness that night rules him out though - he was practically unconscious by the time he got home."

"Which is why Sandra had to be working with him," Ray said.

Mark stood up. "I can't talk about this now – I need to give it some thought. Besides, you were right when you said there's nothing we can do about this for now. Let's just focus everything on solving the last clue and then we can decide what to do." Mark yawned and stretched which set the other two off. "Look, I know I said it wasn't my business but we've only got a few days left. Couldn't you arrange to…uh, keep each other company when this is all over?"

"That's rich coming from you! There was a time when you and Kirsty spent more time in bed than out of it." Alice said indignantly.

"We weren't having to sneak around though were we? Besides, that was in our downtime."

"Not how I remember it," Ray said. "Anyway, whatever - we don't need your judgment Mark and you're right that it's none of your business."

Mark rubbed his face and exhaled heavily. "I'm not judging, I'm just…look this is desperate times here. Make sure you're getting enough sleep, that's all I'm saying, so you can get through the next few days."

Alice sighed. "Don't worry, we'll get as much sleep as anyone else."

"Okay then. Good. I'll leave you to it. Ray, will you come and find me in the dining room later – I need your help with something."

"Fine I'll be there soon," Ray said and he shut the library door.

As Mark walked back down the corridor he exhaled deeply, annoyed that he had something else to think about now. The image of

Alice looking dishevelled, and the peep of flesh he'd seen above her stocking top flashed across his mind, erotic in its unexpectedness. He shook his head trying to clear the thought. Alice had great legs but he'd erase the sight as well as the knowledge about her and Ray if he could. She was right that he'd be tempted to say something to Brian too just to wipe the smug look off his face. He wouldn't, but as much because they couldn't afford the distraction than for her sake. Mark wished they were able to work in isolation but more than ever they had to share books and collaborate with each other. It was their last push to crack the clue in these final five days. On top of their own desperation to find the money, there was the blackmailer's threat to expose them if they didn't find it. If the old friend of Tom's really existed they had the stick as well as the carrot to motivate them.

A heavy framed picture on the wall knocked against Mark's elbow as he walked past and he shoved into it, tilting it so that it hung crookedly. He did the same to the gilded frame of the next picture and the next, and by the time he'd reached the end of the corridor he was breathing heavily, his frustration boiling over as he kicked out at a large ornate vase. The vase shattered as it smashed against the wall and Mark jumped as Sandra appeared beside him and put a hand on his arm.
"Oh Mark. I saw you from the drawing room. Is it Kirsty?"
"What? No, it's not Kirsty. Christ."
"Are you alright?"
"Oh, I'm amazing thanks Sandra. Really brilliant actually and how are you?"
Sandra removed her hand from his arm.
"There's no need to be sarcastic. That was a nice vase."
Mark looked at the delicate pieces of porcelain on the dusty floorboards and exhaled slowly.
"You're right, it was. Sorry."
Sandra shrugged. "It's nothing to me. It's Tom's estate people you'll need to apologise to. Fingers crossed Annie didn't have a phase of buying Ming vases hey?" She smiled uncertainly and Mark smiled back.
"Fingers crossed I'll be in a position to replace it if she did. Sorry Sandra. I was just letting off steam really, got a bit carried away."
"I think we're all at that stage now. Frank's a grumpy bugger at the moment and I'm all over the place. I had to go upstairs earlier as I had odd shoes on. Not that anyone noticed of course." Sandra gestured to her floaty sundress and long cardigan.
Mark smiled at her. There was no way Sandra was capable of killing

Joan or faking the attack. She just didn't have it in her, Mark was sure of it.

"How are you doing Sandra?"

"I'd repeat your answer to that question if I were being honest."

"Fair enough. Come on, let's get back to it shall we?"

They walked to the drawing room together, which now held the musty smell of books and old paper. This room and the dining room next door had effectively become their headquarters now. Pieces of flip chart paper were taped to the walls and there were piles of books lining the walls and general clutter everywhere. Mark and Ray had taken over one half of the dining room for churches and cathedrals and the others had taken over the drawing room and the rest of the dining room for their research on World War II. Ray had put a big bowl on the table that was filled with sweets, chocolates and empty wrappers, and there was a map of Sussex on the wall where he and Ray had concentrated most of their efforts. There were crosses all over it as they'd marked off churches with red or green pen depending on whether they'd visited or researched online. As well as local Sussex churches they'd eliminated all the Cathedrals now, visiting anywhere they knew Tom had a connection. They'd all done a lot of travelling for this last clue, but they had needed to be selective as they could only cover a fraction of the churches out there. Ray had focused on web research so Mark had visited most places by himself, visiting as many as twenty churches in one day and glad of the time alone despite the frantic pace.

"Look at this poor place," Sandra said. "Even I can't cope with this level of mess and I have very low standards." She half-heartedly picked up a few mugs from the tables and put them on a sideboard.

"We haven't got time to do it so it just keeps building up," Mark said with a shrug.

"There's no need for that though. Look." Sandra picked up a banana peel from the arm of a plush velvet sofa. "Seriously, that's disgusting. It's the broken window syndrome – do you remember how beautiful this room was?"

"It will be again. I'll book in that cleaning crew once everyone's left."

"Mark, can you believe it's nearly over. I really thought we'd do it too."

"Hang on, we're not having that conversation yet. We know how quickly we can get the answer once we're on the right track."

"If only we'd spotted that bloody ABBA clue," Sandra said bitterly. "We could have cracked that in a day. "

"We could have done this whole thing in a month if we'd had luck on our side."

"I know, but that one's on us – I even saw Mammia Mia in London. Listen Mark, I saw something odd yesterday and I've been wondering whether to say anything."

"Go on," Mark said and she tugged his sleeve and beckoned him over to the window in the corner.

"Right. I went up to get something from my room yesterday afternoon and I saw Alice..." Sandra looked over her shoulder and Mark's heart sank. He knew where this was going. "Well, I saw Alice letting herself into Ray's room and there was something about the way she straightened her clothes before she went in. She didn't knock either. I heard his voice through the open door and he sounded different. I'm not explaining myself very well but I'd say they're having an affair."

"Have you told Frank?"

"No. I wasn't going to tell anyone but it's been playing on my mind and I thought perhaps they're working together. All this blackmailer stuff, you know."

"Sandra, will you do me a massive favour," Mark looked at her. "Please don't say anything to Frank."

Sandra looked astonished, "I'm right then, am I?"

"About the affair yes, but not about them working together, at least I don't think so. I've only just found out myself – I walked in on them in the library."

"No way!" Sandra giggled. "Mrs High and Mighty? That's made my day."

Mark found he was grinning back at her, his earlier bad mood fading away. "The way she talks to him sometimes must be their cover."

"Ooh, I can just see her being all strict with him can't you? She'd definitely boss him around. 'Not there, there!'"

"Don't! You won't tell Frank though, will you?"

"No, I won't - Frank would tell Brian, he wouldn't be able to help himself." Sandra shook her head. "Well, well, well."

"Thanks Sandra - we just need to concentrate for these last few days. How are you getting on?"

"Oh you know, needle and haystack, all of that. How about you?"

"Same." He put his hands in his pockets. "We just need a lucky break though and it can all change."

"And how are you coping without Kirsty?"

"Fine thanks," Mark said casually and Sandra looked concerned.

"I know how much she thought of you," Sandra said. "It wouldn't surprise me if she feels differently about breaking up once this is all over."

Mark shrugged. "We'll see. I'm not really thinking about her, that's how I'm coping. Anyway, let's crack on shall we."

"Got it, subject closed for now." Sandra patted his arm. "Don't give up on her though Mark. It took a lot to walk away from this and from you but she was the sensible one really. I mean we're all of us living with someone who'll bump us off if they get the chance. It's hardly normal is it? She just prioritised staying alive over the possibility of being rich. It's sort of a no-brainer really."

"I understood that. I just didn't like the way she ditched me in the process. But, anyway…"

"Yes, back to it, I know. You are lovely Mark and just keep hanging in there, okay." Sandra held out her arms. "Come here."

Mark's tiredness combined with Sandra's hug and the affection in her voice gave him a lump in his throat. He swallowed his feelings away and patted her back as she held him.

"Thanks Sandra. You're lovely too."

She released him and held him at arms length. "Well, you know where I am if you need me. Especially now there's an older woman thing going on in the house."

Mark looked at her trying to work out if she was joking and was relieved when she laughed.

"Oh Mark, your face. Don't worry, Alice can pull off the femme fatale thing but it's not really my style. Besides, I'm Frank's girl through and through even if he does drive me mad sometimes."

"He doesn't deserve you Sandra, you know that don't you?"

"Of course I know that Mark but the heart wants what the heart wants. Unfortunately."

"Tell me about it."

Chapter Thirty

Mark put his mobile in the back pocket of his jeans and yawned widely thinking of his plans for the day ahead, the final day of Tom's treasure hunt. He was in his bedroom and his hands shook as he tried to button his shirt. He had dressed with extra care this morning, wearing the clothes he'd worn when he first met Tom. He thought of this as his lucky outfit, smart black jeans and a grey shirt that he'd owned for years but wore only occasionally. He'd even been wearing it when he'd first met Kirsty at the library and then again on the night they got together. Mark looked at himself in the mirror and barely recognised the face that stared back at him. When Tom told them all he wanted them to feel they'd earned the money, Mark didn't think this was what he'd had in mind. He wondered what Tom would think if he could see him now. He looked gaunt and his eyes were ringed with dark circles, with the blue irises unnaturally bright in their bloodshot setting. He hadn't shaved but it was more than stubble that made him look older - it was as though the last few months had rubbed away any remaining youthful softness. For a moment he bitterly regretted staying on after Kirsty left. Giving up his claim on the money would have changed everything between them but now it was likely he'd lost her and the money. He turned away in disgust. It still hurt too much to think about Kirsty and he pushed his feelings away for the thousandth time since she'd left. He moved through to the living room and looked out of the window. The sun was rising in a blaze of red and orange and it looked like it was going to be another gloriously hot day. His trousers and long-sleeved shirt were going to be much too warm and he considered changing them, but decided against it. At this stage, superstition was the only thing he had left.

He stepped in to the hall and locked the door behind him at exactly five-thirty. Ray was doing the same and Mark nodded to him, and to Brian who stepped out of his room as they passed. They waited in silence at the top of the stairs for the others to join them and Mark's eye was caught by the fiery sun glinting off the gold filigree on the six vases in the window ahead of them. He walked around the half circle of the banisters to the table in front of the window and stroked the vase nearest him. He felt tempted to throw it over the banisters just for the satisfaction of seeing it smash on the wooden floor below, but took a deep breath and looked out at the woods instead. Was it possible that an old man would train a pair of binoculars on the vases in the window today? Mark didn't think so but felt his stomach clench at the thought of having to handle the threats of the blackmailer on top of his own disappointment.

They had until midnight to work out the clue. After that, Tom's website would expire, along with the information that would tell them where the money was hidden. Seeing that Frank, Alice and Sandra had joined the others he walked back round and followed them down the stairs. In a pack they walked into the kitchen and each began preparing drinks, from hot water and lemon to bitter black coffee. Mark's stomach clenched at the thought of food but he waited while the others made something. Ray put a couple of pop tarts in the toaster and devoured another one straight from the packet while he waited for them to be ready.

"You know those aren't actual food, Ray?" Alice said with disdain. "Just sugar and e-numbers."

Ray shrugged. "They taste nice though."

Brian leant against the counter while he ate a bowl of shredded wheat but Mark wasn't the only one who couldn't eat. A few minutes later they were all seated around the long dining table looking expectantly at him. Brian logged on to his laptop, coughing loudly, and the sound grated on Mark's raw nerves. He didn't know what to say to them and his head throbbed as he waited for inspiration. Brian's coughing morphed into a wheeze that sounded like an engine starting and Mark breathed deeply as he waited for it to finish.

"This is our last day and we're long past rousing speeches because we all know what we've got to do. All we need is inspiration…and luck so just follow your instinct because the answer's got to be here somewhere." Mark gestured to the towering piles of books all around them.

There was a strangled noise and Mark looked over at Brian. His face was animated and he was staring at the screen of his laptop in disbelief.

"Message! It's a message from Tom."

Mark felt hope leap through him and reached for his phone. He scanned the messages on his Hotmail account and there between two junk mails was the real thing, a message from Tom Stevens, with the subject heading 'Need help?' Mark opened it and grinned broadly at the simple message.

"Ever been to Glasgow?"

Brian read it out and for a while it was as though the months of anxiety had never been. They were laughing delightedly, hugging each other and all talking at once. Sandra broke down in tears and was laughing and crying at the same time. Mark was as excited as the rest, but his mind was ticking over even as he shook Brian's hand and clapped him on the shoulder. They weren't there yet. When they had calmed down, Mark said,

"Okay, plan of action. Three of us go to Glasgow. Three stay here. Any volunteers to go?" There was silence and Mark waited, knowing the reason for the stubborn silence. Everyone wanted to stay so they were on site for delivery of the final password. Despite the small cream envelopes that Tom had given them so long ago that meant they needed to be together to work out the password, suspicions remained. The brief moment of trusting togetherness evaporated.

"Right, I'm staying here to co-ordinate everything. That means you have to go Ray, you're the other church expert. Brian, you go with him and you Sandra." At Brian's outraged response Mark immediately said, "fine, Ray, Alice and Frank then." There was more squabbling and Mark shouted above it. "No time for this. Three of you need to be in a car and on your way to Gatwick within ten minutes. Who's it going to be?"

After a moment's hesitation, Brian stood up. "It's all right Alice, I'll go."

"I don't mind going," Sandra said. "I've been to Glasgow before."

"Great, thanks. Have you got your passport so we can book your tickets?"

Ray proudly removed his passport from his back pocket and waved it at him and Brian took his from a pocket of his laptop case

"As instructed." Sandra said taking hers from her handbag. "Here it is."

"Okay. Leave them with us while you get yourselves ready. Ray, I'll get the information together on Glasgow churches."

The three of them hurried off while Frank searched for flights online and Alice booked a hire car for them at Glasgow airport.

Sandra was back downstairs first. She had changed out of her shift dress and sandals and was wearing dark cotton trousers with a blouse and waterproof jacket, paired with comfortable looking trainers. "Reporting for action," she said.

Mark looked up from the list of Glasgow churches that he and Ray had put together, and nodded.

"Looking good Sandra," he said.

Brian was down next in his usual light trousers and shirt but he'd changed into a battered-looking pair of brogues that Mark hadn't seen before and he carried an umbrella.

"Can I take your portable charger?" Brian asked Alice, who nodded as she finished making the booking. He checked it was stowed safely in his laptop bag then put a notebook and some pens into the pockets of the case.

Ray was next and bounced into the room wearing the same trainers, jeans and shirt he'd been wearing before. He had a rucksack slung over one shoulder and looked excited.

"Will you need a jacket?" Sandra asked. Ray turned around smartly and came back from the kitchen moments later with his jacket and a handful of chocolate bars.

"Just in case," He said, putting them into his bag.

Mark took the print outs listing Glasgow churches and handed Ray a copy along with a file of brochures and notes on Scotland. Ray took the unwieldy folder and crammed it into his bag.

"Okay, we won't be able to phone any of these until nine at the earliest, probably later, so read through them on the flight and decide where you're going to start. I'll be researching at this end."

"Cathedral first," Ray said as he zipped up the rucksack and Mark agreed. They always started with the Cathedrals and worked their way through the churches in order of significance.

Frank handed Sandra, Brian and Ray a print out of their boarding passes and their passports.

"You're booked onto the 8.35 from Gatwick so you should be there for ten by the time you've picked up your hire car." Frank turned to Sandra. "Good luck old girl. Have you got everything you need?" He asked.

She nodded and patted her bag.

"Right then, let's go shall we." Brian said, jingling his car keys impatiently. The three of them left in a whirl of good byes and Mark, Alice and Frank watched as the wheels of Brian's dusty looking Jaguar spat out gravel and he roared down the drive.

Mark looked at his watch. Unbelievably it was only ten past six, which left them nearly eighteen hours to input the password to the final clue and access the location of the money. Mark felt adrenaline course through him. It was enough. The three of them would be able to cover Glasgow in that time, while Mark, Frank and Alice supported them online and by phone, eliminating churches where they could, and perhaps even being able to get the answer themselves.

*

Mark's phone rang and he fumbled with it in his race to answer the call. It was Sandra and she sounded out of breath,
"We're just coming into arrivals. The bloody plane was delayed…"
"Sandra…"
"We sat on the tarmac for an hour at Gatwick …"
"Sandra, we've got the password!" Mark shouted.
From the sound of it Sandra had dropped her phone. He heard a clatter and then Sandra swearing and her shout to Brian and Ray to stop.
"Mark, are you there?"
"Yes, I'm here." Mark laughed. "I spoke to a woman at Glasgow Cathedral and she told me all about it. You need to go straight to departures. Frank has booked flights for you with BA. He's checked you in and emailed your boarding passes through so you just need to grab a coffee and you're all set."
The others were obviously standing next to her and as Mark had expected, the next voice he heard was Brian's.
"What's happened?" Brian asked.
After making sure he was already headed towards the ticket desk, Mark gave him a brief outline.
"So what's the answer?"
"It's a ladybird." Mark said. "I spoke to a woman at Glasgow Cathedral and she got it straight away from the clue."
"I thought you and Ray had contacted all the Cathedrals."
"We did. The old guy I spoke to when I rang before didn't know anything about it."
"Well, you should have called back then. I would have thought…"
Mark felt his temper rising. "Ray and I were busy checking the other thousands of churches at the time. We've got the answer now, why are you going on about it?"
"Yes, alright Mark. Sorry. It's just a bit of a shock, that's all. I thought we'd never get off that plane and now…well, it's great news, really great." Mark couldn't remember hearing Brian apologise before.
"It's okay. We're the same here. Just get back as soon as you can and we'll get this over with."
"Hang on, Ray wants a word."

Ray whooped down the phone and Mark held the phone away from his ear, grinning broadly.

"We've done it." Ray shouted. "I can't believe it. What was the answer?"

"Ladybird. It turns out the teeny thing was a ladybird."

"And, what was our bit?"

"Are you on the move?" Mark asked.

"Yes, just following Brian and Sandra. Go on, what was the churches bit?"

"The woman I spoke to said a torpedo boat crew found a ladybird on board and decided it was a lucky omen. Then everyone survived the boat being hit so..."

"Right, and our bit?"

"After the war they gave a chair to the Cathedral with a ladybird carved underneath. That's the highest seat, prayers are said around me bit."

"Brilliant – at least we were on the right track. Shame we didn't get her last time." Ray said. "Wait, what if there's something else under the chair. Tom said to look underneath - it might be the carver's initials or something. We can probably be in an out of the city within an hour or so."

"I don't think you need to Ray. The woman I spoke to was great. I told her how important it was and she called me back. She said she looked underneath with a torch and there was nothing but the ladybird."

"God, I can't believe it. This is amazing!" Ray sounded excited again. "Okay, we're heading for security. I'll ring again when we land. See you later!"

Mark put the phone down and realised that Alice and Frank were standing just behind him.

"You think they'll catch the flight?" Alice asked.

"They should do. With luck they should be back in three hours."

"If only they hadn't gone." Alice said despondently.

"What is it with you and Brian?" Mark asked. "Talk about glass half empty. If they hadn't gone and I'd got the useless old bloke again, we'd have been really stuck, wouldn't we?"

"There's no need to talk to me like that," Alice said haughtily.

There was every need in Mark's opinion but in the interest of getting through the next few hours, he apologised.

"Look we've got a few hours to spare and for the first time in months we've properly got nothing to do." As Mark said it, he realised how much it felt like a weight had been lifted. He rotated his shoulders and stretched, feeling wonderful.

"Mark?" Frank said.

"Hmm?"

"You were saying…"

"What? Oh, sorry I was just thinking. There's nothing we can do now except wait for them. I didn't sleep well last night so I'd rather go for a nap than pace the floor until they come back."

"Go for it. I'm going to go and have some proper breakfast now. I'm starving." Frank said.

"I think I'll go and have a lie down as well." Alice said with a yawn.

Mark let himself into his apartment and automatically locked the door behind him. He sank onto his sofa and sighed. He wanted to tell someone, anyone, Kirsty especially, that they had got the answer. It had been such a monumental moment when the woman at the Cathedral told him about the ladybird, and so inadequate that he had only the others in the group to share it with. The truth was that he could never tell anyone but that was a small price to pay compared to what he stood to gain. Mark had already researched the Swiss Banking system in preparation for reaching this far and one of the first things he planned to do was go to Zurich. With the bearer bonds cashed in and the money safely hidden, he would be free to start his new life. Mark felt exhausted, the weeks of sleep deprivation taking their toll, and his eyes felt gritty and sore. He shut his eyes for a moment and thought of Kirsty, wondering whether to contact her before or after he'd been to Switzerland.

He was startled from sleep by an insistently shrill noise that reverberated though his sluggish mind.

"Where are you?" Mark asked, still stupid from sleep.

Realising what the sound was, he reached forward to where his mobile was vibrating against the coffee table, wincing at the pain flaring in his numb leg.

"Hello?" He said groggily.

"Mark, we're here. Come downstairs. Quick!" Ray said.

Mark looked at his watch and saw it was half-past two. He'd been asleep for four hours. He rubbed his eyes.

"Just coming. Give me a minute." He disconnected and tried to stand up but his leg was now burning from pins and needles. He stood on his good leg and touched the floor with his incapacitated leg, swearing loudly at the pain. He was impatient to find out what was happening and continued touching the floor until the agony subsided enough for him to lurch towards the door.

By the time he got downstairs he was fine and he strode into the drawing room feeling refreshed and full of energy. Sandra was the first to see him and she ran towards him and wrapped him in a hug.

"Isn't it wonderful?" She asked.

Ray was almost hopping with excitement behind her and thumped Mark's shoulder.

"Bloody Glasgow Cathedral hey?" Ray said. "All those little churches we looked at."

"We've got the website up Mark," Brian said, "just need to type in the password."

"Can I do it?" Sandra asked. "I haven't done it yet."

"Go for it." Mark said and she flung herself into the chair in front of the laptop.

Once there she flexed her hands and painstakingly typed 'ladybird' into the box headed 'Next Password'. She looked around at the rest of them who were crowded around her.

"That's right isn't it?"

The password appeared in the box as eight asterisks and Brian said, "I'd be on the safe side and do it again. I couldn't see what buttons you pressed."

Sandra typed it again, with Brian leaning over the keyboard and she was almost hyperventilating by the time she'd typed the final letter.

She pressed enter and a letter from Tom appeared on the screen. She read it out in a quavering voice and Mark scanned it over her shoulder,

Congratulations and well done! I knew you would do it even if you needed a little help in the end. I mentioned to all of you at one point or another that I've always been fascinated by the secrets our country holds. Do you remember? Perhaps it was the most subtle hint of them all but if you look in my study you'll find a copy of 'Secret Britain' that you would have found useful.

Sandra paused and looked pointedly at Brian. He shrugged. "Well, you and Frank did know even if you weren't the only one that Tom told." She rolled her eyes and continued reading,

I always liked the story of the lucky ladybird and it seemed a good note to finish on. I hope you've enjoyed your treasure hunt as much as I enjoyed putting it together. You all brought so much to my last months and it was a nice surprise to have new friends at a time when I most needed them. I wanted to give you a nice surprise in return so you'll find more money than you expected. I said there was five million pounds in bearer bonds but I didn't mention the cash I managed to get together too." Sandra's voice shook and there were gasps of amazement from the faster readers among them. *"It's harder than you'd think to make two million pounds disappear, but I'm sure you'll think it was worth the effort.*

"Seven million quid." Ray sounded awestruck. "Is he saying there's seven million quid?"

"Between six of us," Brian said, rubbing his hands together.

Sandra continued reading the rest of the letter aloud and repeated the last line,

"Before you carry on, make sure you've got those envelopes I gave you to hand."

There was the sound of paper being unfolded. Mark had his and Joan's, Alice had hers and Tony's and Sandra had Kirsty's as well as her own.

"Are we ready?" Sandra asked breathlessly.

Mark nodded and Sandra pressed the button that showed them where they needed to go to find the money. The screen seemed to take an age to reveal itself and Mark realised he was holding his breath. He hoped the location wasn't too far away. A map was revealed and Mark craned forward, along with all the rest. In the jostling and bumping, he couldn't see it clearly but he heard Sandra's yelp of surprise.

"It's here! He's marked the house."

Sure enough, the large-scale map showed the woodland surrounding the house and to the right was the name of the adjoining farm. The Manor was shown, although not named, and had a circle around it.

Mark felt excitement course through him and remembered the instructions that Tom had given him

"Right, the final step is to open our envelopes and the longest password will give us the exact location."

"The money's been here all the time," Ray said. "I can't believe it."

Frank rubbed his hands together. "Good old Tom. He told us it would be safe."

They opened their envelopes and put the nine pieces of paper on the dining table. Each page had three words on it, the password at the top and duplicates below of two other passwords. Mark sat down in front of the paper and wrote a list of the nine passwords with the number of letters noted next to it. When he had finished, he scanned the list of castles. "It looks like it's Knaresborough," Mark said. "Does someone else want to check through, make sure I haven't made a mistake?"

Brian sat down next to him and grabbed for the page immediately, repeating the process of listing the passwords with the number of letters noted next to each word.

"Agreed, Knaresborough it is."

"Whose was that?" Alice asked.

"Kirsty's." Mark said. "Right, are we ready?"

Sandra carefully typed in 'Knaresborough'.

The screen changed again and this time all that was revealed was a number.

295710

Frank was the first to speak. "What the hell is that supposed to mean?" There was a pause before Sandra said, "It could be co-ordinates on a map, the map on the last screen maybe but I don't…"

"The vault!" Ray shouted triumphantly. "Tom told us he used to keep the money in the vault. He never moved it."

Brian groaned. "Why didn't we guess that before?"

"Good one, Ray," Mark said. "That has to be right." They were minutes away now. Everyone started moving towards the kitchen, eager to see that the money really existed.

They walked to the cellar door which creaked as it opened revealing a flight of white-painted stone steps. Brian reached in for the light switch and they descended in silence. Mark had been down here before to fetch wine and had always been in and out as quickly as possible. The vast emptiness and gloomy atmosphere made the hairs on the back of his neck prickle and for once he was glad the others were there. The cellar's musty smell tickled his nostrils and he sneezed loudly.

"Bless you," Sandra said automatically.

Shelves that could hold thousands of bottles held less than a hundred, and the room seemed to throw back muffled echoes of their voices as they whispered among themselves. After walking the perimeter of the room, they found a narrow corridor where the light barely penetrated. There was another small oak door at the end of the room and Mark was relieved to see a large key in its lock. Brian reached the door first and turned the key eagerly, opening the door with a flourish and stepping through.

"Shall I go and get a torch?" Ray asked.

"Hang on, there's got to be a light switch somewhere," Brian said, brushing his hand up and down the wall. A moment later the small room was flooded with flickering light from an overhead fluorescent strip.

"From one extreme to the other," whispered Sandra. They could see the small room was dominated by a large grey safe and they moved towards it in a huddle. The atmosphere in the small room seemed to hum with their combined nervous energy and Mark found himself wiping sweat from his brow despite the cold air. He swallowed with difficulty, his mouth dry, as he bent down to the safe. There was silence and his hands trembled as he set the dial to zero and began moving the dial in the combination that Tom had given them. He moved the dial back to zero as the last move in the sequence and closed his eyes for a moment before trying the large lever. There was a loud clunk and the safe door opened.

Chapter Thirty-one

The kitchen windows were open but the heat of the day still clung to the people seated around the table. They were unusually quiet as they stared at the nine heavy holdalls on the table. Eight bags each contained quarter of a million pounds. Brian and Frank had counted out the money from one of the bags, riffling the bricks of twenty-pound notes and placing them neatly side-by-side. The ninth bag contained a thick stack of bearer bonds and box after box of heirloom quality jewellery. They had opened some of the boxes but it was difficult to work out how to divide these between them. Alice had volunteered to go online for a rough idea of their value but this had led to an argument and they put the boxes to one side ready to sort them out later. Ray entered the room and Mark was reminded that this wasn't the only thing left to do.

"I've put the last vase in the window," Ray said. "I'll bet he was watching, he knows that today is the deadline."

Mark thought that there was very little chance of that but as he'd nearly been poisoned the last time he'd voiced his scepticism, he kept his thoughts to himself.

"So, what now?" Alice asked.

"We wait." Mark shrugged. "I'm sure the blackmailer won't waste any time, he'll be as keen to get this over with as we are. Let's get the two and a half million together so that we're ready."

They counted out a sheaf of bearer bonds and carried the remaining four and a half million down to the cellars, locking the bags of cash and the remaining bonds back in the safe. Mark removed the key to the door and asked everyone to follow him into the drawing room, carrying the bag of jewellery with him.

"If someone wants the money badly enough to kill for it, I'm guessing that burglary won't be a problem."

"At least we're all on our guard." Alice said.

"I'm keeping the blackmailer's money on me and I'll stay in sight of you all. From now on I think we all need to base ourselves here where we can see the key." He stood on a chair in front of the fireplace and, using his full reach, was just able to place the key on top of a large picture frame.

Alice put the jewellery boxes reverentially on the largest coffee table before straightening the richly coloured boxes and lifting or removing their lids. Trying to value the jewellery gave them something to do and for a while they just stared at the contents of the thirty or so boxes laid out before them.

"How do you work out what's worth more?" Brian asked. "I haven't got a clue about any of it but we need to make sure it's fair."

Alice lifted a beautiful emerald and diamond necklace out of its box and as she did the lining of the box came out revealing a receipt tucked underneath.

Frank grabbed the receipt from the box and opened it with great ceremony.

"Right, here you go Brian - guess how much. It's platinum, emerald and diamond. It's from Boodles if that means anything to you and the emerald's 2.74 carats. What do you reckon?"

Brian looked bemused. "Five thousand, something like that."

"Nope. Anyone else?"

"Twenty thousand," Alice said confidently.

"Not even close," Frank said. "Sixty thousand."

"No way," Ray said. "Just for that?"

"It's stunning," Sandra said. "It's really delicate though, I can't believe it cost all that. What about this one?" Sandra picked out a diamond bracelet from a Van Cleef & Arperls box. She lifted the lining and unfolded the receipt. "It's a magic Alhambra bracelet in white gold and diamond, 5.64 carats. Oh my god, guess how much?"

"Ten thousand?" Brian suggested.

"Thirty-seven thousand." Sandra said. "Just for this little thing. Look how it sparkles though." She held it up to a shaft of light from the late afternoon sun and a rainbow of dots appeared on the wall next to her as she moved it.

"How are we going to do this?" Mark asked. "We can work out the costs of everything and then divide it up or we can take it in turns to pick something we like and then add up if we've got roughly the same. I don't mind but I think we need to make a start."

"Can we pick what we like and then see what we've got? That sounds like fun." Sandra said.

"We'll need to draw lots about what order we go in." Brian said.

"Fine. Has anyone got a pen?" Mark grabbed a piece of paper and tore it in to strips, scribbling numbers one to six, before offering them around.

"Right, we'll go around once in that order and then whoever was last goes first next round and we do it in reverse order. Does that seem like a plan?"

They agreed and opened their pieces of paper.

"I'm first." Alice said delightedly.

"Get the emerald necklace." Brian said at once.

Alice looked at him. "You get it if you want it. I like the look of that." She picked up a diamond tennis bracelet in a distinctive red box.

"Lovely. I've always wanted something from there."

"You're not shopping Alice." Brian said sounding exasperated. "You're supposed to be choosing the best option."

"Well, if you knew anything about jewellery you'd know this isn't a bad choice." She opened the receipt. "Thirty-seven thousand apparently and over six carats of very sellable diamonds. Anyway, I might just keep it as a little reward to myself." She put the bracelet on and waved her wrist at him.

"I'm next." Frank said grabbing the emerald necklace. "Sorry Brian."

"You would take that one wouldn't you." Brian said.

"Look, we'll have to swap things around if it doesn't all balance up, so there's no point arguing about it now." Mark said.

Brian shook his head when Frank winked at him but he said nothing. It was Sandra's turn next and she chose a colourful necklace from Bulgari.

"I love this. It's like something from the middle ages." She looked at the receipt. "The Allegra necklace. Oh, twelve and a half thousand. Well I don't care. This might be my treat to myself."

"Can you believe that twelve grand doesn't seem like much now." Ray said with a laugh. "All I know is that diamonds are worth the most and I've heard of Tiffany's so I'm going for that." He picked up a delicate diamond cluster necklace and looked at the receipt. "Yes!" He punched the air. "Seventy-nine thousand. Take that Frank!" He waved it in his face and laughed again.

It was Mark's turn next and he went for a small, shabby looking box from Garrard containing an art deco diamond brooch.

"I'll have that one." The receipt was tucked underneath the pin of the brooch and Mark opened it carefully.

"Six carats. Forty-three thousand. Sounds good."

Brian was the last to go and he looked at the boxes on the table for a while before turning to Alice.

"What do you think of these two?" He pointed to a bracelet made of fat rubies and an emerald and diamond necklace that was next to it."

Alice nodded. "Either of those, yes."

They went round in turn until all that was left was an unassuming turquoise and amethyst brooch which went to Frank.

"Even this costs nearly six thousand. This Bonham's receipt says it's Asprey, from the Sixties."

They spent the next hour playing a kind of monopoly game with the jewellery. If Ray's Tiffany & Co diamond necklace was Mayfair and Frank's vintage turquoise brooch was Old Kent Road then most of the other pieces were somewhere in between the two. They stuck post-it notes to each box and swapped with each other until finally they were satisfied. Mark stretched and moved over to the window. He thought how much Kirsty would have enjoyed what they'd just done. If only she'd stayed on. He smiled ruefully as he realised that even now he'd chosen pieces with her in mind. The art deco brooch had reminded him of her diamond watch, except the diamonds were much, much bigger. He wondered if she'd ever see any of it. Mark was staring at the hills in the far distance, not really seeing the view, but something caught his eye near the Lodge House at the same time as he registered the noise of a motorbike. His position next to the window meant he was the first to see the black-leather clad motorcyclist roaring up the drive. He threw himself across the room, righting himself as he nearly tripped over Ray's legs, and raced to the front door. The others were following, shouting for him to open the door. Mark heard the thump of something being thrown against the door but before he could turn the key he heard the growl of the motorbike revving as it sped back down the drive. Mark yanked the door open and looked out to see the back wheel of the motorbike turn the corner past the Lodge and disappear.

Mark bent down, his heart racing, and picked up the small jiffy bag. He ripped it open as he walked back to the drawing room, keen to return within sight of the key and the money even though everyone else was in the hallway with him. Inside the bag was a single page with their instructions printed in large letters. He read them out, ignoring the inevitable spelling mistakes.

"Get the short fat bloke to deliver the cash at eight tonight. I want him to come alone. Drop the money in the woods opposite the house at the bottom of the hill. If anyone follows I'll shoot him. I mean it. I want everyone else to sit where I can see them in the big window downstairs - the one below the honeysuckle. I'll be watching and if there aren't five bodies there I'll shoot him. Don't try anything."

"Are you all right with that Frank?" Mark asked.

"What? He must mean Brian, I'm not fat." Frank said, attempting to suck in his paunch.

"Come on Frank, you're definitely the shortest. Still if you want Brian to go instead…" Mark said, deliberately testing him.

"I'm not bloody going if he's asked for Frank. Anyway, I'm nowhere near as fat as Frank, it's obviously him." Brian said.

"I think we have to do as he asks, it won't do to antagonise him."

"Oh that's nice Alice." Sandra said. "You don't want Brian to go but it's all right for Frank to go."

"I don't think it's wise to send someone else that's all."

There was an awkward silence and Frank looked at them all in turn.

"So, you're saying I've got to go down there." He shook his head. "What if I don't want to? That wasn't him on the bike was it?" He sounded nervous.

"I don't know." Mark said.

"He might have an accomplice." Brian said.

"Great. That's just great. Why me?" Frank asked.

"Good question." Mark said.

There seemed no more to be said and the atmosphere was tense now that the anonymous messenger gave credence to the blackmailer being real. Mark still couldn't believe that Tom would have told someone else but the evidence of the photo and the motorcyclist together meant he couldn't rule it out.

"Frank, I'm sure it will be fine. He just wants the money and I bet he doesn't really have a gun."

"Easy for you to say. You're not the one who's going to have to walk into the woods knowing he's in there waiting."

"You'll do it then?" Mark asked.

"Yeah, I'll do it. The only thing is he said he wanted half. What if Tom told him how much there really was? With the extra cash I mean."

"Why would he have done that?"

"Why would he have told him about it in the first place? Look, it's my neck on the line I'm not going out there without half, like he asked for."

"But…what give him three and a half million? No, there's no need for that." Ray said sounding shocked.

"I'm not doing it then." Frank said firmly. "I'm not taking any chances. Anyway, we're still better off than we thought we were. Before today we thought we'd be sharing out two and a half million once we'd paid off the blackmailer. This way, we're safe and we still get an extra million to share."

Mark sat down trying to keep his face expressionless. So, Frank was the blackmailer, of course he was. There was no other explanation for him of all people wanting to hand over half their money.

"It's all right Frank, don't worry. The blackmailer mentioned two and a half million in his last note to us." Mark made himself sound as reassuring as possible.

"Did he? Oh I'd forgotten that. Well, that's all right then. Anyway, how would I have carried all that cash?" He let out a great belly laugh. "I tell you what though, if the bastard hasn't got a gun and I get hold of him, he's had it. Not only ripping us off, but calling me a short fat bloke – insult to bloody injury that is."

There were murmurs of laughter and although Sandra was uncharacteristically quiet, the atmosphere lightened considerably. They had three hours to wait and they needed to stay together. After a while they were itching for something to do to fill the time. Layers of smoke from Ray's cigarettes hung in a blue cloud in a corner of the sunlit room and as a fat honey bee droned noisily outside the window, Mark realised he couldn't stand another minute in the stale room.

"Why don't we go and sit outside? We can put some blankets out."

All of them had the unnatural pallor of people who'd spent too much time indoors and they greeted the idea enthusiastically. By the time they had found blankets and grabbed something to eat from their cupboards, half an hour had passed. Mark stretched out on his blanket and soaked up the feeling of the sun on his face. He should be wearing his shorts but he wasn't going to take off his lucky clothes now. He took a swig of his water – it was a poor substitute for the beer he wanted, but he knew he needed to keep his head clear. Blotting out the sound of the others talking, he went over his plan for the handover.

By ten to eight they were back inside and Frank was pacing up and down the drawing room and muttering to himself.

"Are you sure you don't want to take my rucksack?" Sandra asked

"Stop fussing!"

"I was only…. sorry. How will you carry everything though?" Sandra asked.

"In my hands. Christ, it's only a folder of bearer bonds I'm carrying not bags of bloody silver."

Sandra kept quiet after that and returned to her post in front of the window. Mark was there too, looking out towards the Lodge House and the woods.

"Here put the folder in this." Mark handed him an empty holdall. "It's traditional, right Sandra?"

"Fine." He shoved the folder inside. "Right, I'm going to get going." The five of them wished him good luck then moved to the window seat in the corner of the room where the honeysuckle hung heaviest on the wall outside. Mark waited until they were all sat down before squeezing next to Sandra so that he was on the end nearest the corner of the room. By taking a casual walk when they were outside earlier Mark had worked out that it was the one blind spot in the window, especially when seen from the woods.

"Come back soon and don't do anything silly," Sandra said, tears falling down her cheeks.

Frank nodded and waved the bag at her, then squared his shoulders and left the room without a word. Everyone else sat stiffly on the window seat, straining to hear the sound of the kitchen door closing.

"I hate this," Alice whispered after a while. "We're like sitting ducks here if he does have a gun."

"Thanks for pointing that out, Alice," Ray said shifting uneasily in his seat. "Something else to worry about."

"Oh, you must have thought of it, surely," Alice said. "It was the first thing that crossed my mind when Mark read the letter out."

"No, I was thinking more about someone stealing..."

"Right, two minutes," Mark said, looking at his watch. "that's long enough." He edged away the window seat, careful not to move the curtains.

"What the hell are you doing?" Brian asked.

"I'm going after him."

"Mark, no you can't," Sandra wailed. "It's not safe. He said he'd kill Frank if..."

"Stop moving," Mark hissed. "He's safe as long as you sit still. You can't see my bit of the window from the woods."

"But..."

"Look Sandra, it's time to face facts. Either Frank's the blackmailer in which case we save the money, or he isn't. If he isn't, I promise you I won't get close enough to put him in danger, but at least we'll know. I'm sorry, but I've got to know."

Sandra looked shocked and then she smiled and shook her head. "It's not Frank, it can't be." She looked around at all of them but nobody looked at her. "Mark, there's no point in what you're doing. Please don't..."

Mark moved away from the window using the furniture to shield himself as he moved towards the door.

"Be careful Mark," Brian said. "If you're wrong…"

"I don't think I am," Mark said as he reached the door. He ran down the corridor and skidded to a halt before the back door of the kitchen. He inched it open then ran in a straight line up the slope towards the woods at the back behind the house. By the time he reached the safety of the woods, he was already out of breath but he kept going, crashing through undergrowth and causing startled birds to rise up out of the trees as he skirted the edge of the woods. Once he could see the house to his left he slowed down and began moving more carefully. With luck Frank's slower pace meant he wouldn't be too far ahead. Mark stopped and used the trunk of an enormous oak tree to cover himself as he peered down the hill towards the Lodge.

Frank was still only half way down and was moving at a sedate pace as though keen not to arrive early. As Mark watched, he stopped and turned around, looking back at the house.

Mark paused and then once Frank started walking again he resumed his steady jog. He slowed as he got closer to the bottom and once he saw the Lodge House crept forward stealthily tree by tree, being careful not to make any noise. He could hear Frank as he crashed through the undergrowth diagonally ahead of him and followed his movements easily. The blackmailer had instructed Frank to leave the money on an old picnic table near the edge of the woods and to Mark that meant dropping the bag off and getting the hell away. As Frank moved deeper into the woods, far away from the drop-off place, Mark knew he was right about Frank and he abandoned caution, running closer until he could see him a few trees to his right. Frank had stopped in front of a hollowed out rotting tree trunk and dumped the bag to the ground. The noise sounded unnaturally loud in the dark leafy gloom of the woods and Mark moved forward warily. He watched him reach inside the dead tree trunk and remove a spade and a sheet of plastic. Suddenly, Frank swung around.

"Who's there?"

Mark ducked his head out of the way just in time and waited, hardly breathing. He could hear his blood pumping in his ears and jumped as a crow cawed loudly as it flew overhead.

After a moment, he heard a chuckle and the scrape of the spade clanking against a stone as it bit into the earth. He inhaled slowly, trying to calm his breathing, and smelt the cold musty earth as Frank dug more deeply. He wondered what to do next. The rational thing would be to go back to the house and wait, ready to confront Frank who would most likely arrive pretending to be terrified after his ordeal. Just the thought of that made Mark's fists clench. When Frank began whistling a jaunty tune, instinct took over and Mark strode towards him with months of built up frustration behind him. As Frank turned to face him, Mark ran straight at him and drove him to the ground in a fierce rugby tackle. Frank lay winded on the ground and looked up at Mark in astonishment.

"Come on, get up." When Frank didn't move, he shouted at him. "Up! Get up."

Mark was breathing heavily, wrestling with the urge to kick the prone man at his feet. If anyone deserved to be kicked when they were down it was Frank but he looked pitiable lying there with a bewildered expression on his face.

"Mark, it's not what it looks like."

"What, you got lost did you?"

Frank gestured that he was trying to get up. "Let me explain."

"You're digging a hole and whistling instead of dropping off the money. There's nothing you can say you greedy bastard."

Frank held his hand up and started moving feebly.

"I think you might have hurt me," he said. "When you attacked me."

"You're pathetic." Mark spat at him, turning away in disgust. Frank moved faster than Mark would have thought possible and rolled over, lifting the spade that lay beneath him in one swift movement. Mark heard the sound and turned around but he was too late to stop the spade crashing into his leg. A starburst of agony exploded in his knee and reverberated in his skull as he went down. He landed badly on a twisted tree branch that jabbed his kidney so hard he felt a flare of pain that threatened to overwhelm him. Dimly he was aware of Frank standing over him.

"Now who's pathetic?" Frank taunted, lifting the spade over his head.

Despite the pain, adrenaline helped Mark ignore his aching body, and he rolled towards Frank knowing that attack was his only chance. The movement made him feel sick but it had the desired effect of making Frank step back and adjust aim. Those few seconds were all Mark needed. He reached behind him for the twisted branch that had caused him so much pain and swung back with it as hard as he could at Frank's shins. The branch connected with a satisfying thud and Mark heard Frank's yelp of pain at the same time as he heard the whistle of the spade passing his ear. Frank had put so much force behind the blow that the blade was buried deep in the packed earth of the floor. If he hadn't moved it would have killed him. A mix of fury and shock fuelled Mark at Franks intent and, taking advantage of the gasping man's frantic attempts to free the spade, Mark stood up and slammed a fist into his face, putting everything he had behind the blow.

Mark had done some boxing training at the gym but he was as surprised as Frank by the sharp crack of the nose breaking as Frank fell to the floor. He kicked him in the ribs once, using the tree branch to balance, then kept his distance in case Frank came round. Mark watched him for a while as he caught his breath. The sun was starting to go down and there was no heat in the few rays that penetrated the gloom. As his heart rate returned to normal he started to feel spooked by the shadows and the rustling noises around him. His knee was throbbing too and he shivered, feeling chilled and disoriented. He cursed the lack of phone signal and checked the screen again but knew he had to deal with Frank himself. He hadn't brought anything to tie him up so he removed his belt and hunkered down as best he could, grimacing with pain. Mark buckled the belt tightly around Frank's wrists and lower arms then used Frank's much bigger belt to tie his knees together. He lifted Frank's eyelids carefully and sighed in relief when he saw the whites of his eyes - he was still out. It was tempting to leave him and fetch help but he didn't want to risk Frank coming round. Instead, he braced himself and began the slow, painful process of dragging Frank to the edge of the woods and towards the others back at the house.

Chapter Thirty-two

Frank sat at the kitchen table, holding a packet of frozen peas to his nose, with Brian, Ray and Alice sitting at the opposite end of the table. Sandra was in the chair next to him, her face blotchy with tears and Mark was standing by the sink, rubbing his neck and trying to stretch out his overworked shoulders and back. He swallowed a couple of painkillers and knocked back another glass of water.

"Why? I don't understand why you did it." Sandra asked. Frank ignored her, as he had the previous times she'd asked, and stared sullenly ahead. It was fully dark now and the lights were on in the kitchen, illuminating the bruises around the eyes that were already forming on Frank's unusually pale face. It had taken Mark a long time to drag Frank through the woods and he had been sweating heavily and cursing the man's bulk by the time Frank started to come round. They had made it out just as the sun was setting over the hills in the far distance and Mark had finally got a phone signal once they were in sight of the house. He had been relieved to see Ray pounding down the hill towards them with Brian trailing behind and Mark had left them to frog march Frank back to the house while he limped behind. Frank hadn't spoken a word apart from when he told them that Mark had tried to kill him.

Mark wiped his wet face with a towel and winced at the rough fabric dragging against his grazed cheek. He turned around feeling anger simmering inside but took a deep breath and tried to sound calm. "So where do we go from here?"

Frank looked up at the ceiling, ignoring Mark and everyone else.

"It's not like you to be so quiet, Frank."

"Just what the hell have you been playing at?" Brian demanded.

"Oh, stop it. Stop bullying him!" Sandra wailed.

Mark caught the smug look on Frank's face that was quickly masked as he adjusted the frozen peas against his nose.

"What will it take with you Sandra?" Alice asked, sitting down next to her. She took hold of one of her hands. "There's no point standing by him. It's over, and you're worth more than him. I wish you could see it."

Sandra looked surprised at the kindness of Alice's tone and looked between her and Frank.

"But it's not like him, that's what I'm trying to understand. Was it gambling Frank? All those nights you were out, were you gambling?"

239

"I think the real question is how you managed to attack Sandra. That's what's been bugging me," Mark said, moving over to the table and looking down at Frank.

"Don't be silly, Mark. He couldn't have done that. There's just no way." Sandra looked intently at him. "I know what he's done is wrong, about the money I mean, but don't try and pin Joan and the other attacks on him."

"So, how did you do it, Frank? You went out on the town, ate a curry but stayed sober, and then attacked Sandra. Is that it?" Mark moved his face within inches of Frank's. "Is that it? You went and hid somewhere and downed a bottle of Tequila, ready to stumble upstairs. That's sly, even for you. If it wasn't so sick it would be brilliant."

Mark snatched the peas from Frank's hands and threw them on the table where they skittered across the surface and fell on to the floor with a crash.

"Mark, stop it! He's hurt. Frank would never have done something like that. He'd never try and hurt me." Sandra began sobbing noisily.

Frank's mouth twisted into a smile and he tried to hide it but couldn't. "What's so funny, Frank?" Mark asked. "Your wife's crying her heart out and you're smiling."

Frank looked around the table at the disgusted faces watching him and stared at Sandra's red, blotchy face. He shrugged and began speaking, his broken nose making him sound as if he was stuffed with cold.

"It's like having a puppy, rather than a wife. I could do anything but she'd still be there wagging her tail, pleased to see me. Anything she doesn't like she ignores. Other women?" Frank assumed a falsetto whine, "I forgive you. I know you don't mean anything by it. It's just what men do." Frank looked at Sandra. "That's what a man does if he's married to someone like that."

Sandra was looking at Frank in disbelief, so shocked that she'd stopped crying. Alice put an arm around her and glared at Frank.

"So we can add cruelty to your list of qualities now, can we?"

Frank sighed heavily and, taking in the horrified look on Sandra's face, said in a soothing voice,

"Sorry, old girl – I didn't mean it. I might have concussion after what he bloody did." Frank pointed at Mark. "There's your killer everyone. I'm surprised he didn't finish me off when he had the chance…"

"How did you take the photo?" Alice asked suddenly. "The one you sent with the second blackmail letter?"

Frank smiled. "I'll hold my hand up to the blackmail attempt. It's your fault though Brian – you were the one that kept saying the money wouldn't go far between us all, 'not in today's climate'. You were like a broken record about that."

"Blame me - of course. You bloody thief, you would have taken our money if you could."

"How did you do take the photo though?" Alice asked.

"It's not rocket science. I took a snap with my phone when I went out to the hall and used a date stamper app and filters to make it look like a traditional camera shot."

"Frank, I thought…" Sandra tried to speak but words failed her.

"What old girl, what did you think?"

"I knew you had your faults…but I…"

Frank waited patiently, a polite smile on his blood stained face.

"Did you kill Joan?" She said at last and then, her face crumpling, she whispered, "You did. Oh God, you killed Joan."

"Now listen here everyone," Frank turned to them. "I've been a naughty boy, I admit it. Shouldn't have done it I know, but the money's back, no harm done – apart from to my poor nose." Nose sounded like 'doze' but his thick voice didn't stop Frank from speaking with as much charm and conviction as he could muster.

"You're not pinning anything else on me though. Take a look at our precious leader for that - why do you think Kirsty left? She knew there was something wrong with him."

"Leave Kirsty out of it! I saw what you're capable of tonight. If I hadn't changed your aim you would have split my head open with that spade."

Frank shook his head, smiling broadly as if he couldn't believe the lies Mark was telling.

"The night of Tony's funeral…" Sandra spoke hesitantly and Frank's head whipped around to look at her. "I woke up in the early hours and you were gone."

"I told you, I went for a walk."

"It's the first time in twenty years I've known you get up in the middle of the night and go for a walk."

"Yeah well, I wanted a drink."

Sandra laughed, a harsh, bitter sound. "Oh, you've done that before, but normally you bring your drink back to bed, turn the light on and read for a while. Never mind that it wakes me up." She put her head in her hands. "I've been such an idiot. All these years, Frank."

Frank smiled encouragingly at her and reached for her hand, but she snatched it away before saying in a whisper, "I've always loved you more than you loved me but that was the price I paid to be with you. Ditzy old me, married to someone so clever and funny. I've put up with so much from you Frank. So much." Sandra blew her nose. "I thought your ego needed attention elsewhere and that it didn't matter because I was the one you came back to. I was wrong though. You're just a selfish, cruel..."

"So he did definitely do it, then?" Ray asked. "He killed Joan?"

"Yeah, he did it," Mark said."

Sandra nodded and stared at Frank as if seeing him properly for the first time.

Alice leaned across the table and slapped him around the face. Her hand clipped his nose and tears sprang to Frank's eyes in response to the pain.

"What is it with you people?" Frank looked furious. "I put her out of her fucking misery! Same as we did with Tom, it doesn't make me a murderer. Christ that hurt Alice, I'd slap you back if I wasn't such a gent."

He gestured to Sandra to pass him the frozen peas on the floor but she ignored him.

"Is that what it was?" Mark asked. He kept his voice calm as he spoke. "You put her out of her misery? Okay, so just how did you do it?"

Frank got up and retrieved his ice pack from the floor. He paused for a moment and looked at them all.

"What is this - Scooby Doo? I would have got away with it if it wasn't for you meddling kids, right?"

"It's not funny, Frank," Brian said but Mark held his hand up.

"Just let him talk Brian."

Frank slumped back in his chair and sighed loudly. "Fine, so I did it but I'm not a murderer. Joan didn't suffer. I just let myself into the house and gave her some Valium and sleeping pills mixed into a mug of hot chocolate. That's all." He shrugged. "It was peaceful for her, nice, and I sat with her while she drank it."

"Didn't Joan wonder what you were doing there in the middle of the night?" Brian asked.

Frank shook his head. "She was completely out of it. I let myself in using the key she told us about and it took ages to wake her up. I told her she'd phoned the house and that Kirsty sent me ahead to make hot chocolate and to wait with her until she arrived. She was confused, but she drank it down and that was that. I tucked her in and put the letter beside her and she went peacefully."

"Why?" Sandra asked, tears pouring down her face. "I still don't understand."

"I told you, I was putting her out of her misery. She wouldn't have lasted a week in Spain and what did she have to live for over here? If she'd known what I was doing she would have thanked me for it."

"So the argument we had about giving Joan her share of the money had nothing to do with it?" Mark asked.

"I just felt sorry for her. It's not all about money you know, whatever you might think." Frank sounded indignant.

"Right, and you tried to kill Sandra, because…?"

"I did not try to kill Sandra. I was just…"

"You were just, what?" Mark demanded.

"Oh all right," Frank said irritably. "I was just trying to scare off Kirsty that's all. Listen, you were never in any danger old girl."

Sandra stared at him coldly.

"I'm sorry if I hurt you. I'd already downed a quarter of the Tequila by then and I might have been a bit rough. Kirsty was getting on my nerves saying she was leaving but then staying. I knew she'd go eventually - I just wanted her to get on with it, that's all."

"Yes, I suppose she was dragging morale down a bit," Mark said, failing to keep the sarcasm from his voice. He took a deep breath. "What about me, Frank? What had I done?"

"Now that wasn't me. Really it wasn't."

"Oh, I apologise," Mark said. "I hope I haven't offended you. It just seemed like the sort of thing you'd do. You know, cowardly." Mark slammed the table and Frank flinched. "It happened the night after I said the blackmailer was one of us. Didn't it Frank?"

"Yeah, well you didn't drink it did you. Anyway, I wasn't trying to kill you. It was only a couple of sleeping pills, just to shake you up a bit"

"What by sending me to sleep?" Mark asked, but Frank ignored him.

"Anyway, what's cowardly about the things I did? I think I've shown a lot of flair. Putting the ladder up outside the window so you thought it was an intruder…"

"Really subtle Frank. That confirmed it wasn't an intruder for me."

"Easy to say that now Mark but what about the blackmail photo? That kept you guessing - and the courier?" Frank looked wistful. "Cost me two hundred quid that bloke did. Worth it just to see the look on your faces though. And do you have any idea how hard it is to swig down half a bottle of Tequila? I hate Tequila." Frank pulled a disgusted face. "You don't have long before it kicks in, I'll tell you that."

Mark looked at Frank whose normal air of bonhomie was returning to him as he recounted his adventures.

"Thanks Frank but we need to decide what we're going to do with you."

The grin faded from Frank's face. "What do you mean do with me? You can't do anything without bringing yourself down. You know that."

Mark nodded to Ray who pinned Frank's arms from behind and pulled him up.

"Put him in the cellar for now," Mark said.

"Get off me! I'm not going down there on my own."

"Too late for that," Brian said. He helped Ray get Frank as far as the steps of the cellars. They slammed and locked the door behind him.

"Sandra, are you all right?" Mark asked, ignoring the sound of Frank hammering on the door.

She stared numbly ahead of her and grimaced, "I will be I suppose. Can we get out of here? I can't stand to hear him."

They stood up at once and Mark checked the door was locked tightly. "Let's go," Mark said, putting an arm around Sandra as she walked with him towards the drawing room. With his limp, the support was mutual and Mark collapsed on to the sofa with relief, stretching his leg on to the coffee table.

"How are you, Mark?" Alice asked. "Did he really aim for your head?" Mindful of Sandra sitting next to him, he raised his eyebrows and gave her the briefest of nods before saying, "I'll be fine." His swollen knee was throbbing and he had a dull ache in his back, but in Sandra's fragile state, it didn't seem tactful to list his injuries.

"So what are we going to do about him?" Ray asked, lighting a cigarette with shaking hands as he stood near the window.

Mark tugged at his hair as though willing his overloaded brain to work.

"What can we do?" Brian asked. "He's right - if we go to the police, he'll take us down with him."

There was silence apart from the tap of the honeysuckle against the window and the whistle of wind coming down the chimney. Mark shivered.

"Ray, would you put some lights on? I'd do it but..." He pointed at his leg.

"No problem."

Sandra moved as though to help but Alice shushed her and began drawing the heavy drapes closed. The enormous room felt cosier with the lamps lit and curtains drawn, but Mark still felt cold. It must be the shock, or perhaps exhaustion was catching up with him. He thought of the blankets they'd had outside earlier. Someone had, improbably, brought them back inside and put them in a neat pile in the hall but he couldn't be bothered to go and get one. He would have asked someone else to fetch one but Mark realised he wasn't the only one who looked exhausted. They needed to get this over with.

"Brian's right," he said. "We've been here before and if we were going to do anything without the possibility of jail time, we had our chance after the inquest. That's when we knew that Joan didn't commit suicide. As soon as we kept that from the Police, on top of everything else, we were in trouble. So, what we have to decide is whether we think Frank will kill again."

"I still think he's just a greedy bastard who got carried away because of the money." Brian said.

"Are you willing to stake someone else's life on that?" Mark asked. "He doesn't seem to feel any remorse for what he's done."

"So what are you saying?" Alice asked.

"I'm saying that we need to decide whether to hand him over to the police."

"But you just said we'd be seen as accomplices."

"We would."

Ray leaned forward. "Mark, I don't want to go to prison."

"Neither do I, believe me, neither do I. We've come a long way from helping Tom to die though. If we let him go after he's got away with murder who knows what he'll go on to do."

"Hold on a minute Mark," Brian said. "We're talking about Frank here, not some axe murderer. I understand what you're saying, really I do. Very noble it is too but my view is that Frank won't kill again. We've all been under a lot of strain and I can even - sort of - see his reasoning about Joan. Even though he was wrong, obviously. The thing with Sandra and then putting something in your drink, all that was just him trying to get the numbers down."

"We can't believe a word he said - you heard him," Alice said. "Sandra had to fight for her life…"

"And who knows what was in my drink," Mark added. "It was a big risk if all he wanted was to put sleeping pills in my drink. I agree with Alice - we can't trust anything he says. Sandra what do you think, you know him best?"

"Do I? That would almost be funny if it wasn't so bloody tragic."

Mark tried again. "You're right, sorry, but you are the one who's spent twenty years with him. Can I ask you some…some personal questions?" She nodded and Mark wondered where to begin.

"Has he ever hit you?"

"No, never."

"What about…was he, er, was he rough with you when you…"

Sandra looked almost as embarrassed as Mark. "Not really," she said in a small voice. "Nothing untoward, I mean we had our moments but no…"

"Right, thanks Sandra – that's fine," Mark interrupted. "Does he get into fights?"

"No. That's why part of me still can't believe what he did. A small part that is," she added, seeing the look on Alice's face. "I don't know what to think. Frank's very selfish and I suppose he can be manipulative. If he wants something he goes after it and he's very good at justifying things to himself."

"See, that's what worries me. I read something about sociopaths once, about how they think…"

"He's not a sociopath, Mark." Sandra laughed hollowly. "There are a lot of names I could call him but not that. I think what Brian said about him getting carried away by the money is right. I can't see him hurting anyone else though." Sandra wiped away the tears that had started to fall again. "We always had such adventures together - he makes…made me laugh so easily. Maybe that's why I put up with so much."

"Not in the future though?" Alice asked, looking alarmed by Sandra's mournful expression. "It's over between you now?"

"Oh, it's over, don't worry about that. I don't even want to see him again."

"Right. So, what now? We can't just leave him in the cellar."

"If it wasn't for the money down there, that would be the most appealing option," Brian said.

Mark's eyes flicked to the picture frame above the fireplace and he was relieved to see the edge of the large key that opened the heavy iron door leading to the safe.

"I think we all need time to get away, especially you Sandra." Mark said. "We also need to find some way of punishing him and I was thinking earlier, when he asked for a drink, what about making him go to rehab?"

Brian chuckled. "I like the thought of that. It needs to be voluntary though, doesn't it?"

Mark shrugged, "Not if we tell him he has to do three months and we'll be checking that he's still there every day…"

"And if he leaves, we'll tell the police what he's done," Ray said.

"Exactly. The punishment hardly fits the crime but I reckon maybe that, combined with losing all claim on the money, will go some way towards it."

Sandra was hugging herself tightly but looked at Mark and nodded.

"I agree. Frank's not an alcoholic as such but three months without a drink would be unbearable for him."

"Right, let's go and tell him." Mark stood up and the others, apart from Sandra, trailed behind.

Mark felt the colour drain from his face when he walked in to the kitchen. The wooden door to the cellar was wide open. He ran over to it and descended the stairs carefully. The floor was covered by smashed wine bottles and Mark ran to the small corridor that led to the safe, feeling icy prickles of sweat break out all over him. He hung on to the locked door for support and wiped an arm over his forehead.

"He didn't get the money," Mark called out as he walked slowly back towards the others.

"How did he get out?" Ray asked, surveying the debris of broken bottles.

"Up here!" Alice called from the top of the stairs. They moved back into the light of the kitchen and Alice showed them the long shard of glass and the crumpled poster that lay at the top of the stairs.

"We left the key in the door, didn't we?"

Mark shook his head at his own stupidity, he'd checked the door was locked but he hadn't bothered to remove the key. Frank must have pushed the key through onto a piece of paper, then pulled it back under the door.

"Shall we look for him?" Ray asked.

"My bloody car keys are gone," Brian bellowed.

He was pointing to the board where the keys were kept.

"He's taken my Jag… bastard!" Brian sounded as though this was the worst crime yet.

"It's hopeless," Mark said. "He'll be long gone now. He must have rolled it down the drive when we had the curtains closed." Seeing the distress on Brian's face he added, "you can buy another car Brian."

"That's not the point."

Sandra walked into the kitchen. "What's going...oh God, he's gone hasn't he?"

She swayed and Ray caught her and moved her towards a chair. Alice ran over to her cupboard and fumbled with the combination to open the door. She brought out a paper bag filled with apples and dumped them on to the counter.

"Here, breathe into this. Nice deep breaths now."

Sandra obeyed and after a minute looked up into the sea of concerned faces.

"Sorry, it's all a bit much."

"Sandra, don't apologise for anything. You're being really brave but I think we need to get you away from here. Have you got anywhere to go?" Mark asked. "You need to be somewhere he wouldn't think to look for you. I'm not saying he'll hurt you but he'll want to get at the money and..."

"I know. You don't need to spell it out." She was silent, frowning in concentration, before she said, "I have got somewhere to go, I think." She smiled. "My French client has told me I can stay with him anytime, at his house I mean not just the hotel..." Sandra's face fell and she stopped talking. "Oh Mark, I haven't told you."

"Told me what?"

"No, it's good news don't worry - really good news. I wasn't going to say anything until after the blackmailer had been dealt with but then with everything that happened..."

"What, Sandra?" Mark said impatiently.

"You won't be happy with me but go easy because I'm not in a good way. Promise?"

"Yes, whatever. Just tell me so we can move on. We've still got stuff to do."

"Did you ever think the way Kirsty finished things with you was a bit sudden? Maybe a bit over the top?"

Mark felt suddenly winded and sat down heavily. He already knew what she was going to say – Kirsty's break up had never rung true. He nodded.

"It was my idea Mark. I talked her into it because I knew she wouldn't stay until the end – I think we all did. I said if she clung on and then left when things were looking bleak you might be tempted to go with her."

"What did you say that for? I wouldn't have left," Mark said angrily.

"That's what she said but if she hadn't finished things with you don't you think you might have decided to follow her? Maybe when you were at your lowest ebb and you were missing her, and it looked like we weren't going to get the money anyway?"

"No, not even…why would you even think that? I'm not some love-struck teenager Sandra - I was never going to give up. Apart from anything else I promised Tom to see it through."

Sandra's face fell. "Oh Mark, I'm sorry - this is my fault. Kirsty really didn't want to do it but I persuaded her that unless she knew she could stay until the end, no matter what, she risked you leaving too. Then the lost money would always come between you in the future. She wasn't convinced but I told her a clean break would keep you focused, without having to worry about her. She did it for you, Mark."

Mark felt like shouting at Sandra, wondering if she had any idea how miserable he'd been. Even functioning enough to get through the last few weeks rather than moping had taken a monumental effort. He saw how fragile she looked though and took a deep breath.

"I'm sure you were acting for the best."

"I was. I really, really was." Sandra sounded relieved. "Kirsty and I have kept in touch – she's been so worried and she's desperately missing you. She's asked me to tell you she'll take you away whenever you're ready to that place in Norfolk where you had dinner on your last night. It's good news isn't it?"

He remembered their last night in Norfolk where they hadn't made it out of their hotel bedroom. As the news sank in that Kirsty only pretended to break up with him he realised he was smiling.

"Yes it's good news although she's got some serious making up to do. She was horrible."

"Oh don't blame her Mark – I told her she needed to be horrible or you wouldn't believe her. I really am sorry…"

"This is all very touching," Brian said, "but…"

"Yes, you're right." Mark felt suddenly energised. "Come on then, what's the plan?"

After that, everything moved quickly. They divided the money between them, all seven million of it, and Mark was surprised but gratified when Sandra insisted that Kirsty should have some of Frank's share. Brian tried to argue that Frank's share wasn't Sandra's to give away but Sandra prevailed and with so much money floating around he accepted the general consensus with good grace. By midnight they were all ready to go. They'd packed everything they needed, having already moved much of their stuff back home already, and Mark had agreed to deal with everything else. It would have been easier to leave in the morning but there was no chance of anyone staying any longer than needed now. In the end, the goodbyes were swift but a lot harder than Mark expected. He had wanted to get rid of them for so long that he never imagined he would be sorry to see them go. Alice and Brian had booked a trip to the Cayman Islands and their flight left the following afternoon. He waved them off and Mark didn't know how he felt at the thought of most likely never seeing them again. Next to go, also together, were Sandra and Ray in Frank's car. With Frank on the loose they were headed straight to a hotel in Gatwick. They planned to fly out to Zurich in the morning and try to make sense of the Swiss banking system. From there, Ray would escort Sandra to her client's house in France before heading back to America for a while.

Mark said goodbye to Ray and Sandra with some fondness but once they left and the house was his again, he felt nothing but relief. It was time for him to get his life back and he didn't need a mirror to tell him he looked more like a prisoner than a wealthy bachelor. He needed to get some good food inside him and then some sleep and fresh air. More than anything, he needed to call Kirsty but the sensible part of him decided to wait until morning. A darker part of him wanted to keep her waiting after what she put him through - what had she been thinking, but he missed her too much. He felt a kind of exhausted relief mixed with euphoria at the thought of seeing her again. Maybe she could even help him get the house ready to hand over to Tom's lawyers. Looking at his phone he saw it was nearly half past one and on an impulse he decided to call Kirsty after all – he couldn't wait until morning, but her number went straight to answerphone. Disappointed, he got a beer from the fridge and sat down at the table to compose a text. He couldn't think what to say and realised that his head was spinning. He was shattered and in the course of one day he'd become a millionaire, captured a murderer and let him escape before discovering that it was back on with the woman he loved. It was no wonder his brain was fried. He sat for a while holding the cold beer bottle against his bruised hand and then he typed, 'Again, I thought you said you couldn't act?! I'll call you in the morning once I'm up. Exhausting day but all done. HINT – Tom would be pleased! ;) XX'. Mark found it hard to imagine him being pleased about any of it as there was so much they'd done wrong, even without Frank. He took a long swallow of the beer and exhaled noisily. It was over now and there was no point dwelling on the past. A good sleep and a shower was what he needed and then it was time to look to the future. He felt a fizz of excitement at the thought of seeing Kirsty again and stood up ready for bed, already planning his best sleep in months.

OCTOBER

Chapter Thirty-three

Mark turned his pillow over and sank back onto the cool side with relief. The ceiling fan whirred above him, but the night was so hot the fan was just circulating the humid air. He hated air conditioning but the open window and fan weren't enough so he padded over to the control panel and turned it on. He couldn't remember the last time he'd slept peacefully for a whole night and when he did get to sleep he was often woken by bad dreams that left him shaken and sweating. His mouth was parched and he reached for the bottle of water beside his bed and downed half of it with a couple of ibuprofen. He felt slightly better although his head was still pounding and he lay back down wishing he'd gone easier on the whisky. In the months since he'd left the house he'd got into the habit of a few drinks before bed, just to take him halfway there - anything to stop him thinking. Exhaustion often pushed him into long naps during the day and those were his favourite times, especially in a shady spot next to the pool or on the beach. He sometimes left his wallet in clear view while he slept, just a cheap wallet with cash in it, and it had become a kind of game with him to see if it was still there when he woke up. He'd been beaten up quite badly on an isolated beach on St Kitts, and in Bali he'd had his T-shirt and towel stolen too, but he found it gratifying that the wallet was usually still there when he woke up. Sometimes he'd even find it tucked carefully under his towel and he appreciated these small kindnesses from strangers.

He scratched a mosquito bite on his side and felt the sharp outline of his ribs. His calorie intake lately was probably more liquid than solid. Tomorrow he'd make sure he had a good breakfast though and start the day right at least. For a moment he had to think where he was and he smiled at the concept of being so well travelled that he couldn't remember. He was in the Grenadine islands now and had spent the last few weeks drinking, sleeping around and island hopping. He'd done his first bungee jump last week, persuaded by a girl he'd met on the beach, but even the fear he'd felt when looking down beforehand hadn't really touched him. He was still numb and what he'd done lurked in the back of his mind, robbing him of peace and ready to ambush him whenever he felt a burst of any happy feeling. He'd become skilled at keeping it at bay during his waking hours, but it waited for him when he let his guard down, and in his nightmares Mark had no choice but to pay it full attention. He sighed and turned his pillow over again.

The last time he'd been truly happy was the night when everyone had left the house. He remembered texting Kirsty and feeling a burst of excitement about the future. Before turning in for the night he'd wanted to look at the art deco brooch for Kirsty, thinking to give it to her when he saw her. He hated going down into the cellar on his own but he was on such a high that he was humming to himself as he went down the stone steps. He remembered vividly how fast that had changed when he heard the door slam shut above him followed by Frank's triumphant shout. Even now, whenever he had a bad dream it was usually overlaid with that same sensation of claustrophobia and panic. He'd felt it last night when he dreamt that Frank was taunting him from the kitchen while blood and red wine poured down the cellar steps towards him. In his dream Frank opened the door at the top of the steps and Mark found he was trapped at the bottom, unable to climb towards him because he was drowning in a gelatinous red river. Mark had woken up gasping. The reality had been different all those months ago when Frank had returned to the house but he still remembered feeling trapped while listening to Frank ranting about their betrayal of him. He'd agreed to Frank's demands to hand over the money from the safe but he'd managed to grab a handful of Frank's shirt when he opened the door. Frank had stepped forward to push Mark back downstairs but he'd stumbled over the bag of money. As Frank tumbled down the stairs Mark grabbed the bag and locked him back in the cellar behind him.

Mark knew he should be grateful it was only that part of what he'd done that touched his dreams but he still found it hard to sleep. The air conditioning was taking effect now and he reached for the red-haired woman lying beside him. For a moment he couldn't remember her name but it was a comfort to have her there and he was glad she'd decided to stay the night. He pulled her towards him like a child with a blanket. It still bothered him that he hadn't talked to Kirsty. At first he couldn't call but later he'd ignored her attempts to contact him because he didn't deserve her, or anyone. There was no way of explaining himself though so in the end he'd written her a note saying only, '*I changed my mind - you were right about us. I'm sorry.*'

Angie, the red-haired woman was called Angie. She worked in a bar at the hotel and she wasn't Kirsty but she seemed nice and she'd kept him company after her shift finished. They might spend tomorrow together if she was free but then he'd move on, perhaps somewhere urban next. She murmured something and he wondered about waking her - he'd be grateful for the distraction. It was the only way he knew to take him out of himself and find some peace but she moved away from him and started breathing deeply again. He looked at the alarm clock and saw it was four am, the time that people were at their weakest apparently. He shivered and was reminded of how he'd shivered uncontrollably after killing Frank. As he hugged himself, he knew he couldn't ever tell anyone what he'd done. It was the way he'd done it that haunted him as much as anything. Once he'd escaped from the cellar he'd moved the heavy Welsh dresser against the wall, ignoring Frank's shouted pleas for help. The tyre iron on the kitchen table had given him pause as he imagined Frank clutching it while waiting for the others to leave. Mark put it into the umbrella rack before going upstairs cradling his beer in one hand and his duffel bag of money in the other. Feeling shaky he'd taken a hot shower and swallowed three of Sandra's sleeping tablets before throwing himself into bed and sleeping for twelve hours straight.

Two nights after locking Frank in the cellar Mark had woken up in the early hours, knowing that he couldn't put it off any longer. Frank had stopped shouting and banging on the door the previous afternoon and he had heard nothing from him since, even when standing right next to the door. Still wearing the pair of shorts he slept in, Mark had moved the dresser away from the door feeling jittery and sick at the prospect of opening the door. Finally, clutching the tyre iron in one hand he'd pulled the door open and found Frank curled in a ball at the top of the steps. The stench had been almost unbearable and he'd gagged at the cold, fetid atmosphere of the cellar. Checking Frank's neck he had felt the feeble thread of a pulse and swore under his breath. Mark remembered feeling unnerved by his disappointment that Frank was still alive, noticing that about himself even as he looked at the pile of wine bottles next to the body. He'd hesitated, confronted by the reality of what he was doing while hazily aware that it still wasn't too late to change his mind. He could just phone for an ambulance from the airport and be out of the country before Frank was awake. Now, months later lying in bed in a strange country next to someone who wasn't Kirsty, he saw that decision as his watershed moment. If he had made that call where would he be now? Possibly in a jail cell, possibly in bed with Kirsty somewhere. He looked at the alarm clock

254

and wondered if he'd get back to sleep.

Mark remembered rationalizing his decision as he'd sat with his back against the cellar door, trying to find the courage to take either of the two options that were open to him. Eventually, as the sunrise bathed the kitchen in warm yellow sunlight, Mark stood up, his decision made. Going outside, he was surrounded by the inaptly cheerful racket of birdsong from the woods as he walked to Tony's shed at the back of the house. In the shed he'd found a roll of gardening sacks and a bag of peat. Next he'd fetched a long tin bath from the attic and placed it at the far end of the cellar. He stood for a long time looking at Frank's unconscious body, working out whether he could actually kill him. In the end he'd just taped him within the large plastic sacks, killing him by default. He gagged when lifting Frank's body into the bath, especially when he had to bend his knees to make him fit. In the following days, numb and broken, he'd created a false wall in the cellar that he painted white and covered with one of the wine racks. After that he called in the cleaning crew again. Between handing over the newly scrubbed house to Tom's lawyers and making his travel arrangements he became used to the dull ache where his heart was.

Mark moved Angie's hair out of the way where it was tickling his nose. It looked black in the moonlight but he'd noticed the rich auburn colour as soon as he saw her. He wondered if he was going to turn into some creepy guy who pursued someone only because she resembled the girl who once broke his heart. Although, adding to his guilt, he supposed that he'd probably broken Kirsty's heart. No doubt she hated him now but he was glad they'd at least been able to give Kirsty her share of the money. He wondered what she was doing and whether she was also lying in bed next to someone but he pushed the thought away. He'd decided that losing Kirsty was the price he had to pay for his actions and there was no point wallowing in it. The way he'd been spending his time since he left the house was starting to sicken him though. He'd been trying to recover himself while travelling around as if he was on some kind of extended holiday, drinking and picking up women along the way but not connecting with anyone. It was a sham of a life, a young man's dream on the surface but he needed to change things before he lost himself entirely, so sickened by what he'd done that he gave up altogether. It was the cowardly way he'd dragged out Frank's suffering that he couldn't get past. As he felt himself drifting off to sleep he knew he couldn't go back home but he wondered if he could find happiness somewhere else or if he'd spend his time drifting from one place to the next until the money ran out. He squeezed his eyes shut as a wave of loneliness and heartache threatened to overwhelm him. As it receded exhaustion settled over him and he pulled Angie closer to him again. His breathing slowed and he felt his body relax as he experienced the brief moment between wakefulness and sleep where, for an instant, he was holding Kirsty tight in his arms. He smiled as he sank into sleep.

FIVE YEARS LATER

Kirsty's hands were shaking as she smoothed down her black dress and adjusted the neckline. She added a silver necklace and as she applied another sweep of mascara she noticed the fine lines forming at the corner of her eyes. She frowned at her reflection but dismissed the thought easily. She remembered turning thirty the previous year and there was a lot to be said for being comfortable in your own skin, something that had eluded her throughout her twenties. She put on some lipstick and looked again at her watch. Ray was going to pick her up in twenty minutes and she couldn't remember being ready this early for anything in her life. She put on a pair of black patent heels and took another deep breath.

It was Brian's funeral and Alice had surprised her by calling last week to ask her to come. After she'd agreed Alice had said, "I'm so pleased Kirsty - that's wonderful. It would have meant a lot to him to have you there, and the others from that time if anyone can make it." Kirsty could tell from her voice that she'd been crying. "It's funny but he became quite nostalgic about everything we went through, as if we had been the Famous Five on a treasure hunt."

"I think that's what Tom meant it to be - he would have loved that. Do you want me to ring everyone else?"

"Would you? Thanks Kirsty, are you still in touch?"

"With Ray yes and I know he talks to the others. Sandra's in France now and I think Mark still lives in Salvador. I'll let you know once I've spoken to them but I'll definitely be there."

After jotting down the funeral arrangements she'd called Ray who had agreed to come and offered to call Mark and Sandra. He and Kirsty still caught up over dinner a couple of times a year and she counted him as one of her good friends. They didn't speak often these days but thanks to Facebook she was up to date with photos of him and Emma with their two girls and she saw his posts from all around the world.

Kirsty swapped her everyday watch for the diamond watch Ray had given her – it seemed fitting and it might annoy Mark. She smiled to herself and took a deep breath. Today was not about seeing Mark again. The watch was still one of her favourite items of jewellery and she was glad she hadn't needed to return it. These days Ray was a successful property developer who could have bought a watch like that for every day of the year. He'd built up a good portfolio in the UK but his main interests were international and she knew he and Mark caught up when they could. A few months ago she'd seen a photo of Mark on Ray's timeline and for a moment she hadn't been able to breathe. It was taken at a waterside bar and Mark had an arm slung around Ray's shoulders. He'd looked relaxed and happy and even more handsome almost as if he'd grown into himself.

The months spent with Mark seemed a long time ago now but the friendly text he'd sent, his last, had obsessed her for a time and she still regretted that she'd missed his call that night. It was just one of her many unanswered questions about him. Most hurtful of all was his terse break-up note although it had, uniquely, arrived by courier along with quarter of a million pounds and a label saying, 'from Sandra, with love - your share'. She'd cried her eyes out, not least because back then she'd blamed Sandra for persuading her to break up with Mark so she swamped by feelings of regret, sorrow and elated gratitude all at the same time. Thinking about that time she retrieved the Art Deco brooch she'd also received that day and pinned it to her dress. This was her favourite piece of jewellery but she rarely wore it and said it was from Etsy if people asked. It was like something the queen would wear so nobody ever realised the gems were diamonds rather than crystal. Kirsty liked to think Annie would be pleased when she wore it, and it looked perfect today with the black dress that was an understated but beautifully cut present to herself from Givenchy.

She'd forgiven Sandra a long time ago for her bad advice and now only gratitude remained. It still amazed her what a difference the money had made. She loved the choices it gave her, and of course the improvement in her circumstances, but mostly she valued what she and her lovely team had achieved since then. It had taken a while and at first she'd been reeling from the emotional overload of everything happening at once. On a whim she'd gone over to Montpellier to visit a friend who was working out there, partly to catch her breath but mostly to escape from the empty flat which reminded her too much of Mark. It wasn't until she got there that she realised what a perfect place it was to recover, overflowing with bars and clubs thanks to the big student population. Imogen, her friend, seemed to know all the best places and they'd spent long balmy evenings flitting between the bars and clubs around Place Jean Jaurés in the old town. As the weeks went by her heartbreak was touched by anger until one night she'd met someone interesting in a club. When he said his name was Marc she was tempted to walk away, but she liked the look of him and he was charmingly persistent. At the end of the night they'd gone home together and she'd seen him a few times. It was nice but nothing serious, really just a way of drawing a line between her and Mark while she decided what to do next. In the end she spent the whole summer in Montpellier, getting a job in a café to improve her French and going for trips to the beach with Isobel at the weekend.

When Kirsty finally returned to Brighton she drifted for a while until she saw a charity poster that said a million older people went a month without speaking to anyone. This sparked something in her as she remembered Tom's loneliness when she first knew him. From there after a lot of research and hard work she started Wise Voices, a social history project that recorded the memories of older people for posterity. She still loved seeing how people come back to life as a result of sharing their stories and being part of something again. Kirsty had been due to visit a school today with two Wise Voices regulars in their eighties, Evelyn and Mary, who both loved the spotlight. She sent a quick text to Kelly, her assistant, to wish them luck from her and idly checked Facebook while she was on her phone. Noticing a friend request she opened it and saw the name Mark Granger. She stared at it in shock and immediately felt butterflies in her stomach. She knew it was ridiculous to feel like this after five years but the call from Ray to confirm that Mark was coming to the funeral had stirred up a lot of old feelings. She accepted his request but before she could look at his profile the doorbell rang.

"You're early," she said, opening the door to Ray.

"Lovely to see you too," Ray said, holding out his arms. Kirsty laughed and gave him a tight hug.

"Sorry Ray, it's always lovely to see you. Come in."

Ray walked through the bright hallway and into the living room. "Very nice. Fantastic views too."

Kirsty's most recent move was to an apartment on the upper floor of a Regency terrace. It was right on Brighton's seafront and she loved watching how the sea changed colour throughout the day.

"I love it here. This might be my last move."

"I've heard that before."

"Maybe but this really feels like home. Besides, I'm fed up with doing places up - that was always more Steve's thing than mine. I nearly bought a new-build when we broke up just because I could."

"You rebel."

"I know. Have I said thank you lately by the way? I couldn't have afforded something like this without you."

Ray waved away her thanks as he always did but she meant it. Her original stake had grown through partnering with Ray on a few of his property projects and he was Wise Voices' most generous supporter.

"How are you feeling about seeing Mark?"

"I'm fine. He's just sent me a friend request which is the first contact I've had from him in five years so that felt a bit weird."

"I was working out on the way down here that this is the first time in the last few years that you've both been single at the same time."

"Let's not go down that path Ray," Kirsty said. "Just seeing him today after the way it ended will be strange enough. Anyway I'm not interested. He's the bastard who never called me back. Remember?"

"As if I could forget," Ray said, but they were both smiling.

"Anyway, I thought it was serious with Gabriela."

"No that ended a while ago. From what he was saying on the phone he's getting ready to leave Brazil too. He's missing the UK."

"He's coming back?" Kirsty asked.

"Apparently. He's just in the process of handing everything over. I was thinking we could all get together for dinner when he's properly back."

Kirsty looked at Ray for a moment. "Let's see how today goes first. Anyway, how are Emma and the girls?"

As they left they carried on chatting but Kirsty's thoughts were elsewhere.

*

Mark sat in a pew near the back with Sandra and tried to be subtle as he looked around him again. She definitely wasn't here.

"Where are they?" Sandra asked, mirroring his thoughts.

He felt a knot in his stomach at the thought she wouldn't show up. It was cold in the crematorium and he shivered, wishing he'd worn a coat on top of his suit.

"You all right?"

He nodded. "I'm not used to these temperatures."

She patted his arm and Mark thought how well Sandra looked. Living in France suited her and she looked very expensive, from the cut of her clothes to her immaculate hair and make-up. The biggest change was to her confidence though. Her self-assurance was new and she no longer had the air of someone who was eager to please. Mark wondered if Kirsty would have changed as drastically.

He remembered Ray showing him her Facebook page when

260

they caught up over dinner in Salvador a few months earlier. Mark had never bothered with Facebook but when he asked Ray about her, he'd handed across his phone. Mark had scrolled through her photos finding it hard to look at pictures of her with a man who looked like some kind of male model. Mark handed the phone back.

"She obviously got over her thing about men with good looks."

"If you're jealous then you deserve it after the way you treated her," Ray said, pointing at him with his knife.

"I put myself into exile back then, it wasn't just Kirsty. Then I left it so long I didn't know what to say. Anyway she finished things with me."

"No she didn't, she pretended to, so don't give me that."

"Yes alright, I know. Why do you think I've been making amends ever since."

"Not to her you haven't. Anyway, how's it going?"

"Good, although it feels like I've about served my time over here. Is it definitely finished with that pretty boy?"

"You don't deserve to know where she's concerned. Besides she's big into her charity work. The pair of you put me to shame - Mother Teresa and Gandhi."

"I'm probably nearly as broke as Gandhi was now," Mark said.

"I don't know why you won't let me help."

"You do help and now that you're supporting the charity, it means I can hand it over and get out of here. I've had enough now - I'm ready to go home."

Mark spoke about serving time but Frank's death didn't trouble him any more compared to what he'd seen in Salvador's shantytowns. Frank had at least deserved to die and Mark had forgiven himself for the manner of his death a long time ago.

He looked at the stained glass windows of the Crematorium and thought about the idea of redemption. After what he'd done over the last few years he felt he'd earned the right to try again with Kirsty, if only to know where he stood. She had been the real deal for him. He and Sandra stood up as the service began and Mark started singing the words of *Abide with Me*. Halfway through the hymn he saw movement in the corner of his eye and turned to see Ray usher Kirsty into the pew, both looking harried. It was not how he had imagined seeing her again but she was more beautiful than he remembered and he beamed at her, the hymn forgotten. She and Ray both smiled back perfunctorily as they got themselves organised and Mark's smile faltered. Throughout the next half hour he tried to focus on the service rather than the nearness of Kirsty but he could smell her perfume and feel the wool of her black coat against his thin suit jacket. Finally the service was over and the four of them stood outside.

There were hugs and handshakes all round and they stood apart from everyone else, waiting for their turn to see Alice.

"We were caught up in an accident. One of those ones where you stop complaining because you're so glad you weren't in it," Ray said.

"Just look at you Ray. Every time I see you I can't get over how much you've changed." Sandra was looking him up and down.

"Same with you though - you look great Sandra."

She smiled. "Thanks. I think living with a Parisian has rubbed off on me. Besides I love fashion now whereas I used to be scared of it." She looked around at them all. "Well haven't we changed? Although black was always our colour, wasn't it – it's sad but I've been to more funerals with you three than I have without you."

"Have you ever heard anything from Frank?" Kirsty asked.

"Nothing." Sandra's bright expression faded. "For a long time I was sure he'd find me. I moved around a lot to start with, right up until I met Adrien. I've shown him photos and he knows not to go near Frank if he ever turns up. That's all I've told him of course." She shuddered. "I hardly think of him these days but God I was under his spell."

"He could be very charming," Kirsty said.

"Especially to beautiful young women." Sandra shuddered again. "Ugh, enough about him. What's happening with you? I remember Ray telling me you were quite serious with someone?"

"No, that finished a while back," Kirsty said. "Nobody at the moment, which suits me for now."

"I always thought it was a shame you two didn't get back together," Sandra said, looking at them both. "You seemed trés amoureux back then."

Ray laughed. "Don't be shy Sandra. Anyway you were the agent of doom on that one."

Sandra looked mortified. "Oh, I'm sorry. I really thought it would be best for both of you. I never expected it to be permanent, you do know that, don't you?"

Mark shook his head. He'd never understood her thinking, nor Kirsty's in going along with it - but then they'd all been under a lot of strain at the time, as he knew only too well.

"It was a strange time," he said inadequately. "How I behaved afterwards didn't help."

Ray patted him on the back. "Bit of an understatement there but yes."

At that moment Alice came over. She looked as elegant as ever and seemed composed as she hugged them in turn.

"Thank you so much for coming. I can't believe you all made it, really I so appreciate it and I know it would have meant a lot to Brian."

They spoke for a while about Brian, and Mark said, "I never realised how much he'd done."

"Well, he was a very popular man when he was safely in his world - president of the golf club, rotary club member and all of that. He wasn't at his best in the house. I think he felt completely at sea a lot of the time and of course he was already suffering with his heart although we didn't know that at the time."

"But he always seemed so... confident." Mark chose his words carefully.

Alice sighed. "Yes, attack is the best form of defence - isn't that what they say? He did think a lot of you all though when it came down to it, especially in hindsight." She looked around, noticing some more people waiting to talk to her. "I have to go. You're welcome back at the house of course, but if I were you I'd grab a drink somewhere instead. There's quite a crowd coming and you won't know anyone."

"Are you sure?" Sandra asked.

"Honestly, I'm surrounded by help. There's no need. I'll see you soon though, I hope. Perhaps we could have lunch before you go back? Thank you again for coming, I'm so glad you did."

They arranged that Sandra would call Alice in a couple of days to organise something and passed on their condolences again.

"Where to then?" Ray asked, after she'd gone.

"You can come back to mine if you like," Kirsty offered. "Or there's a pub I know not too far from here."

"Let's go to yours shall we?" Sandra said. "Pubs are always such depressing places in the early afternoon."

"I can give you a lift," Mark said. "I'll just need to know where we're going."

"Let's swap," Ray said. "If you give Kirsty a lift she can show you the way and I already know where I'm going. Come on Sandra."

Once they were out of earshot Mark said, "it's hard to remember them isn't it, how they were?"

"I know. I'm used to the new Ray now but Sandra's unrecognisable."

"The car's this way, I'm just about used to driving on the left again."

Mark led the way to a grey Audi A3 and breathed in the new car smell of the hire car as they got in. "I booked this online while I was waiting at the airport. Hertz have all these different sections on the website, dream cars, super cars, fun cars you name it. I was seriously tempted by an Aston Martin as a welcome home present to myself."

"So why didn't you get it?" Kirsty asked.

Mark shrugged. "I couldn't do it in the end. The way I've been living in Salvador I couldn't spend that much a day on a hire car. Do you remember when Tom said that people would think the money was wasted on people like him and Annie?"

"Yes, although Annie did buy up half of Bond Street and then they bought Downsview Manor."

"True, good point," Mark laughed. "I had a few crazy months myself to be honest but I think the conversations we had about doing good with the money rubbed off. Anyway, a lot of it's gone now - I've got enough but I don't feel the need to spend it like I thought I would."

"What about where you live?" Kirsty asked

"It's fine. It's in a safe part of town and it's got security and all of that but it's nothing special. Mind you, it would have felt strange commuting to the slums from a mansion."

"Is that what you were doing over there - working in the slums?"

"Sort of - that's where a lot of Tom's money went. We ran programmes to get to kids before the gangs did and tried to get families out of the shantytowns. The way some people have to live, you wouldn't believe."

Mark turned out of the car park.

"Ray just told me you were working over there but I had no idea about any of that."

"Yes, well Ray's not my biggest fan when it comes to you. Anyway, what about Wise Voices? I saw the website link on your Facebook page. It looks great."

"Thanks. The social history thing is what we do but usually the cup of tea and chat is just as important. That and the follow up stuff."

"Tom would have liked that."

"I hope so, although it feels a bit tame compared to rescuing slum kids."

"Probably less chance of getting shot at but otherwise you know how it is - never compare. My friend works on a charity that helps bats and she's very eloquent on that point."

Kirsty laughed. "Well, when you put it like that. So how long are you back for?"

"Not sure yet. I'm working out what to do next and where to live."

"That must be a weird feeling."

"It is. It really is but I was telling Ray how difficult it was and he asked if my diamond shoes were pinching."

"He's quite direct these days isn't he?"

"Just a bit."

"So how will you choose what to do next?" Kirsty asked.

"There are some conversations I need to have first then I'll have more of an idea."

"People to see, places to go." Kirsty said.

"Something like that." Mark looked across at her and smiled.

They drove in silence for a while and Mark felt awkwardness building between them. The tone of their conversation so far had been that of two acquaintances catching up. Nobody would ever think they'd once been lovers. Mark's fingers drummed on the steering wheel as he wondered how to get past the chat to what he really wanted to say. Just then he felt the vibration of a text and heard a beep from Kirsty's phone.

"It's Ray," she said. "I don't believe this. Apparently Sandra's got the early signs of a migraine so Ray's taking her back to the hotel. He says he'll head home after that as he's out later."

"They've bailed on us," Mark said.

"Apparently. He says to sort out a date in a couple of days. Look, if you've got stuff to do don't worry about me."

"No. I'm fine if you are. It will be good to catch up." Mark tried to sound casual.

"I know but it's okay, we can do all that when we see the others. I could do with getting back to work anyway. Where are you staying?"

"I'm at the Hotel du Vin."

"Great." Kirsty looked at her watch. "If you park up at The Lanes my office isn't far from there so I can just go straight from the car park. Look, the turning's just up here."

They parked in silence and Mark couldn't think what to say as they got out of the car.

"Thanks for the lift Mark and it really was good to see you again." Kirsty spoke brightly.

"You too. I was looking forward it, even if the circumstances weren't the best."

"I know. Sad really that we never saw that side of Brian - I didn't recognise the person they were describing."

"No, he kept that side very well hidden in the house," Mark looked at Kirsty and a smile passed between them as he caught her eye.

"Well, I'd better get going," she said. "I'll see you once we've sorted out a time with Ray and Sandra."

"Okay. I'll look forward to it. See you then."

Kirsty casually kissed his cheek then walked off through the underground car park. It had all happened so suddenly. He leaned back against the car with his hands in his pockets and watched her as she walked away. When she went through the door to the staircase without turning back he knew he had his answer. They were together for a few months five years ago and whatever had been between them had gone. Maybe he was only ever a distraction for her anyway, someone to pass the time with while they were stuck in the house. He folded his arms, feeling cold again, and thought of going back to the bar at his hotel. He'd booked there because he thought it was the sort of place Kirsty might like but he couldn't picture himself alone on the low velvet sofas. He'd be better going to a pub and fulfilling Sandra's idea of them as depressing places in the afternoon.

He walked out of the car park and found himself enclosed by the uninspiring architecture of council offices and the back of a big hotel. A wave of sadness passed over him. He'd known not to get his hopes up but it was hard to accept there was nothing between them any more. She couldn't get away from him fast enough and he felt foolish for thinking that the chemistry between them would still be there. He stood for a while but as seagulls reeled overhead he was taken back to their first morning as a couple when he'd woken up in Kirsty's flat and felt dazed with happiness. This memory sparked something in him as he realised that in his jet-lagged state he'd missed something vital. He couldn't believe he'd been so stupid but he hadn't actually apologised so how could he know where he stood. He laughed out loud as he berated himself for being an idiot and smiled at a young woman who looked at him suspiciously as she walked past. He felt a surge of excitement – there was still a chance. He ran diagonally across the square, into the Lanes, following the direction she'd gone. He was now in the warren of narrow streets that made up the Lanes and there was no sign of her. A pack of tourists was walking maddeningly slowly as they spanned the narrow passage, looking in the windows of the antique jewellery shops on either side. He shoved past them and halted as he reached a crossroads. There was no sign of her.

Mark stood frozen in place as people bumped into him. He couldn't wait until he met up with her along with everyone else. He needed to speak to her today, now. He got his phone out to see if Wise Voices listed an office address.

"Mark? I was just dropping my watch off for a new battery." Kirsty pointed at the shop he was standing next to. "What are you doing here?"

"Thank God. Kirsty I thought I'd lost you."

"What's wrong?"

"Nothing. Or everything, it depends on what you say but I was so nervous about seeing you I forgot to apologise."

"All that seems a long time ago now."

Mark shook his head. "I know but I can't tell you how sorry I am that I didn't explain myself back then. In my head I've already told you that but I haven't have I?"

"Are you alright Mark?"

"It was never about you…"

"Don't, please. You know, for a long time I thought you must have met someone else?" Kirsty said, folding her arms. "I decided that was the only thing that made sense."

"What? God, no." Someone bumped into him and he steered Kirsty back towards the shop window so that they were out of the way. "It got really bad after you left, I mean really bad. I lost the plot for a while and once it was all over I felt like I didn't deserve to be with you, I mean I genuinely thought you'd be better off without me. I just didn't know how to tell you without it sounding trite – it's not you, it's me. The longer it went on the worse it was."

She looked taken aback by his intensity and it was a while before she said anything.

"Why didn't you try to explain? I wish you'd at least spoken to me. One minute I get a lovely cheerful text and the next I hear from you it's over."

"I couldn't. I didn't trust myself to contact you in case you talked me round."

"Why would that have been so bad?" Kirsty looked angry. "That's what didn't make sense. Do you know how much time I wasted trying to work out what happened?"

"I've got a good idea how it felt. Your performance by the lake was pretty convincing you know."

"Yes, well - It was never for real though, not like you. Was it for revenge? Is that why you never contacted me?"

He shook his head. "What? No, why would I...look, there's nothing I can say to explain myself, nothing that will make sense."

"Try Mark," Kirsty said. "You owe me that at least."

"I've already told you. Things got really dark and I just felt like I didn't deserve you. No worse than that...it was like I didn't want to pollute you."

"You didn't want to pollute me?" Kirsty sounded puzzled.

"I told you it wouldn't make sense but that's how I felt back then. If it's any comfort most of my work the last few years has been for you, well, driven by you - by wanting to be good enough for you." Mark shrugged. "I mean outside of the work itself obviously."

"For me?"

Mark couldn't read her expression but he nodded anyway.

Kirsty looked at him and he held her gaze, knowing there was nothing else he could say. It felt like he could hardly breathe but after a while she nodded and unfolded her arms, revealing the brooch he'd given her.

"I never thanked you for this," she said, gesturing towards the brooch. "You liked it?"

"I loved it." She smiled at him and Mark smiled back.

"Even more than the watch Ray gave you?"

Kirsty laughed. "I'm not answering that until I've decided if I'm forgiving you."

They looked at each other again and Mark felt something pass between them. What they'd had was still there. "So how do I go about earning your forgiveness?"

Kirsty looked him for a beat longer and then she smiled.

"You can start by buying me a drink."

Mark exhaled. "I'll even buy you dinner," he said. "I know a good Italian place if you don't mind domineering waiters."

Kirsty reached up and stroked the scar on his jawline.

"One step at a time. You've got some serious making up to do before we get to any Italian restaurants."

"I know."

"It is really good to see you though."

"You too."

Mark couldn't take his eyes off her and found he was grinning. After a moment Kirsty beamed back and he saw the shine of tears in her eyes. He held out his arms and it was enough just to hold her. They clung to each other tightly, lost in a sea of tourists, before heading away from the crowds towards the start of something.

Acknowledgements

My sincere thanks to all those who played a part in this book coming together. The support has been above and beyond - from my grandmother, June Fryett, joining me on a research trip, to my wonderful friend imbuing a manuscript copy with JK Rowling stardust while on a trip to Edinburgh!

After many re-writes I am hugely grateful to those who gave their feedback and suggestions particularly Louise Hindley, Jonathan Carroll, Dominic Patteson and Maggie Carroll, as well as Araminta Hall and the group from the Beach Hut Writing Academy. Thanks also to Revd John Smith and to Gavin Lewis for their patience in answering my questions – any errors are my own.

My biggest thanks though go to my parents, Peter and Christine Davies, for their infinite supply of encouragement and support, to my son, Euan, for cheering me on throughout and to my steadfast and loving husband Jon for, well…everything over the very, very long writing and editing period of this book – it really is finished now I promise!

29254800R00151

Printed in Great Britain
by Amazon